Harriet Smart was born and brought up in Birmingham. She attended the University of St Andrews, specializing in the architecture and applied arts of the eighteenth and nineteenth centuries. The research for her degree thesis into a firm of church furnishers in Birmingham inspired her first novel, *A Garland of Vows*, which fulfilled a life-long ambition to write historical fiction. After graduating in 1988, she married a fellow student and they now live in Edinburgh.

Also by Harriet Smart

A Garland of Vows
Green Grow the Rushes
The Daughters of Blane

The Lark Ascending

Harriet Smart

KNIGHT

First published in 1995
by HEADLINE BOOK PUBLISHING PLC

First published in paperback in 1995
by HEADLINE BOOK PUBLISHING PLC

This edition published 1999 by
Knight an imprint of Brockhampton Press

10 9 8 7 6 5 4 3 2 1

All characters in this publication are fictitious and any resemblance to real persons, living or dead, is purely coincidental.

ISBN 1 86019 6977

Typeset by Keyboard Services, Luton, Beds

Printed and bound in Great Britain by
Mackays of Chatham PLC, Chatham, Kent

Brockhampton Press
20 Bloomsbury Street
London
WC1B 3QA

To Suse Coon

Part One
Rankeillor, Forfarshire, August 1912

1

Chris Adam looked down at the empty sheet of manuscript paper and groped for the thread of melody which had been tormenting her all day, singing to her like a plaintive child: 'Write me down! Write me down!' Yet now that she had managed to extricate herself from various domestic duties and sat finally alone in her room with a pencil in her hand, the voice seemed to be fading fast. In a minute or two she feared she would no longer hear it.

She plunged in and sketched out the barest pattern of notes. On the stave, that tiny snatch of song looked unimpressive when in her head it had sounded beguiling. She hummed it aloud and smiled, hearing again the chords that suggested themselves as an accompaniment. She scribbled them in as best she could and played them through in her mind. It was a start but it would not do. There was still a gap between what she had imagined and what was in front of her. She wondered how she was going to pull down and shape into plain black marks on the stave those dream-like sounds which had filled her head. She clutched at the pencil in her hand in frustration at her lack of skill. She felt like a man with a vision of an unbuilt house, a person who had a hod of bricks and a pail of mortar but no real knowledge of how to transform them into a house. 'I must learn to build,' she told herself, and reached out for one of the harmony books she kept on her table. But she hesitated to open it, distracted by the view from the window. The great beech trees which edged the Manse garden, she noticed, seemed tired with their late summer burden of leaves. Her little piece of music ran in her ears again and she realized that she would not find her answer between the covers of those books. She had to work out for herself what she wanted: conventional exercises in four-part harmony did not make the sort of music she heard in her head. She had to discover her own musical language.

But how hard that was! Why did she always have to be left alone with that impossible task, with no one to encourage her, no one to tell her even it was worth while? Sometimes it seemed more like a curse than a gift, that desperate desire in her to make something out of nothing. 'But I will do it,' she told herself.

She leant back in her chair and closed her eyes. She took her notes, and experimentally imagined them played on the fiddle. Then, quite wonderfully, she heard the answering phrase played on the flute. That was it: flute and fiddle – the two voices weaving together, twisting and turning to form a conversation.

'Chris, you won't believe who's here!' Her sister May's voice tore into the web of sound she had been creating. 'Oh, did I make you jump?'

'Yes – I wish you'd learn to knock,' said Chris. 'I was . . .'

'Miles away,' said May glibly. 'Daydreaming.'

'I was not!' exclaimed Chris, and wondered why she needed to justify herself to her younger sister. 'So who is it? It better be good, mind. I'm busy.'

'Oh, in that case . . .' said May, now off-hand. 'I just thought you might be interested, that's all, interested that Guy Lindsay is sitting downstairs.'

'Guy? Surely not?' Chris could not help sounding enthusiastic.

'I thought you'd be pleased,' laughed May. 'And he

only got back yesterday. I call that pretty keen.' She was heading for the door. 'I'll leave you to get changed, then.'

'Changed? Why on earth?' said Chris. 'Oh May, don't be daft. We're just friends. You're the one who's been daydreaming.'

'Oh, but wouldn't it be wonderful?' said May. 'He's so braw . . . and all that money!'

'Father would be horrified to hear you talking like that,' said Chris, but May ignored her and went instead to open the press. 'I'm not dressing up,' Chris added, firmly.

'Just a fresh blouse,' pleaded May. 'That one is so . . .'

'No,' said Chris. 'He can take me as he finds me.'

In the chilly Manse drawing room with its skimpy chintz curtains and shabby furniture, the girls found their mother giving Guy Lindsay a regular interrogation. She had sat him opposite her on an uncomfortable little chair by the empty grate and Chris observed an expression of pained politeness on his face. However, an instant later, when he had realized she had come in, it changed. He grinned broadly, leapt to his feet, and strode over to her. He seemed to fill the room with his handsome broad-shouldered presence, as if the wind from the moor were gusting through an open door.

'My dear Christina, it's so very good to see you again,' he said. She put out her hand and he clasped it with both his, with extraordinary enthusiasm. For a moment she was at a loss, and then remembered herself.

'Hello, Guy. Welcome back. We didn't expect you so early. Christmas, we heard . . .'

'Well, I thought I should surprise everyone.'

'Did things not work out?' she could not help asking.

'Not exactly,' said Guy.

'I don't know why you went in the first place,' said Mrs Adam, with typical forthrightness. 'The Continent is such a terrible place. Your mother must be so pleased you're home again. May, go and tell Phemie to bring in the tea now. You must be longing for some proper Scottish food, Guy, I shouldn't wonder.'

'I did miss Arbroath smokies,' he said, sitting down again. 'You can't get those in Vienna.'

The tea, by usual standards, was lavish: shortbread and treacle scones as well as bread and butter, and Guy was enjoined to eat as much as possible. Chris could not help being amused at her mother's treating him like a returned prodigal. He had not gone abroad in disgrace, after all, but to study music.

'Another scone, Guy, won't you? They won't keep.'

'I couldn't, really. But they were delicious,' he said. 'In fact, I feel a bit cheeky now, having eaten those. I brought you this from Vienna. I hope you don't mind.' He extracted a brown parcel from a little pile by his feet.

'Oh, but you shouldn't have . . .' said Mrs Adam.

'Open it, Mother, please,' said May, leaning over in excitement.

'There's one for you too, May, and you, Chris,' he said handing out the other two parcels.

'Well, Guy, I really don't know . . .' began Mrs Adam. A present for her was one thing, but for her unmarried daughters quite another. She contemplated the morality of it for a moment and said, 'I suppose there can't be any harm in it, can there? Rather wicked of you, though, I think.'

'Guy only meant to be nice, Mother,' said May, enthusiastically ripping the paper from her parcel.

Chris sat with her parcel on her knees, wondering slightly at this gesture. She found herself thinking that the presents for May and her mother were simply a justification for giving one to her. There had been something portentous in the way he had given it to her.

'Oh Guy!' May suddenly exclaimed, lifting the lid from a slender, striped pink and white box. 'Oh but . . . How did you know I collected fans?' She took out a folded fan and spread it over her knees. It was a pretty, sugary thing, painted with harlequins and Columbines. Guy had judged May's taste perfectly.

'Chris mentioned it once,' said Guy.

'I hope it wasn't too expensive,' said Mrs Adam. Chris repressed a smile.

'It's the most beautiful thing I've ever seen! Thank you so much!' said May, jumping up. She fanned herself with it for a moment, a parody coquette, and then leant over and kissed him on the cheek. 'Thank you.'

'Sit down, dear,' murmured Mrs Adam.

'You haven't opened yours yet, Mother,' said May.

'Very well,' said Mrs Adam, who was clearly enjoying this, despite her puritanical instinct.

It was a large box of bonbons at which she made a little exclamation of delight.

'Not Scottish, I'm afraid,' said Guy, with a grin.

Mrs Adam was beyond words. In a moment the ribbon had been torn off and the box handed round. Chris wanted to laugh. Guy was undoubtedly a genius.

'Aren't you going to open yours?' he asked her, moving over to sit beside her. Mrs Adam and May were not listening. They were examining the painted fan.

She found she was nervous as she attempted to unfasten the knots.

'Here, let me.' He produced his penknife from his pocket and cut through the string.

The string cut, the paper bounced open. There was no elegant box beneath to open, simply a pile of miniature scores with bright yellow covers.

'Mozart . . .' she said softly. 'Mozart . . . oh Guy!'

'*The Marriage of Figaro*,' he said, '*The Magic Flute*, *Così*, and *Don Giovanni*. I saw them all, and when I had I bought the scores for you. It was the nearest thing to your being there. I know you would have wanted to see them.'

'You saw them all?' she said.

'What have you got, Chris?' said May breaking in. 'Oh, music. How dull.'

'You wouldn't say that if you heard these, miss,' said Guy, rapping May playfully on the forehead with *The Magic Flute*.

The other scores still lay in Chris's lap, glowing in their intense yellowness against the dull tweed of her skirt. She wanted to plunge herself into them at once, but did not quite dare to, fearing an almost immediate interruption. She would save turning back the covers until she had time and privacy to drown in their music.

'If it wasn't for the German lettering, they'd look like French novels, wouldn't they?' remarked Guy.

The mention of French novels drew Mrs Adam's attention.

'Really, Guy, I should not be able to thank you if that's what they were. I just hope that there's nothing too salacious in them. Opera can be so . . . well . . .'

'When did you ever see an opera, Mother?' Chris could not help asking, irritated.

'When I was a girl – when I was staying with the Macrae cousins in Glasgow. A most improper thing it was, full of half-naked women. Aunt Jeanie and I did not know where to look. We left after the first act.'

'Are you sure that was an opera, Mrs Adam?' murmured Guy, with a glance at Chris. She swallowed her laughter – it was all too easy to imagine her mother and Aunt Jeanie Macrae scandalized by the sight of dancing girls in pink tights in some second-rate musical burlesque which they had unaccountably mistaken for an opera.

'It isn't the story in an opera that matters, anyway, Mother,' she said. 'It's the music.'

'I'm not sure I agree with you,' said Guy. 'Admittedly, the stories can be absurd, but on occasion, well, the mixture of wonderful music and powerful sentiment is quite marvellous. Take *The Marriage of Figaro* – there's a quite extraordinary scene set in the Countess's bedroom, for example, which . . .'

'In her bedroom?' said Mrs Adam. 'Well, that just confirms everything I ever thought, doesn't it?'

'What happens?' said May eagerly.

'Haven't you anything useful to do, May?' said Mrs Adam, swiftly. 'There are still the things to be sorted for the Dorcas meeting aren't there?'

May went, albeit reluctantly, recognizing censorship when she saw it.

'Mother, you shouldn't be so . . .' said Chris when she had gone. 'She's nearly seventeen.'

'That is not the point,' said Mrs Adam. 'Really, I'm not sure this is the sort of thing I want discussed in my house.'

'I'm sorry,' said Guy. 'I didn't . . .'

'Well, you'll have to remember this is Scotland, Guy,' she went on. 'What goes for Vienna, doesn't go here.'

'I'll try and remember,' said Guy getting up from his seat. 'Well, I'm afraid I had better cut along. Roddy's coming down from town today and my mother will be cross if I'm not there to meet him.'

'I'm very glad to hear that,' said Mrs Adam. 'It's been such a time since he was at the Castle. People have been remarking on it, in fact. Some of the tenants – well they are my husband's congregation and one does hear things – they feel, well, that the Laird ought to be here. They expect it. I thought I should mention it.'

Guy looked uncomfortable and made his excuses to go. Chris followed him into the hall.

'Look, do you fancy a walk? It's so nice out,' he asked.

'What about Roddy?'

'He won't be here for hours, I only said that as an excuse,' he said, with a slight grin. 'I wanted to walk with you. Go and get your coat and then we can have a proper talk.'

'Yes, why not?' said Chris.

They took the lane which lay between the church and the Manse, and left the neatness of the village behind them as they climbed up the wooded slopes of Rankeillor Hill.

'Best to avoid the village,' Guy had said. 'People are beginning to look askance.'

'Because of Roddy?' said Chris. 'What my mother said was idiotic . . .'

'No, not really. It's no more than the truth, is it? You've been here. You must have heard things.'

'Yes, but I haven't honestly believed it. It just seemed more Rankeillor nonsense.'

'Rankeillor nonsense!' he repeated with a laugh. 'I like that.'

'I think I've had more of it than I can stand. Every little thing blown up out of all proportion,' said Chris. 'This last year . . .' She sighed. 'Well . . . you saw what my mother was like. Sometimes, it's simply insufferable.'

'You must wonder why I've come back, then.'

'You must tell me,' said Chris. 'Only if you like, of course.'

'I think you are the only person I can tell who might understand,' he said, with sudden gravity that unnerved her. The remark struck her, like the present of the scores, as designed to touch something deep and quiet inside her.

'Oh, I don't think so!' she laughed. 'What about your Oxford friends?' She remembered the glamorous young men that Guy had brought to the Castle a few summers ago. They had seemed to her like a group of gods who had lifted Guy up to their sacred level, making him leave behind the insignificant friends of childhood. She had been sixteen, and he nineteen and a vast gap had opened between them; he was a young man, while she was still only a schoolgirl. He had been as kind as ever, but remote from her. She could no longer understand his experiences, for he had the world now, while she still only had Rankeillor and boarding school. She had felt at the time that a door had shut in her face, and yet now, Guy seemed to want to open that door again, back to the intimate conspiracy of their childhood, but there was still that great gulf of experience. She had left school now, a full year ago, but she had not left Rankeillor. She felt frozen in time, unable to keep pace with Guy.

'Oh, I haven't kept up with them much,' he said, surprisingly.

'I'm sorry,' said Chris. 'You all seemed so close, that summer.'

'That summer, yes . . .' he said with regret. 'Ah well, that's life, I suppose. Nothing lasts particularly except . . .'

'Except what?'

'Rankeillor nonsense. That hasn't changed.'

'I wish to God it would!' Chris exclaimed, with real feeling.

'My poor child, is it that bad?'

'I'm suffocating quietly,' she said, as brightly as she could. 'One day, they'll find me lying on my bed choked to death by it.'

'I hope not,' said Guy.

'I know it's wrong of me, of course, not to be able to settle to this life. I ought to be grateful, I know, but sometimes I think if I have to teach another girls' Bible class or make any more useful, plain clothes to send to the poor in Dundee I shall simply explode. There has to be more to life than that, doesn't there? There's so much I want to do.'

'Such as?' he asked, as they reached the point of their walk where the trees cleared and the valley spread out in front of them with the village, the church and the Castle.

She hesitated. She had found in the past it was not a good idea to admit to her real ambition. It was generally greeted with open scorn or polite indifference. She glanced at Guy. He had sat down now, his elbows resting on his bent knees, his chin on knotted hands, and those unsettling blue eyes regarded her rather than the view. He was waiting, it seemed quite expectantly, for her to speak and Chris decided she would risk it. Here with Rankeillor subdued and distant, it felt safe. 'I've been writing a bit of music lately, when I can, and I've found what I really want – and I know this probably sounds silly but what I want is to be a composer.'

There now, she had said it.

'It doesn't sound the least bit silly to me. I'm not at all surprised, really,' he said. 'You always were so musical, more than I am, certainly. And, how wonderful to have such a clear idea of what you want out of life! That's the hardest thing, I find,' he went on. 'To have a clear sense of purpose. It's something I've never had. I'm afraid I'm a bit of a drifter, a dabbler if you like . . .'

'I wouldn't call your playing dabbling,' she interjected. 'And that's why you went to Vienna, surely, to study, to be a real musician at last.'

'Is it?' he queried. 'I suppose I thought that, but it didn't take long for me to realize I was fooling myself. I'm no more a musician than . . .'

'But you play wonderfully,' went on Chris, horrified. 'What on earth happened?'

'Why don't you sit down?' he said. 'You make me feel guilty about it, standing there like a reproachful angel.'

She complied.

'So what happened?' she asked again.

'I was thoroughly humiliated. At first, it was wonderful. A beautiful city to get used to – a new way of life – those coffee houses – I thought it was all so civilized. I couldn't believe my luck. My German was improving and my teacher was indulgent. I worked hard, I thought – there was a marvellous piano in my digs, and it was easy – I was doing four or five hours' practice a day. I began to believe

I was getting somewhere until . . .' He broke off and stared out over the valley. 'Do you think the estate is really such a mess?'

'I don't know anything about that,' said Chris. 'Anyway, it isn't your responsibility. It's Roddy's.'

'I think it is,' he said, with a sigh. 'I've got off the point, haven't I?'

'If you don't want to tell me, you don't have to,' said Chris.

'I do want to. I just feel such a fool. It's all that terrible male pride one is raised to have. It can't take too many knocks.'

'Guy, what happened?' she said.

'A ten-year-old, a little girl, in fact. A very pretty child actually, in a white muslin dress – the sort you used to wear on Sundays. Her mother had brought her all the way from Hungary to see my teacher. She arrived just after my lesson, and I stayed to hear her play.'

'And?'

'She was extraordinary – she is extraordinary. She'll be famous in a few years, I imagine. I don't think I've heard anyone play quite like it. It was as if she had the soul of a seventy-year-old, and put seventy years of experience into her playing but mixed it with the energy of a child. She played Schubert, and I sat there, in the room next to the music room – the rooms had double doors between them, so I could hear perfectly – and I think I cried. And then I noticed the mother. She was sitting across the room from me, a thin, shabby creature in black – she looked like a widow, and she looked as though she'd starved herself to get her daughter to Vienna. I knew then the game was up. I hadn't even begun to learn how to be a musician. It wasn't in me. I was simply on holiday, being self-indulgent.'

'I think you are being too hard on yourself,' said Chris.

'You wouldn't if you'd heard that child.'

'She's an exception, surely, a freak. It shouldn't have made you give up. It should have inspired you.'

'To continue with something that was utterly pointless?' he responded. 'I don't think so. The next day I asked my teacher what my chances were, what they really were. He was quite brutal: "You will never be anything more than an accomplished amateur, Herr Lindsay." And that was it. So here I am, again.'

'Well, if you can still bear to touch a piano,' she said, 'we could do with you at the village concert. Or have you lost your nerve utterly?'

'No, not entirely,' he smiled. 'I'd like that.'

'It'll be good for you. People will appreciate your playing here – and they should. You play beautifully. You shan't change my mind on that.'

'Thanks,' he said. 'Perhaps we should do some duets – just like the old days. Some of the Dvŏrák Slavonic Dances? Or Grieg?'

'I shall have to get some practice in,' she laughed. 'I haven't been able to get more than an hour a day in, lately.'

'Then come up to the Castle,' said Guy. 'Better to practise together, don't you think?'

'Well, your lovely Bechstein is a temptation but I don't think my parents would be too keen. It isn't as if we were still children.'

'That's Rankeillor nonsense,' he said. 'And you don't listen to that. Besides, my mother will be there. You know how she loves to interfere. There won't be a chance of our being left alone, unfortunately.'

'I should be wary of you,' laughed Chris, getting up. 'And I ought to get back to the Manse. My mother . . .'

'Yes, perhaps,' he cut in. 'Or you'll find she's confiscated your Mozart on the grounds of impropriety.'

'You never did tell me what happened in the Countess's bedroom,' she said.

'It really is too shocking,' he said, with mock solemnity. 'Especially for your innocent, Manse-bred ears. Run along now.'

'You're not coming just now?'

'I need to think a bit.'

'Well, don't get too gloomy. It doesn't suit you.'

He smiled at that and stretched to catch her hand. To her surprise, he kissed it. She looked down at him, amused but flattered by this little piece of gallantry.

Letting go of her hand, he said, 'Off you go now.'

She went, a little reluctantly, she found, and turned to see him wave to her. Further on down, she turned again, and he was still just in sight, but he did not see her. He was staring forward again, his chin resting again on his knotted hands, his craggy face locked in some grim pattern of thought. She felt his disappointment then as if it had been her own. When he had left for Vienna she had wished for his success although she had envied his opportunity. She had lived vicariously through the very fact of his being there, and to find that he, of all people, had failed seemed to dash her own hopes harder than ever against the rocks of circumstance. If ever a soul was destined to succeed in what he set out to do, she had thought it would be Guy Lindsay, but now he was back at Rankeillor, like a whipped dog. What chance then did her ambitions stand?

When she got back to the Manse she had a chance to look at the miniature scores he had brought for her. She turned to the first of them: '*Die Zauberflöte – The Magic Flute*. The name pleased her – she had long believed that music was a form of sorcery. Opening the score, she saw it was rather meanly type-set, with no thought for clarity or elegance, but to her such things were immaterial. It was the patterns of the notes which electrified her, and as she read the first few bars of the overture, she found herself quite entranced.

Three sets of sustained chords rang out in those first few bars of the overture, each set punctuated by, it seemed to her, daringly long pauses. She felt those chords with their deeply satisfying harmonies echo through her, sending a prickle of excitement through her nerves. After them was a brief section of development, resolving it seemed all the tensions that the chords had awoken, and then a fugue broke out, a delicious, mischievous fugue on a pattern of rapidly repeated quavers . . .

She closed her eyes for a moment, dizzy at it. She had realized some time ago that she could read a printed piece of music and hear it playing in her head, but never had anything she had seen before affected her like that. She knew the *Messiah* backwards and loved it dearly, but there was nothing in it like this. This was not like the few pieces of Mozart's piano music she was familiar with but something entirely different and compelling.

She knew she would be wanted downstairs, and she was about to close the book, but those opening chords tantalized her again. She could not resist turning the page to see what lay beyond. A bold, rising melody confronted her, hooked her indeed, and soon she was lost utterly in the wonderful music of the first act of *The Magic Flute*, where three women sang in extraordinary harmony to save a man from a dragon. Nothing could disentangle her now from such enchantments. Not even Mrs Adam at her most persistent could follow her into this world.

2

That evening as he was dressing for dinner, Guy found he was still thinking about Chris. The memory of her presence resonated in him, like a striking set of harmonies. He had found seeing her again both strange and attractive. She had changed so much in his absence: he had left behind a girl and returned to find a woman, a beautiful, self-possessed young woman touched with quiet determination. She wanted to write music!

She was remarkable, that child of the Manse. But perhaps the austerity of the Manse itself was in some way responsible for it. There were generations of ministers in her family, he recalled, and perhaps she had their puritanical stubbornness in her blood, but wished to use it, by some magic, for a very different purpose than preaching to the godly.

She had looked exactly like a minister's daughter in her neat, sensible and hard-wearing tweed coat and skirt, and a respectable, ugly hat, no doubt chosen, like everything else, for durability and economy. She was pretty as well, as a country girl could be pretty, far prettier, in fact, than he remembered, with bright, clear skin and ripe corn-coloured hair that looked inviting to the touch. No one would have noticed anything strange about her. But he had looked into those grey-green eyes and seen the spark in them when she had said, 'I want to be a composer.'

He was sitting in his dressing gown, contemplating this, as the bath water ran and the room filled with steam.

As he got into the bath, he heard the rumble of the brougham on the gravel outside. Roddy was back then. Guy let his head sink back against the high back of the bath, trying to extract every shred of relaxation he could from the hot water, but it was not much good. Roddy's voice, raucous with drink, was now calling out a florid greeting to the staff. It was, Guy supposed, too much to hope that Roddy could stay sober on such a long train journey.

Five minutes or so later, there was an urgent rapping at the bathroom door, which did not surprise him.

'Guy, Guy, are you there?' It was Isolde, his sister. 'You must come down at once. It's Roddy, he's being . . .'

'I'm in the damned bath!' exclaimed Guy.

'Oh, but you must! I don't know what to do with him.'

'Can't Malcolm and Johnny cope with him?'

'Please, Guy, please . . . We can't let Mama see him like this.'

'All right,' said Guy. 'What a waste of bath water,' he muttered in addition.

'What?'

'Nothing,' said Guy, reaching for the towel and climbing out.

'I'll go and order some coffee,' said Isolde. 'Don't be long, please.' He heard her shoes tapping along the passageway.

'A bucket of cold water might be more to the point,' said Guy, rubbing himself dry as best he could. It was suddenly freezing, and he pulled his dressing gown on, hoping the plaid wool would dry the rest of him adequately. With wet hair, and wet feet, he set out to deal with Roddy.

His brother had always been a heavy drinker, but recently the habit had become a problem. Guy had seen him briefly in London on his way back from Vienna and had been shocked by the change. If Roddy had been wild before, now he was quite out of control.

Isolde was hovering in the hall, waiting for him. She was all dressed up, just as he had expected, in a shimmering grey silk dress, and she was trembling with anxiety so that she reminded him, in her pale slenderness, of a frosted leaf shaking in a chill wind of winter.

'Where is he?' he said, pulling his dressing gown round him a little more tightly. Isolde was easily embarrassed by any show of male nakedness.

'In the billiard room,' she said. 'Drinking brandy. You were right, Guy, absolutely right. I didn't really believe you when you said those awful things about when you'd seen him in town . . .'

'We ought to start locking the brandy up,' he said, as he went in.

Roddy was lying in state on the large sofa, which was at right-angles to the fire, a disreputable piece of furniture at the best of times, being old and saggy, and the favourite home of the family dogs. But Roddy, in his shirt-sleeves, his crimson face propped up on the cushions with one of the dogs salivating over his chest, did little to improve the picture. In one hand was a thin cigar, in the other a brandy balloon.

'Ah, just the fellow . . .' he said, as Guy came in. 'I need a refill, and bloody Dido here' – he nudged at the red setter with his elbow – 'won't shift. She's pinned me down, the infernal hound . . .'

'Come here, Dido!' said Guy, and the bitch came obediently to his side, and began to lean against his legs in her inimitable fashion.

Roddy sat up slowly, as if his large frame were made from lead and not flesh. Perhaps the flesh was heavy enough, for there was a great deal of it suddenly. His face particularly, always broad, had filled out, and a large double chin was developing. He looked older than twenty-eight, quite gone to seed in fact.

'Now, I can get a bloody drink,' he said.

'Do you think you ought?' said Guy.

'Spare me this, Guy, for God's sake,' said Roddy, waving his cigar, so that a large piece of ash landed on the sofa. 'Issy has put you up to this, I know. She's been dashing about like anything since I got back, worried I'll offend Mama.'

He staggered towards the table where the decanters and glasses were set out. Guy stepped nimbly in front of him.

'Oh, come on, Guy,' said Roddy. 'Give a fellow a chance . . .'

'You're absolutely sotted, Roddy,' he said. 'You . . .'

'Shut up,' said Roddy with utter indifference. He pushed past him, and with alarmingly unsteady hands poured out two large brandies. 'Here. Drink.'

Guy shook his head. In some ways, there was nothing he would have liked better than a stiff drink just then, lining the cold, strained pit of his stomach, but how could he? One did not fight fire with fire.

'Thanks, but no,' he said. 'And you shouldn't really . . .' and he attempted to wrest the glass out of Roddy's hand.

'What the devil?' exclaimed Roddy. The glass went crashing to the floor, spattering brandy over Guy's bare feet. 'You little . . .' and with a heavy, surprisingly well-aimed hand he whacked Guy across the face, and sent him reeling backwards slightly. This made Roddy laugh with delight.

Guy, although his face was stinging, knew he could not give up.

'Very amusing,' he said. 'You bloody sot. Oh, for God's sake, Roddy, look at yourself! It's disgusting, really.'

Roddy lunged for him. Before Guy knew what had happened, Roddy had pinned him to the wall by the shoulders. Guy was strong, but Roddy, even when roaring drunk, was stronger. Much of that flesh was still hard muscle. And then, in one swift, horrible movement, he had kneed Guy in the groin. Guy yelped out, and then bent double, unable to ride the pain, feeling the automatic tears come streaming down his face. He found himself wondering if he would ever get upright again, let alone father any children.

'Serves you bloody right,' said Roddy. 'You bloody prig!'

Guy heard the door open, and through a mist of tears he saw Isolde run in. Guy, who was crouched against the wainscoting, bellowed out, not particularly for her benefit but for his own, 'He's a lunatic!'

She looked horrified and Guy wanted to vomit. He could not believe how much pain he was still in. It was getting worse, rather than better.

'Ah, hello again, Issy,' Roddy said. 'Fancy a drink? No . . . oh well, all the more . . .' Guy heard the refilling of a glass.

'Guy dear, are you all right?' Isolde had come over to him.

'No!' he exclaimed. 'Of course not!'

'Well, I suppose I should go and dress for dinner,' said Roddy, his s's well slurred by now. 'Don't worry about him, I was just administering a little friendly fraternal guidance. I shall see you all at dinner.'

Guy managed to lift his head enough to see him go. It was with such a swagger that Guy was surprised he did not fall flat on his face. He certainly wished that he would, preferably on to some hard, pointed object.

Isolde helped him up and into a chair. She brushed cool hands over his sweating temples and wondered if they need call out the doctor.

'For Roddy, more to the point . . .' Guy managed to say.

'Yes,' said Isolde. 'We really have to do something about him.'

'You can lock him up and throw away the key, as far as I'm concerned,' said Guy, 'if he's going to carry on like that.'

'I believe there are sanatoriums...' Isolde said tentatively.

'But how would we get him there?' said Guy, making a valiant effort to get to his feet. 'Oh God . . . aaah . . . look, I'm going to lie down for a bit . . . I may not make it to dinner.'

'Do watch out for that glass, Guy,' said Isolde, but it was too late. If it had not been so painful, he might have laughed at it.

An hour later, the Lindsay family were assembled at the dinner table, keeping up appearances. Guy, with a dull ache in his groin and a yard or two of gauze bandage on his foot, had managed to struggle into his evening clothes and get downstairs again. He was not entirely sure why he had made the effort. Lying on his bed, in the soft, dark comfort of his room, well dosed with laudanum (kept in the house for his mother's migraines), he had felt careless and indifferent to what had happened. Roddy's problem had not seemed his problem at all. Why should he care, when his elder brother had behaved so badly?

Yet, as he gazed across the room, and saw the ranks of his lead-soldier armies, which were set out on all the available surfaces, his carefully collected dragoons and hussars, he knew he could not ignore the matter. It was his duty to sort Roddy out, no matter what it might mean to him personally. If Roddy hated him for it, so be it. His father, who had given him many of those soldiers, tiny symbols of duty and tradition, would have expected that of him, and his father's memory was something he could not disappoint. He would have to stay and fight, even if Roddy kicked him in the groin every night.

His father had wanted to be a soldier. He had wanted to command an Indian Regiment and live a life of exemplary courage and honour. But his health had never permitted it, and he had stayed at home running the Rankeillor estate with the same care with which he would have commanded a regiment. Yet he never lost his love of military things, and had passed it on to Guy. Together they had set up the lead soldiers to fight the great battles of the past: Waterloo, Blenheim, and, most loved of all, Salamanca, because there the Forfarshire Contemptibles had distinguished themselves. At thirteen, Guy had decided that Sandhurst would follow his time at Rugby, and together they had pored over the entrance regulations. Then, quite suddenly, during his first half at Rugby, his father had died. His mother had arrived in full mourning to impart the news. Nothing in his life, he felt, could ever have equalled the pain of that moment. It was as if God Himself had died.

'A really honourable man,' his father had once said to him, 'is the one who can make sacrifices cheerfully for the common good. It might not be easy but you must always try.'

And so, for Isolde's sake, and for his mother's, he had to make the effort and go down to dinner. They could not be left alone with Roddy. To stay in his room, sheltered by the faded crimson bed hangings, was an act of selfishness, and, more important, not in the least constructive.

So he found himself sitting uncomfortably in the dining room, watching Roddy guzzling oxtail soup. The prospect of dinner seemed to have sobered him up slightly – he was as fond of his food as of drink, especially the rich autumnal food which was being served that night, all of it awash with cream and heavy sauces.

His own appetite spoilt, Guy put down his spoon and turned to look at his mother. Lady Lindsay was apparently quite indifferent to the sight at the other end of the table, but Guy knew she was exercising her iron self-restraint. She would make no hint that one of the people at her dinner table, her darling elder boy, was unacceptably drunk.

She was dressed elaborately, as ever, with that touch of theatricality, which sometimes made the more conservative ladies in the county stare. Tonight, she was in her lilac cloud of gauze, all ruffled and spangled and ethereal – a costume which always reminded Guy of the Queen of the Night. Perhaps, he reflected, it was not only the dress. There was something terribly regal about her, with her determinedly impassive face, more handsome now in middle age than in youth. If she had been a singer she would have made the role her own.

'So, Guy,' she enquired. 'Have you thought any more about what you will do with yourself now?'

'After his Viennese fiasco?' snorted Roddy, contemptuously. 'I could have told you that was a rotten idea twelve months ago.'

'Roddy, that isn't kind,' said Isolde. 'Guy wasn't to know that.'

'Trust you to waste a bloody year having piano lessons,' Roddy said.

'I hardly think you spend your time any more usefully,' murmured Guy. He could not resist this jibe.

'What do you mean by that?' said Roddy.

'I mean that you're making a fine mess of running the estate,' said Guy.

'Guy . . .' said his mother, reprovingly.

'No, it's about time he heard a few home truths,' said Guy. 'The whole estate will go to ruin unless he starts working at it. Father would be shocked to see what you've done – or rather what you haven't done. You've got responsibilities. That's the price you have to pay for the honour of being Laird, for sitting there in Father's chair. You have to work for that. He always said that, didn't he?' He cast round with a glance to Isolde and Lady Lindsay, hoping they might back him up, but they remained silent; Isolde struck with fear, he suspected, while his mother was outraged at such plain speaking. 'The fact is,' he went on, determined to carry on whatever, 'you're ruining yourself and the estate, and if we don't all do something soon about it, well . . .'

'Well, what?' said Roddy.

'Have you heard of dipsomania?' he asked. 'Apparently it's a horrible way to die.'

'Guy, really, this is hardly the time . . .' said Lady Lindsay.

'No, Mother, I think it is. It's about time Roddy faced up to the fact that he's drinking himself into oblivion, and if we don't do something about it, well . . .'

This was too much for Roddy. Like some ancient sea monster, dredging itself out of the depths of the water, he heaved himself up from his seat.

'This isn't a pulpit, man!' he exclaimed, thumping his fist on the table. 'It's a dinner table!' He spat out the words with such vehemence that Guy saw a glob of spittle fly across the table. 'Did ever a man have to deal with such a' – he paused to look Guy over with utter disgust – 'a pious little prick!'

'Roddy, dear, please . . .' said Lady Lindsay, with an elegant gesture of entreaty and a touch of steel in her voice.

But Roddy shook his head, pushed back his chair with such a kick that he knocked it over, and stumped out of the door. Guy leant back in his chair and stared despairingly at the ceiling, thinking of the row of decanters in the billiard room.

'Well . . .' said Lady Lindsay, with only the slightest of sighs, as if it had been only a minor accident which had upset the careful ritual of dinner. 'I think you can serve the fish now, Malcolm,' and then she turned again to Guy.

'What will you do then?'

'Oh, I don't know,' snapped Guy, irritated by the way his mother seemed so easily to side-step the real issue. 'Malcolm, will you have someone take the decanter tray out of the billiard room,' he added quietly as the butler was at his elbow, offering him the dish of fried trout.

'I'll certainly try, Mr Guy,' said Malcolm, as he spooned out almonds and parsley over the trout. 'But we may be too late, sir, if you catch my meaning.'

'Well, in future, I think it had better be put away.'

Malcolm nodded and disappeared.

'You must have some idea, surely,' said Lady Lindsay, responding to his earlier remark.

'I haven't really had any time to think. And now with this business with Roddy – someone ought to look to the estate, don't you think?'

'Oh, the estate!' exclaimed Lady Lindsay lightly. 'Roddy can look after that.'

'Mama, dear,' ventured Isolde, 'what Guy says is right, you know. Roddy's terribly ill and . . .'

'I don't know why we are all getting so vulgarly concerned about this,' said Lady Lindsay. 'My father was a hard drinker, and so was your father's father. No one would have dared to presume to call them ill. How middle-class this obsession with temperance is! Roddy may be a little wild just now but . . .'

'Oh, do stop fooling yourself, Mother,' said Guy, sharply.

'I'll pretend I didn't hear that,' she said.

'I'm sorry, but it's true. You are fooling yourself, Mother.'

'Well, really,' she responded. 'I don't know what your father would have said to hear you talking to me like that.'

'He wouldn't have let things get so out of hand,' said Guy.

'So I am to blame for all this, am I?' she said.

'We all are, I suppose,' said Guy. 'But I for one am not going to sit here any longer and do nothing about it. We can't, any of us. It's our duty.'

'Your duty is to make something of yourself, Guy,' said Lady Lindsay. 'I can't sit here and allow you to waste yourself like this. If the estate needs a land agent, then let Roddy employ one. You would be wasted here. Your father and I had such plans for you, Guy . . .'

'My duty is to help Roddy,' he cut in, firmly.

She shook her head and then clasped her hands in front of her mouth for a moment of intense thought.

'No, you're mistaken,' she said. 'You simply haven't had a chance to think this out properly, to consider the alternatives there might be for you.'

'What alternative do I have?'

'Well, Quentin's offer in New York still stands, of course . . .'

Guy could not help scowling. This was a pet scheme of Lady Lindsay's with which she had often taunted him. His American uncle, having no sons of his own, wanted someone in the family to come into his bank and carry on the blood line.

'He needs someone like you,' she went on. 'Only in his last letter, he was begging me to ask you again if you'd consider it.'

'If he's so desperate, why doesn't he ask one of those cousins on the farm in Kentucky, then?' responded Guy. 'They'd probably jump at the chance.'

'Don't be facetious,' she said, tartly.

'I'm being quite serious,' he said. 'I thought they didn't have two ha'pennies to rub together.'

'Exactly,' said Lady Lindsay. 'Quentin would no more let one of Nelly Kennedy's boys into Horton's bank than the hogs which they raise. Whereas you . . .'

'I'd be a monkey in a silk hat,' said Guy.

'Whereas you,' she repeated, 'would belong, quite

beautifully, you'd belong. You could do so well, Guy. And New York would welcome you, I'm sure of it. There would not be a door closed to you.'

'I don't want to go to New York,' said Guy. 'I dislike the place intensely. I'm a Scotsman. Can't I live in my own country?'

'I should hope that you might regard America as your country too,' said Lady Lindsay, with a slight sniff. 'And as for your disliking my birthplace so . . .'

'I'm sorry, Mama, I didn't mean to slight you,' said Guy, 'but you have to understand I can't feel the same way about it as you do. I'm sure you don't feel the same about Rankeillor.'

'I don't think you know anything of what I feel,' said Lady Lindsay, 'from what you've said tonight.'

'How was your visit to the Manse, Guy?' said Isolde, valiantly attempting to change the subject.

Her question was innocent enough but Guy felt as though he had been prodded by a sharp stick. Chris's face and eyes were with him again, disconcerting him. He searched for a moment for something bland to say.

'Oh, it went well enough,' he said. 'Mrs Adam interrogated me pretty thoroughly. I think she imagines the Continent will have corrupted me.'

'Perhaps it has,' said Lady Lindsay.

Guy was about to respond, but Isolde flashed a warning glance across the table at him. Instead he said, 'I asked Chris up to practise some piano duets – it'll be quite like the old days, won't it?'

'Christina's so pretty now she's put her hair up, isn't she?' said Isolde, artlessly.

'I suppose so. I didn't really notice,' he responded, with as little colour in his voice as he could manage. He attacked the food on his plate, realizing then just how much he had noticed.

3

'Oh my goodness, my goodness me!' said Mrs Adam, coming into the back sitting room which the family used as a general workroom.

Chris looked up from her hemming.

'Who was it?' she asked, and then saw the yellow telegram in her mother's hand.

'A little boy!' exclaimed Mrs Adam, staring at the telegram. 'Ann's had a little boy – oh, but . . .' She sank down into the nearest chair. 'I meant to be there and . . .'

Chris got up and took the telegram from her mother.

'A. DELIVERED OF A SON THIS MORNING. BOTH DOING V. WELL. J. CHISHOLM.'

She could not help smiling at the economy of the announcement. Her brother-in-law might be delighted at the birth of his first son, but he was not going to waste pennies on an extravagant telegram.

'It's three weeks early, isn't it?' said Mrs Adam. 'Something might have happened, and I wasn't there.'

'I'm sure John's mother was there,' said Chris.

'Yes, but that isn't the same at all,' said Mrs Adam. 'I was there for Margaret's birth and I know how much it helped. Oh, poor Ann, I hope it wasn't too long.'

'John could have given us a few more details couldn't he?' said Chris.

'Where's your father?'

'In the study.'

'I shall have to go there, won't I? I can't possibly stay here. I have to see she's all right. She'll need me.'

'Of course . . .'

'But your father won't like it.' Mrs Adam considered the point. 'It's such very short notice.'

'I can manage things here.'

'Can you?' said Mrs Adam, quite unconvinced.

'You know I can. In fact, why don't you take May as well? She'd love that.'

'Oh, I don't know . . .'

'Be reckless,' said Chris. Mrs Adam shook her head at that. 'It is your first grandson,' she added.

'I know, but . . .'

'But me no buts!' said Chris. 'Go and tell Father that you and May are going down to Dundee for a few days. He won't mind, I'm sure. He'll be glad of the quiet, I should imagine.' And so shall I be, she could not help adding mentally.

'Yes, you're right,' said Mrs Adam. 'May would be useful. I'll go and tell him . . .' She got as far as the doorway. 'The packing,' she said. 'I'll have to start packing . . .'

'It'll wait a few minutes. Go and tell Father he's got a grandson.'

'Oh yes, yes, of course,' said Mrs Adam, breaking into a broad smile. 'Isn't it wonderful!' she said, as she went.

Ann had always been the favoured child. Chris could not remember her sister ever being in trouble with their parents. She had always effortlessly done everything right: from making beautiful button-holes to marrying an eminently suitable, rather serious young man with just the right amount of money (neither too much nor too little) and settling to a life of unblemished domesticity in Broughty Ferry. Now she was producing children, and being, as far as Chris could judge, a perfect mother. Mrs Adam constantly held up Ann's life as the model upon which she and May should form their own futures.

She retrieved the piece of cloth she had been hemming – a baby dress as it happened, not intended for Ann's baby, but for some poor child in a Dundee slum. Looking at the uneven hem, she decided that the poor did not deserve shoddy workmanship disguised under the sacred name of charity, and she picked up her scissors and ripped out the stitches. An hour's work vanished before her, and she felt the frustration of her own futile endeavour. How much better she could have spent that hour at the piano, methodically working through some five-finger exercises, instead of pushing a needle through a wretched piece of cheap cloth. That baby dress was an insult, with its horrid rough calico, an insult really! How could anyone persuade themselves that making such things was good work? She threw it down on the table, and went into the dining room where the piano was.

It was a large, north-facing room, dominated by the long table with its covering of green baize and the carefully marshalled tablet-back chairs (bought by Chris's great-grandfather in a rare fit of extravagance). The piano, at one end, seemed uneasy in the room, its pale wood carving and inlay too frivolous and too feminine. It had been a wedding gift to her parents from some now-forgotten friend or relative to whom Chris had often offered a secret prayer of thanks: it was a good piano, as well as a pretty one.

She opened the lid and began to play the Arabesque by Schumann to unstiffen her fingers. As she stumbled she realized she would need to put in a great deal of work if she was going to play the Slavonic Dances with Guy. His playing had always dazzled her, and his time in Vienna, whatever he might say about it, was sure to have improved it further. She was glad it was only the indulgent village who would be their audience. They would not expect perfection, no matter how much she wanted to give it.

'Chris!' Mrs Adam had come into the room and sounded irritated. 'The packing.'

'Yes, I'm just coming.'

'You're coming now. The train is at three. I've sent May to wire them, so you can pack for her.'

'She won't like that...' Chris tried to protest. However, Mrs Adam was insistent and Chris was chivvied into a chaos of hat boxes and petticoats.

When at last Mrs Adam and May had been dispatched to Broughty Ferry (not without much commotion) Chris found herself blessedly alone. Her father retreated to his study and informed her he would not be out until dinner. She was amazed at her sudden leisure. There were tasks which she had been left with, but nothing was urgent, except her own desire to get some real work in. She collected her manuscript book and a pencil and settled in the dining room to try again to capture her little thread for flute, fiddle and piano.

It went well. She became utterly absorbed in it, and the ideas seemed to flow out from her so that she was at times surprised by her own ingenuity. The notes she wrote down began to form sounds which were as rich and as haunting as those in her head, and she found that she had, in the space of two hours, half a dozen pages of music in front of her which had not existed before.

She was interrupted suddenly by Phemie the housemaid, coming in with a lamp. She was startled by the brightness of it. She had scarcely noticed that the light had gone.

'You've a visitor, Miss Chris,' said Phemie. 'Mr Lindsay's here.'

Before she had time to answer he was in the room with them, presumably having followed Phemie and her lamp. She got up to greet him and found her legs shaking. She realized she was exhausted.

'Guy – how nice . . .' was all she managed to say, before sinking back on to the stool.

'I'll bring you some tea, shall I?' said Phemie.

'Please,' said Chris.

'Are you all right?' said Guy, when Phemie had left them. 'You look quite done in.'

'I've been working, and I lost track of time, I think.' She could not help smiling. There was something marvellous in being able to say that. This tiredness she felt was satisfying.

'May I see it?'

'Play it if you like,' she said, getting up from the piano stool to give him a seat. She pulled out one of the chairs at the table, and sat down, her elbows resting on the green baize.

Phemie had left the lamp on top of the piano, and Guy sat in the pool of golden light which it cast. It made his fair hair shine, the waves of it illuminated crisply, so that they resembled the carved mane of a wooden lion she had once seen. He is braw, she could not help thinking.

'Rhapsody for violin, flute and piano,' he said, reading aloud the title she had scrawled on the first page. 'What a wonderful combination. Why a rhapsody?'

'Because it doesn't go anywhere in particular,' she said. 'I hope you can decipher it all.'

'It looks clear enough to me. So we start with the flute, alone . . .' He played the opening theme and she was surprised to see how well he interpreted it. It was as if she'd told him exactly how she wanted it played, with that easy, elegant grace. She wanted it to flow, like a burn, without any particular purpose, except to go forward with wonderful fluidity. 'That's quite lovely,' he murmured, and played on, to the section where the fiddle answered, a little lower, but still as plaintive. Then he got to the part when all three instruments played together for the first time, and because he was skilled he managed to put in some of the flute and violin lines as well as the piano. Chris heard, then, for the first time, her creation played by someone else, and it seemed familiar and yet odd, as if she had had nothing really to do with its creation. It stood alone now, an independent thing with a life of its own.

He broke off suddenly and turned to her.

'You know this is simply . . .' he began and shook his head.

'Is it all right?'

'All right?' he echoed. 'Chris, it's incredible. I don't know how you do it.'

'I'm not so sure myself – I just had this urge and that's it . . .' She got up and went over to the piano. 'Do you mind playing on? I can put in the other parts for you. I'll stick them an octave up, then I won't get in your way.'

'Yes, let's,' he said, moving up the piano stool to make room for her. They began again, and Chris, hearing the fullness of the whole thing, was filled with a restless longing to do nothing but work on this piece. When it ended, abruptly and without ceremony, she burst out, 'I must try and finish this, of all things, I must.'

He laughed at that, a warm, robust laugh that pleased her as much as the dying echoes of the piano, and then, suddenly, he took her hand and, holding it rather firmly, looked keenly into her eyes.

'You know,' he said, 'I really think you will do something wonderful.'

She swallowed, a little taken aback at this. She did not quite understand it. If some other fellow had done and said such a thing, she would have been sure that he was making love to her, but it seemed ridiculous that someone like Guy Lindsay should think of making love to her.

'You think so?' she managed to say.

'All the signs are there. You'll be a meteor, Chris, ascending the highest heights and no one will stop you, will they?'

'How can you know that?' she said, withdrawing her hand gently, but reluctantly.

'An instinct,' he said, and turned away from her, back to the keyboard. 'What shall I play now?'

'Surprise me,' she managed to say.

'All right,' he said, 'do you recognize this?'

He played a sustained chord, and she smiled as she realized what it was; the opening chord of *The Magic Flute*. 'Not quite the right thing for the piano,' he said.

'Oh I don't know,' she said. 'Carry on.'

But as he played, she found she was not really listening. Her usual easy concentration was upset. She was watching him, feeling a fool for doing it, but doing it all the same. Every inch of him fascinated her suddenly, from the rough, tweedy back of his jacket to the suggestion of stubble on his cheek. She felt if she had dreamt of a perfect man, she was seeing him now. She was stirred up in her very guts by it, although her rational mind shouted at her to put those ridiculous feelings aside. There was no place in her life for such feelings. They would get in the way of what was really important. But wasn't this important, her soul whispered back, wasn't feeling like this important?

He broke off suddenly, in the middle of a passage.

'I'm playing like an idiot. I can't concentrate,' he said, staring resolutely ahead of him. He rested his hands on the music shelf and bowed his head, shaking it. 'It's ridiculous . . .' He began to laugh, and she could not help but laugh too. She was not sure why they were laughing, but she felt good, liberated by it, like an animal let off a short tether. Then all at once he turned again to her, and the laughter died between them, as quickly as it had come.

He leant forward and touched her lips with his: it was the tiniest, most insignificant kiss, but she felt slaughtered by it. She saw that he too was shaking. They sat there, breathing rather loudly, the deep, cool silence of the dining room all around them.

The door creaked open behind them, and Chris instinctively slid a little along the piano bench, putting some distance between Guy and herself. She turned, as Guy did, to see her father standing in the doorway. She felt discovered, as if he knew what had just happened, which he could not know. She expected, when he opened his mouth to speak, that some reproach would be issued, but instead he said, 'What was that music you were playing just then?'

'Mozart, sir,' said Guy, jumping guiltily up from his place.

'No, not that. I know Mozart when I hear it. Christina plays it enough. Before that. That strange thing . . .'

'Your daughter wrote that,' said Guy.

Mr Adam looked at Chris for a moment and she felt he looked at her as if he had only just made her acquaintance.

'Did you like it?' Chris had to ask.

As was his habit, he did not answer at once but gave the question due consideration.

'I found it . . .' he said, and then stroked his beard for a moment, 'I found it unsettling.'

'Unsettling?' said Guy, 'But Mr Adam . . .'

Mr Adam held up his hands to stem Guy's words.

'I've no time for a debate just now, young man,' he said. 'I've a visit to make – to Kilbraddie Farm, in fact. You know they're thinking of emigrating, I suppose?'

This last remark was offered as a reproach. Kilbraddie was one of the farms on the Castle estate.

'No, I didn't,' said Guy.

'Apparently they think they stand a better chance in Canada,' said Mr Adam. 'Which perhaps they do.'

'You ought to dissuade them from it,' said Guy. 'That family has had that lease for years.'

'Oh, but I can't mend their roof for them, can I?' said Mr Adam, putting on the hat which he had been holding. 'Perhaps though if your brother were to call and reassure them. They'd be a great loss to the parish.'

'I'll speak to him about it,' said Guy.

Mr Adam smiled approvingly and began to retreat.

'Just one thing, sir,' Guy put in suddenly. 'I wonder, would you let Christina come up to the Castle tomorrow night? We'll have the house full of people and dancing after dinner and I thought . . .'

'I can't see any great harm in that,' said Mr Adam.

'I'll send a carriage for her.'

'And see to it she isn't back too late?'

'Of course.'

'Then you may have her for your party,' said Mr Adam. 'And I must go, as you should too, Guy. My wife isn't here at present, you understand, and I can't leave you here alone in the house, can I? I'll be back for dinner, Chris.'

And with that, he ushered Guy out. It was only when they had gone that Chris quite realized the significance of what had happened. Standing alone in the dining room, she touched her lips where he had kissed her, but the gesture had been so slight she could not trace it. He had not bruised her lips with sudden passion but rather had left a mysterious whisper of something intensely significant.

She walked to the piano and looked again at her manuscript, at the music which her father had found unsettling. Well, so he should! she found herself thinking, for she knew then she had created something of real worth, too complicated for mere words. She felt alive with music as she stared at what she had written and was filled with longing to weave a web of such beautiful sound that everyone hearing it should feel as she did then, alive to the possibility of everything.

Guy returned to the Castle to find his mother's guests installed in the drawing room for a late cup of tea. On being introduced to them he found they were pretty much as he had expected: smart, rich people, adept at 'fitting in'. The men were neatly tweedy and hopeful of some good shooting while the women struck him as quite consumed by their elegant but complicated clothes. He had, of course, seen such groups of people before and was generally entirely comfortable with it. But that afternoon he could not slip into the usual game, or at least his heart was not in those conversations about the merits of various gun-makers or in dissecting the doings of the previous season. He found he was looking at them with cruel objectivity and could summon up very little tolerance.

Of course, superficially everything was the same; the usual elegant luxuries for which his mother had such a genius were all in evidence, from the blue and gold Sèvres tea-service to the antique lace ruffles which dangled extravagantly from the wrists of her tea-gown. She was making her customary perambulation about the room with the silver tea-pot, an act of affected simplicity which would have been better left to the butler, but which gave her a chance to burst into the most interesting conversations. In the meantime, Isolde, who had none of Lady Lindsay's easy confidence, was proving her absolute virtue to any man who might be watching by being attentive to the two well-crusted and ferocious ladies who could never be omitted from a guest list. Roddy, for his part, was deep in with the principal guns of the party, in a conversation which involved extravagant gestures and hearty laughter. He was, astonishingly, behaving rather well. Better than I am, Guy reflected, for he was not even half attending to anything that Mrs Vane and her daughter were saying to him. But this shooting party was Roddy's element entirely whereas he felt quite dislocated, as if he had left all the important things about himself in the austerity of the Manse dining room with Chris.

Mrs Vane moved nearer to him and he caught an overpowering whiff of the strong, exotic perfume she wore. He remembered suddenly how Chris had smelt of lavender and he wished he could drown himself in that sweet, simple smell again instead of sitting there choking in such artificiality. He took up his cup and saucer but found he did not want to drink – he did not want to wash the taste of Chris's lips from his own. Had he really kissed her? He began to feel the truth of it slipping away the longer he sat there.

Mrs Vane went to speak to someone else and he was left with the daughter, Mary, a handsome, expensively dressed girl of about Guy's age. 'Do you shoot much?' she enquired, predictably. 'Is it good shooting here?' Her voice struck him as precise and lifeless. He found himself longing for Chris.

'You'll have to speak to my brother about that,' Guy said. 'He's the sportsman of the family.'

He saw his mother smiling in their direction. He knew she would approve of Miss Vane. She would probably push her in Roddy's direction. She would regard a soldier's daughter as just the thing to straighten him out – he could hear her saying it. Guy found himself almost believing it. She looked strong-willed.

'Of course,' she said. 'I'm so interested to see the house – it's very beautiful.'

'I suppose it is . . .' said Guy lamely, never having really considered the point. He could imagine, however, that Miss Vane would look everything over with an appraising, acquisitive eye. She looked like the sort of person who mentally redecorated other people's drawing rooms. 'So, Miss Vane, what do you do?' he asked.

'What do I do?' she said, clearly a little nonplussed by the question. Guy felt his heart sinking. She obviously did nothing seriously. 'Oh,' she went on, back in her stride again. 'I simply adore lawn tennis.'

'Do you play in championships then?' he said. She looked pained, as if he had said something rather vulgar, and he felt obliged to go on and explain himself. 'It's just you sounded so keen.'

He realized then how much Chris had got to him. She had become his standard for women. He now expected all girls to be as modern and as ambitious. He liked it so much in her that he wanted to see it everywhere. It was 1912 after all! How could Miss Vane sit there being so stuffy and old fashioned?

'I don't think my parents would like it if I went into public competitions,' said Miss Vane.

'But wouldn't you like to?' he asked. 'I mean, if you like a thing passionately, you should pursue it passionately.'

'That sounds like self-indulgence to me, Mr Lindsay,' she said, primly.

'I should say it was rather using one's talents to the best end – like the parable.'

'Yes,' admitted Miss Vane, 'if that is appropriate. But there are many cases where it is not appropriate, especially for a woman.'

'I think that's nonsense,' said Guy. 'It's a lie put about by men to keep women down.'

'You obviously wish to de-sex women, Mr Lindsay,' she said coolly, 'which is hardly honourable.'

'No, no, I don't see that at all,' he said. 'There's no reason why taking on a man's challenges should de-sex a woman. In fact I think intelligence and ambition enhances a woman. It makes her more complete, more lovely . . .'

'I do believe you must be in love with Miss Pankhurst!' laughed Miss Vane with considerable derision.

Her remark came in a little lull in the other conversations and the others heard it. The laughter became general and Guy found himself having to smile nonchalantly, the butt of the joke.

'As if anyone could be in love with those harridans!' someone said.

'Has my little brother been spouting his usual rot, Miss Vane?' said Roddy coming, over. 'Let me offer you an escape. How would you like to see over the house before it's time to dress?'

'Oh yes, how lovely!' she exclaimed, jumping up from her seat. 'If that's all right, Mama?' she said, turning briefly to Mrs Vane.

'But of course . . .' murmured Mrs Vane.

'Are there dungeons, Sir Roddy?' Guy heard her asking him as they left the room.

The party began to break up after that and Guy was hoping to slip away to his room, but his mother restrained him with a light tap on the arm.

'I want a word with you,' she muttered, and then turned quickly to another guest.'I've put you in the Duff room, Alice. I know how much you like a garden view.'

'You're too thoughtful, Marianne,' said Lady Seaton. 'It's such a shame that I couldn't bring my little grand-niece, as we planned.'

'Ah, yes, Miranda,' said Lady Lindsay. 'Such a pretty name – how is she bearing up?'

'Quite well, I think. Her sister did insist on making an unfortunate marriage – a Jew, you know,' she added in a whisper, 'and I should prefer Miranda to live with me now, but she won't hear of leaving her sister. But next year at Bayreuth, we shall be there together, I will insist on it. She's so keen to go – she has such a passion for the Master. It's quite wonderful.'

'If she's as beautiful as the photograph you sent me . . .' said Lady Lindsay.

'Oh, twice as beautiful,' said the Countess, with a smile at Guy. 'You young men will have to watch out when she comes out.' And she swept past them, leaving them alone.

'You won't upset the Vanes, will you, Guy?' his mother said.

'Why on earth do you think I'd do that?'

'You can be funny sometimes,' she said. 'And Roddy's keen on her. You can tell, can't you?'

'Do you think he should be encouraged?'

'Of course!' she said. 'How stupid you are. This is a far better thing than all your dramatic talk the other night of a sanatorium. Nothing settles a man like marriage. It's a well-known fact.'

'But I dare say that Mary wouldn't thank you for marrying her to a drunkard.'

'Shush . . . goodness sake. You are going to be difficult, aren't you?'

'No, but . . .' he began.

'Good. I want this thing sorted and settled. I had a long hard talk with Roddy this morning and he quite saw my point of view.'

'What did you say to him?' said Guy. 'I find it impossible to talk to him.'

'Because you don't know how to manage people at all. You're like your father in that respect,' she added. 'You think that plain speaking solves everything. Well, it doesn't.'

'I'd no idea you were a disciple of Machiavelli, Mama,' said Guy.

She shook her head at that and then said, 'So you promise me, no scenes like the other night?'

'I'll try.'

'Good. Well run along. I've things to do.'

'Just one thing. I was at the Manse this afternoon . . .'

'Yes?' she said, suspiciously.

'Well, I happened to ask Christina up for the dancing tomorrow night. She has such a dull time, and I thought . . .'

'Oh yes, I suppose that's all right,' said Lady Lindsay. 'But are you sure she'll fit in?'

'Of course,' he said, irritated by this show of snobbery. 'What, do you think that she doesn't know which knife and fork to use?'

'No, I don't mean that. I simply mean that girls like that don't have a great deal of polish. They find things awkward.'

'Who needs polish?' said Guy, thinking of Mary Vane, who seemed glitteringly insubstantial.

'I hope you are not being silly and falling in love with her,' said Lady Lindsay.

He was about to answer, but found he could not. It would have been the easiest thing to say no, but he did not want to.

'Oh Guy, really,' said his mother, shaking her head as she went past him to leave the room.

For a moment he cursed his silence and then he understood what it meant. To say no would have been a sort of betrayal, because he was falling, falling fast. Why else would he have kissed her?

4

'Very pretty,' said Mr Adam, as Chris came into dinner the following evening. 'I didn't know my daughters had such a stock of finery.'

'Hardly a stock,' said Chris. 'I've just not had the chance to wear it. But I wore this at New Year, don't you remember? It was a present from you and Mama.'

'Ah well, I have very good taste then,' said Mr Adam. 'It reminds me of Annie's wedding dress.'

'It's the same stuff. Duchess satin.'

He nodded and bowed his head slightly to indicate the conversation was over and that he was about to say grace. Chris stood at her place and, as usual, did not listen to his lengthy exhortation over the soup tureen. Her father was inclined to ramble on such occasions. He did not mind his soup tepid, whilst the others might. She remembered, with an inward smile, often tapping a restless, hungry finger against her knuckles as the grace laboured on. She did not know what had first put the idea into her head of God not existing, but since that time she had never been able to persuade herself that it was not the truth. God, to her, did not exist, no matter how sincerely her father might pray to Him.

She looked down at her hands as he prayed on, thinking of the solitary pair of long evening gloves lying still on their tissue paper upstairs which she must endeavour not to forget. Despite her father's compliment she was certain she would feel shabby. Her dress might be made of nice heavy white satin, but it was carefully modest, with little to decorate it except a few tucks and two flat bows on each shoulder. She did not even have the customary string of pearls for her neck.

Her father finished his grace, and it was time to serve the soup – her task tonight, in her mother's absence, and she was scrupulously careful at it, for there was no alternative to the white satin dress. She noticed her father was watching her.

'You did that very elegantly,' he said, when she had finished. 'They'll all notice you at the Castle.'

'I don't think so.'

'Well, certainly Mr Lindsay will notice,' said Mr Adam, dipping his spoon into the soup. 'He is . . .' he began, and then drank the spoonful, 'I suppose . . . er . . . keen – is that the word of the moment?'

'Keen?' she repeated.

'Yes, keen,' he said.

'I don't know . . .' she started.

'Well, of course he's always struck me as a nice, sincere young man, but the main trouble is, don't you think, that he doesn't do anything? I always think a young man needs something solid to do. His late father would agree with me, I think.' Mr Adam had now forgotten quite about his soup and had left the spoon in the bowl. 'You ought to talk to him about it.'

'Me?' said Chris.

'Of course. You have a responsibility here. If he is . . . if he finds you . . .' Mr Adam was too delicate to state the facts.

'You mean if he likes me?'

He nodded. 'Exactly. Well, you have influence. There's no denying a woman has a tremendous influence over a fellow in such a condition . . .'

'You make it sound like an illness.' Chris smiled.

'To a certain extent it is. So you must be careful,

Christina, that he is, well, led – led towards something purposeful.'

'Such as?' Chris could not help enquiring.

'He's a good mind and a sense of duty,' said Mr Adam. 'He'd be a great asset to the Kirk.'

'Guy, a minister?' she said, rather astonished. 'Oh Father, surely not . . .'

'The Kirk needs men from all walks,' said Mr Adam. 'Of course, if you feel diffident, my dear, I could speak to him.'

'Well . . .' she began, but Mr Adam was now well lost on his own train of thought. 'It might be just the thing. A little gentle encouragement and . . . You'd have to wait for him, though. It would take time before he'd finished his studies but . . .'

'He's only asked me to a dance, Father, not to marry him,' Chris protested, but with little effect.

'Now, did he not read classics at the university?' said Mr Adam, unable to let go of his fantastic construction. In a moment, Chris reckoned he would be predicting Guy's election as Moderator.

Phemie came in saying, 'Mr Lindsay's here, sir, for Miss Chris. He asks if he can come in for a minute.'

'Of course. Lay another place will you, Phemie.'

Guy came into the dining room, looking very different from the other afternoon. He had exchanged his usual tweed suit for a kilt and jacket of considerable magnificence, but the effect was rendered very odd by his obvious embarrassment at interrupting them, and the fact that he was carrying a brace of grouse.

'I'm so sorry, I'd no idea you were eating. Oh bother – it's just that we're one short at dinner and my mother is so superstitious that she doesn't like an odd number at table. I thought I might catch you before you ate. I brought you some grouse as well,' he added inconsequentially, gesturing with the dead birds. 'I shot these myself.'

'Phemie, would you take those to the kitchen please,' said Chris, who wanted very much to laugh.

'They'll need hanging...' Guy called out to her as she went.

'You'd better get ready to go, Christina,' said Mr Adam.

'But you've begun...' said Guy.

'Just a little soup,' said Mr Adam. 'Besides, it's a fair exchange, a brace of grouse for a dinner companion.'

'You're very sporting, Mr Adam,' said Guy.

'I shall read a book. Always a pleasure with a meal for me,' said Mr Adam. 'And something which my wife never allows.'

Chris could not resist planting a kiss on her father's bald spot as she passed by him. He looked up a little startled, but Chris scarcely cared what he thought. Guy's wonderful absurd appearance delighted her and she was really glad at the chance of dining as well as dancing at the castle. It stimulated her curiosity and she was glad her mother was not there. None of it would have happened then. She would not have permitted it.

She ran upstairs and fetched her gloves without even hesitating to glance in the mirror. She returned downstairs to find Phemie expounding on the merits of the grouse to Guy.

'Lovely plump birds, they are,' she was saying.

'I picked them out especially,' said Guy.

'How could you?' laughed Chris. 'You shot them.'

'Easily. I looked up and saw these two fat ones, and I thought, that's just the thing to take to Phemie at the Manse. So I shot them.'

'Well, you know how the Minister likes a bit of grouse,' said Phemie.

'We'd better go, hadn't we?' said Chris, shrouding her white satin in her black wool cape, an unexciting but practical garment.

'We don't sit down till eight,' said Guy. 'That's why I thought . . .'

'And we dine at seven. Well, now you know how provincial we are,' she said, as they went out through the front door. 'Goodness, you've come in the motor!'

'You haven't been in this, have you?' he said.

'I've never been in any one – except a 'bus, but that's not the same is it? Oh, it is lovely. I like the thistle on the front.'

'Isn't it patriotic? Hop in.' Mackie, the chauffeur, held the door respectfully open for her.

Guy sat down beside her on the large rear seat and covered her knees with a Lindsay plaid.

'It isn't that cold,' she said, smiling at the attention.

'You look delicate in that dress,' he said.

'I'm as strong as an ox,' she said. 'You know that.'

'I can believe it,' he said. They moved off and Guy remarked, 'I thought of learning to drive one of these things.'

'To give you something to do?' She found she was laughing. 'Oh Guy, you should have heard my father just now!'

'What did he say? Something very amusing, clearly.'

'I don't know if I ought to tell you. You might be offended.'

'You'll have to tell me now,' he said.

'He was telling me that you ought to find something useful to do.'

'He's probably right. What's so funny in that?'

'Well . . .' she began, but laughed again. Guy in his flamboyant kilt with those dead grouse fitted so ill with her father's image of Guy in the sober robes of the Kirk. 'He thinks you'd make a good minister.'

Guy snorted with amusement.

'Where on earth did he get that idea?'

'Who knows? He lives in quite a different world, you know that.'

'Well, I shall have to do something shocking then to disabuse him of the notion,' he said, looking at her significantly. 'Shan't I?'

'Perhaps,' she said, glancing down at her bodice. 'Oh bother . . .' she murmured. She had just remembered she had decided to pin a blowsy silk rose into her waistband to give the dress a spot of colour.

'Bother what?'

'Bother nothing,' she said.

'It sounded a fair bother to me,' said Guy.

'It was a silly one. I forgot something.'

'We can go back.'

'No, no, it's not worth it. I just meant to put a silk flower on and I forgot, that's all.'

'Oh, you shouldn't wear silk flowers,' he said. 'I've a much better idea.' He picked up the speaking tube and addressed Mackie. 'Would you stop at the glass houses first, please.'

'It doesn't matter. It was just a thought . . .'

'Yes it does. I should have thought of it myself. It would have made a better offering than a brace of dead grouse. What sort of devil comes courting with game, eh?'

She was rather astonished by his reference to courting. Was that what they were about, a courtship? She supposed that was how it must look. Her father had thought it and Guy clearly thought it – so then why did she feel any surprise?

'Here we are,' said Guy. 'Donald ought to be around. The lights are still on. I never knew a man so devoted to his plants . . .'

They climbed out of the motor and walked along the path towards the steam-house door. Donald, alerted by scrunching on the gravel, came out to greet them.

'Oh, it's you, Mr Guy, and Miss Christina too. What can I do for you?'

'Flowers,' said Guy. 'The best you have.'

Donald looked Chris over with a well-practised eye.

'That would be a dead white satin, Miss, would it? Ah, yes . . . then cream won't do, will it? But I wonder if there might be something else.' He went back into the glass house, and Chris and Guy followed him.

'He's a complete genius, you know,' whispered Guy.

Chris wondered if Donald, like his plants, could truly exist outwith of this exotic world. She had seen him in the church on Sundays, of course, but she decided that Donald, in his sober best suit, was a wraith. This place, dramatic and sensual, with its lighting of storm lanterns flickering across dark, shiny leaves and picking out here and there some mass of perfect flowers, was Donald's real home and the real Donald was the soft-haired little man, in moleskins, with string dangling from his pocket.

'Here we are. Now usually, Mr Guy, I wouldn't part with these. I had intended them for the luncheon table tomorrow, but well, they're rather more forward than usual. Tomorrow they'll be too far gone, but tonight . . .'

He removed a loose sacking cover from a bucket to reveal a beautiful cluster of roses, deep red-purple in colour and the head crumpled and ruffled like old velvet.

'Madame Isaac Pereire,' said Donald with a sigh of satisfaction. 'Good stock this rose . . .' He picked out three or four of the larger flowers.

'Don't you hate to have to cut them?' Chris could not help asking.

He shrugged his shoulders, and picked out another, shaping the flowers in a moment into a perfect display. Guy reached out to take them from him, but Donald shook his head.

'No, I'm no finished yet, Mr Guy,' he said. 'They won't last just like that. Besides, have you seen the thorns?' And he set off again, into a little room that clearly served him as potting room and living room.

There was something entrancing about the skill of those old, nut-brown fingers. Guy and Chris watched him strip off the thorns and wrap the stems in a web of moss, before he bound them all up in a piece of ribbon, to create a seamless sheaf.

'There we are, miss, that should see you through all the dancing,' he said, handing the flowers to Chris. 'If you want a pin, I've a packet here.'

She buried her face in them for a moment. The smell was intoxicating – of honey and vanilla.

'They're almost too beautiful to wear!' she exclaimed.

'Nonsense,' said Guy. 'Now, shall I pin them on for you?'

'I'll put them in my belt,' said Chris, moving back into the plant house where the black glass of the door could serve her as a mirror. She caught sight of herself with a slight shock – a shadowy, distorted figure, distinguishable as her only by the dazzling whiteness of her dress, where her cloak fell open. And behind her Guy hovered, as strange and as distant as her own reflection, a tall, very male presence who towered over her protectively. She felt in that moment that she did not know him at all. The Guy of her childhood was quite vanished, to be replaced by a Guy who kissed instead of teased and presented her with flowers instead of insults.

'Come on,' he said. 'We'll be late.'

'I'll do this up at the house. I can't see quite straight in here,' she said, looking still at her swimming image in the black glass. It felt, too, as if her own self had vanished, at least the self to which she was accustomed.

'Good idea,' he said, taking the door handle. 'Thank you, Donald!' he called out as they left.

As they returned to the motor she was filled with sudden reluctance to carry on up to the Castle. She was not afraid of social difficulties, rather it was the ease of it all that frightened her. This business of the car and flowers, so different from the usual scheme of her life, was like a cloak of luxury thrown down on the floor for her to walk across. Dinner and dancing at the Castle could only provide more of the same. She would be a young woman in a pretty white dress, with beautiful flowers at her waist and a cavalier in attendance, with nothing more to think of than her own enjoyment. But what was wrong in that, she told herself fiercely, irritated that the spirit of John Knox could haunt her still, when she had thrown out his wretched theology. She determined, then, as they drove into the forecourt, that it would not haunt her that evening – she would be a complete hedonist if she liked. Yet she could not disabuse herself quite of the notion that it was wrong, to strip thorns from roses – it might lull one into a sense of false security.

Guy found that his mother, in a rare fit of benign humour, had put Chris across the table from him and he would have the pleasure of looking at her through dinner.

She was, it seemed, beginning to take up permanent residence in his mind. He had found himself thinking about her at the oddest moments, and in the oddest way. He was not at all sure about what was happening to him. He had been in love before and it had not been the least like this. He had, for a year or so, lamely worshipped one of his sisters' friends (chiefly for her pretty face and enticing body, he suspected now, though at the time he had ascribed himself the purest of motives). He had even gone so far as to ask her to marry him, and had, thankfully, been declined. He had been utterly convinced of his love then – it had seemed to come over him so very suddenly, rather like an attack of influenza, and he could do nothing about it. It had been entirely irrational.

With Chris he did not feel that sudden fever, that

ridiculous switching from sanity into hopeless passion. He had known her for so long, after all. Rather, he felt the fascination of opening a dusty old book which had sat on the shelf for years and finding the contents to be quite brilliant. Her gifts had stunned him into admiration. It might be easy to forget she was a woman, with those gifts. Yet he did find himself remembering her womanliness, constantly. Her undoubted loveliness spoke to him in quite a different language from her music and this evening it disturbed him more than ever. She had dressed that extraordinary hair in a new way, and she wore a square-necked evening dress which showed her neck and chest to some advantage. He was rather disgusted to find himself wondering what her breasts might be like. It did not seem right to think of her like that, when she was so obviously a superior being, but he could not help himself. He looked down at his plate to distract himself but with little success. He looked at her again, and she caught his eye and smiled at him, as if she could read the very thoughts in his head. The temptation of pursuit rocked him then, and he could do nothing about it.

He could not help thinking then how ridiculous Lady Lindsay's imputation of awkwardness had been. She belonged there perfectly, smiling and chatting politely with her neighbour, whom Guy knew to be a boring fool, having spent a morning in the butts with him. She might have been one of them – and why should she not be?

The idea of marrying her jumped wonderfully into his head, while his own neighbour wittered on. After all, there was nothing to stop them, was there? He was twenty-two and had control of his fortune. Nothing could stop him. If he were to marry Chris, well . . .

Of course, his family would not be thrilled about it, but what could they do, and did it matter? He would have the moral high ground. He would know he had done the right thing.

He could set her free so easily. It would be like letting a bird out of its cage. As his wife, she would have all the time which his eight hundred pounds a year could buy. She could write symphonies, operas, concertos . . . the thought of it made him dizzy. For the first time he felt he had a reason for being, a purpose – his purpose was to let Chris do what she must. He was her golden key. Only he could lift from her shoulders all the stifling burdens of her life, and how he longed to do it.

His imagination raced on this theme. He pictured them roaming about Europe from one lovely spot to another. He pictured large scores with 'Christina Lindsay' printed across them. He pictured an orchestra applauding her latest triumph with even more enthusiasm than the audience. And all the time she would sit, as she sat now, looking so lovely in that candle-white dress, smiling at him, loving him as he would love her. It felt so real, so possible then, that he felt he could touch it as easily as he could touch her hand across the table.

The women were getting up now to go to the drawing room, causing a sudden silken fluttering, like the wings of large birds. Chris went among them, of course, the whitest, palest, most luminous figure of them all, her gold hair catching the light, like the halo on a medieval saint, as if nature were determined to signify her greatness to them all. He felt sad at her going, but only slightly, determined now that their separations would soon be only temporary affairs. Besides, soon they would be dancing together.

With the departure of the women, the atmosphere in the room became that of the schoolroom deserted by its overseer. Riot was instantaneous, even among the older men, who swallowed back their port eagerly, as if it would rejuvenate them. Guy drank deep of it also – it would have been impossible and churlish not too, and it fed his euphoria about Chris. The moment began to seem as glorious as the wine: sweet, rich and good-humoured. He became quite convinced, as he sipped and talked inconsequential but amusing nonsense, that he was destined for success, not only with Chris (that, he was sure, went without saying. How could she refuse him?) but in everything he did. The humiliation of Vienna dissolved in the haze of cigar smoke, and he even went so far as to bet a Guards officer called Colston ten guineas that his bag the following morning would be larger.

'You're quite insane, Guy,' said Roddy, leaning on the back of his chair. 'You saw him this morning.'

'The only fellow who's ever beaten me, you know,' remarked Colston, lazily dragging on his cigar, 'is the King, and then of course I was simply being polite.'

'The King is a crack shot though,' said Roddy.

'Oh yes,' said Colston. 'But I am better. Doesn't that sound unpatriotic?'

'Well, I feel lucky,' said Guy, pouring out another glass of port and then pushing the decanter towards Colston. He sniffed his glass before putting it to his lips. 'I suppose I should go easy here if we're to do any dancing tonight.'

'Oh dancing – of course!' exclaimed Roddy with deep contempt. 'Dancing – I'd quite forgotten about that nonsense. God, how I loathe dancing.'

'The man's lying,' said Guy to the rest of the table. 'He's a miracle on his feet. Our governess used to say . . .'

'No you don't, little brother,' said Roddy, and slapped his hand across Guy's mouth like a gag. 'Goodness, what soft skin,' he teased, rubbing Guy's chin. 'Perhaps I ought to ask you to dance.'

Guy, who was past caring, could not resist playing up to this. He held his hands to the side of his face in a gesture of mock-affectation. 'Oh, Sir Roddy, I don't know what to say . . . This is so sudden!'

'Brute!' said Roddy, laughing, and dragged Guy to his feet. 'What shall it be then?'

'Could we manage a waltz?' said Guy. 'Who'll lead for God's sake?'

'I will!' roared Roddy, and to the delight of the rest of them they began to waltz furiously up the room until they could get no further and fell apart, their will destroyed by their own hilarity.

'Encore!' shouted someone and began to applaud.

'No, 'fraid not,' said Roddy, finally regaining himself. 'Time for a toast.'

Guy found he could only stand up with the support of the sideboard and decided that he would drink the toasts in seltzer water. He did not want to dance that badly with Chris. He turned and filled up a glass from one of the siphons, wondering vaguely how long it would be before the siphons began to be squirted about the place. That was a usual development at such affairs.

Roddy was climbing on to his chair and demanding silence for the toast. His face was now puce, like the satin dress of the woman next to whom Guy had been sitting, and in one hand he held a brandy glass, the contents of which slopped from side to side. Guy wondered if this was an entirely wise venture on Roddy's part, but the rest of the men seemed to think it a splendid piece of bravado and were stamping their feet in appreciation as Roddy straightened himself up.

'Ah ha!' he exclaimed with triumph, and then downed the brandy. 'Another!' He surveyed the room for a moment, and laughed like an imbecile. 'I can see who's goin' bald, you know, up here!' He bent down a little to allow his nearest neighbour to refill his glass, this time with twice as much as the previous one. So much for Mama's long hard talk, thought Guy, watching Roddy salivate over the brandy. But then, he concluded, I'm no better, am I?

'Toast then, Lindsay!' shouted one of them, and there was a chorus of, 'Hear Hear!' Roddy beamed at them. There was nothing he liked better than an audience.

'I need a cigar . . .' he began inconsequentially.

'Oh, come on, man!'

'All right then, gentlemen, I give you our noble adversary' – he really had to struggle with 'adversary' – 'the damnable Grouse!' With the final words he swept both arms into the air with a great gesture, and then suddenly the chair tottered, fell backwards and Roddy went crashing to the floor.

It happened so quickly that for a moment Guy was not sure it had. He was not at all sure how they had got from Roddy standing on a chair to Roddy lying there in a distorted heap on the floor, his limbs and clothes crumpled up, lying so very still.

He went forward to help him up.

'Are you all right, old man?' he found he was saying as he crouched down beside him, but all the time, the utter stillness of his brother was clutching at something inside Guy, pulling at some terrible communication cord to his brain. He was prompted into quicker action. And then he saw it. Roddy's head, which was turned away from him, was suddenly lying in a little pool of crimson.

With shaking hands, Guy bent over him and turned his head. That crimson liquid which he was unwilling to acknowledge as blood flowed over his hands and cuffs. Involuntarily he let go and Roddy fell back, his head knocking dully against the cast-iron fender where it had been lying.

He looked up questioningly to the crowd of suddenly sober men who had formed around him.

'Someone get a doctor!' he shouted. 'We must do something . . .'

He saw Colonel Vane shaking his head.

'I know a dead man when I see one,' said Colonel Vane. 'I've seen enough of them. I'm sorry, Lindsay. There's nothing that can be done.'

5

'Chris! Chris!' Guy shouted out, as he came to the foot of the main stairs and saw her standing alone in the hall, her back to him, already wrapped in her black cape. She turned at the sound of his voice, and seeing her face was like being comforted.

'They said you were leaving,' he said.

'I am,' she said. 'I think it's for the best. I can't do anything useful, can I?'

'No, I suppose not. I'd better take you home.'

'You should stay,' said Chris. 'Your mother . . .'

'Oh, she's being looked after, and to tell the truth I need to get out. I'll walk you back.'

'If you're sure you won't be missed . . .'

'I don't care,' he said, putting out his hand to her. 'I need to get out.'

She took his hand, and he clasped it with desperation, aware of her strength and his own weakness. She stared up at him, her eyes wide with a kind of numb shock.

'Oh Guy, I'm so sorry . . .' she murmured and laid her other hand on his shoulder. He felt his face twitch a little at this gesture. He felt close to breaking then, in the sight of her kindness. He forced it back though, and instead brushed his hand across her forehead, and managed a tiny, grim smile.

'Let's walk,' he said.

His determination was fierce and they set off at a good pace down the long avenue which led up to the Castle, under a brilliant canopy of stars. When they got to the great wrought-iron gates he stopped and said, 'I wish we could walk all night. Out here it doesn't seem anything's happened, does it? It all looks just the same. But it isn't, is it?' He looked up at the sky, at the suddenly painful beauty of the stars. 'Do you know, I didn't realize that the passage between life and death could be so brief . . . That's what you can't get hold of . . .' He reached out and tentatively touched the wrought iron of the gate. 'A fender – Chris, a fender!' he exclaimed suddenly. 'It's so bloody stupid, isn't it? If you read this, you'd laugh, wouldn't you? And I could have stopped it.'

'I'm sure it's not your fault.'

'But,' he said, turning to her and putting his hands on her shoulders, 'I saw him get up on that chair, and I thought, "Oh Roddy, that's not a good idea, is it?" So why, why didn't I say anything? I wasn't that drunk! I could easily have said something. Just a word or two. That would have been all it needed . . .'

'Guy, it's not your fault. It's nobody's fault. It's just a horrible thing that no one could do anything about.'

'Bloody hell!' he said, and pulled his arms around him.

'You must be freezing,' she said. 'Go back and go to bed.'

He shook his head.

'I don't want to. I can't face any of it. I don't think I'll ever be able to eat in that dining room, or sit in that bloody chair – it's my chair, now, of course. It's all bloody mine, every lock, stock and barrel of it.' And he grabbed the gate and shook it, violently. 'But I don't want it! I don't want any of it. All I want is for it to be three hours ago, with us standing in the glass house . . . and you looking so . . .'

He let go of the gate, his rhetoric exhausted, and looked at the pale black and white figure in the moonlight.

'At least you still look the same,' he said, coming closer. 'Thank God.'

Gently he pulled her into his arms, pressing his lips to hers. He had meant only to hold her for comfort, to kiss her a little, but the nearness of her overwhelmed him. The soft, clean smell of her skin, the warmth of it, provoked him. He felt he was clutching at life itself with her in his arms, and he could not let go of that. He wanted suddenly to quite possess her, for with each kiss, with each caress, he felt the spark of his own life-force igniting.

He felt her respond. She seemed to slacken in his arms, and he felt her own kisses on his lips. They fell back on to the steep grass verge behind them, on to a carpet of new-fallen leaves, in an eager tangle of limbs and clothing. He pressed himself against the full length of her, feeling the satin of her dress slippery beneath him. He put his face to the bare space above her bodice and heard her heart beating as fast as his. He felt her fingers in his hair, and he wanted to shout out with the sheer physical joy of it. It was triumphant and desperate in one, that drive inside him towards consummation. He would spit in the face of death in this act of wonderful life!

Then suddenly a gust of sharp, brisk wind surrounded them, whipping over them like a harsh, cold slap of the hand. He felt her shiver at it, and he too shook, as if it had been Death's bony hand in that wind crossing over them. They remembered. Guy remembered, and saw Roddy's head on the floor again, lying in the pool of crimson which he could not believe was blood. A wave of nausea swept over him. He flung himself away from her and began to retch into the ditch.

Chris found she was crying. She folded herself in her cloak and rolled on to her side, as if to hide herself from the harsh, accusing eyes of the stars. She heard Guy vomiting and she shook with harder sobs, tasting her own bitter self-disgust. How could they have done such a thing? How could they have let themselves go?

She had felt powerless in his arms. When he had looked at her, she felt he stripped the flesh from her bones. Something had overtaken her and she had not in the slightest wished to resist. She had returned every kiss. She had not even tried restraint. It was as if they had been possessed for those moments by an evil spirit, but that spirit, she knew, was of their own making, conjured up by their own fleshly weakness.

She struggled to her feet, looking down at the terrible sign of her crushed dress. What would her father think? What would she say to him?

Guy straightened up and turned to her.

'I'm sorry . . .' he said in a hoarse whisper.

'I think I'd better go,' she said, swallowing back her tears. He nodded and she began to walk back to the Manse, as briskly as she could, scraping the tears from her face with her handkerchief. She did not once look back at him. She did not dare to.

Everything about the Manse seemed calm and still, as if it were under water. She pushed open the door and stood for a minute on the threshold, looking into the familiar neat hall, at its black and white flagstones shining slightly in the darkness and at the crack of light shooting out from the gaps about the closed door to the study. It looked like the light from Heaven in coloured Bible pictures.

Shutting the front door behind her clearly raised her father. He came out carrying his lamp and held it up to catch her in its light, as a missionary in the slums might do over some fallen woman.

'Christina – you're early? Is there something wrong? I didn't hear the motor – I thought . . .'

The innocence of his enquiry floored her. She began to cry, stood there sobbing helplessly. She was remembering

Roddy suddenly, how he had been years ago. Once, when he was fourteen and she five, he had lifted her up on to a pony and led her round on it. Before that she had been afraid of horses.

'My dear child,' said Mr Adam. 'What is it?'

'It's Roddy Lindsay. He's dead,' she blurted out.

'Oh, dear Lord,' he said, putting down the lamp. 'Oh . . . tonight?'

She managed to nod.

'My poor child,' he said, and put his arms a little awkwardly around her. 'What a terrible, terrible thing . . .'

He led her into the study and sat her down in his special chair by the fire. Here she found she broke down utterly, consumed by rage and shame and sheer confusion.

'You've clearly had a dreadful experience,' said Mr Adam, bewildered. 'If only your mother were here . . . Oh dear . . . Can you bear to tell me how it happened?'

She swallowed hard and looked across at him.

'It's ridiculous, that's the worst of it.'

Her father looked puzzled.

'He fell off a chair – he was standing on it, making a speech or something, and he fell off and hit his head on the fender. He was very drunk, they said . . .'

Mr Adam shook his head slowly and sank back in his chair.

'His poor mother . . .' he said, at length. 'I shall go up to the Castle first thing tomorrow. And you, my dear, I think you had better go down to the Ferry for a few days, to your grandmother. You've had such a shock. Seeing your new little nephew will help, I'm sure.'

Guy got back to the Castle, and then wished he had not gone back at all. He wished he could have walked away for ever, into the numb blackness of the night, walked on until he ran out of land under his feet. He could imagine himself marching out into the sea, welcoming the cold purification of the water's embrace, knowing there would soon be oblivion.

For it seemed to him, then, standing in the bedroom where Roddy's body had been laid out, decorously hidden by a sheet, that human life was entirely meaningless. All human endeavour seemed pointless, because it led only to this terrible blank end. It could not be defied. It always won. Nobody could escape it.

Isolde was sitting on a little chair, sobbing into her hands. His mother had not been able to get into the room even. She was locked in her own private hysteria, and Guy knew he would soon have to go back to her, and do what he could, which was little.

Suddenly Isolde was looking up at him, pleading with her sodden eyes for comfort, and he went to put his arms about her. She clutched on to him, shaking like a bird in the cold, her face buried against his stomach. Her soft, feminine warmth invaded him, although it was not really hers, but the ghost of Chris's. He wanted desperately to cling to her and weep, as Isolde wept, but he knew it was not possible. He had destroyed any chance of intimacy between them now. This was all that remained for him, this room, with Roddy's corpse, as obvious as anything, despite the sheet, and his sister's tears and his own terrible sense of futility.

Mrs Vane came into the room and told them that Lady Lindsay now wanted to see Roddy.

'I'll bring her in,' said Guy.

He found his mother in the next room, sitting bolt upright in her chair, still in the magnificence of her dinner dress. She said nothing, but took his arm, and allowed him to lead her into the other room. She felt to him as stiff as a wooden shop dummy.

'Show me him . . .' she said, quietly and with fierce control.

He felt he was hitting his mother as he drew back the

sheet from his face. Someone had cleaned up the blood, but the sight was still dreadful.

He turned to his mother, hearing her gasp. He saw her shaking and grabbed on to her, feeling her composure cracking. She fell down on to her knees, throwing herself over Roddy, attempting to embrace him.

'My baby ... No, no ...' she bleated. 'Not my baby boy ...' She was crying into his chest, stroking his hair with a fevered hand. 'This can't be ...'

Behind him Guy could hear Isolde crying with renewed violence. He wished he had these women's easy gift of tears, but he was too angry for that, too consumed by the black fires of raging confusion. What on earth was the point of his mother ever having brought Roddy into the world, only to lose him because of an unstable chair and a cast-iron fender? How could life be at heart such a terrible deception? It was all a filthy trick and he had no means to deal with it. Not even love could help it. Love only made it fouler, more pointless. It would be better to die now than suffer this agony again. He had felt this when his father died, and now Roddy was dead and the pain was there again. It could only come again and again to take from him everything he cared for and heap him with suffering. The road was too bleak to go along. He did not want to take another step.

Across the room, above the fireplace, he saw the face of one of his ancestors, a gentleman who, despite his periwig, had a strong look of Guy's father about him. It was a quietly stern face that seemed to address him: You cannot give up. It is your duty to go on. They need you. You are the Laird now.

'Come along, Mama,' he said, bending over her, and putting his arms around her. She seemed to fall gratefully into his living embrace, relinquishing Roddy as if she had now accepted the game was up. 'You need to rest.'

6

'So,' said Aunt Minna, snipping a length of embroidery silk. 'How is your music getting along? Are you still writing? I did so like those wee things you used to write.'

'You did?' said Chris, looking up from the score of *The Marriage of Figaro*.

'Oh yes, those dances for the piano. Very clever I thought those were. That waltz tune – I still hum it sometimes. So you won't stop, will you?'

'I've no intention of doing so,' laughed Chris. 'Why on earth do you think I would?'

'Well, your sister, she was so clever with her needle, and now she's quite lost interest. I always think whether a woman is married or not, she needs something constructive to do, on her own account.'

Aunt Minna Ronaldson was Mrs Adam's elder sister, who had never married but stayed at home to tend to her parents. It seemed to Chris that she had organized this role for herself a good deal better than other women had. Too often the spinster daughter lost control of everything to bullying parents, whereas Aunt Minna had become the head of the household, on old Mr Ronaldson's death. She managed the house and her mother impeccably, and spent her free time doing large quantities of beautiful, fine embroidery which would have destroyed other women's eyes years ago. She was an elegant, crisp little bird of a woman, always alert to the world.

'Ah, Annie would never be as good as you,' said Chris,

getting up and going to the bay window where her aunt sat at her frame. 'This is quite exquisite,' she said, admiring the design of scarlet flowers on black silk. 'To embroider on silk – I don't know how you do it. What will it be when it's finished?'

'Oh, I don't know,' said Aunt Minna. 'Perhaps an evening shawl for my favourite niece,' she added, and reached up and touched Chris on her cheek.

'You shouldn't have favourites,' smiled Chris.

'I know, but I can't help it. You and I, Chris, see eye to eye. I'd ask your father to let you come and live here with us, if it wasn't being selfish.'

'It wouldn't be,' said Chris, rather charmed by this suggestion. 'I'd be more use here than at Rankeillor. I'm sure I'm an awful thorn in Mother's side sometimes.'

'Oh, I don't mean you should stay at Rankeillor,' said Aunt Minna. 'You are simply wasted there. No, it would be selfish to keep you from studying, which is what you ought to be doing, isn't it?'

'I'd love too, but you know . . .'

'Yes, I know. Your mother and father are so very conservative. Living up there they don't see things have changed. Girls take degrees now, just like the men. Oh,' she added wistfully, 'how I should have liked that chance in my time. That's why I think you should have yours.'

'Is it really possible?' said Chris. 'Really?'

'I see no reason why not. If you were a clever boy, everyone would be jumping to help you. It's only a question of finding a hundred pounds or so a year, after all.'

Chris could not help laughing.

'You've obviously gone into all this pretty thoroughly!'

'Well, yes,' she said. 'I am splendid, aren't I? If you look in the top right-hand drawer of my bureau you'll find a little brochure. I took the liberty of writing off for you, I hope you don't mind.'

Chris opened the drawer and took out a small buff pamphlet. Across the front was printed, in bold, Gothic lettering: 'The Royal Caledonian Academy, Edinburgh'.

'The Caledonian Academy . . .' said Chris. She shook her head. 'Aunt Minna, I'm sure I'm not good enough for that.'

'Oh course you are. They sent a sample entrance examination paper and I'm quite sure you could do it standing on your head. You might even win a bursary. Some of them are quite generous.'

'The Caledonian Academy,' Chris repeated. 'But that would be . . .'

She sat down and began to study the prospectus. The details dazzled her: 'All students receive two hours of tuition for each instrument a week, as well as a weekly lecture on the History of Music. There are also compulsory studies in Harmony and Counterpoint', and then: 'There is an orchestra as well as numerous chamber groups. Concerts are frequently put on, and each year an opera and an oratorio are performed.'

'Oh, we appear to have a visitor – in a motor, no less,' said Aunt Minna from her bay-window vantage point.

'Mmm?' said Chris, who was now deep in the list of entrance requirements.

'It looks like Mr Lindsay,' said Aunt Minna. 'Or should I say Sir Guy, now?'

'Guy?' said Chris.

She had not seen him since the night of Roddy's death. In Broughty Ferry she had thrown herself into family business, admiring Annie's baby and helping her aunt in an attempt to squash that evening out of her consciousness. But it had hardly been successful. There had always been a nervous irritation, a little rash of shame mixed with confusion which would not go away. At night, as she had tried to get to sleep, it had been a positive high fever of self-torture.

'Well, I don't suppose he's come to see me,' said Minna getting up from her seat, 'but I shall open the door to him, I think. I don't trust young Susan to do that yet.'

Chris wondered if she should ask her aunt to turn him away. She was afraid to see him, afraid of that horrible complication which now, she was sure, must fester between them. It would have been the easiest thing to do, of course, to refuse to see him, but she realized it stank of cowardice and she did not like to think herself a coward. This thought spurred her enough to follow her aunt into the hallway.

The hall was filled with the strong blast of a low afternoon sun, and Guy, in the open doorway, stood against the light, making a dark, sharp figure in an immaculate suit of such dull blackness that it seemed to throb of mourning against the bright colours of the tiled floor and patterned wallpaper. Chris hid herself while he presented himself to her aunt, at once aware of a change in him. His shoulders seemed bowed, and his manner gravely nervous. She could not help remembering the bonny cavalier in his kilt, who had appeared in the dining room swinging grouse.

'Come in, come in,' Aunt Minna said, warmly. 'Christina's just in the drawing room – no, she's here . . .'

Chris, now flushed, managed a crooked smile. She felt a fool but couldn't think what to say. Neither, it appeared, could Guy.

Aunt Minna left them alone together in the drawing room, which Chris was sure her mother would never have managed to do. But Aunt Minna was more sensitive about such things. She would have noticed at once the embarrassing awkwardness between them.

'Won't you sit down?' Chris managed to say, as if he were quite a stranger. He perched on a chair, still clutching at his hat, and looking restlessly about him. He looked as though he did not want to be there at all, but if that was the case why on earth had he come all the way from Rankeillor?

She sat across the room from him, with equal diffidence, her hands clasped in her lap, wishing that the terrible smell of that night would leave them, and that everything between them could be as before. She wondered what she might say to do that, to bring back their old easiness. She found she was quite lacking in inspiration.

'I . . . er . . . see you've been studying the Mozart . . .' he said at length, catching sight of the little score she had left on the table.

'Yes, though not very thoroughly yet,' she said quickly, immensely relieved by this safe topic. 'But it's glorious stuff.'

'I knew you'd like it,' he said, and then looked up at her, searchingly. 'Oh Chris, this is ridiculous! Why must we have small talk?'

'Because we're embarrassed,' she ventured. 'Aren't we?'

'Do you think what happened was terribly wrong? Between us, I mean?'

'I don't know,' she said lamely.

'I was rather afraid you wouldn't want to see me. When I heard you'd gone, I thought it was because of my being so brutal . . .'

'My father sent me here. I was upset, over Roddy, more than anything.'

'So, you aren't too angry with me?'

'Not angry,' she said. 'Worried. You look tired.'

'I am,' he admitted. 'I haven't had much sleep – things are terribly complicated. Well, my mother for one . . . she's in a rotten state and . . .' He got up from his chair suddenly and began to pace up and down. 'And all the time I've been so worried about you, terrified that I'd ruined everything. I was so stupid that night . . . so bloody stupid!' He threw up his hands with this exclamation, and then turned to her. 'Can you forgive me for it?'

'There's nothing to forgive,' she said, and in saying it she found a marvellous relief. It did not matter. It was only a few minutes' indiscretion, after all, brought on by a horrible situation. It had only been the life in them, she realized, shouting out that they still lived. It was nothing to feel guilty about. She felt a certain triumph in acknowledging that, as if in her mind she had overturned a heavy piece of moral furniture.

'Are you sure?' he said.

'Quite,' she said, and smiled. She saw his whole frame relax.

'Thank God,' he said, and sat down again. 'I'm glad I came today. It's my last chance for a while. I've got to go up to town and see people.'

'About the estate?'

'Yes, lawyers and brokers . . . the lot. The tax alone is going to be a nightmare.'

'You'll manage, I'm sure.'

'I suppose I will, though it isn't quite what I'd planned.'

'Are you still regretting Vienna?'

'A little, perhaps. The freedom of that life more than anything. I'd got used to thinking I could go anywhere, for as long as I liked. I'm rather tied down now. Rankeillor needs me.'

'I'm sure you'll rise splendidly to the challenge,' she said.

'I don't know. I'm not sure I'll manage alone,' he said. 'Oh Lord, I don't know how to start on this, Chris, but one of the reasons I was anxious about what happened that night was that just before Roddy had his accident I'd made up my mind to ask you . . .' He broke off, and got up from his chair again. 'I can't think sitting down,' he said.

'To ask me what?'

'To ask you to think about throwing your lot in with

me,' he said. 'Oh God, how ungracious that sounds! What I mean is, as my wife. It made a lot of sense then, and now it makes even more sense, at least I think it does.'

She leant back in her chair, folding her arms across her, breathing hard suddenly.

'You look as though I've just asked you to go to hell with me,' he said.

'It's just a bit of a shock,' she managed to say.

'Yes, it must be,' he said. 'It was a shock to me, when the idea first occurred to me, actually, but now I'm sure it would be so right. And of course I'm not asking you to say now. You must think about it. You couldn't possibly give me an answer now.'

'No, I couldn't . . .'

'So I shall go up to town tomorrow, and when I come back, you can tell me.'

'Can I?' she said. 'Oh Guy, I'm not really . . .'

'Shush . . .' he said, coming over to her and pressing his finger to her lips. 'Just think about it, please.'

Chris heard the creak of the gate and the sound of her mother's voice, saying something to May. Guy heard it too, for he moved instinctively away from her.

'They'll be back from Annie's,' she remarked.

'Ah yes,' said Guy. 'The baby. What's it like?'

'Like all babies,' said Chris. 'They're calling him Jamie.'

'I suppose I should send something. A silver mug – isn't that the usual thing?'

'Why?' she could not help asking.

'Because if we . . .' He broke off and she was glad he had restrained himself. Of course, if he had asked her, he wanted a positive answer from her, but he had no right to assume such a degree of success. He clearly thought of himself as her putative fiancé, who had, therefore, an obligation to her nephew. His confidence frightened her. There was something cold in it to which she could not respond, as if he were acquiring a possession rather than a wife.

'Guy,' she found she must ask, forgetting quite that her mother and May were in the hall, taking off their hats and coats, 'you are in love with me, aren't you?'

'Of course I am,' he said, dropping suddenly on to the chair beside her, and taking her hands in his. 'I shouldn't dream of asking such a thing, if . . . Oh yes, I do love you. I've never felt the way I do about you about anyone. You've turned me quite upside down. The moment I saw you when I was just back, everything went . . .'

The door flew open and they stared across at Mrs Adam, who was for once rendered quite speechless by the sight that met her eyes. Her mouth opened and she seemed to be struggling to find the words, but nothing emerged. Aunt Minna, wise to all situations, instead darted forward saying, 'Oh Agnes, I'm glad you're back. Mother's been asking for you all afternoon . . .' She hustled her out of the room, leaving Chris with Guy's confession burning in her ears, the sincerity of it scorching her.

'I think I ought to go,' he said. 'I don't want to but . . .' They got up from their seats and suddenly he grabbed her and kissed her fiercely. 'I can't bear to go,' he said, between kisses, and when he did release her she felt the same regret, as though she had just left a warm fireside. His physicality upset her internal balance, just as it had done the night of Roddy's death. To be held and kissed with such feeling set something alight in her which she could not suppress.

'May I write?' he said, as she opened the front door.

'Yes, do,' she said, and then felt moved to kiss him goodbye. He clutched her then with grim strength, as if he were leaving for something very terrible, like death itself, instead of appointments with brokers and lawyers.

She watched him stride down the path, and felt quite drunk with his last embrace. There had been something sweet and intense in his closeness, like a draught of legendary wine, and it went to her head. She shut the door and leant against it, breathless.

'Did I just scc him kiss you?' said Mrs Adam, appearing from the rear of the hall. She sounded accusatory and interfering, and Chris was certain that the last thing she wished to do was talk about what had just passed between Guy and herself. For one thing, she was hardly sure herself what had happened.

'Mother, this is none of your business.'

'Oh, is it not? I find my daughter being pawed over by a young man, and it isn't my business? What is going on between you?'

'I'd rather not discuss it, if you don't mind,' said Chris, crossing the hall and making an attempt to go upstairs. However, Mrs Adam caught her arm.

'Well, I'm afraid you are going to have to,' she said, almost marching her into the drawing room. 'Do you think this is a light thing?'

'No, of course not!' exclaimed Chris, turning her back on her. She stood in the bay window to watch Guy's motor move off down the street. 'But it is private.' Mrs Adam exhaled vehemently and Chris turned back to see her standing tapping her fingers together in irritation. 'Can't you understand that?'

'You're talking as if you had something to be ashamed of,' said Mrs Adam, 'which I hope you haven't.'

'No, of course not!' She found she snapped the response out.

'Then what is your difficulty?' said Mrs Adam.

'Because as I said, it isn't any of your business,' she said.

'Has he suggested something indecent to you?' said Mrs Adam, going on relentlessly.

'Oh, Mother, for goodness sake, I told you . . .'

'You haven't told me anything,' said Mrs Adam sitting

down. 'And I shan't let you out of my sight until you've told me everything. I have a right to know.'

'I can't think how you can imagine that,' said Chris, pacing back into the bay-window. The street was empty and quiet again, the great shining motor quite vanished. She wished her mother's nosiness could disappear as easily. She pressed her hands against the sun-warmed glass and stared out, determined not to speak.

'At least you could have the grace to tell me how serious he is,' said Mrs Adam. 'Has he talked about marriage?' Chris kept resolutely silent, but Mrs Adam interpreted the silence as assent. 'Ah, then he has . . . Really, Chris, how strange you are . . .'

'For wishing to keep it to myself?' she retorted. 'Mother, this is my private business.'

'Marrying someone like Guy Lindsay is hardly a private matter,' said her mother.

'Who says that I will marry him? He's only asked me to think about it, for heaven's sake!' Chris blurted out.

'Ah, but you do like him, don't you?' said Mrs Adam. 'You let him kiss you, after all. It seems to me you've given him reason to hope that you'll accept. You must like him pretty well.'

'Of course I do. I always have, you know that.'

'Then why on earth are you so cross about this, dear?' said Mrs Adam. 'You should be the happiest girl on earth to get an offer like that from a man you like.'

'Because . . . because . . . Oh, I don't know!' said Chris. 'I suppose it's because I hardly expected it.'

Suddenly Mrs Adam became conciliatory.

'Yes, it would be a shock, especially at such a time, with all that dreadful business with poor Roddy . . .' She came and put her arm about Chris's shoulder. 'But I dare say you will get used to it soon enough.'

'Will I?' said Chris.

Mrs Adam gave Chris's shoulder a little squeeze and

said, 'Yes, with time.' She let go of Chris and drifted across the room towards the door. 'I suppose Miss Adam to Lady Lindsay is more of a leap than any of us have quite anticipated . . . Perhaps,' she said, her hand on the door now, 'we should buy you a few new clothes, dear . . .'

Chris let this pass, more anxious to end the interview than to challenge Mrs Adam any further. She sat down at the piano and began to play a Chopin *étude*, which she could not help remembering that Guy played with a great deal more brilliance than she could ever manage. As she fumbled through it, she seemed to hear his performance as vividly as she still felt his kisses on her lips. There was the same passion, the same tenderness, the same sheer irresistible beauty. Guy was like the *étude* itself. And, now he was offering himself to her, a tempting gift of easy pleasure! Lady Lindsay – she could be that, and happy as that, with the simplest nod of the head . . .

She stopped playing Chopin and clenched up her fists suddenly, for a moment, and then released them again, to play a few strident discords that, in the rapid, rhythmic succession that she improvised, exhilarated her. The sound was rough, horrible even, and certainly did not have the winning charm of Chopin, but there was fire in it and something primitive and terrifying, that made her think of that furious struggle of an embrace that she and Guy had had by the gates of the Castle. She thumped them out again, and then decided she must record them.

She dragged the piano stool across to the table where she had left a notebook and pencil. As she picked them up, she noticed the prospectus for the Caledonian Academy again. She scribbled down a bare outline of those chords and then flicked open the prospectus, unable to resist doing so, as if it were a rash to be scratched.

'Students of outstanding ability are invited to study in the Principal's advanced composition class.' She read these words and they seemed to escape and smoulder inside her, like a glowing cinder that had fallen from the fire on to the hearth rug. Their smoke filled her nostrils, and she recognized the smell as being of her own ambition, a stench so powerful that she could not ignore it.

7

Chris watched Mrs Adam and Annie worshipping the baby, for that was how it struck her, this daily, silent adoration of the sleeping child in the lace-hung cradle. Their faces were rapt with concentration, as if little Jamie were divine to them, rather than simply another, ordinary baby. There were, of course, things that Chris found interesting and admirable about Jamie – his tiny feet, for example, had delighted her – but she could not manage the sense of wonder which so consumed her mother and sister. The child exerted no mystic fascination over her. She merely wondered what sort of man he might become as she hung on the threshold of the room.

There was a thudding of small footsteps in the passageway outside, and Margaret, Annie's two-year-old daughter, crept past her skirts into the baby's temple. Chris bent to take Margaret's hand, but the child would not be restrained and pushed forward towards the cradle. She stared at the rapt faces of her mother and grandmother, and, clearly sensing she had lost her monopoly of attention, began to whine.

'Oh, get her out of here, quick, Chris,' said Annie. 'He'll wake up again.'

Chris squatted down and lifted a fiercely reluctant Margaret into her arms. She wriggled and turned the whine into a wail, and Chris could feel her jealous frustration shaking through her thin little bones.

'You have to be quiet,' she muttered, as they left the

room. She ran a useless hand over her head, in a vain attempt to soothe her. 'You'll wake your brother. Here,' she said, pushing open the nursery door from which Margaret had escaped. 'Shall we play with your bricks?'

With very little ceremony Chris dumped her down on the hearth rug by the fire and searched for the box of bricks, while Margaret stood, it seemed dangerously on the brink of a real tantrum. However, the act of tipping out a large heap of bricks in front of her melted away her anger. She was soon picking out a large yellow arch and handing it over to Chris as if it were something deeply significant.

'Thank you,' said Chris. 'What's this for? What do you want us to build? A big arch?'

Her questions got no response. Margaret was still a child of very few words. Chris sat back on her heels and wondered how long it would be before they could have a properly intelligent conversation.

'Oh, we've got the bricks out have we? What fun,' said Annie as she came in. Margaret responded at once to her mother and went to embrace her legs, gurgling delight. Chris found herself amazed again at the quickness with which her mood changed. In another moment, she supposed, she would be crying again, for no apparent reason.

'No, go back and play with Auntie Chris, dear. Mummy's got to sit down,' Annie said, turning her back towards Chris. This was the first day she had got up from her bed since the birth and she sat down in the nursing chair by the fire with visible relief.

'Oh goodness, I still feel so tired,' she murmured, smoothing the pink woollen folds of her dressing gown. She leant back and smiled at the sight of Margaret, who had begun to pile bricks into a rudimentary tower. Then she yawned, and retied the ribbon that decorated her long fair plait. She seemed to Chris like an animal then, deep in her contentment at having fulfilled nature's demands by reproducing. It had made her beautiful, with her pink cheeks and swollen, milk-full breasts which even her modest and matronly dressing gown could not disguise.

'I hear you had a visit from Guy,' said Annie.

'Oh,' said Chris flatly. 'What's Mother been saying to you?'

'Well, she did say . . . that he seemed pretty keen . . .' said Annie, coyly.

'There's no point trying to have secrets in this family, is there?' said Chris.

'Oh come on, you can tell me,' said Annie. 'Did he ask you to marry him?'

'What makes you think that?' said Chris, defensively.

'Well, Mother was rather excited and it does make a great deal of sense. You always were close and – it's logical, isn't it? Of course, he's quite young, but when you're the Laird, it doesn't matter, does it?' expounded Annie, and then added, 'And she said she saw him kiss you.'

'One kiss doesn't make an engagement,' said Chris.

'But he has asked you, hasn't he? Oh, do tell me, Chris, please.'

'Yes,' said Chris, lamely. 'He did ask me.'

'I knew it!' exclaimed Annie, clapping her hands with delight. 'So, when's it to be? I suppose we'll have to wait. He'll be in mourning till the spring – oh yes, late spring. A June wedding would be glorious!'

'I'm only thinking about it,' said Chris, stemming her flow. 'I haven't said one way or the other.'

'Oh, but you wouldn't turn him down, would you? How could you?' At that moment Margaret deliberately toppled the tower she had been building. She laughed with delight at her act of destruction. 'Oh Margaret, what a silly girl you are!' exclaimed Annie. 'Why build a tower just to knock it down? Silly girl.'

Chris could not help feeling she was being addressed as much as Margaret, for dithering over Guy. She began to gather Margaret's fallen bricks, to help reconstruct the tower.

'So you will, won't you?' said Annie, addressing her again.

Chris laid two red three-inch blocks in a neat parallel on the rug.

'I don't know,' she said.

'But you'd be so happy,' said Annie. 'You're so well suited and . . .'

'And he's got lots of money, and I'll never have to worry about anything. Yes, I know all that. Mother has been shouting it at me, but that isn't the point. I'm not sure I want to marry anyone.'

'Don't be silly,' said Annie, as if Chris were two years old and had knocked down her tower. 'How can you not want to marry, especially someone like Guy? He's perfectly charming.'

'Yes, of course he is. But that's nothing to do with it. It's what I want inside that matters, and marriage seems to me such a terrible surrender.'

'Surrender? What do you mean?'

'Of myself. I wouldn't be just me, I'd always be someone's wife, or someone's mother, never someone in my own right.'

'But as Lady Lindsay you'd be someone in your own right, Chris! You'd be invited everywhere.'

'You don't see it, do you?' said Chris. 'That would be only because I was his wife. I should feel like a performing monkey.'

'That's daft!' said Annie, laughing. 'I can't believe you're thinking all this, Chris. You can't seriously think you are going turn him down?'

'I don't know yet. I haven't thought about it enough yet.'

'There's nothing to think about. It would be wonderful for you. You'd be a fool not to marry him.'

'Perhaps I'd be a fool to marry anyone, let alone Guy. Perhaps I'm not suited to marriage. There's so much about it that I find difficult.'

'Oh, you shouldn't worry about that,' said Annie. 'You get used to that. At first, it's hard, but I'm sure Guy would be quite gentle . . .'

'I didn't mean that side of things. Oh, that doesn't bother me,' she said. 'In fact, I should think it would be quite interesting.' Annie looked vaguely shocked at this and pointed discreetly at the child. 'You raised the subject,' responded Chris, and went on, 'no, what bothers me is the consequence of that: motherhood. I'm not sure I want that at all.'

'You don't want children?' exclaimed Annie. 'But that's wicked! It's what marriage is about . . .'

'Exactly. So how could I marry, when that repels me?'

'Repels you?' said Annie. 'Is it the pain that worries you? It isn't that bad, and the result is so overwhelming, so wonderful . . .'

'That you can't think of anything else? That you become a mother, and nothing else?'

'What more could a woman want?' said Annie, a shade piously.

'Exactly what a man might want,' said Chris. 'A chance to act, to create, to do something really worth while.'

'Oh, children are not worth while, are they?' said Annie, defensively.

'For you, yes. You're a genius at it. It's what you should do. But I can't feel it, I can't see it. It doesn't set me on fire, and one has to feel that to do something well. There has to be a passion for it. I wouldn't be happy doing it. I'd always be looking out of the window, when I should be tending them, wishing that . . .'

'You'd have help,' said Annie. 'I'm sure of that.'

'That isn't the point!'

'I don't understand you at all,' said Annie. 'I think you are just being selfish.'

'Is it selfish to turn Guy down, if I thought I was not going to be happy? Because if I'm not going to be happy, he certainly won't be.'

'But you will be happy,' said Annie. 'Believe me. I know it seems a big step, but you'll find it all falls into place. I'm sure you will, if you love Guy, and you do, don't you?'

'I don't know if I do,' she said. 'He upsets something very deep in me. I feel very tempted but . . .'

'But what?' interjected Annie. 'He's not tempting you to do something wrong, Chris. He's offering you the greatest gift a man can give a woman – his hand. It's a wonderful thing. He's offering you the sun and you're quibbling.'

'These are not quibbles!' said Chris. 'It's not an easy thing to choose between two states of life. I have to decide which I want.'

'You want to be unmarried, like Aunt Minna?' said Annie, contemptuously. 'She has money, of course. You won't. Will you get a job? I can't think anything you could do would quite match being Lady Lindsay. You might spend the rest of your life regretting it. What on earth have you to do that is so important you can't marry Guy?'

Chris got up from the floor, needing to command a vantage point over her sister and niece. She looked about the room, at the frieze of nursery rhymes, at the toy cupboard, at the little clothes airing on the large fire guard. This nursery was Annie's entire world. It was a place of sacred significance to her. It gave her life meaning, but Chris would not have that. She would not be defined by her being a woman with a capacity to bear children. She was determined she would not let it happen.

She had too much real work to do. There was too much music inside, waiting to be expressed, for that.

'What then?' asked Annie again.

'You wouldn't understand,' said Chris.

Annie shook her head and turned her full attention to the child.

Chris walked back to her grandparents' house alone, needing Aunt Minna's sane counsel through a world that seemed to shriek of domestic virtue. From her sister's house to her grandparents' she passed a succession of neat villas which kept their distance behind stone walls and which were set in careful gardens, where respectful men raked up the glorious mess of autumn. She passed shining perambulators with diligent nursemaids, and small children bowling hoops with great earnestness. She did not look at them with longing or regret. She had decided to embrace her exile cheerfully. She would do what she had to do, and throw all that up for her own private dream.

There was a letter from Guy waiting on the hall table which she took and twitched between still-gloved fingers, afraid to open it and experience the bombardment of affection that she was certain it contained.

Aunt Minna came out and found her standing there with it.

'Are you all right?' she said.

Chris shook her head.

'Ah, this is about young Sir Guy, I take it,' said Aunt Minna, putting her arm about Chris's shoulders. 'Has your mother been . . . ?'

'Annie,' said Chris. 'They all think I should marry him.'

'And what do you think?'

'I think not,' she said carefully, and then burst out, 'but it's so cruel, isn't it? To have to say no?' She held out the letter despairingly. 'I don't want to lose a friend, but I'm sure I will.'

'It is a difficult thing to do,' agreed Aunt Minna. 'Believe me.'

'This has happened to you?' said Chris.

'Oh yes, though not for a very long time. But quite a few times, actually.'

Chris sighed with relief.

'It is possible then?'

'Everyone thought I was quite mad,' said Aunt Minna, taking her into the drawing room. 'One of them was really quite wealthy but I knew that it wasn't right. And then, of course, there was . . .' She hesitated for a moment. 'I'm not sure if I should say this but, oh, why not? Your father even asked on one occasion.'

'My father – he didn't!' Chris could not help smiling at this revelation. 'But that would have been . . .'

'Quite dreadful, yes, I know,' said Aunt Minna bluntly. 'I told him that, and he took it very well. He wasn't really very much in love with me. It was just I was the eldest girl, I suppose. He soon realized that your mother was the one he should be looking at.'

'Were you ever really tempted by any of them?'

'Very,' she said. 'Especially the wealthy one. Well, you see, being married gives a young girl status, doesn't it? Instant prestige. I would have liked that very much but there was too much else that I didn't want. I'd seen so many friends lose themselves in marriage and my will would not permit that – well, you know how determined I am. It's a trait we share, I think. We are not naturally submissive, are we, Chris?' Chris nodded. 'I needed more than anything to preserve my sense of self, which no man I had met was prepared to allow me to do.'

'Annie thought I was being selfish. Is it selfish of me?'

'To develop your own talent?' said Aunt Minna. 'That's what this is really about, isn't it? Your music.'

'Yes. I'm worried that there would be nothing left for it. I'd be so busy with babies and parties. I think I'd be squashed. Although I do like Guy a tremendous amount, I don't think I love him enough to be able to give it all up.'

'Then don't. Ignore everyone else and do what you think is right,' said Aunt Minna. 'He'll be miserable at first, but it will be better than you marrying under false pretences.'

'That's what I thought,' said Chris. 'I'm still frightened to read this letter though. I'm terrified he'll say something so lovely that I can't not say yes.'

'You won't. You've enough real purpose to resist. It won't be easy but . . .' She went and rang the bell for some tea. 'Well, why don't you leave that a minute, and we'll write a letter to the Academy. I think we ought to arrange an interview for you.'

'But . . .' began Chris, thinking at once of the financial ramifications.

'I know what you are thinking,' said Aunt Minna. 'And I've been to see my bank manager this morning. I've decided I shall give you a hundred a year if you pass the entrance exam – I know, of course,' she added, with a wicked smile, 'that Guy would have probably given you that a quarter for your hats alone, but . . .'

'Are you sure? Oh, Aunt Minna . . . Thank you.'

'Hush,' said Aunt Minna. 'I shall enjoy it. It rather appeals to me to be a patroness of the arts. Come, let's write this letter. No, I'll write the letter, and you can study your harmony books. You have an exam to get through, after all.'

Later that night, Chris found the courage to open Guy's letter.

'My dearest Chris,' he began, with a bold black line underlining dearest:

It is a joy to be able to write to you. I'm sitting up in my dressing gown – it's about one in the morning, I think, but I'm not sure, because I've had such a pile of papers to get through that time has become meaningless. I'm supposed to be getting the early train to Edinburgh tomorrow and then that dreadful crawl up to London, but I can't actually believe I'm supposed to be doing it. The only thing that seems real to me at the moment was the time we spent together this afternoon – all of half an hour, wasn't it? The rest is quite meaningless still. I can't accept any of it, although we've had the funeral, and there are dozens of letters of condolence and all this administration to keep reminding me what has happened. But I don't believe it yet, not in the heart of me, because to accept it is to accept that life is pointless and I won't have that . . . Oh, I have to beg your indulgent ear on this, Chris, you're the only person I can talk to about it. With you today, I felt like a child – I felt safe and understood. You forgave me for that awful business – and you understood, thank God! Everything about you seems to me utterly perfect, and I'm helpless before it. I'm a peasant falling down on my knees in front of you, and you are my guardian angel, a darling, gold-hair Flemish angel, who by some miracle I can touch and hold and pour out my heart to. Oh Chris, if I didn't have you to think of now, to hope for, I don't know what I would do.

Chris threw the letter down on to her bed, unwilling to read any more. The strength of his love seemed to flood over her, an overwhelming, inevitable, irresistible tide. All the resolutions she had made earlier were washed away in the force of it, like mere pieces of driftwood, on to which she could not grip and keep afloat. There was only the sea of his passion remaining to drown her and she could find no resistance to it. It was so much simpler, was it not, to let herself sink into the water than struggle for air. Who was not to say that life in the sea would not be sweet? A soft drowning in solicitude and love – was that not what everyone wanted deep in the core of themselves? And who was she, Christina Adam, to question the received wisdom of so many? Wasn't her mother happy, wasn't Annie happy – and why should she not be happy, wonderfully happy with Guy, who had spread out his soul for her to walk across?

She sank back on her pillows and stared up at the ceiling, where the candle flame cast a pool of light. She was rigid with indecision, clenching and unclenching her fists, as if in a fit, trying to think clearly about it. Yet as she lay there, it felt as though he was lying stretched on top of her like an incubus. She could imagine him kissing her, the warm, male smell of him invading her nostrils as he did so, and she could almost feel the touch of those unnerving fingers, through the thin stuff of her night gown. She felt herself begin to twitch with desire, just as she had done on the night of Roddy's death, and she was ashamed of it, but she could do nothing to stop it. The heat of her own nature as a woman rushed over her, and she longed for some relief.

The fingers that touched her, she told herself, were Guy's, and she muffled her cries in the pillow. Oblivion overpowered her, and she slept with Guy's letter lying on the counterpane.

8

Glancing at his reflection in the glass, as he washed his hands in the gentlemen's lavatory at the Caledonian Station, Guy saw again the stranger in the dark suit. It was the same young man whom, in London, he had observed with the detachment of a servant in the corner of the room, meeting with various grave, grey-faced gentlemen in panelled offices for invariably complex discussions. Guy had often felt sorry for this stranger, but was glad that this masquerade felt able to assume his name and go through these games, by which he had felt repulsed. He felt much obliged to this dry, dutiful young man, who bore it all with such wonderful forbearance when his own blood boiled.

The stranger rested his blue eyes upon Guy and the trick of detachment collapsed like a house of cards. He was himself again, and with all that implied. He could no longer escape into that secret haven in himself which had been his refuge for all the time he was in town. He had to face facts, and accept that this was his new life, that he was Sir Guy Lindsay of Rankeillor. The signature which he had had to use to amend so many documents lately was his own.

He dried his hands on the coarse towel, dropped a farthing in the attendant's dish, and went out into the station again. He took out his pocket book and consulted it – he had an appointment at two, and then the late afternoon train up to Rankeillor, but he suddenly could not face the thought of hanging about in Edinburgh for so long simply for the convenience of a bank manager. He had had enough of these people with their respectful sympathy and coyly obsequious manner. He decided he would cancel the appointment and get back to Rankeillor on the first train there was. And of course if he was at Rankeillor, he could see Chris again! That was enough to set him pounding across the station to find a public telephone.

But he stopped, wondering if he should not take a detour and go to Broughty Ferry first. She was quite likely to be at her aunt's still. Yet if he went there, she was sure to be at Rankeillor and it would have been a wasted journey. He became utterly undecided on the matter, his eagerness to see her complicating the whole issue. It had only been five days, but it had seemed like an eternity. Every night, lying in the masculine arms of a Pall Mall club, he had thought of lying in her arms. If she had been there, it would have been bearable. He would not have needed to invent the stranger to carry the burden for him.

As he debated what to do, a train pulled up and disgorged its load of passengers on to the station. It was a busy, mid-morning train, full of ladies coming up to Edinburgh to search for ribbons and gloves, and the station seemed to ring with the clear and yet delicate tapping of their high-heeled shoes. Guy found he was watching them, this amazing flux of womanhood, who in their very diversity struck him as being as exotic and extraordinary as the inhabitants of some Eastern bazaar rather than women coming into Edinburgh. He watched, hypnotized by it, for some minutes, and then began to realize that there were faces in the crowd he recognized. He thought for a minute it was his imagination, because the coincidence seemed too wonderful, too lovely to be believed. He wanted to see her there, surely that was it?

But it was her: it was Chris, that tall girl, in the green tailor-made, and the woman beside her, small and dapper, was definitely Miss Ronaldson, who did not have the sort of mien one could forget in a hurry. He shivered with excitement – this glorious piece of chance seemed so significant, as if the higher powers were really working on their behalf. He did not rush up to them though, partly because he still was not quite certain that it was true, and partly to savour the sight of her coming up the platform. Now he had identified her, she seemed to shine out, as obviously the most handsome woman there. She reeked of style, with lace ruffles at her throat and wrists, with a marvellous broad-brimmed hat. She looked very different in this Edinburgh attire, and he could not resist picturing her at all the county functions which in the course of his new life he would have to attend. He could see her at once giving out the prizes at the Rankeillor Games, and dancing, with consummate elegance, an eightsome reel at the Caledonian Ball. And he could hear the congratulations of other men: 'What a charming woman Lady Lindsay is!'

He ran forward through the oncoming crowd to greet her.

Chris felt guilty the moment she saw him. She felt he had caught her with another man, in the act of doing something unspeakable. Her nerves were in a state as it was – she felt quite sick with apprehension at the exam and interview that afternoon – and suddenly to see Guy dashing towards her, looking as if all the riches of the world had landed in his lap, she found herself wondering what she had done to deserve such torment. And then, without quite knowing how it happened, she found she was in his arms and being kissed with a complete lack of inhibition.

Aunt Minna coughed, and Guy remembered himself. He stuttered an apology and managed some more respectful handshaking.

'I don't think you need to apologize to me,' said Aunt Minna. 'It's Chris whose jabot is crushed out of all recognition,' and she flicked out her hand and adjusted the lace jabot that decorated Chris's collar. Their eyes met as she did it. Be strong, Aunt Minna's seemed to say. You've made your decision.

Chris wished again it were that easy. When Guy was not there she could cope with him. She could dismiss him, turn him down with kindly, well-ordered, reasoned words, but now he was here again, having caught her in the act of betrayal, she did not know if she could manage it. There was something in her which told her that she wanted him badly, a voice as insistent as that which told her she did not.

'So what brings you up to Edinburgh?' said Guy.

Chris hesitated to speak. She could not mention the Academy. It would be too callous. He deserved a full, calm explanation of her reasoning, not a sudden deduction of her duplicity. Fortunately Aunt Minna filled the silence.

'Oh, dreadful women's fripperies,' she said. 'I find you get a better class of frippery in Edinburgh. Are you on your way through to Rankeillor?'

'I've time to kill. I've an appointment this afternoon but nothing till then. Perhaps I could help you?'

'You're not serious, I hope,' said Aunt Minna laughing. 'You'd be driven quite to distraction. I couldn't inflict that on a young man. It would be too cruel.'

'I've stood it with my mother,' said Guy.

'Oh, but she's an intelligent woman,' said Aunt Minna. 'Not a old dithering ninny spinster, like myself. No, you shan't come with me. But I think perhaps you two ought to go and have a quiet talk over a cup of tea, don't you think, Chris?'

Guy's face lit up at this suggestion.

'Are you sure, Miss Ronaldson?'

'I think you should. Chris has something to say to you.'

Chris silently cursed her aunt for that. She felt she had been forcibly marched to a hated appointment at the dentist.

'You do?' Guy said, with enthusiasm.

She realized she had said nothing to him yet, and could only manage, 'Let's go and sit down first, shall we?'

They left the station and crossed over Princes Street to Maule's.

'There's a tea room here, I believe. I shall come for you in an hour, Chris,' said Aunt Minna and disappeared in the direction of the drapery counters.

'Your aunt is a good sort, isn't she?' said Guy.

Chris wondered whether he would think that of her in an hour's time, if she managed to say what she had to say to him.

The tea room at Maule's was hardly the place Chris would have chosen for such a difficult conversation. It struck her as a place full of staring eyes and flapping ears – the women at their tables seemed to scrutinize them very thoroughly as they came in and sat down. Chris felt she might be wearing a large paper sign saying 'Jilt' round her neck. Already she could sense their unspoken sympathy for Guy and their contempt at her utter foolishness.

Guy was grinning broadly, obviously enjoying hugely the chance to be alone with her. He ordered sandwiches and scones, declaring how hungry he suddenly was.

'I've hardly had an appetite since . . .' he said. 'But now I feel . . . Well, seeing you, it's like waking up, you know.'

'I'm sorry I didn't answer your letters,' she said, thinking that this, as anywhere, was a good place to make a beginning.

'I didn't expect you to,' he said, laying his hand over hers. 'You told me once how you hated letter-writing.'

'I did?' she said, surprised he had remembered such a trivial admission. 'That isn't really why I didn't. I feel rather bad about it but I found . . .' She hesitated. 'I found I couldn't. I wanted to but . . .'

'It doesn't matter,' he said. 'I've told you.'

'It does,' she answered. 'You have to let me explain – if I can.'

'What is there to explain?' he smiled. 'You don't like writing letters. That's simple enough. I think music is your preferred language. I should imagine Beethoven was a rotten correspondent . . .'

'No, it isn't simple, Guy,' she said. 'That's why I couldn't write. I didn't know what to say, how to answer. Your letters were so . . . so confusing.' Now he looked confused. He knotted his brow for a moment in a puzzled frown. 'It was a little like being shot at,' she went on. 'It might have been easier if you hadn't written them, perhaps . . .'

'Easier for what?' he said.

'Easier for me,' she replied, and would have gone on but the waitress appeared with their order. The teapot and milk jug were put in front of her, and she poured out for Guy without much thinking about it.

'You remember just how I like it,' he said, accepting his cup.

'Oh,' she said flatly, 'just because it's the same as I take it.' However, he smiled as if she had remembered something of real significance to him. 'Look,' she said, realizing she had better get as quickly to the point as she could, 'there's something I really should tell you, before we go any further.'

'Fire away, then,' he said, innocently, and Chris did feel exactly as if she held a loaded rifle at his head. Guy, however, hardly seemed aware of it. He was attacking a plate of beef sandwiches.

'I've an interview at the Caledonian Academy this afternoon,' she said, pressing her finger on the trigger. 'And an exam – for a bursary.'

He looked at her again, a little confused, but not yet aware she had just lodged a bullet in his head. She found she was waiting for the yelp of pain.

'The Caledonian Academy?' he said, putting down the sandwich he had raised to his lips. 'The music college, you mean?'

'Yes.'

'The place that Henry Mackenzie is the director of?' he said. She nodded, unable to speak now. 'And you want to study there?'

'Yes,' she managed to say. 'More than anything . . .' she found she blurted out.

'More than anything,' he repeated. There was a leaden edge to his voice. He dropped the sandwich on to the plate. 'Oh Chris . . .'

'This hasn't been easy,' she protested. 'This hasn't been easy at all.'

'But I thought . . .'

'You assumed,' she cut in. 'Rather too much. You told me to think about it, but you'd made up your mind, hadn't you, that I would say yes, that I couldn't possibly say anything else?'

'Because you seemed keen, as keen as I was. I felt it, Chris, when you kissed me!'

She stared down into her tea-cup, thoroughly ashamed of herself. She could not find any words to excuse herself and decided she had best be blunt with him. She gave him a nervous glance and said, 'I don't think that was love, Guy, it was . . . curiosity.'

'Curiosity?' he said. She hated the faint tone of disgust in his voice. 'What do you mean?'

'I mean I was . . . You tempted me. I was excited, intrigued, I suppose. You overwhelmed me and I couldn't help myself, just as you couldn't that night.'

He grimaced and slumped back in his chair, staring at the ceiling.

'But Chris,' he burst out suddenly. 'Chris, I need you.' He looked across at her again, and she saw the blind panic in his eyes, like that of an animal in a snare.

She shook her head vehemently, washed over by a terrible mixture of pity and self-disgust at her own cruelty towards him. It would be so easy to help him, to make him happy, but she could not. The price was too high.

'I need you,' he said again.

'You don't, not really. You just think it, because you're bleeding inside . . .'

'I knew this before Roddy died, I knew,' Guy pressed on.

'You were bleeding then, because of Vienna. You want someone to lick your wounds, Guy, not a wife.' It came out sounding very harsh and he stared at her, but she felt she must go on. 'It would be madness for us to get married. You won't see that now, but you will. I'd be a rotten wife to you. I'm not made for marriage. I'm made for my work, for music. You must see that!'

'Do you think I'd stop you?' he said. 'What do you think I am, some sort of domestic tyrant? I shouldn't stop you for one moment. I want you to be great, Chris, I want you to write all you can.'

'Then leave me be!' she exclaimed. 'I have to do this alone.'

'Why, for God's sake, why? I don't seem to remember that being married bothered Bach or Mozart.'

'Because they were men! Marriage is quite a different affair for men than women. Very little changes for a man when he marries, but for a woman everything does. It's a job for her, and a job I'm not prepared to do. I'm sorry, but I can't.'

'I don't know what you mean,' he said.

'You couldn't,' she said. 'You're a man. You've never felt the invidious little pressures of being a woman. If I became your wife, Guy, I should have to do it thoroughly.

There would be no other way. It's my training, I suppose. I'd have to squash myself to make a decent job of it.'

'I shouldn't let you,' he said, grabbing her hand. 'This is terrible nonsense you're talking, Chris. I should make you work, I promise.'

She felt his hands about hers, warm and strong, and saw the powerful sincerity with which he delivered those words. Inwardly she wavered. How simple it would be to say yes, and believe him. But she was not sure it would be possible.

She shook her head and gently withdrew her hand.

'I can't have any distractions,' she managed to say at length. 'I have to take this path alone. I can't say why, but I only know that's how it has to be. I know it hurts, because it hurts me, as well as you, but it's the only thing I can do. The music – it's too important to leave to chance. You must accept that, Guy.'

'I wish I could,' he said, 'but I really can't. I don't see why you feel obliged to sacrifice yourself on some altar for the sake of art when we could be happy, really happy for the rest of our lives.'

'Because we wouldn't be happy!' she said. 'I'd make you miserable. I'd always be regretting that I never tried, that I never pursued the one thing I know I'm here for. I'm not here to be a wife and mother, very pleasant though that might be, but to compose music. That's all I know for certain. It's my duty, my responsibility to do it. You know the parable of the talents, I'm sure.'

'Always the daughter of the Manse, aren't you?' said Guy bitterly. 'I suppose I should be damned glad you are not throwing me over to preach to the heathens in China. You sound just like a missionary.'

His sudden sarcasm startled her, and she felt her heart sinking even more. She had made an enemy of him, just as she had feared.

'Guy, please try and understand,' she pleaded.

'How can I?' he said. 'All I can feel is abandoned.'

'It'll pass, I'm sure it will. In time you'll see I was right.'

'What comfort is that to me now?' he snapped. 'Honestly, Chris, I don't think you have the least notion how I feel.'

'Or you of how I feel,' she felt forced to retort. 'Which proves it, doesn't it? That we should be a disaster together.'

'We can't know that unless we try, can we?' he said.

'Marriage isn't an experiment,' she said. 'What if it did fail, how would we get out of it? You know as well as I that you can't simply get out of a marriage if it doesn't work.'

'Then we'd make it work. I'm damn sure I would, for one,' he said, leaning across the table, his whole body tense with sudden earnestness. 'And so would you. Oh Chris, can't you see it at all, see how marvellous it would be?'

'I don't have your faith,' she said simply, and pushed back her chair from the table, as coolly as she could. She had decided it was time to stop this conversation. She could no longer stand the way his eyes were burning into her, blazing with such anger and passion that they seemed to scorch the very insides of her. She was sure that any minute his control would go and he would explode at her and force her into submission. She had to get away.

She stood up, gathering up her gloves and music case.

'I'm going to find my aunt,' she said.

'Go on then,' he said, with a feeble show of indifference. She attempted to slip past him, but in a moment he had jumped up and was holding her, discreetly but firmly so that she could not get away.

'Guy . . .' she protested in a mutter. 'Let go.'

'Don't think for one minute I'm giving up on this,' he said, his face so close to hers that she could feel his breath on her cheek. 'I don't give up that easily on anything.'

'And neither do I!' she retorted, rather louder than she

had intended, so that she noticed the ladies at the next table were exchanging fascinated glances. She managed to wriggle out of his grip and turned away from him at once, to make a hasty but decorous exit from the tea room. Yet she found she was shaking as she went, and that her eyes were blurring with irritating tears. How ridiculous that was!

She found Aunt Minna deeply engrossed in the choice of an evening blouse.

'Ecru or ivory, Chris?' she asked. 'I really can't decide.' Chris shrugged her shoulders lamely. Aunt Minna, reading the gesture, at once said, 'Have you this in black? I should like to see it in black,' and sent the shop-walker scurrying away.

'Did you do it?' she asked in a whisper.

'Yes,' said Chris, sitting down on a chair by the counter.

'Well done,' said Aunt Minna, stretching out her hand to her and giving her arm a brief squeeze.

'No, it was not,' said Chris, with a sigh. 'Not well done at all.'

9

'So, Miss Adam, I see from your application that you wish to study piano and composition,' said Dr Bradley, the admissions secretary.

'Composition and piano,' said Chris. 'Composition to be my principal study.'

'I see,' he said, looking very pointedly at her through his gold-rimmed pince-nez. 'Are you quite certain about that, Miss Adam?'

'Yes, Dr Bradley,' she replied with all the firmness she could manage. 'Quite certain.' She did not want to have a run-in with this man. Why did everyone have to query her motivation? She had had enough battles for one day, and she could not help thinking that the inhospitable Dr Bradley was in secret league with Guy to thwart her. He would refuse to give her a place and she would have to go back and submit, after all, to her proper destiny.

'Well, that is unusual,' he said. 'Most young ladies come here seeking to be performers.' He said it contemptuously and Chris felt herself bristle. 'You do understand that the composition course is very ... er, demanding?'

She wanted to ask him if he would have said that to a male candidate, but contented herself with saying, 'Good,' which startled him, she could tell.

'Humm ...' he said, looking down at the papers on his desk. 'Well, I suppose I ought to give you a fair trial, though I can't imagine you will be up to scratch. We'll start with testing your sense of pitch. I think pitch to a musician is like the pulse. Without a good clear notion of it, he's quite lost.'

His rudeness was so breathtaking that she wished she could laugh at it, and that his opinion did not matter. But she was horribly aware that she had to do everything she could to impress him. As he stumped over to the large black piano which dominated the room she studied him. He was a short, balding man in middle age, with a puffy and unattractive face that was made worse by a disagreeable frown. He was leaning on a stick, gripping the top of it with a claw of a hand. Chris felt whatever calm she had conjured up vanish.

The door opened suddenly then, with a noisy rattle, and a girl dashed in, dressed somewhat spectacularly in a clinging dress of violet velvet and a vast black hat from which trailed a cream lace veil that was almost bridal in length. Yet her clothes, striking though they might be, were muted by the appearance of the girl herself. She had the kind of beauty it was impossible not to stare at. It was the sweet, sculptural perfection of a Renaissance madonna, especially now, as she made her excuses to Dr Bradley, putting her whole body, it seemed to Chris, into an elegant line of submission to which no man could possibly remain indifferent. Except, of course, Dr Bradley.

'Who are you, madam?' he asked, addressing her as though she were a recalcitrant housemaid who had come in with smuts on her face.

'Carlingford,' she said. 'Miranda Carlingford.'

'And you are a candidate for admission?' he said.

'Yes,' she said.

Dr Bradley consulted a piece of paper on his desk.

'I see . . . yes. Miss Carlingford. You were supposed to be here at two o'clock.'

'Yes, I know but . . .'

'Two o'clock, Miss Carlingford,' Dr Bradley said. 'And it is now three o'clock. You wish me to admit you to a serious course of study and yet you cannot even manage to be on time for a simple appointment, ten minutes away from your place of residence?'

'Oh, I know,' she said, putting out her black-gloved hands in a gesture of appeal that was positively operatic. 'It really is unforgivable of me.'

'Sit. I will get to you in a moment,' he said, indicating a chair at the side of the room. 'I was just about to give Miss Adam here an aural test and then I will test you, Miss Carlingford.'

Miranda Carlingford turned to Chris.

'I really am so sorry,' she said. 'Do you mind sharing like this?'

'No, not at all,' said Chris.

Dr Bradley looked at them both and then sighed heavily as he sat down at the piano, propping his stick at the treble end. He beckoned Chris over.

'Now, sing out nice and clear, girl. There's nothing I detest so much as timid women singing.'

She felt physically sick at that, sick enough to want to make a dash for the door. Surely the indignity of cowardice was better than the ignominy of failing. She knew she was being irrational but she could not help herself. She put out a hand to the piano to steady herself.

'Look away from the keyboard if you please, miss!' barked Bradley. She turned away and her eyes met those of Miranda. She gave her an encouraging smile from beneath the broad brim of her hat and Chris forced herself to remember that her sense of pitch was pretty trustworthy. She had nothing to fear but Bradley's deviousness – and she was convinced he was capable of that.

'Right, scale of G major – sing me a fifth above the tonic please.'

Well, that was easy enough. She obliged.

'And a third . . . and a seventh. Right, C minor now, a fourth please, and . . . the seventh. Hmm . . . You seem to have that knack off quite well. What's this interval then?'

'A sixth,' she said. 'And it's D major, isn't it?'

'No need to get cocksure,' he said. 'But it is. And this is?'

He tested her for at least five minutes, progressing from intervals to identifying triads and the keys of inverted chords. Although she did not make any mistakes, when she had finished she felt as if she had been hauled over the coals.

'That was good,' said Bradley, in a mildly surprised tone as she sat down. 'Now Miss Carlingford, it's your turn.'

'I'm afraid,' Miranda said, 'that I shan't be able to match that degree of accuracy.'

'It would be surprising if you could,' said Dr Bradley. 'Perfect pitch is extremely rare.'

Chris sat reeling slightly at what she took to be a compliment. At least that part of the test she had passed with flying colours.

Miranda was fumbling and she longed to help her out as she stood there groping for the right answers. On most occasions she got there, but it took her some time.

'That was no more than barely adequate,' said Bradley. 'I'm sure you do very well on paper, Miss Carlingford, but really, it's the idea of the note in the head that matters. Too much piano playing, I imagine, has made you over-reliant on an artificial means to locate you. Now, I have written out some exercises here,' he went on, taking some sheets of manuscript from a folder on the piano. 'Have you both something to write with?'

Miranda produced an elegant little pen from her reticule while Chris dug for the stub of a pencil which she usually carried about her, and they began the paper. As they worked, Bradley sat glowering at them from his chair, his hands resting on his stick, convinced perhaps that they might attempt to collude. There was no need to. The exercise was not taxing – a melody to transpose and another to harmonize. Chris could see from the speed of Miranda's pen that she had no trouble with any of it either.

The next hurdle was sight-reading on the piano. Miranda here was the clear winner. She read effortlessly, and without any visible mistakes. Chris, on the other hand, found her hands were shaking and that she took the whole thing too fast out of nerves, so that the left-hand fingering went quite disastrously awry. There were too many wrong notes to be ignored and Bradley, rapping his stick on the ground, interrupted her.

'Spare us the rest, Miss Adam. I am quite relieved to hear that you do not wish to be a concert performer, but to compose . . .' He paused for a moment, and then began in a slightly more kindly tone, 'My dear young woman . . .'

'I'm quite serious,' she cut in. 'I've written a few things already, actually.' She had not wanted it to sound apologetic but it came out that way.

'Have you now? What sort of things?'

'Songs,' she said. 'Settings of Shakespeare's songs. I've brought them with me.'

'I rather feared you might have.'

'I don't mean to sound disrespectful, Dr Bradley,' piped up Miranda, 'but you can't possibly judge until you've heard what Miss Adam has written, can you?'

'Oh can I not?' said Dr Bradley. 'If you had been presented with as many feeble compositions by benighted amateurs as I have, you begin to get a trifle cynical.' Chris now felt like a small worm crushed under the tip of his stick. 'Settings of Shakespeare . . .' he went on with a sigh. 'Well, I suppose I must comply, Miss Carlingford. I should hate you to think me unsporting. Play something, Miss Adam.'

She got across the room, and was fumbling to open her music case.

'This is a song for soprano and piano,' she said, scrabbling for her manuscript. '"Full fathom five thy father lies" – from *The Tempest*.'

Bradley looked bored at this, but Miranda jumped up and said, 'Shall I sing for you? Would that help?'

She nodded thankfully. She did not think she could do even her own music justice in these circumstances, and as she was sure this was the best thing she had done, she did not want to ruin it with her own less than marvellous singing voice. Miranda's voice even in the limited display of the aural test, had struck her as good. She spread the sheets of music across the stand for her. 'I hope you can read it all right.'

'Perfectly,' she said, and Chris began the introduction.

She had written a slow sequence of deep chords, in C minor, to accompany the song, like a funeral dirge, and the voice part began on a high repeated E to which she had fitted the opening words. Miranda came in with confidence, with wonderful attack, in fact, startling Chris slightly with the lovely purity of the note. Her voice was perfect for the song, exactly the voice Chris had imagined singing it, and she sang with real feeling, understanding the demands of the music. Chris could not have asked for a better interpretation and she knew then the song was good. Her belief in herself and her ambitions was confirmed. It was worth struggling on, no matter what objections threw themselves in her way.

She played the last three chords, that echoed the closing words, 'Ding dong bell', so softly that she felt she was caressing the keys. Then after a pause she repeated them.

'"That strain again! It had a dying fall,"' quoted Miranda. 'What an exquisite song!' she exclaimed.

Dr Bradley coughed and said loudly, 'Don't get too carried away, young lady.'

'But it is delightful, you must concede that,' said Miranda, bubbling with such enthusiasm that Chris felt she could have kissed her for it.

'It shows promise,' said Dr Bradley carefully. 'But promise that can only be fulfilled by a great deal of hard work.'

'So I have a place?' Chris felt bold enough to ask him directly.

'I will let you know,' he said airily. 'And you, Miss Carlingford,' he added in answer to Miranda's unspoken question, 'will also hear from me presently. You may go.'

They scrabbled together their things.

'Oh, leave that song, will you, Miss Adam? I trust you have a copy,' he added, just as Chris was about to pack it away. 'I'd like to show it to the Principal.'

'To Sir Henry?' Chris said in astonishment.

He clearly did not wish to elaborate and instead gave a dismissive wave of his hand.

'I am a busy man,' he said. 'Go and trim hats, young ladies!'

When the door closed behind them, Chris and Miranda exclaimed simultaneously, 'Oh, what a dreadful man!' and then laughed.

'I knew I shouldn't have worn this hat,' said Miranda, as they walked down the empty passageway. 'It's all wrong, isn't it? "Go and trim hats!" She gave a creditable impersonation of him. 'Oh, the cheek of the man. Now if I had worn something sensible, he would not have been able to say that, would he?'

'I'm sure he says such things all the time,' said Chris. 'I think he has a low opinion of women.'

'Well, he has a low opinion of us, of me, certainly,' laughed Miranda. 'I suppose I've ruined it for myself now. I shall never get in.'

'I think he liked your playing,' said Chris. 'I certainly

did. And thank you for helping me out. I don't think I've heard my song sung so well before.'

'Do you think so?' she said, earnestly. 'I do so want to do this thing, but people simply won't take me seriously. They laugh at me, even when I know that it's the one thing I am really any use at.'

'I know,' said Chris, thinking again of the morning with Guy. 'That's half the struggle, isn't it?'

'But it must be easy for people to take you seriously,' said Miranda. 'When you make such lovely things.'

'I think it disturbs them more than anything. It's such a departure from what's regarded as normal for a woman.'

'Oh, but that's exactly it!' exclaimed Miranda, clapping her hands together. 'I do hope we both get in, Miss Adam. I'm sure we'd be great friends. Perhaps we should be friends anyway after that little experience. You will let me write to you, won't you? You must let me take your address.' She stopped in the middle of the passageway and began to dig in her reticule. At last she produced a little notebook, with a pencil attached.

'Write it in here,' she said, flipping the book open.

Chris obliged and handed it back. 'Oh . . .' said Miranda, reflecting on it for a moment. 'You're from the country.' Then she giggled and said, 'Do you know, I've just had the most splendid idea.'

'Yes?' said Chris, a little bemused.

'I don't suppose you've any lodgings fixed up in town, have you?'

'Well, that rather depends on . . .' She gestured back towards Dr Bradley's door. 'Doesn't it?'

'Yes, but if you do get in, which I'm sure you will, do you have anywhere to live? Some flock of cousins you'll have to roost with, for example?'

'No, not a soul.'

'Then I can recommend excellent lodgings.'

'Oh, you can?'

'Yes, my house.'

'Your house?' Chris queried it, because the way Miranda spoke the words suggested she owned a house, which seemed impossible.

'Well, it's not entirely my house. It's half my house. My father left it to us, my sister and me, that is. It's a wonderful great barn of a place in Royal Circus and we don't have the money to run it properly – my brother-in-law is just starting out as a doctor, you see, and doesn't get paid much – and we don't want to sell, we love it too much – so we thought we'd take people in as lodgers.' She laughed. 'It does sound a bit odd, doesn't it? But we thought it would be amusing.'

'So you live there with your sister and brother-in-law?'

'Oh yes, now Antonia's married, it's horribly respectable. Funny what difference a wedding band makes, isn't it? You will think about it, won't you? It won't be expensive, really.'

'Of course I shall,' said Chris, though she was not at all sure she would be able to afford such grand quarters. Judging by Miranda's dress, she could guess that their standards of what was and was not expensive might differ. But the idea of it, the sheer unorthodoxy of it, delighted her and she hoped she could afford it.

But as she reached the main hall where Aunt Minna was waiting for her, perched on a gothic-style bench, reading a dull-looking magazine, she realized she was getting far ahead of herself. For one thing she did not know she had a place, and for another she did not yet have the approval of her parents. Those were large things still to be overcome, and then there was Guy. The last thing he had said to her was, 'I shan't give up,' and she found herself shivering at the thought of it.

'How was it?' said Aunt Minna.

'I don't know,' said Chris. 'He took one of my songs to show the Principal.'

'He did? That's good,' she said. 'Who was that girl I saw you talking to?'

'Her name's Miranda. She's took the exam with me.'

'Someone to compare notes with. I'm sure that helps. But you know something, Chris, I'm sure you beat them all hands down.' She laid her hand on Chris's arm affectionately. 'There's nothing to worry about.'

'Isn't there? What about Mother and Father? I wish we could have been more honest about this.'

'When you hear you're in, I'll sort them out, I promise,' she said. 'You've had enough sorting out of your own to do.'

10

It still annoyed Guy that he had let her go, that he had let her run off like that, past all those dreadful staring women, leaving him with a half-eaten plate of sandwiches while he plummeted into despair. He ought to have gone after her. He ought not, when he had actually had her in his grasp, to have let her go. Instead of feebly touching her and telling her he was not going to give up he should have shown her. He should have crushed her in his arms and kissed her with all the passion in him, until she was no longer able to resist him, until all the barriers of her defiance had collapsed. That would have been the right thing to do.

Yet he had not. He had let her go, and had sat there for some time afterwards, numbly eating those sandvwiches and drinking the tea, while inside he had felt himself cracking in two. He would have liked to roar out his pain, to kick over chairs, smash china and rip off the table-cloths, anything to awaken all those smug genteel bitches around him to the intensity of his anger. But the invisible but steel-like threads of good behaviour held him fast in the place and made him powerless. Perhaps he should not be so surprised that he had let Chris go. He was an impotent, dry thing, a cipher of his class, unable for the sake of appearances to do what was necessary. No wonder she had not wanted him.

He stopped his futile, restless pacing of the library and threw himself into a chair by the fire. Outside, a foul storm, very appropriate to his state of mind, moaned drearily on, rattling the window frames and lashing rain again the glass. He detested then the warm shelter of his house. It seemed like a comfortable prison in which he had been trapped for too long. Awful things might happen, but the storm never truly got in. The icy rain-water never spoiled the old tapestries with damp hands and the wind, however fierce, never blew away the comfortable certainties of the lairds of Rankeillor. He, Guy, was only another of them, a new incumbent perhaps, but of the same old stuff. He had failed to be any different, for all his struggling. Vienna had told him that – that he was not made for anything but this life. There seemed, in that moment, something horridly inevitable about Roddy's death. What else could he, Guy, have done in his life but be the Laird? He was fit for nothing else than to be the ostensible master of Rankeillor, fit in truth to be its absolute slave.

If I had not been this, he wondered, might she have wanted me then? Yet he knew he would not have been Guy, then, but some stranger. Chris's not wanting him was inescapable, her rejection had been unequivocal. He had to accept that, but God, how could he? He kicked the fender in his anger, and woke the sleeping dog on the hearth rug. Dido staggered to her feet and came to him, pressing against his legs and staring up at him with dumb, animal devotion.

'I shall go and see her,' he said to the dog. 'I told her I wouldn't give up, and I shan't. It's probably stupid but . . .' He got out of his chair and went to the door, deliberately not imagining what might happen when he did see her. The act of doing, of going, was in that moment enough.

Just before he got to the door, Isolde came in.

'Oh, here you are,' she said. 'We were worried when you didn't come into luncheon.'

'I wasn't hungry,' he shrugged.

'You should eat something,' she said. Her solicitude, indeed her appearance needled him. It was as if she had arrived expressly to deter him from going to see Chris. She noticed an empty glass on the table. 'Oh Guy, you haven't . . .' she began.

'It was seltzer water,' he exclaimed. 'Do you think I'm that stupid?' In fact, he would happily, over the last few days, have drunk himself into senseless oblivion. Indeed, he had only just managed to stop himself from doing so.

'No, no,' she said, putting up her hands defensively. 'Of course not. It's just . . . Oh, I'm so worried about you, Guy.'

'You don't have to be,' said Guy. 'I'm as right as can be, given the circumstances.'

'But it's more than that. You seem so angry.'

'Well, of course I'm angry! The whole thing is so senseless, isn't it? I have to be angry.'

'It isn't good for you. You must try and be a little resigned, Guy. You have to accept that God . . .'

'Don't, Isolde,' he cut in. 'Please!' If there was one thing he could not bear it was a religious homily on the theme of Roddy's having gone to a better place. His mother and sister had been clinging to this wilful piece of self-delusion and it appalled him. 'You know my views on that.'

'Yes, but I can't help thinking that you'd feel much better if . . .'

'If I lied to myself? No, Isolde, I can't and that's an end to it. Anyway, I'm going out just now. I haven't got time to discuss this, not that there's anything to discuss, of course.' He brushed past her towards the door.

'Where are you going?' she asked.

'To the Manse,' he said, and seeing her look of mild surprise, he added, 'And it isn't to see the Minister, if that's what you're hoping.'

He dashed down the turnpike stair, deciding whether to

order the covered gig or the motor. The motor won. He wanted speed suddenly, and there was always a chance that she might still be in Broughty Ferry at her aunt's. Well, he would go all that way if necessary, even in this storm. He had to convince her of his seriousness.

While he fretted in the hall, waiting for the motor, Malcolm, nanny-like, insisted he put on an overcoat.

'Such a terrible, driech day, sir. Are you sure you must go out? Her Ladyship will worry about your motoring in such a storm.'

'Mackie will be driving, not me,' said Guy, impatiently pulling on his coat.

In the back of the motor, as Mackie drove him along the castle drive, Guy suddenly remembered how he had made that short journey in reverse, with Chris sitting beside him, and how beautiful she had looked that night, in her white dress, with the plaid blanket spread over her knees. He touched the plaid now, as if by touching it he could touch her. A futile act, he realized, but perhaps the closest he might get. The old despair came creeping over him. What on earth was he doing?

When the motor drew up at the Manse, Guy was reluctant to get out and go in. But he had to get out. Poor Mackie was standing holding the door open for him, the rain pelting down relentlessly.

'Thanks, Mackie,' he said, as he climbed out. 'It's in a good cause, I assure you.'

The rain had soaked the crisp stone façade of the Manse into a dank grey, making it appear more austere and forbidding than usual. He felt intimidated, and hesitated on the step of the dripping porch before ringing the bell.

Phemie opened the door to him, but a moment later Mrs Adam appeared.

'Who is it? Oh Guy, it's you! Well, I'm very glad to see you. How are you managing?' She spoke in a hearty fashion he had observed in her before, a manner of cheerful sympathy reserved for invalids and the bereaved. 'I'm afraid my husband's not here at present, but then you probably don't want to see him, do you?' she added, with a significant laugh.

'Well, yes, I did come to see Chris, actually.'

'Of course you did,' she said.

'She's busy,' said Phemie, bluntly, 'kneading.'

'Well, that will keep, won't it?' said Mrs Adam. 'Go and get her, will you, Phemie, and you, Guy, come in here. There's a nice fire.'

'I'll fetch her myself,' said Guy, realizing he would never get a private word with her in the Manse sitting room.

'Well, if you like,' said Mrs Adam, a little mystified, clearly, that Guy should want to go into the kitchen. 'Don't be long.'

He had not been in the Manse kitchen for many years and its cheerfulness surprised him. The range was blazing out heat, there was a smell of something good boiling and in the centre of it all, stood Chris, at the large deal table. She had rolled up the blue flannel sleeves of her dress, and put on a striped apron, that was no doubt hum-drum enough, but that struck him as picturesque. Her cheeks, like her fingers were pink, as she pummelled a large piece of dough.

She looked up and stared at him as he came in, stopping her work. She gazed at him with clear discomfiting eyes and he felt awkward at once.

'You look like a Vermeer,' he said. She grimaced a smile at this attempt at a compliment, and returned to her kneading.

'I have to finish this,' she said.

'Yes, yes, of course . . .' he said airily, and they fell into silence.

The rhythm of Chris's kneading hypnotized him, and he could sense her own fierce concentration on it. There was a pulse to it. She worked with exquisite regularity as if she were marking out the beat of some unheard melody. It was beautiful, and he ached to see it, wanting to possess those strong white hands and feel them touch his own bare flesh as they touched that lump of bread dough. Impulsively, though the breadth of the table separated them, he leant across and tried to catch one of them.

'No!' she exclaimed, stepping back and twisting free.

He had held her hand for only a moment, but it had been enough for him to feel the warmth in it, enough to make him angry. In that moment it seemed to signify all his loss.

'Why?' he shouted, smacking his rejected palm down on to the table so that the bowls and jugs on it rattled. 'Why?'

'You know why,' she said. 'I've told you.'

'I know but . . . but . . .' He found he was staring at the wood of the table-top, at the little scattering of flour over its surface, at the white-grey piece of bread dough, at anything, in short, rather than at her. 'But I'm damned if I can understand.'

The door opened behind him and he heard Mrs Adam say, 'Now, Chris, come along. I'm sure Guy doesn't care to stand talking in the kitchen.'

'We were just finishing,' said Chris sharply. Now he looked up at her. 'In fact you might as well stay and hear, Mother. I've something to say to you both.' He watched her wipe her hands on her apron and dig in her pocket. She brought out an envelope. 'I haven't found the moment to tell you this, Mother, and since this concerns you too, Guy . . . Well, this letter is from the admissions secretary at the Caledonian Academy. They're offering me a bursary – fifty guineas a year, actually . . .'

'What are you talking about?' said Mrs Adam, quite bewildered.

'The Caledonian Academy, Mother, in Edinburgh. It

was Aunt Minna's idea that I try for it, and I know we should have told you, but really, I wasn't at all sure I would get in at all and . . .'

Mrs Adam reached out and snatched the letter from Chris. She glanced over it, shaking her head.

'Do you mean to say . . .' she began, 'that you and Minna have gone behind our backs and organized this? How can you possibly imagine that your father and I would agree to such a thing? And Minna too! This is . . . conspiracy – that's what it is. I simply can't believe that you could stoop to that!'

'Then you'd better try to,' said Chris.

'I shall not!' said Mrs Adam. 'And if you think that I shall let you go on with this preposterous nonsense – goodness, I don't even know how you could begin to think . . .' She broke off and gestured at Guy. 'The best offer you could get, and you're talking of bursaries and colleges . . . where's your sense of duty, child?'

'I won't have her marry me out of duty,' said Guy, appalled by that suggestion. 'But if you love me, Chris,' he said, striding round the table to her, 'I won't let you deny it, not for all the scholarships in the world. I won't!' As he approached her, she shook her head and held up her hands as a barrier against him. But this time he would not be deterred. He grabbed her into his arms and held her tight, just as he should have done that morning in Edinburgh. 'Now tell me you don't love me.'

'I don't,' she said, in a whisper.

'I don't believe you.'

'I don't!' she said. 'I don't love you! I don't love you! How many times must I say it? I don't! I can't! I won't!'

He released her. There could be no doubt about the angry confidence of her words. They stabbed like knife blades into him. He took a step back, winded by the finality of it.

'Christina!' said Mrs Adam in a shocked tone.

'Not a word more, Mother,' said Chris, and then she bolted out of the room. Guy heard the back door slamming shut.

'Go after her, for heaven's sake,' said Mrs Adam.

He went, but he hardly knew why. He saw her at the end of the garden path, through the grey veil of sodden air, and felt the cold embrace of the rain on his own face. It was like a cold, realistic embrace. He felt himself awaken with it, felt the tears of knowledge in his eyes, and yet he still ran after her. His body was still intent when his heart already knew that he had no right.

From the garden into the muddy field beyond they went, but he found he walked now, slowed by the driving rain. She soon vanished from his sight completely and he wondered if he had only dreamt of that dark figure against a dusky sky. What more could she be to him than that, after all?

And then he found her again, at the top of the field, by a collapsed wall, collapsed herself amongst a heap of stones. She was lying in the mud, her skirts twisted and clinging, her face and hands stained with the earth, the rain dripping from her hair. The sight of her moved him desperately – that she was so determined to be free that she could bring herself to this.

'I can't get up!' she cried out. 'I think I've twisted my ankle. It's so stupid . . .'

He was glad that the rain hid his tear-stained face as he bent to help her. She tried to stand, but she was wavering terribly.

'I'll have to carry you,' he said, and lifted her into his arms. She was stiff with fear, he could feel it. 'Don't worry,' he said. 'I'm not going to do anything, or say anything. I understand now.'

'You do? Oh, thank God!' He felt her relax in his arms. 'You won't regret it, I promise.'

'I will,' he said, truthfully. 'But I see now you're the fox that shouldn't be caught. It'd be wrong to force you. But you must promise me one thing.'

'That depends,' she said, cautiously.

'You'll be able to manage this,' he said.

'What then?'

'That you do your best, your absolute best. That you do something worth while, something' – he looked down at her lovely, rain-soaked face; 'life-giving. If you don't, I'll never forgive you.'

'I'll try,' she said. 'Look, I think I could walk from here.' They were at the garden gate.

'Are you sure?' She nodded, and he set her down gently. She held his arm for a moment and then took a tentative step away from him.

'Yes, I'll manage,' she said.

He stayed with her until they reached the door of the house, but he felt that the slight physical distance between them was in fact opening up like a great chasm. She might physically be limping by his side, but in truth she was a bird, wheeling high in the sky, way beyond the reach of him, a song bird who could not be confined by his cage, even when the bars were made of love. In it, she could not have sung, and what was the point of her without that?

11

The room pleased Chris at once, with the faded crimson toile-de-Jouy that covered its walls and the large, solid pieces of mahogany which comprised its furniture. If she were to have imagined her ideal lodging, it would not have been much different from this high, square room, with a black marble fireplace and a view of trees lying like a layer of black lace against the Edinburgh dusk. And there was even a piano.

'It used to be our day nursery,' said Miranda. 'Does that bother you? I mean, if you don't like it, there are always others, but you see we thought you'd like the piano. It isn't wonderful, but it is in tune.'

'It's lovely,' said Chris. 'Perfect.'

'You are sure?' said Miranda. 'It's rather shabby and I wonder if you oughtn't to look about a bit. I don't know if we're even asking a fair price. I think I press-ganged you that day. We'd just thought of the idea the night before, you see.'

'I'm used to shabbiness,' said Chris. 'And this isn't. And the price is very fair – especially with a piano thrown in.' She walked over to the old square piano which sat on shapely legs between the two windows. 'May I try it?'

'Of course,' said Miranda.

Chris sat down and played a few experimental chords.

'Goodness . . .' she said. 'It's an interesting sound, isn't it?' She tried a few bars of Schumann. 'Oh, I like that.'

'You do?' said Miranda. 'I learnt on this one, of course, but I always preferred the one downstairs.'

'This is so quiet, and sweet-toned . . .'

'Yes, but you can't get the effects you can on a modern piano, and the tone is very uneven. Listen.' She played a descending scale at the treble end. 'It's quite different from the middle, isn't it? I suppose they didn't know how to make it even.'

'I rather like that,' said Chris. 'It's unusual. I wonder how old it is. I mean, perhaps it's the sort of piano that Schubert wrote for, or Beethoven.'

'It can't be!' said Miranda. 'I think Beethoven sounds ridiculous on it. It simply doesn't have the same effect as a good modern piano.'

'Do you want me to take this room?' laughed Chris.

'I suppose I'm not being very persuasive, am I?' said Miranda. 'Now what can I say that's good? Oh, well, it gets plenty of sun and there's a new mattress on the bed. That was Jack's idea. He's very practical – it's being a doctor, I suppose. You can take those awful bed curtains down, if you like. I hate bed curtains.'

'I don't mind them, really,' said Chris, glancing at the bed which was sheltered by a red damask tent.

'It was Antonia's idea to put that in here. She says it matches the piano.'

'I'll take it,' said Chris, getting up from the piano and looking about her. It was the sort of room she had always dreamt of escaping to, with its piano, its sunshine, its sweet-smelling polished boards and faded rugs. There was a generous bureau-desk to one side of the fire for her to work at and an old armchair on the other to relax in. She saw herself working there already, composing, creating, just as she had always hoped.

'You will – oh, how splendid! I'll go and have your boxes brought up,' said Miranda, going to the door.

Chris sat down on the bed, and relished her aloneness.

Things at the Manse had been difficult as she had got ready to leave. Although Mr Adam had not objected at all to her going her mother had been resentful. She had said nothing, of course, she would not have dreamt of contradicting her husband, but Chris could tell from her face, indeed from the very set of her shoulders, that her anger had bitten deep. She knew she would not be forgiven lightly for throwing over Guy. In fact, Guy might forgive her more easily for it than her mother.

Chris noticed that there was no Bible by the bedside, which would have shocked her mother profoundly, but which hardly mattered, as her father had presented her with a fresh one, as well as with a Greek New Testament with which she had no idea what she was supposed to do. She would have enough things to study at the Academy without attempting to learn New Testament Greek. She would probably not even manage to read the daily portion. It was a habit she had always easily fallen out of when she had been away from home before. In truth, she found the Bible boring.

How extraordinary it was to sit in this strange but very handsome room, and realize that she had, by coming here, this short distance from Rankeillor, changed her life so very profoundly. She had succeeded in liberating herself. Her mind now she owed to no one. It did not matter if she did not read the Bible every night. Neither did it matter if she sat until three in the morning reading something disreputable, or, better still, sat working at her music. Her mother would not be sniffing with disapproval at her every action and she would not have to suffer the puzzled yet resigned disappointment of her father. Sometimes it had seemed that he looked at her as if she were some foundling, not at all his child, and it was how she had felt. She had not believed she belonged at all. She saw it now, standing there, quite alone, beginning this adventure. She belonged only to herself and she had chosen that. She could so easily have belonged to Guy, after all, but then she would never have felt this wonderful sense of freedom.

'It's time for tea,' announced Miranda, breezing in. 'Antonia's finished working.'

'What does she do?' said Chris, very surprised to find a married woman working.

'Oh, she's trying to finish my father's book – the great classical dictionary,' said Miranda. 'It's very silly of her really. She's quite crushed under it, I think. She has to typewrite all the entries that my father had written by hand – and you should see his handwriting. Horrible! And of course, since he only got to L, there's an enormous amount of research still to do. I think it's revenge on her part. She wanted to take classics at the university, but he would never hear of it. He would never hear of anything like that. So now she's trying to prove that she's twice as brilliant a scholar as he ever was. What is the point though? He's dead. He'll never know.'

'But she will,' said Chris. 'I can understand that.'

'I suppose I do, really,' said Miranda. 'My father was not an easy man at all. He wouldn't let me study music properly either. He wanted us both to marry well, that's all.'

'I wonder if that's all parents think we are fit for,' said Chris, with a sigh.

'That sounds intriguing,' said Miranda. 'That sigh was very heartfelt. I hope you don't think me inquisitive . . .'

'I think you are,' laughed Chris. 'But it doesn't matter. There was this fellow who was keen to marry me, and my mother thought it would be splendid too.'

'Was he well off?'

'Horribly.'

'It must have been difficult.'

'Slightly,' said Chris, aware that this was an understatement. 'In fact, sometimes I can't quite believe I have got away, and that tomorrow we start lectures.'

'DV,' said Miranda, crossing her fingers. 'Unless your chap comes dashing up on a white charger to carry you away.'

'I hope not,' said Chris. 'I don't think he would go quite so far as that. I think he understands now, even if my mother doesn't.'

'Well, at least you made him understand,' said Miranda. 'That's something.'

'I'm not so sure it doesn't make it worse. I mean, I think I would feel less guilty about the whole business if he'd been angry with me, instead of being so handsome about it.'

'Was he very tempting then? I mean apart from the money?'

'Yes, he's a very good man. An ideal husband, which is why my mother is so angry with me.'

'What a heroine you are!' exclaimed Miranda, jumping up from the bed. 'I don't think I should have managed it. I suspect I have the feeblest will.'

'Well, you had better strengthen it,' said Chris. 'I shall need you to take the lead in my first opera, shan't I?'

'You're going to write an opera?' said Miranda.

'One day,' said Chris, conscious that she had never admitted this ambition to anyone before. 'When I've learnt my trade.'

'How can you call it a trade?' said Miranda. 'It's a great art – the greatest art, I suspect.'

They went downstairs to the drawing room. It was a large, pale room, running across the front of the house. The curtains were not yet drawn against the dwindling sun, which filled the room with a soft pink and grey light, which touched individual things with soft fingers, rather than lighting the whole room, catching the imperfections of the panes of glass and the sheen of the silver teapot.

There was a solitary spot of intense colour in the grate, where logs had been set to burn, filling the room with a scent of wood-smoke.

At the tea table sat a lean, tall woman in her early twenties, who wore a dark, plain dress that for all its simplicity struck Chris as extremely smart. She bore a strong resemblance to Miranda, with that same, dark, lustrous hair and those high, well-made cheek bones, but her beauty had a quieter, more masculine stamp, and her eyes seemed distinctly sharper. She rose and put out her hand to Chris.

'Miss Adam? I'm Antonia Rosenberg.'

'Mrs Rosenberg,' said Chris, shaking her cool, thin hand.

'Must we be so formal!' exclaimed Miranda.

'Perhaps Miss Adam would prefer it,' said Mrs Rosenberg.

'Actually, I prefer Chris,' said Chris, and got a smile from Mrs Rosenberg that was slightly surprising in its warmth.

'Of course,' she said. 'And I prefer Antonia.'

'Thank goodness for that!' exclaimed Miranda. 'I can't bear stuffiness of any sort, you know. We've only so long on the earth. Why waste it with formality?'

'Formality has its uses,' said Antonia, returning her attention to the tea-tray. 'It papers over awkward cracks in situations. Everyone can be at their ease at once because they've a fixed set of rituals to follow.'

'Antonia, that's quite horrid. Papering over cracks indeed,' protested Miranda. 'I think formal manners are just an excuse for not living, for not breathing properly. If people were natural, we shouldn't need the silly rules.'

Chris reflected that she would not have been there if Miranda had not behaved 'naturally' as she put it. But there was a great deal in what Antonia said too. What a strange pair of sisters they made – alike in looks, but clearly not in character. Miranda was sitting on the sofa, her shoes kicked off, and her feet tucked under her, while Antonia kept to her seat by the tea table on a chair with a back as straight as her own.

'Besides, you've just knocked your own theory into a cocked hat,' said Miranda, reaching out and taking a sandwich. 'By admitting you prefer Chris to call you by your name.'

'There were no cracks to paper over,' said Antonia, simply. 'I felt it at once.' And she handed Chris a cup of tea. 'Isn't that so?'

'I think so,' said Chris, wondering where these women had learnt the secret of such charm. If she had been a man, she imagined it would have been impossible to be presented with them as she saw them now and not resist them. They were like the lamps set about the room on various tables, making out pools of intense and radiant light into which she wanted instinctively to dive and drown.

'Chris is going to write an opera,' Miranda announced calmly. 'Isn't it splendid?'

Antonia looked with intense interest at her. Chris found herself blushing.

'One day,' she said, as she had done to Miranda. 'I'm not ready to do it yet.'

'But the ambition is there,' said Antonia. 'It's so unusual.'

'I suppose so,' said Chris. 'Perhaps it's foolhardy. But I have this feeling, deep inside, that that's what I'm supposed to do. It would be cheap of me not to try.'

Antonia leant forward and rested her chin on her hands.

'Why is it, do you think, that there are no great women composers?'

'Because it isn't thought ladylike,' said Miranda.

'There's something in that,' said Chris. 'Women have always been allowed to serve music, like its handmaidens. Music has always needed women as interpreters – great singers and pianists – think of Clara Schumann or Madame Nilsson. That's considered all right, because she is always a servant to the music, never creating it in her own right, always letting it be her master. Just like the rest of life, really, I suppose . . .' She finished lamely, aware that she had never made such a long speech on the subject to anyone, let alone this pair of strangers.

'Go on,' said Antonia. 'Please . . .'

'I'm not sure I'm making much sense,' said Chris.

'Perfect sense,' she smiled. 'So you think women have been afraid to master music, to make it for themselves?'

'Not just afraid, but unable to. Besides, it's satisfying enough to be an interpreter, isn't it? It's a great deal better than being a nothing, passive sort of woman. It's more than most women can hope for. It's an achievement enough to do that much. I suppose it takes a special sort of arrogance to think one has to go further and break into male territory.'

'You're not arrogant, you're brave,' said Antonia. 'And so clear-sighted.'

'Sometimes it feels like sheer perversity,' Chris reflected. 'To be kicking over the traces so thoroughly. It would be so much easier if one could settle for less.'

'Don't ever do it,' said Antonia. 'We need women like you.'

Chris leant back on her cushions, feeling drunk and dazzled at being so thoroughly and so quickly understood. She was accepted entirely for what she was and what she wanted to do. It seemed incredible.

'But you too, you're working too,' said Chris to Antonia. 'Miranda tells me you're trying to finish your father's book.'

'Oh, that's not real work,' she said dismissively. 'I'm doing it to educate myself really, for better things.'

'So what do you want to do?' Chris found she must ask. 'Since we're talking of ambitions.'

'Ah yes,' chipped in Miranda. 'True confession time, I think.'

'You start then, Miranda,' said Antonia.

'I don't know. I'm not clever like you two. I just want to sing and sing brilliantly. I like the idea of ravishing people with my voice alone. Isn't that wicked? But think of the power of it!' They laughed and Miranda went on. 'So we have an opera, in which I shall be lead soprano. What will you do, Toni? Run up the costumes?'

'That would be very respectable, wouldn't it?' smiled Antonia. 'No, I should sit in the audience and let all your combined talent wash over me and light up those dark spots in me, so that I could rush home and work on my translation.'

'Your translation?' said Chris

'I think it's like your opera. It's my mountain, that I have to climb, my particular piece of arrogance. I want to do the best modern translation of Virgil's *Aeneid* that there is, a real poetic translation that does it justice for once.'

'When did you think of that?' said Miranda. 'You've never mentioned it before.'

'I've had it mind for a while,' said Antonia. 'Perhaps I just needed a jolt to admit it. It's difficult to be as strong-minded as you'd like, isn't it?'

'Then you should stop bothering with Father's book,' said Miranda.

'Oh, I can't,' said Antonia. 'It's a terrible waste not to do something with it. It was his life's work – and it was good. I have to try. I owe it to him.'

'I can't think how you can bear to,' said Miranda. 'After the way he treated Jack, you can't think you owe him anything, surely.'

'That doesn't matter now,' said Antonia. 'Yes, I do think the way he treated us was unforgivable, but it's all over now. And it would be petty-minded of me to deny that his work was good and worth continuing because of that. He was a great scholar, even if he was a less than perfect man.'

'What an understatement,' said Miranda. 'You should have heard the rows. And that time Father threw Jack out . . .'

'Please, Miranda, I don't want to remember. It was all very embarrassing and unnecessary.'

'I don't know how you can say that,' said Miranda. 'What would you have done if Father hadn't died when he did? You were at breaking point. You were desperate.'

'I don't know,' said Antonia, sharply. 'And I don't see there is much point speculating. Could we please talk about something else? I'm sure Chris doesn't find this interesting at all.'

'Am I the only lodger so far?' Chris managed to ask, after the awkward little silence.

'Yes, yes, you are,' said Antonia. 'We're only going to let a few rooms, of course . . .' The door opened and everyone looked round. 'Oh Jack, you're early!'

'I cut loose,' said the young man coming in. He went straight over to Antonia and kissed her, quite as if there was no one else in the room. 'I had a row with Holloway.'

'Oh no . . .' said Antonia. 'What about?'

'The man is a fossil. He won't accept anything I say. If I hit him round the head with the evidence, he wouldn't see it. He'd just go on doing things the way he was taught – treating hysteria with cold water. I don't believe for one minute he wants to treat any one of them successfully. He wants to punish them for being abnormal, or at least abnormal by his standards. I suspect some of them are saner than he is.' He gripped his folded arms tighter around him and shuddered slightly. 'Bloody man.'

'You won't make your revolution without a fight, Jack,' said Antonia.

'I begin to wonder if I'm up to it,' he said with a sigh. 'Everything I do seems destined to failure at the moment. At every step I find myself facing these pompous, middle-aged Christians who want to send me back to the ghetto. I can't think which of them is worse, MacIver or Holloway. They both should be . . .' He turned slightly and caught sight of Chris. 'Oh, I'm so sorry. You must be Miss Adam. Miranda mentioned you at breakfast. I quite forgot . . .'

'That's all right,' said Chris, shaking his hand. 'I think you had a hard day.'

'Oh, not really,' he said, sitting down close to his wife. 'I shouldn't grumble – especially not so publicly.' He looked very embarrassed and Chris decided she liked him at once. 'Well, then, another musician in the house. That's wonderful. Music is the nearest thing I get to religion these days.'

'Jack has a marvellous singing voice,' said Antonia, with pride.

'Well, it's rather rusty these days. I used to sing a lot more,' he said. 'My grandmother hoped I'd be a cantor in the synagogue, but I preferred to sing Schubert. But the Jewish chant – have you ever heard that, Miss Adam? It's something quite . . .'

'I doubt it, Jack,' said Miranda. 'Chris is a daughter of the Manse.'

'Oh.' He looked crestfallen. 'Then I apologize again for what I said just then.'

'It doesn't matter,' said Chris. 'I don't believe in anything much except music.'

'Bravely said,' he smiled. 'Will all our lodgers be as bright as this one, Antonia?'

'I don't know,' she laughed, 'but I think we should have

a condition, don't you? That they should be doing something worth while – and I don't mean working as missionaries. They should be painting or writing or something . . .'

'Then I'd better leave. I'm just a dull old doctor,' said Jack.

'We'll make an exception for you, Jack,' said Miranda. 'Your general culture is so high. Besides,' she added with a laugh, 'we need someone to do the accounts, don't we?'

12

'Well, young man, do you have anything to say for yourself?'

Angus Bretton wondered how often that particular phrase, and variants on it, had been offered to him, and how often he had stood, as he stood now, before his interrogators, with his hands behind his back, knowing that there was no adequate defence and that he would not escape punishment. Well, at least, as a houseman of twenty-four years old, hauled up before the Medical School Disciplinary Board, he knew that they could not beat him, although the man who posed the question looked as though he might want to. Bloody little sadist, he thought, and purposely put his hands into his pockets, detachedly watching their reactions to this deliberate piece of disrespect.

His judges were three in number, sitting along the length of a polished table, wearing smug black suits and expressions. One was thin, the other two fat, and he pictured them in the dress of Inquisitors, with crucifixes and instruments of torture to hand. God, they would have made a fine job of that, better than the originals, these grotesque Edinburgh physicians.

'Well, I suppose you have not,' said one of them. 'The evidence is quite conclusive.'

'I was composing my defence,' said Angus. 'You don't give a fellow much time for rhetoric, do you?'

'Rhetoric, sir?' said one of them angrily. 'What do you

think this is?' Angus was glad his flippancy had hit home. 'You do realize we are obliged to send you down for this offence?'

'So why ask me to defend myself, since I'm already condemned?' Angus answered.

'We are obliged to,' said another of them, the thin, Jesuitical one, 'in the interests of justice.'

'I suspect you want to know if I am repentant.'

'It would be to your advantage if we could see that you did at least regret your actions.'

'But you'll still send me down,' Angus put in.

'I'm afraid,' said the Jesuit, without any hint that he was the least sorry about it, 'we must do that. But if you were to wish to resume your studies at some other institution abroad, the notes of this Board would of course be forwarded. A decent show of regret would perhaps help such an application.'

'And what exactly is a decent show of regret?' said Angus. 'Shall I weep and say that I fear I have broken my mother's heart—'

'Bretton, I don't think you realize the seriousness of this,' interrupted the third judge. 'This is your career at stake, a career which might have been very brilliant, judging by your academic record. We do not wish that to be squandered, and if you can convince us that this unfortunate business was a temporary lapse which will never occur again, then we can at least present a report which will not damn you entirely in the eyes of other institutions. I am sure there are places in the Empire which would be very glad of your talents.'

Angus had to repress a smile at that suggestion. He attempted to picture himself in some up-country hospital in India, quietly finishing his training, heroically accepting the necessity for this exile. He knew his father would suggest that at once.

'Well, I'm afraid, gentlemen,' he said, 'I can't dissemble, even if it would be to my advantage to do so. I remember too little about the incident to regret what I did. That's the great thing about whisky, I find. It makes one marvellously forgetful.'

He had enjoyed saying that. It was a little like dropping a dozen raw eggs on to the table-top and watching them break and gush all over it.

'There is no point continuing this interview,' said the Jesuit, getting up from his seat. 'Kindly understand you are sent down forthwith, Mr Bretton.'

'Indeed,' said Angus, taking up his hat which he had left on a stool at the edge of the room. He smiled broadly and bowed deeply to them, flourishing the trilby like a dandy's tricorn. 'I thank you, gentlemen, for my freedom.' And he turned and went to the door.

He heard them making little clucking noises, like a group of poultry who have seen a fox. And then one of them spoke.

'Your father will be very saddened by this, Bretton. He always had such high hopes for you.'

Angus turned and stared. It was the smallest and plumpest of the judges, the one he had reckoned a sadist, and he was not surprised he should be a crony of his father's.

'Oh no,' he said, with all the gaiety he could muster. 'You know he won't be saddened. He'll be bloody furious!'

It was a relief to get out of the portentous medical school building, and he plunged straight into the Meadows, running along the long avenue of trees that skirted the Royal Infirmary. He could not help running, and there was so much sudden joy in him that he wanted to shout to every passer-by the ecstasy he felt. He was free, at last! When he had thanked them, he had meant it, although he had said it to mock them. In truth those vile fellows had done a wonderful thing. And he ran faster to put behind all those wasted years of grinding study, those years of fitting himself to a mould for which he had not been formed. Seven years it had been, seven years of agony to please his parents! No wonder he had got so blinding drunk and behaved so disgracefully on the ward. It had been out of desperation. He had wanted the glorious ignominy of being thrown out. No one, not even his father, with all his powerful friends, could argue with the Edinburgh University Medical Schools Disciplinary Board. If he had asked his father to let him leave, he would have been bullied back, but he could not be bullied back now. He was well and truly sunk!

He stopped and stared up into the tree above him, into a fabulous canopy of golden, dying leaves. The wind shook them and some of them drifted down about him. He spun around and around, flinging his arms up, trying to catch as many of them as he could, giddy with all that sudden beauty. The moment was incomparable. It must be fixed, he decided, in words, and now he had a chance to do that, a chance at last to dedicate himself to being what he had to be: a poet – and he would be nothing more and nothing less than that. He would heal more people with his poetry than a thousand pompous physicians. Great art was the only medicine the world needed!

Now he was faced with this sudden blankness, this open, uncharted road in his life, he realized how much he had craved it. Why, then, had he done nothing about it, but had gone on meekly like an ox under the yoke, lumbering through the deep mud of other people's expectations for him. And he had not even had the courage to cut himself free – they had turned him off instead, seeing he was unfit for their uses.

He wished he had done it himself, with lucidity and calm courage. A simple letter would have been enough to extricate himself. 'I have decided not to continue with my studies, etc., etc.' They could have sent back his father's cheque for the year's fees. He wondered what happened to the fees if you were sent down – probably the university sat on them as an additional humiliation. His father would not like that. He would probably demand that Angus make good his wasted cash from his own income.

Thank God for Cousin Flora! he thought suddenly. Angus was not much given to gratitude to his relatives, but Cousin Flora's generosity in the Bretton family demanded it. Sometimes, in fact, he mentally promoted her to a minor goddess who walked around Olympus, still dressed in the neat silk dresses of sombre hue that she had always worn in life. She had had no children of her own, and having been the widow of a Glasgow ship-owner there had been a fair parcel of money to hand out. Servants and charities had all been scrupulously remembered, but the surprise had been that the bulk of the capital went to her cousin's children, Angus and his sisters, in the form of a handsome, well-managed trust fund, which, like a well-made fruit cake, had good proportions of consuls, gilt-edged and government stocks. Cousin Flora, he realized, had by her kindness freed him long ago, long before the disciplinary board. It only remained for him to free himself, to actually walk out of his prison and stumble into the light of his life, his very own life. He knew, however, he had not quite done that yet. It would not be done until he had spoken to his father.

Ecstasy under a gilded tree was one thing, Dr Bretton quite another. He left the Meadows and pushed up Marchmont Road, leaving the benign gaze of trees for the scrutiny of those hard-faced, highly respectable tenements, which seemed to him like a prelude to the apotheosis of his parents' house in Grange, with its high, secretive, snobbish walls. Those in Marchmont no doubt aspired to Grange and to those fortified, bourgeois villas of unremitting driech stone, but all his life Angus had dreamt of escape.

Perhaps now was the moment. Perhaps he should simply turn round and never go back. It would be so easy and there would be no awkwardness, no blistering row, no tears from his mother – and she would cry, he was sure of that. Why should he have to face that?

He was at the end of Blackford Road, where the Bretton house occupied the large corner site, and he hesitated. He would have to go in, he knew, but he was sick with reluctance at the thought of it, like a schoolboy hauled up before the dominie.

He went in by the tradesmen's gate and up the flagged path that was hidden from the house by a laurel hedge. He had a latch key for the front door of the house – the odd hours of medical school life had permitted this liberty – but he preferred to use the kitchen door. He had done this always as a boy, because Ellen the cook would always have something for him to eat. She still often did, as if she, like the rest of them, could not accept he was a grown man. He supposed the youngest child in a house often met with this prolonged childhood.

'Ach, you're early today. You didna say you'd be back for lunch – I shall have to make extra,' she said.

'I don't think I'll be hungry,' he said.

'You, not hungry?' she laughed. 'You're no sickenin' for something, are you? There's no knowing what you might catch in that hospital.'

'No, I'm fine,' he said, 'it's just . . .' He wondered if he should tell Ellen first, test her reactions. But she was absorbed with a pot on the fire.

'Well, I'll make more anyway,' she said. 'It is your favourite, collops.'

'Don't bother, please, I shan't be in for lunch.'

'Well, make sure you eat something decent. You have to keep your strength up with all your studying. No one ever became a great doctor on an empty stomach.' She went on stirring her pot.

'Ellen . . .' he began.

She turned and looked at him kindly. 'Yes, dearie?'

'Nothing,' he said, and made for the kitchen door. How well she had swallowed the family line. The inevitability of his becoming a doctor was obvious to her. She believed in it, just as he had once believed in it. He had hated it, loathed it, but he had never until now realized that his fate was avoidable. Even in the depths of those bitter depressions, when he had drunk to make his soul sing again, he had not thought he could escape. He began to wonder again if he really could.

He went into the hall and found his mother fiddling with the large vase of dahlias on the hall table.

'Oh Angus, my dear, I didn't know you were home,' she said. 'I don't seem to be able to get these to settle at all.' Her hands moved restlessly through the flowers, pushing the stems back and forth. 'How awful they look.'

'They look fine to me,' he said.

She smiled. 'Thank you, dear, for saying so, but I know men don't really notice such things. A few daisies in a pail would look perfect to your father and you, I dare say . . .' She bent forward and tweaked another flower. How he hated to be bracketed with his father like that. 'Your minds are on much more important things. There, that's better,' she said stepping back. 'All finished.' She put out her hand to him. 'Are you very busy today? Have you time to fill me in on all your news? You're so busy, I never seem to hear it.'

'Mother,' he said, taking a deep breath but not her proffered hand, 'there's something I need to . . .' He broke off. The door to his father's consulting room had swung open and Dr Bretton came into the hall.

For a moment they stood and stared at each other. Angus realized from the cold sharpness of his father's gaze that he must know. The genial smile of the fashionable doctor could not be guessed at.

'Rosneath telephoned me,' said Dr Bretton. 'I've been sitting there for half an hour trying to make sense of this, but . . . but . . .' He threw up his hands. 'It's not true, is it?'

Angus stuffed his hands into his pockets and said, 'Why would Rosneath lie?'

'Is that all you can say?' said Dr Bretton. 'You've been sent down for disorderly conduct on the ward – which is an understatement, I gather – and that is all you can say?'

'Sent down?' said Mrs Bretton. 'Oh Angus, no, there must be some mistake.'

'I wish to God it was,' said Dr Bretton shaking his head.

'I don't!' said Angus vehemently. 'As far as I am concerned, this is a good thing.'

'Have you gone quite mad?' exclaimed Dr Bretton. 'You have just ruined yourself utterly and you consider it a good thing? Rosneath said your conduct at the disciplinary board was disgraceful!'

'I don't understand this,' said Mrs Bretton. 'I really don't.'

'Neither do I,' said Dr Bretton. 'And I don't expect I ever shall.'

'No, you won't,' said Angus. 'You couldn't possibly. Your mind is narrow, Father, so complacent that you could not possibly imagine that I might be different from you, that I might want something different from life than pandering to rich patients who like to think they are ill!'

'I beg your pardon . . .'

'That's all you ever do – smile sympathetically and take their bloody fees! I might respect your profession if you practised it decently.'

'Oh Angus, really,' said Mrs Bretton. 'This is . . . Please apologize at once. You didn't mean that, you can't have.' She had interposed herself between them, but Angus stared over her shoulder to his father, whose face was now grim with rage.

‘I meant every word of it.’ He was surprised at the calm of his voice, and the giddy feeling of triumph that was jumping up in his guts.

‘My own son – this is beyond belief,’ said Dr Bretton. ‘After all that I’ve done for you, you think you can . . .’ He stepped past Mrs Bretton and attempted to slap Angus across the face. But he missed, for Angus was too fast for him, and dodged him.

‘What have you ever done for me?’ he retorted, moving backwards now, because his father was stalking him. ‘You’ve starved me, imprisoned me and beaten me! You’ve starved my soul, imprisoned my mind and beaten down my spirit! But not any more. No!’ They were facing each other now across the hall table and Angus was riding high on the tide of his angry rhetoric. ‘Not any more!’ he said again, and with a broad, deliberate and powerful sweep of his arm he swept the vase of dahlias off the polished table-top.

The vase hung in the air before crashing down on to the bright tiles. The water shattered like the crystal, dispersing in a great swathe across the floor. Mrs Bretton screamed and then clapped her hand over her mouth as if she had said something obscene. She sidled towards Dr Bretton, clearly terrified as to what he might do next.

‘I’ll give you half an hour to get out of this house!’ said Dr Bretton, breathing so hard that he almost wheezed. ‘Half an hour and then I don’t want to see you here again. Do you understand?’

‘Lionel, no, no, you can’t do that,’ said Mrs Bretton. ‘You’re both angry and . . .’

‘Half an hour,’ said Dr Bretton and turned towards the consulting room. Mrs Bretton followed him part of the way, making ineffectual gestures and noises. But the door was shut in her face.

‘We’ll sort something out, we will . . .’ she said, coming back towards Angus. She put out her hands and then withdrew them, clutching them together against her chest, still afraid of him.

'I'm going,' he said, his foot on the first stair.

'Oh Angus, Angus . . .' she cried out. He turned back, moved to pity by the anguish in her voice. She looked at him for a minute and then said, 'That was Waterford you know. One of my very favourites.'

13

Chris hated to admit it but certain aspects of the Academy were a disappointment. That afternoon, as she sat in her harmony class, while the whey-faced Mr Scrabister droned on, with very few deviations from the standard text-book, she felt no sense of challenge. They were studying simple three-part harmony, a subject that held no mystery for Chris. She wished she did not feel so bored, it seemed ungrateful, but bored she was. She would have to endure this for the rest of the term as well, before she was allowed to take a counterpoint class.

The only other woman in the class, an earnest body called Gladys Ross, who seemed to write down everything that Mr Scrabister said, was asking yet more questions, silly questions too. Christ twisted her pencil in her fingers and tried to assume some sympathy or at least a little interest. But it was so obvious – surely she could see it? What on earth was Gladys Ross doing there if she could not grasp such a fundamental point? Chris began to feel sorry for Mr Scrabister for all his lack of charm as a teacher.

Fortunately it was almost four o'clock and the torture would soon be over.

'Would you please work through exercises fifteen to twenty-five in Williams,' said Mr Scrabister, 'and leave them in my pigeon-hole by Tuesday.'

What a surprise, thought Chris sourly. She had worked through Williams during the summer. At least it would not take long. She would have plenty of time for her piano practice and those fiendish five-finger exercises Madame Lindstrom had prescribed to improve her technique. Then, she decided – for she reckoned she should be philosophical – there were all those interesting books at Royal Circus to read; books of a sort that would not have got across the threshold of the Manse, let alone into her hands. If, at present, she was not learning much from Mr Scrabister, she could broaden her education elsewhere.

After the class she found Gladys Ross accompanying her to the women's cloakroom.

'He goes so fast!' she wailed. 'I shall never keep up.'

Chris took pity on her, her father's conscientious kindness weighing for a moment on her shoulder, like the pressure of his hand.

'I could help you with it, if you like,' she said. 'I've done this stuff before.'

'Oh would you? That would be so kind. I'm in such a state about it.'

'Well, perhaps tomorrow, in the library. I've nothing on till ten.'

'Shall we meet at eight then?' said Gladys. Chris grimaced discreetly. She was not sure her patience would last a full two hours.

'Nine?' she suggested, taking her coat from its peg.

'Yes, of course,' said Gladys. 'You really are too kind.'

Chris glanced around, looking for Miranda. There was no sign of her, so she would walk home alone, or at least she hoped she would, and that Gladys Ross was not going in her direction. For she was still by her side, as they came out of the women's entrance. Suddenly Gladys said, 'Don't you miss your home, Miss Adam? I should, I'm sure.'

Gladys, she recalled, lived across the town with her parents.

‘No, not really,’ she said honestly.

‘Well, Mama and I were thinking,’ – and Chris was appalled to think she had been a topic of conversation with them – ‘would you like to come to tea on Saturday? We just thought – another Manse – well it isn’t quite the same, of course, but lodgings must be so dreary.’

‘They’re very jolly actually,’ said Chris. ‘And they’re not lodgings in the strict sense.’ Then she realized she ought to be a little more gracious. ‘But thank you for thinking of it.’

‘So you’ll come? My father says he remembers yours so well from St Mary’s. You’d be very welcome.’

‘Then thank you. I’ll be glad to,’ said Chris, annoyed that the Church should have dug its talons so effectively into her. The last thing that she wanted was tea in a Manse drawing room.

Gladys Ross went off happily though, and as Chris walked down the hill to Royal Circus she realized how much a month had changed her view of the world. She did not miss the Manse in the least. She wrote her letters home, of course, but she could not manage to be quite sincere about her regret at not seeing them. She had found a way of life that suited her perfectly. If the classes at the Academy were a little slow, life at Royal Circus was certainly not. There was always good talk to be had there, and also the chance for solitude. That, she reckoned, was the best of it. Since she had come, she had felt like a plant moved into the sunshine for the first time. She felt well rooted and she felt she was growing. Mr Scrabister and Gladys Ross apart, life was good.

She reached for her latch key and let herself into the house, relishing for a moment the simple fact of having a latch key.

The house and its peculiar, book-filled serenity embraced her. Even Miranda’s most frenzied pianistic performances never seemed quite to destroy that calm. It was a solid thing, like the old furniture and large pictures, and Chris loved it. Her father had often said that in silent prayer he saw things more clearly, and she knew in the depths of silence lay the profoundest music. In utter tranquillity, where the mind was free, she could hear clearly enough to write it down.

She went straight upstairs, feeling although she was tired there was that itch in her to do a little writing – nothing spectacular, but a few notes, a scrap of melody, some cadences which had been travelling with her during the day. She thought, as she reached the top-floor landing, of the notebook on the piano, which each day seemed to gather more material, like the bag of scraps that Phemie saved to sew into crazy quilts when her duties in the kitchen were finished.

She came in and would have gone straight to the piano, and the open book on the music stand, but a large suitcase and a portmanteau blocked her way. She looked around and realized that her room had been occupied. Sprawled out on the counterpane was a man, a young man for that matter, in a deep sleep. His tweed jacket was tossed on the floor and his boots, judging from where they had landed, had been roughly unlaced and kicked off. She found she was examining his feet, in her surprise, gazing at thick wool socks that had been darned by an expert, and then at his body in its casing of thick tweed trousers and a waistcoat that had twisted about him in cumbersome folds. One blue-flannelled arm hung over the side of the bed with the hand displaying a heavy signet ring while the other was crumpled up by his head. And what a head it was! She could not help marvelling at it. For all that it was clearly flesh, it seemed sculpted from stone, with hard, clean, elegant lines. Even the curls of his dark hair lay with the crisp regularity of marble tendrils. Yet it was the impassivity of his features that fascinated her. He resembled, with his eyes closed, the blank-socketed bust of a Roman patrician. He did not seem to sleep for indolent reasons, but for reasons of state.

She wondered that anyone in sleep could compose himself so – it struck her as almost self-conscious, but the carelessly flung boots and his trailing hand belied that. What could be more careless, more lacking in composure, than his being asleep on her bed?

She smiled at the absurdity of it. A strange man on her bed, lying there for all the world as if he belonged there. Reputations were destroyed by such accidents but Chris did not really fear for that. Rather she felt annoyed that her territory had been invaded, and that she felt obliged to stand and look at that invader as if he were a work of art. An invader, she reckoned, ought to look less dignified. At least he should snore, instead of lying there, so beautifully, like a fallen Roman warrior, who needed only a few weeping women and a stoic soldier leaning on his spear to complete the picture.

She touched him gently with her still gloved finger, as if to check he were not a phantom. She realized it would take more than that to wake him. She reached out again, grabbed his shoulder and shook him a little. She saw him stir and at once stepped back.

'Uuggh?' His sleepy eyes opened and focused on her. 'Who are you?'

'I might ask you that,' she said, folding her arms. 'What are you doing in my room?'

'Your room?' he said. 'No, no, this is my room. First on the right, Jack said. Up the stairs and first on the right.'

'Well this is first on the left,' Chris pointed out.

Slowly he propped himself up on his elbows.

'It is?'

'I'm afraid so,' she said, repressing a smile, as he sank back on the pillows, a Roman warrior no longer, but a very fallible human.

'I never did know left from right,' he said, and laughed

briefly but deeply. 'Oh God, my head . . . Too much damnable moonshine.' He struggled up again. 'Well, I suppose I had better get out.'

'If you think you can manage it,' she said, laughing.

'Have pity,' he said, swinging his feet to the floor. 'Haven't you ever had a hangover? No, I don't suppose you ever have.'

He reached out for one boot and winced. Chris handed him the other.

'Thanks,' he said. 'What's your name, neighbour?'

'Chris,' she said, bluntly. There did not seem much point in standing on ceremony.

'Chris, just Chris. I like that,' he said, regarding her for a moment. 'And thanks for not screaming the house down. Some girls would have, if they'd found a strange fellow in their bed.'

'You were only on it,' said Chris. 'And I'm not the screaming type.'

'No, I don't imagine you are,' he grinned, and put out his hand to her. 'Angus Bretton at your service, ma'am.'

She found she was laughing again.

'Yes, I'm afraid I am an absurdity,' he said, getting to his feet. 'Where's the nearest bathroom? I always find that a bath is the best cure for a hangover.'

'I'd better show you since you don't know left from right.'

'Very sensible.'

She showed him to it, and he promptly disappeared inside, locking the door. She returned to her room and realized he had not removed his bags. She went back on to the landing where she could hear the hot-water geyser wheezing in its familiar style. There was nothing else for it than to move them herself.

They were surprisingly heavy – especially the portmanteau, which felt as if it were packed solid with books. She pushed open the door and peered around into the dark room after setting the bags down. It was the old night nursery, she imagined, and there seemed to be little that was remarkable about it. She went back to her room, pleased that she had such good quarters. She hoped Angus would not be disappointed in his.

Angus lay back in the steaming water, immersing every part of him that he could, so that the water even lapped into his ears. A hot bath, next to a good glass of wine, seemed to him then one of the pleasantest things in the world. Of course, there were plenty of finer things, like great poetry or paintings which set something grumbling in the pit of the stomach, which spurred the blood about the body, but there was only so much high art that a man could stand, especially with a hangover and run-in with his father still ringing in his ears. It was then that simple physical comforts came into their own. Of course, he had overdone the good wine – in fact, it had not been good at all, but pints and drams in excess which had been foolish. This bath, at least, was wholesome and sensible.

He reached out for the soap and sniffed it: lavender. He wondered if it was his neighbour's choice. Lavender would suit those sensible, discreet clothes but it hardly went with those green eyes and the laughter. When he had opened his eyes and seen her, he had thought for a minute that he had reached judgement and that a handsome, vaguely disdainful angel was about to decide his fate for all eternity. He would rather be judged by such a creature, he remembered thinking, than any of those oafs on the disciplinary board.

He thought of all his good resolutions in the Meadows about writing. Why had he got drunk then? It was the same destructive urge that had made him break that vase. 'It's Waterford,' his mother's voice bleated and he sat up and splashed his face, scooping up the water in his cupped hands. He did it again and again, as if the breaking of the water against his skin might bring him into the wakefulness he would need to do this thing. If he were to get anywhere he would need to find his own discipline, a self-imposed regime. He realized he had only ever dabbled before, never plunged deep into the pool of some big, important work, and it would not be easy to do it. He knew his own weakness too well. He gloried in it, even. The only discipline he had known had been imposed upon him, brutally. They had put calipers on his legs and now they were broken he would have to learn to walk in his own right.

He still felt sick and his head ached but he felt the water had purified him mentally. The old symbols are always the best, he thought, as he climbed out of the bath. A chalk-white tiled bathroom, lit by a gas mantle, was hardly the spot the ancients would have envisaged for a moment of watery self-knowledge. But why should there not be a sacred pool in a bathroom, a cast-iron pool set amongst the commonplaces of towel horses and lavender soap and condensation on the window? The very modernity of this idea enthralled him, and he wrapped himself in the bath towel, his mind awash with images.

He burst out on to the landing, determined to find a piece of paper. He would not waste this. He would not waste such things ever again. Then he heard the music.

It was piano music, which generally moved him very little. He had heard his mother and sisters work their way through an endless stream of insipid rubbish, but this was different. It flowed, and flowed, as their music had done, but this was pungent and restless. He had never heard anything quite like it before. It was coming from the room where he had fallen asleep, from the girl's room.

He knocked and, only just waiting for a reply, he went in. He forgot that he was only just decent in a bath towel and was dripping with water. He only remembered when she swivelled on the piano stool and stared at him.

'What was that?' he blurted out. 'That music?'

'Oh, it hasn't got a name,' she said. 'Er . . . your bags are in your room, if that's what you're wanting.'

'Thanks. I'm sorry to bother you like this – you don't have some paper do you?'

'Of course.' She was smiling. 'On the desk there.'

'I have to write something down, before I forget it,' he said, crossing the room. 'God, you must think I am mad!'

'No, it happens to me all the time,' she said, and turned back to the piano and began to play that same bizarre music. He scribbled for some minutes and then suddenly her remark struck him.

'It does? Do you write then?'

'I write music,' she said.

'Did you write that?' he said, amazed.

'Yes. I suppose it does sound rather odd.'

'It sounded savage,' he said. 'Oh goodness, I've dripped all over your floor.'

'It doesn't matter. I'm sure your idea is more important. Perhaps though, you should keep a slate in the bathroom.' She looked at him for a moment. 'Savage – is that really how it sounded?'

'Oh yes. Something primitive, certainly, something relentless, inescapable!' He laughed, struck by the oddness of their conversation. 'You're not shocked, are you?'

'I said I wasn't the screaming type,' she said. 'Besides, I'm a great one for saving scraps.' She pointed to his piece of paper. 'One never knows – it might be the germ of something.'

When he had gone, Chris found herself mopping up his small pool of drips with her handkerchief. It was a calm, rational activity, but she felt neither calm nor rational. She felt like a dry bale of straw that had been put to the torch. The man's behaviour was too extraordinary! She supposed she should have been shocked, rather than fascinated, but she could not manage the appropriate degree of moral repugnance. Why should such spontaneity be punished and why should she be repulsed by beauty? For in the classical draping of that towel, he had seemed magnificent, as braw as man could be, with strong shoulders and arms. His maleness had been overwhelming. And it had been so unconsciously displayed. He was not a peacock putting up his tail feathers to impress her, but a man lit up by some inspiration and not caring about anything except the business of capturing that blazing idea.

She wanted to know what it was he had been writing – and more than that. She was consumed with curiosity about him. Clearly he was some friend of Jack's – and quite a close one to use his first name. She wanted to dash downstairs and quiz Antonia about him but that would be daft. There would be plenty of time for that later and she did have better things to do just then – like writing out that music, for example. He had seemed to admire it, after all, and she would not waste it.

14

In Jack Rosenberg's house – or, rather, his wife and sister-in-law's house, as Jack was careful to point out – Angus felt he had fallen on his feet. It was a piece of damnable good luck after so much ill. The atmosphere was so different it seemed he had travelled a thousand miles instead of merely across town. It might not be Edinburgh at all. It was true that they had sat down to dinner at eight in a dining room that was heavy with the usual paraphernalia of Edinburgh dining rooms: namely the gilt-framed pictures, the enormous sideboard, the deeply shining table and the well-polished, extremely solid silver candlesticks. But no one had dressed for dinner – Antonia Rosenberg had outlawed that, and this would be a clear indication to any upholder of bourgeois practices that something was seriously amiss. There again, one would only have to look at the faces around the table to know that, for there was not a soul amongst them above the age of thirty. Where was the grey-haired gentleman or gimlet-eyed lady of a certain age whose duty it was to cough loudly or protest when the conversation became too frank? They were nowhere to be seen amongst this very unusual group of young people eating game pie served by a maid who did not live in.

Mentally, Angus reviewed them all. At the head, a trifle uneasy in the chair of the master of the house, he suspected, was Jack, the brilliant young doctor who was all set to upset the profession by practising those wild new ideas from Vienna which were so scoffed at by Dr Bretton. His wife at the other end, neglecting her food for the conversation, was clearly a patrician's daughter, but not the least bit fettered by it. Miranda, her sister, a voluptuous innocent, sat equally at ease, but in quite a different way. She was tracing patterns with her finger on the table-top and gazing into nowhere, her lips very slightly parted. So much for his hosts – now to his fellow lodgers. The other new arrivals of the day, apart from himself, were an odd Welsh couple, Richard and Megan Lloyd-Church, he all beard and stutter, studying Celtic literature and explaining it with some difficulty, while she, a birdy, little creature, had a bewildered air (as well she might, for Angus was sure this was not the sort of lodging she was used to). Then there was his neighbour, Chris Adam, who in some ways seemed the strangest and the most wonderful of them all.

And what can she think of me, he wondered, a reprobate medic who wants to be a poet? The man who was so drunk he could not fall asleep in the right room? He asked himself this because he caught her looking at him. He grinned and she looked hastily down at the plate, as if the vegetables were of much more interest, and she blushed, he noticed, very slightly. He was pleased by this. After her earlier calm at his admittedly bizarre behaviour and that wild music she had played he had begun to wonder if she were quite human. That little touch of red in her cheeks confirmed it.

'Perhaps we should take more pride in our own national myths,' Antonia was saying, in response to Lloyd-Church's remarks.

'I think we do,' said Angus. 'Think of Jacobite sentimentality over the Forty-five – the king over the water!' he added, gesturing a toast with his claret glass. 'There are myths enough in Scotland for dozens of ridiculous operas.'

'They needn't be ridiculous,' said Miranda. 'I think a

Scottish Wagner would be a good thing. A Scottish *Ring*, although it wouldn't be the *Ring* of course, but a cycle like that telling all the great Scottish stories. You could have Malcolm Canmore being converted by St Margaret, or Robert the Bruce, or even King Alexander being saved from the stag.'

'Are you sure that wouldn't be ridiculous?' said Angus. 'But that's the trouble with opera – it is ridiculous. I can't take it the least bit seriously. The stories are always so absurd.'

'Be careful what you say,' said Antonia. 'Chris here has operatic ambitions.'

'You have?' he said.

'Even more so now,' she smiled. 'I'm determined to prove you and your sweeping statements wrong.'

'But you must concede that some opera is utterly daft? Wagner particularly. A friend in London dragged me to Covent Garden and I had to sit through hours of plump Hausfraus wailing and pretending to be Rhine-maidens and so forth. Is that supposed to be art?'

'Of course it's art!' exclaimed Miranda. '*Das Rheingold* is magnificent. If you'd seen it at Bayreuth you'd understand.'

'Perhaps,' said Angus, 'but I really don't see why opera always has to take itself so seriously.'

'It doesn't,' said Chris. 'Mozart never does. What about *The Marriage of Figaro*? That was based on a comic play, and there are no gods or goddesses in it. Just ordinary people.'

'But that's an absurd story too,' he said. 'A farce in essence.'

'Yes, I know,' said Chris, 'but the music does something to the story. It turns it into magic. It doesn't seem absurd. It gives it meaning.'

'I'm not convinced,' said Angus. 'The thing is, I don't believe words and music are really compatible. You can never hear the words in opera, thank God, for they're usually rubbish, but I've heard dozens of songs that pretend to be settings of Shakespeare or Goethe and are really pieces of butchery.' He glanced around the table to gauge who might support him in this way. He was enjoying being provocative. 'Poetry gets a damnable deal from music, wouldn't you say? Come on, Lloyd-Church, you're a words man, don't you agree?'

'I'm afraid I can't,' said Lloyd-Church. 'In Welsh literature, the song is the highest form. We are bards, remember.'

'And what about the human voice?' said Miranda. 'One of the finest instruments there is. What better way to display words but sing them?'

'If it's an instrument, why does it need words to sing?' said Angus. 'Why can't a voice be simply like a violin or a cello and use melody alone?'

'It's an interesting idea,' said Chris.

'Oh no,' said Miranda. 'It's absurd to think of standing there singing to la all the time.'

'Why?' said Angus. 'You'd get used to it. And one wouldn't have to worry about hearing or understanding the words. Poetry could go back to being an art in itself instead of being the slave of music.'

'It isn't a slave,' said Chris. 'It inspires music.'

'It doesn't need too,' said Angus. 'It has its own music.'

'That's why composers want to set it,' put in Chris. 'Can't you see?'

'I'm losing here, aren't I?' said Angus, laughing.

'I think so,' said Jack. 'Besides, I'm sure if someone wanted to set your verse-epic to music, you'd be flattered, in spite of yourself.'

'A verse-epic,' said Antonia. 'This sounds intriguing. What's it's about? Not gods and goddesses, I hope,' she added.

'No, it begins, would you believe, in a dissecting room.'

He thought he detected a faint shudder from Megan Lloyd-Church.

'Oh yes,' said Jack. 'And what will you make the rest of it from – laundry lists?'

'There's an idea,' said Angus and then, seeing Jack's face, added, 'I'm not serious. But really, your idea of poetry is so limited.'

'I know,' said Jack. 'For me there has to be something in it to escape into, something of extraordinary beauty or power. There's none of that in a dissection room. I know it's feeble of me, but I don't want sordid things in poetry. I see enough of that elsewhere.'

'I take your point,' said Angus, pouring out another glass of wine. 'But I can't see that the thing is worth doing unless you deal with that sort of thing – all the wretched filth of life. It isn't all cowslips. Besides, there is a good deal of beauty in the dissection room.'

'I wish you'd been there to point it out to me,' said Jack.

'So what happens?' said Chris. She had rested her chin on folded hands and was looking at him intently.

'Well, there's a man looking down as the medical students paw over his body, with their inept scalpels.'

'A ghost story, then?' said Megan Lloyd-Church.

'In a way. He's a disembodied soul.'

'So what will you call it?' said Antonia.

'*Everyman*. Because we're all disembodied, we're all gazing at ourselves from a distance, uncomfortable with the world and everything in it. He moves all over the city, seeing everything, hearing everything, but unable to change anything. He sees his wife, weeping at his death, but he can't comfort her. He sees his partner ruining his business, but he can't stop him. He's powerless. All he can do is feel and observe and suffer.'

There was a little pause and then Chris Adam said, 'Now that's a subject for an opera.'

He wondered if she, as he had been earlier, was merely

being provocative. Those clear green eyes were fixed on him but they did not look mischievous.

'I think not,' he said.

'Why not? It's a drama, isn't it? And if your Everyman can only feel, and observe and suffer, what better way than music would there be to express it?'

'Because the words would be lost and that would be intolerable.'

'Not if he spoke them above the music,' the girl went on. 'It would make him different. His wife would sing, his partner, your students in the dissecting room, but he wouldn't, he couldn't, don't you see? He'd be divorced from music, as he was divorced from life.'

'It's an interesting idea,' said Jack. 'An opera with the main part in speech. Where did you come on that?'

'It just popped into my head,' said Chris.

'Well, what do you think?' said Antonia.

'I'm not at all sure,' said Angus. 'I don't want to be a librettist.'

'Then perhaps you should try it,' said Antonia. 'If you hate existing forms so much, perhaps you should try breaking them and doing something fresh. You should collaborate, you two.'

'Perhaps this isn't really fair,' said Chris. 'We've stolen your idea, haven't we? It just sounded so . . .'

'You've not read a line of my verse yet,' he said, pleased by her conciliatory approach.

'But the idea is so exciting. I've been looking for a subject,' she said. 'I don't really approve of gods and goddesses either.'

'Well that settles it,' said Antonia. 'You will have to do it. I insist. We shall make it a condition of your staying here that you attempt the thing together. I can't give it a name, can I, because it won't be an opera. There, does that pacify you, Mr Bretton?'

'I don't know what to say,' he said.

'That you'll try, of course,' said Miranda. 'You have to do something now you've been sent down – something to make your name as a poet. You'd better write a good part for me, though.'

'I'll bear it in mind,' said Angus. 'But you shan't get a pretty frock, if I've anything to do with it.'

'So you'll attempt it?' said Jack. 'I think it might be splendid. I've heard some of Chris's music and it is quite remarkable.'

'I know,' said Angus. 'I shouldn't even contemplate it otherwise.'

'Well,' said Antonia, with a slight air of triumph, as she plunged a spoon into a dish of stewed pears, 'we await a masterpiece. In the mean time, who's for pudding?'

After dinner everyone dispersed, and Chris, having climbed upstairs and made up her fire, wondered how she was going to settle to her Academy work when such tempting ideas were dangled in front of her. She was not sure she was ready to begin such a large thing, but the idea of Everyman and his journey through a hostile city set something itching inside her. She managed to begin to write out her harmony exercises but her mind was really racing over the thought of the scene in a dissecting room, with a macabre chorus of medical students.

There was a knock at the door, and she turned to see Angus Bretton hovering in the doorway, a good deal more diffidently than he had done in his bath towel.

'More paper?' she enquired, and realized how delighted she was he had come to see her.

'No, no, I've found some,' he said. 'Can I come in?'

'Of course,' she said, and wondered what her mother would think of her entertaining a young man in her bedroom. Well, Mrs Adam would never know.

'I think,' he said, 'I owe you an apology.'

'For what?'

‘For this afternoon, all of it, and this evening. I was fairly bumptious.’

‘No, it was interesting. A lot of what you said makes sense to me, at least. Opera can be ridiculous. Sit down – please.’

He took the armchair by the fire, and she turned her own towards the hearth.

‘I think there was a lot of sense in what you said. Music can give an extra layer of meaning and *Everyman* is theatrical. So shall we try?’

‘I should love too but . . .’

‘Yes?’

‘Well, it’s a few things really. I mean, you should really be certain that’s what you want. It is your creation, I should only be tampering with it, and you might hate that. I wouldn’t want you to think I’d been butchering.’

‘I’m prepared to risk that. What else?’

‘Well, I’m not at all experienced. I’ve been working on orchestration on my own, but the silly Academy won’t let anyone take classes until they’ve done all the basics, so I’m really a novice feeling my way. I can’t guarantee that everything will be . . .’

‘Well, so am I,’ he said grinning. ‘An utter novice. Being a medical student doesn’t leave much time for anything else. Besides, surely the best thing to do is to learn by doing.’

‘And if we fail?’ she asked.

‘Does that frighten you?’

‘More than anything,’ she said. ‘You see, when you’ve set out to prove something – something that people think is well nigh impossible – the thought of their being proved right all along is horrible. I want more than anything to succeed.’

He laughed and said, ‘Do you know, you’re quite terrifying when you say things like that.’

‘You wouldn’t be terrified if I were a man,’ she said

bristling. 'It would be quite all right for a man to say such a thing, but me, no . . .'

'I meant it as a compliment,' he said, holding up his hands. 'Honestly.'

'I'm sorry,' she said. 'I'm too used to having to defend my position.'

'Well, perhaps I should get some advice from you. It's something I shall have to learn to do, I suppose. I shall have to face my family again at some point and justify myself.'

'Do you think it will be difficult?'

'Impossible,' said Angus. 'They are people without any imagination. They understand only what is conventional and respectable. They would not understand this, for example,' he said, gesturing at her and the room.

'That's funny,' she smiled, 'that's exactly what I was thinking of my mother when you came in – how horrified she'd be.'

She stretched in her chair and was vaguely conscious that she was doing it slightly for the effect, and glanced at him to see if he reacted. But he was dreaming into the fire, which showed her what an idiot she was to think of such things. But she could not deny that she wanted him to admire her in that way, to look her over the way she had seen Guy look at her.

'So you're not bothered yourself about being sent down?' she ventured.

'No, I was glad really,' he said. 'It's odd, I know, to stick something for so long and then . . . Well, in a year, I'd have been qualified – God help the poor patients if I'd made it. No, it's far better this way.' He got to his feet. 'And I ought to start as I mean to go on,' he said. 'I have that itch to write.'

'Good luck,' she said, but felt disappointed that the conversation was ending. She felt she could have talked to him until the small hours.

15

The Academy orchestra was rehearsing the overture to *Don Giovanni* and Chris sat in the organ gallery of the concert room, with her copy of the score deliberately closed. It was all very well to look at a score and see how the effect was achieved, but she wanted to analyse the texture of the sound alone, to work it all out for herself without a prop. It was perhaps not the best piece for the exercise. The Haydn symphony with which they had begun the rehearsal had been much better. The Mozart had too much in it to distract the emotions. It was hard to break it down. It defied such cold treatment, but spoke straight to the heart, thrilling and shivering it with real force. She had made a few vague mental notes about the coupling of French horns and the percussion, but in the end the thing overwhelmed her and she simply listened on the simplest, deepest level. The artifice was there, she knew. She could look at the score later and work it all out, but now there was only the music itself. It was like some beautifully crafted garment which gave no evidence of the mundane nature of the construction: not a thread hung loose and the illusion was complete.

Sir Henry Mackenzie, the Principal, who was conducting, signalled them to stop, and proceeded to harangue the string players for raggedness. Chris wished he had not stopped them. She knew they were ragged, but she wanted the rest of the music, and felt cheated. She fumbled for the score, and leafed through to find the page at which Sir Henry had broken.

She heard the door to the gallery open behind her, and she looked round to see who had come in. Usually other students came to hear the orchestra rehearse, and she had been surprised to be alone that afternoon. But it was not a student, she saw at once, but Dr Stewart, the assistant principal.

He stood in the doorway for a moment, dressed for outdoors, in that flamboyant hat and cloak which immediately identified him, although his features were not quite visible to her. Chris wondered if she should acknowledge him. She had never spoken to him – she only knew him from lectures on form and history in the large lecture theatre which they all attended.

In the end it was he who spoke.

'Aah, only one acolyte this afternoon,' he said. 'Tut-tut. Miss Adam, isn't it?'

'Yes, Dr Stewart.'

'Have you seen a few Bach scores lying around up here? I was taking an organ lesson, and I appear to have mislaid them . . . most annoying . . .' he said, approaching her. He made a little effort of looking about him for the scores, but Chris could not help thinking that he was looking more at her.

'Are those they?' she said, indicating a few grey-covered scores on the bench to the side of her.

'I think so,' he smiled. 'Would you be so kind as to pass them over?' he added, and she felt his black eyes search over her again. He was handsome, she had to concede it, in the way middle-aged men could be handsome, with his black beard and hair just touched with grey.

She picked up the scores and held them out to him. He took them, but then to her surprise sat down on the bench beside her. The rehearsal had begun again.

'Ah, *Don Giovanni*,' he said. 'It's a shame we can't get up a whole production of it, but I'm afraid the Board would never have it. That's Edinburgh for you, isn't it? Afraid of anything that is slightly . . .'

'*Don Giovanni* gets his retribution,' Chris said. 'Surely they couldn't object to the morality of that?'

'But he never repents, does he,' he said, 'which I'm sure, as a daughter of the Manse, you know is the crucial thing.'

'How do you know that?' she said. 'If you don't mind me asking.'

'No, not at all. It is my business to know. You are one of our bursary students after all. How are you finding things?'

'Oh, fine thank you,' she said, and was aware that she did not sound as enthusiastic as she might. Perhaps she should be quite honest with him. 'I mean, mostly it's fine, but really, I find the harmony rather dull.'

'I thought you might,' he said. 'When we were discussing your entrance, I proposed that you should be put straight into the counterpoint class, but Dr Bradley likes to do things properly.'

'Oh,' she said, very flatly. 'I suppose one has to get a good grounding.'

'You have one,' he said. 'You got one hundred per cent in the entrance test, you know. That's quite rare.'

'I did?' she said.

'I think I shall have to speak to Dr Bradley again. Perhaps you should have some extra work, something to provide you with a challenge.'

'I really want to learn orchestration,' she said, encouraged by his suggestions.

'You are eager, aren't you?' he said. The orchestra had begun to play the overture again and they both gave it their attention, or at least she did, for she could feel his eyes on her, burning her with their attention. She felt she were a picture in a gallery to which he kept returning. She realized she was being observed for his aesthetic pleasure.

'I wonder,' he said, when the orchestra broke again, this time because of inefficiency on the part of the woodwind section. 'If you were to come to me for an hour or two a week we might remedy this situation.'

'Really?' she said, turning to him. 'You could . . . I mean . . . ?'

'Two hours a week would be no problem for me. It's my duty to encourage talent.'

'Well, thank you.'

'It will be a pleasure,' he said, getting up, patting the grey-covered scores he held with an air of satisfaction. 'Shall we say Tuesdays and Thursdays at five o'clock?'

'Yes, of course.'

'Excellent. Well, I suppose I should give you something to be going on with, shouldn't I? Well, what shall it be? Ah, yes, of course. You know the Mozart piano sonatas, I presume?' She nodded. 'Choose a movement from one and orchestrate it for me. For these sort of forces—' he said, indicating the orchestra below. 'Do you think you could have a go at that?'

'Yes, I don't see why not,' she said, with all the confidence she could manage, though the thought was in reality somewhat daunting.

'Good. Until Tuesday then, Miss Adam,' he said, and swept up the steps to the door, his cloak flapping out behind him.

After the rehearsal had finished, Chris found herself dashing toward Royal Circus with her news, filled with whooping euphoria at this advance in her fortunes. She felt she had been lifted into the lap of the gods, for Dr Stewart was something of a god with the students, with his charismatic lecturing style and his reputation as a composer. Chris had never heard any of his music but she had heard good reports of it. And he had picked her out of the crowd for special notice – it was simply wonderful!

She let herself into the house and decided she must tell Antonia straight away, so went straight to the study door. 'Antonia?' she said, pushing it open quickly, worried by a horrid, suspicious smell of burning.

The room was foggy with smoke that at once stung her eyes. Chris saw through instantaneous tears that the grate was overflowing with burning paper and that Antonia was about to heap on another great pile. She was standing over the fire, the flames almost licking at her skirts, her arms stretched out with the papers, holding them above the burning mass beneath, as if this were a sacred ritual. A large ball of flaming paper rolled off the fire and on to the hearth but Antonia was apparently unaware of it. Rather, she seemed to lean even closer, as if she could not feel the scorching heat of the fire.

'Antonia!' she called out. 'The fire . . .' She did not hear and Chris rushed forward and pulled her away. Antonia resisted silently, like a wooden dummy in Chris's arms, and Chris was obliged to march her across the room. She managed to press her into an armchair, and then rushed back to the fire and set to work with the poker to try and get the fire within bounds of the grate again.

When she was satisfied, she turned and looked at Antonia, who had not uttered a sound, although she herself had been spluttering and coughing. She was sitting deadly still, her hands gripping the arms of the chair, her expression white and stark, the eyes fixed straight ahead on some invisible point. The lively, poised Antonia had quite vanished. This person was a stranger.

Chris pushed up the sash and wondered what on earth to do. She looked about her. The room was in ruins – books pulled from the shelves, papers thrown about everywhere, as if Antonia had been suddenly possessed of a devil. She approached her chair tentatively.

'Antonia ... are you all right?' A daft question, she knew, the moment she had said it. Antonia jerked her head round and stared at her, with wide, fearful eyes. 'Antonia, it's all right, I'm here.'

At last Antonia seemed to recognize her. She shook and jerked and suddenly exclaimed, 'Oh God, what am I doing?' She closed her eyes tightly. 'No ... no, I haven't...' Still with her eyes closed she went on, 'I was there again, on that brink ... and...' She opened her eyes and looked at Chris again. 'If you hadn't come in, God knows what I would have done!'

She buried her face in her hands and then looked up and began to glance around her at the disorder in the room. 'Oh God...' She leant back in her chair and began to cry.

Chris put her arms about her, and she accepted the embrace gratefully, vigorously even, clinging to her with a certain desperation.

'I didn't think it would happen again,' she sobbed. 'I thought this was something in my past, not now, not when I'm supposed to be happy. I should be happy. I am happy, aren't I?'

'Don't worry,' said Chris. 'I'm sure everything will be quite all right...' She tried to sound convincing.

'No, you don't know, you can't know,' said Antonia, breaking free of her. 'You don't know what I'm like. This thing, this curse on me...' She began to walk listlessly around the room. 'You see it just comes, like a great black cloud, clogging me up, until I don't know what I'm doing. Look at this—' she said, looking towards the fire. 'I've burnt books – God help me!'

'A few books don't matter.'

'But they do!' she exclaimed. 'Burning books – it's a desecration!' She spat out the word and then put her hand over her mouth, as if she were trying to stem a tide of nausea. Then, in a thin little voice, she said, 'When I was fifteen I tried to cut myself. I had a knife, and I would have done it, but one of the servants found me. I wanted to hurt myself, destroy myself . . . and, oh God, I didn't think it would happen again. I thought that Jack, and everything, it would be different, that I was better. I don't want to destroy myself. I don't!' She began to cry again, this time hysterically. 'But I'm no better than those poor souls in Jack's asylum, am I? How he'll hate me now, for being mad!'

'He won't hate you,' said Chris, taking her hands, terrified now by her state. 'Of all the things I can be certain of, I know he won't hate you. I can see how much he loves you. It's obvious. He'll help you, I'm sure, he'll make everything better. I promise. Now, why don't we go upstairs and you can lie down, and I'll get some tea.'

It seemed a feeble remedy, but Chris could think of nothing else.

Antonia, still crying, allowed herself to be led upstairs to her bedroom. Chris got her on to the bed and watched her subside into a deep, impenetrable well of her own private misery. She lay, a distorted, shaking heap, her face pressed to the counterpane, howling like an animal. Nothing Chris said or did would comfort or quiet her, and Chris, although trying to stay as calm as she could, felt the wings of panic rising inside her.

She would have to look for help. Miranda would be the person, but a knock on her door revealed she was not back. She ran upstairs and thumped on Angus's door.

'Oh, thank God,' she said, seeing him emerge. He was unshaven and dishevelled, in shirt-sleeves and braces. He blinked at her, as if he were emerging from a trance. 'You've got to help me. It's Antonia. She's nearly burnt the house down. She's had a fit or something – I don't know what . . . But you've got to help.' She was already at the top of the stairs again.

'What?' he said.

'You must know what it is. You were nearly a doctor.'

'Well . . .'

At Antonia's door she paused. 'She won't stop crying and I can't do anything. And if you'd seen her before in the study. She was so close to the fire, I had to pull her away. It was as if she couldn't feel it.'

He grimaced and followed her into the room.

'What should we do?' she asked. She was desperate by now for an instant prognosis.

He did not answer, but went over to the bed and sat on the edge of it. He put his arms round Antonia and pulled her up to face him. She was virtually screaming as he did it.

'Water,' said Angus, as if he were addressing a nurse.

Chris filled a glass from the carafe by the bed and handed it to him. To her surprise, he threw it in Antonia's face. She stopped screaming, and he laid her back gently on to the bed.

'What is it?' whispered Chris.

He folded over the counterpane to cover Antonia and Chris noticed how her hands clutched at it.

'God knows,' he said. 'Hysteria. I don't know . . . I know nothing about this sort of thing.' He glanced back at her. 'It's . . .'

Chris nodded, and clutched her arms around her. She was frightened.

'We'd better get Jack,' Angus went on. 'What's the time? Is it worth telephoning the asylum?'

'No, he'll probably be home soon,' said Chris. 'I'll sit with her.'

'We both will,' said Angus. 'I don't like this at all. If I were my father I suppose I'd give her a sedative, but I'm not sure . . .'

Fortunately they did not have to wait long for Jack to get back.

'Physically she seems fine,' Angus explained. 'But she was severely hysterical. The water calmed her, Jack, but really, I don't know . . .'

'Don't worry,' said Jack. 'Thanks anyway. I'll see what I can do.'

'I had better check on that fire,' said Chris.

It was bleak and cold in the study. The fire had burnt itself out, and all that remained was the mess of papers and books.

'I wish I hadn't been so engrossed upstairs,' said Angus. 'I didn't hear a thing.'

'It's a solid house,' said Chris, stooping to pick up one of the papers.

'Looks like her father's stuff . . . Yes, it is.' He snapped shut a notebook and put it on the desk. 'I suppose this is some sort of breakdown.'

'But she seems so level-headed, so poised,' said Chris. 'Why should she break down? I mean, she said it had happened before, that once she tried to cut herself. I can't reconcile that with the person she usually is . . .'

Angus shrugged his shoulders.

'You'll have to ask Jack that,' he said, sitting down. 'Now you've seen why I'm no loss to the medical profession. I don't suppose throwing water at the patient is a particularly advanced treatment.'

'It worked. I mean, it stopped that crying.' She found she was shaking at the recollection of it. 'I've never heard anything like that. It was as if she wanted to cry herself to death . . .'

'To oblivion at least,' said Angus.

A few moments later Jack came in. They looked up at him anxiously, Angus half rising from his seat.

'Well?' they asked, almost in unison.

'She's sleeping,' said Jack. 'I gave her something.'

'So will she be all right?' asked Chris.

'I don't know yet. The last time, it took some months,

apparently. After her mother died, when she was fourteen. Not immediately after, about six months later . . . She doesn't remember a great deal about it. She described it as falling into a great pit. I suppose I've half been expecting that it might happen again. It's about six months since the Professor died, after all.'

'So it's grief – delayed grief?' said Angus.

'Not grief,' said Jack sitting down. 'Anger. He made her life intolerable those last couple of years. She went through agony. He wouldn't hear of our engagement, and he worked her like a dog at that book. I was never allowed into the house, of course, so we used to meet furtively. It was dreadful for her. If he had got wind of it, well . . . I think on occasions he hit her. She hasn't told me that, but I've a strong suspicion . . . Anyway, the crisis is here now.'

'So how can we help?' said Chris.

'You've helped already. She might have burnt herself to death if you hadn't intervened. I'm glad it was you, Chris. I don't think Miranda would have been so level-headed. She is not the stablest person either, to be frank.'

'What are you going to do then?' asked Angus.

'At this stage, to be frank, I don't know. Anyway,' he said, getting up again, 'I'd better go back to her.'

Angus said, 'I need a walk. Do you want to come?'

It was a surprising request, but Chris realized it was what she wanted.

'That's a good idea,' she said.

He fetched his coat and they set out into the quiet, gas-lit crescent. It was still and cold, and they both glanced up at the windows of the house they had left, as if they were a little afraid of it.

They walked in silence, down the hill to Stockbridge. Angus, with his hands stuffed deep in his pockets, and his coat collar turned up, walked briskly, but Chris kept pace with him easily enough. When they reached the bridge, at the centre of the village, he stopped and propped his elbows on the parapet, staring down into the almost invisible waters as if he read something of great significance there. The gush of the Water of Leith filled her ears.

At length he said, 'If you were a fellow, I could ask you to come for a drink, couldn't I? I could anyway but it wouldn't do.'

'No,' she said, feeling regretful that she was not able to go and sit in some smoky howff and talk the night into oblivion. She did not want to go back to the house.

'We'll walk to the sea instead then,' he said. 'Is that all right?'

She assented, and they walked on, still saying very little, past the hefty villas of Trinity, and down towards the shore at Newhaven. She knew it was odd, this walk of theirs, but there was such strange ease in it that she felt she would have walked wherever he wanted, for as long as he wanted.

'Are you hungry?' he said suddenly.

'Yes,' she said, laughing, realizing she was almost faint with it.

'Good, so am I. Let's eat then.'

He took her to a cheerful, bustling supper room, where the lights shone with incredible brightness and the air was hung with the smell of freshly fried fish.

'I've never been anywhere like this before,' she said, as they sat down.

'I'd be surprised if you had,' he said.

'What'll it be, hen?' the waitress asked Angus.

'Two fish suppers,' he said. 'Don't ask what that is. You are here to learn, Miss Adam.'

'That walk was a good idea,' she said. 'I feel much calmer.'

'So do I,' he said. 'Something like that, well, it makes me realize how close we all come to anarchy, to self-destruction. So, one comes to a place like this and sees real life again and real people.' He looked around him with satisfaction. 'Perhaps we should have brought Antonia.'

Chris looked about her too, at the faces of all those ordinary Edinburgh working men and women, who, in fact, did not look ordinary at all, but rich in character and experience. She felt they all might tell her extraordinary stories.

The waitress brought a tray with a large brown teapot and thick cups upon it. Chris suddenly thought of how she had last sat with a teapot in front of her pouring for a man. It had been with Guy, at Maule's, in what seemed another epoch of her life. What would Guy have thought to see her now, sitting with this strange man, with his stubbled chin and collarless, open shirt, in a working-class supper room? But he would never know. There would be no need for anyone to know about this. She had, she realized, a private life, at last. At least while she was in Edinburgh, and outside the walls of the Academy, there was no one to whom she must answer.

'Were you working when I fetched you?' she asked.

'I've been deep in it for days,' he said. 'I don't know if it's any good, but I feel driven by it.'

She nodded, understanding him, and he smiled and said, 'You know, I think it's really splendid of you to go along with me.'

'Well,' Chris said lightly, 'I seem to be making a profession of rule-breaking just lately.'

'They're not actually rules,' he said, 'if that's any comfort. Conventions, rather, which suggest they're not worth observing. Do you know it was quite common two hundred years ago, before this town got so damned genteel, for women to go to the howffs and join the disputes with their men-folk? Now that would be unthinkable, wouldn't it?'

'Things may be changing again. When women get into Parliament...'

'Ah, you're a suffragette then. Of course you must be, to say when rather than if.'

'Not an active one. I don't find politics too interesting, I have to confess. But the principle of it is quite sound.'

At this point the waitress arrived with the fish suppers. Chris could not help squeaking with surprise at the size of the plate put in front of her. The fish, in its puffy gold casing of batter, was too long for the plate, and the thick, faintly glistening chips looked as if they had been measured out with a shovel. Angus laughed at her reaction.

'How will I ever eat all this?' she said.

'You said you were hungry,' he pointed out.

'Yes, but...' She was laughing too, now, at the gloriousness of sitting in the sort of place that her mother would have crossed the street to avoid, in the company of a young man she hardly knew, about to eat food which Mrs Adam would have considered highly vulgar.

For an extra penny (clearly he was a man of liberal means) Angus commanded a quartered lemon and proceeded to spray its juice about everywhere.

'Shall I?' he said, indicating her plate.

'Mmm...' she assented.

She watched his hand squeezing thc lemon with delicate strength and precision, and, fearing suddenly that he had squeezed too much, she touched his hand.

'Enough?'

'Enough,' she answered, but did not lift her two fingers from his hand. They were face to face suddenly and she was drowning in the depths of his brown eyes. She wanted to touch his face and brush away the lock of hair which had fallen over his forehead, fallen, she felt, quite purposely to tempt her to do it. She wanted to touch the rough stubble on his cheek, indeed to press her own cheek to it and smell, with intensity, the maleness of him, which now, at this tiny distance between them, whispered to her, unsettling something in the pit of her stomach.

She pulled herself back from the brink of this abyss, the abyss of her own weakness which had caused Guy so much agony. She had no time for such things. She had forsworn them after all. But glancing at him again she realized that whatever she had felt for Guy had been only feeble compared to this. She wanted this man, this stranger, with all the primitive desire of an animal. Her body ached for him.

'This'll be getting cold,' she said, hastily picking up her knife and fork and putting all her concentration on to the food.

16

Angus laid the bunch of flowers in Antonia's lap and with one slender finger she touched the curling petal of rusty chrysanthemum. She smiled wanly and acknowledged his presence with a flicker of her eyelids. He looked across at Jack who was perched uneasily on the foot of the bed. He did not meet Angus's eyes either, but looked down at his hands, anxious, it was obvious, to conceal his own despair.

Antonia, lying back on her pillows in her absolute stillness, resembled, now he had laid his tribute of flowers on her, one of those wax effigies of saints that he had seen in Italian churches. All she needed was a coronet of silk flowers to dress her long black hair and a rosary dangling from her fingers to become a virgin martyr. No wonder Jack was in despair. Of course, he could easily enough describe his wife's symptoms in the reassuring gobbledegook of medical language, but the reality of it was not at all comfortable. Jack was not an ambitious young neurologist here, but a husband of only a few months. To see his wife so withdrawn was cracking the calm surface of the professional practitioner. He was scratching at one of his knuckles with his fingernail, as if he meant to draw blood.

'I'll put these in a vase,' said Miranda, breaking the twitchy silence and taking the flowers up in her arms. As she did so, she brushed her hand across her sister's forehead, but there was no reaction, except from Jack, who sighed, got up and walked to the window.

Angus followed him and asked, 'Will you get a second opinion?'

'Who, for God's sake?' said Jack. 'There's not one of them I'd trust with such a case normally...'

'So what will you do?'

'Wait. From what Miranda can remember about the last time it seems she'll come to, eventually.'

'But what is it? I mean, to be so withdrawn...'

'I've seen something similar. A woman who'd seen her husband stabbed. She was silent for months, and then ... it's a defence mechanism.'

'But surely she hasn't seen anything like that?' said Angus.

'No, very likely not. But Antonia has an exquisite sensibility. She feels things very deeply. It's one of the things I love about her but it makes her more vulnerable – unfortunately.' He glanced back towards the bed. 'It's as if the scales have been tipped. There was too much for her to bear any more.'

'Well, I wish you luck,' said Angus. 'Both of you.'

'Thanks, I think we'll need it.'

He left the room and plodded upstairs. On the landing he found Chris, in her hat and coat, about to go out. She was holding her music case in folded arms in front of her, but whether it was for comfort or defence he could not tell. The morning light from the roof lantern shone down on her, and made her face glow. It was a reassuring sight.

'Have you...?' she ventured.

'I've just been in.'

'And?'

He twisted his hands equivocally.

'Jack says it will take time,' he added, seeing how she bit her lip in dismay.

'I wish there was something we could do,' she said.

'I know,' he said, and without much thinking about it

reached out and put his hand on her shoulder. 'It's just a question of patience, I think.'

'Just?' she said, and moved past him towards the stairs. 'Oh, I have to go now. I feel I should stay but . . .'

She hovered on the first step, looking up at him, as if asking for guidance.

'Jack doesn't need the house full of people fretting,' he said. 'Go.' And he waved her away. 'Work.'

'You're right,' she said, and went downstairs.

He leant on the banister and watched her go. At the bottom she turned and looked up at him, and he hastily retreated. He did not want her to think he might be flirting with her, though it was possible he was. He was not sure about this thing at all. He had never been friends with a woman before, indeed, he had never been intimate with a woman in any way. They were puzzles to him, but not the sort of puzzles he was anxious to solve. Yet Chris Adam did intrigue him. She was so companionable that he could forget she was a woman. She did not talk nonsense like other women. Women's minds had always seemed to him to be made up of bits of frippery, of scraps of silk and gauze and misplaced sentiment. But in Chris he perceived a hardness, a will, that was not conventionally feminine. There was steel in her, something ruthless that challenged all his preconceived notions, that upset him inside.

He went back to his room and looked at the piles of paper on his desk: blotchy, inelegant stuff, in medical scrawl, but sifting through it now he was surprised at the extent and the occasional quality of what he had achieved. He had seemed to pour the stuff out on to paper, a frenzy of fresh ideas leaping about in his mind, demanding he give them all due attention with the nib of his pen. He had written until his arm had ached, and then done more, as if he were a mute who had suddenly found a voice and had the accumulation of a life of silence to express. Well, he had been a mute of sorts, he reflected, as he pulled out his chair and sat down at the table under the window.

But the concentration of the last few days deserted him. He had emptied his mind with it, and he felt stale and tired. He could not help thinking of Antonia. The step between sanity and madness was slight. Any one of them, at any time, could take it. Perhaps that should be Everyman's ultimate fate, the city mad-house, the only place where he would feel comfortable, amongst all those other disembodied souls. A music-drama which began in a dissection lab and ended in an asylum – well, it would not be the usual fare that the middle classes in their smart evening clothes came out to see. It would probably never be staged, but he was not in the business of crowd pleasing, and neither was Chris Adam if he had read her right. They would do what they wanted, however strange it might turn out to be.

But he knew he could not do any that day. He needed to drift, like Everyman, and observe and feel apart from the city. Yet he knew when he pulled on his overcoat that he had changed somewhat from the old Angus who drifted. This time, he put a notebook rather than a novel in his pocket.

So it was, a few hours later, with a neat book-seller's parcel beside him, and an agreeable sense of having loafed very satisfactorily, he sat down in a booth at the Café Royal, for an early lunch. He had come there in the interests of balance. If the previous night had been low life, then this was high. The men who lounged about here, behind their newspapers, smoking cigars and drinking champagne from half-pint tankards, smelt of their money and power much as the poor smelt of poverty. It pleased Angus that he could move between these worlds, belonging to neither, but observing each as carefully as he could. No doubt he looked just like the men there, for he was wearing a dark suit from a good tailor, and his cufflinks and signet ring had the required solidity. These signals made the waiter duly deferential. Dressed as he had been last night, having not shaved for days, he would not have been allowed in the place.

'I can recommend the salmon today, sir,' said the waiter, putting down his tankard.

'Oysters,' said Angus. 'A dozen, please. And some bread and butter.'

'Yes of course, sir. By the way, sir, it is Mr Bretton, isn't it?'

'Yes . . .' Angus was a little surprised. He had never been an habitué of the place.

'It's just there's a gentleman at the bar asked me to send over his card. He says he knows you.'

The card was held out decorously on the waiter's silver tray. Angus took it up and laughed.

'Good God!' He turned in his seat towards the bar and saw it was indeed Hugo Doyle standing there. 'Tell Mr Doyle I'd be glad if he'd join me.'

The waiter did so, and in a moment or two Hugo was settling himself on the banquette opposite.

'What a palaver!' said Angus still laughing. 'Why didn't you just come over?'

'I wasn't sure it was you,' he said. 'It has been quite a while. Three years, is it, or four? Besides, this is hardly the place I should have expected to run across you.'

'I suppose not,' said Angus. 'So what are you doing here? I thought London had claimed you for good.'

'Oh it has,' he said languidly, 'entirely. But one is forced back occasionally. A family funeral, for example.'

'Oh, I'm sorry.'

'Don't be. It was a tedious old uncle – something I have rather a plethora of. He won't be missed a great deal. But that's too dreary. Tell me what you have been doing. You must have qualified, I imagine. You have that respectable look about you.'

'Nothing could be further from it,' said Angus. 'Look, we need more to drink, don't we?'

'We do, indeed,' said Hugo, and signalled to the waiter with a flamboyant wave of his hand. He had not changed much in three years. He still wore immaculate clothes, which were slightly too fashionable to be quite those of a gentleman. His pale golden hair was still swept back from the high, almost bony forehead, and his white hands still made their beautiful gestures. Angus felt the past slip away, and he was a boy of sixteen again, on the edge of a cricket pitch, watching this vision in white flannels running and bowling with extraordinary grace. Hugo Doyle, his corrupter, his saviour, and his first lover, was sitting in front of him again, as gilded and as irresistible as ever. He could see the high blue Perthshire sky above him, smell the sweetness of the grass and hear the other boys talk the banal rubbish of schoolboys, while he sat, his knees tucked under his chin, lost in his silent adoration of the wonderful Doyle. He had not hoped to be noticed, not even dreamed of it, but he had been, and one night, after an illicit bathe in the burning cold of a highland stream, they had held each other and Angus had awoken from innocence. Their bodies had been slippery with water still, as they lay together and kissed fiercely, in a rough bed of heather. 'We're like the Greeks,' Hugo had said, and it had seemed ancient and primitive, that passion of theirs. He remembered creeping back to his narrow iron bed in the dormitory and lying there, half ashamed, half ecstatic, unable to make any sense of what had happened to him.

And now here he was again, the beautiful Doyle, appearing as he had done intermittently over the years since they left school. So they sat and drank, very naturally, a good deal of champagne, the hours passing as Hugo talked very divertingly of his life in London, where he was making a name for himself as a belle-lettrist. They had a good complicated argument about literature over several cognacs, and staggered out into the four o'clock dusk. Angus realized he had drunk more and talked less than Hugo and found he could hardly walk.

He woke up some hours later, and found himself lying naked in bed in Hugo's hotel room. The details came back to him, in a rush of uncomfortable shame, accompanied by an equally uncomfortable headache. He groaned softly, rolled over and tried to go back to sleep. But Hugo had spotted him.

'Time for dinner, old man,' he said.

Angus struggled to lift himself up on to his elbows and saw Hugo standing before the glass, tying a white tie with perfect composure, quite as if nothing had happened. The sight made him sink back on to the pillows, closing his eyes.

'You always were a lazy beggar,' said Hugo. 'And you never could hold your drink either, could you?' He came over to the bed and ripped the covers off. Angus tried to grab them back, but Hugo was unrelenting. There was nothing for Angus to do but to jump off the bed and start to find his clothes. He found himself dashing around the room, like a hunted rabbit.

Hugo laughed and said, 'Anyone would think you were ashamed of yourself.'

'Well, perhaps I am!' snapped Angus, pulling on his shirt.

'Don't be an idiot,' said Hugo, sitting down and lighting himself a cigarette. 'There's nothing to regret here.'

'Oh, do you not think so?' said Angus.

'You sound like an Edinburgh spinster,' said Hugo. 'I thought you fancied yourself as more broad-minded.'

Angus put on his trousers and said, 'Look, I was bloody drunk. I lost my head. I haven't done much of this since school.'

'I guessed as much,' said Hugo, smiling. He got up and came over to Angus. 'Not even with a woman, eh? You have been a poor little Protestant monk, haven't you?' He reached out and caressed Angus's hair with a lazy hand. 'Perhaps we ought to give you a tonsure.'

Angus would have moved away but Hugo had slipped his hand down on to his neck and was stroking it in a way that seemed to drug his body.

'Hugo, I don't think . . .' he managed to protest.

'You don't think what?' said Hugo, coming a little closer and putting his other hand about his neck. 'That it's right?' With gentle fingers he began to massage his shoulders. 'How can this not be right? How can something so pleasurable be wrong? Remember dear old Epicurus, Angus.' And he kissed Angus gently on the lips.

Angus attempted to stiffen, attempted to resist, but it was useless. The wonderful Doyle had caught him again.

'So you'll come to London then? You're simply rotting here, you know,' he said. When they broke their embrace Angus found that he had to say yes.

17

At Dr Stewart's door, the institutional character of the Academy vanished. Stepping inside his room was like stepping into a private drawing room. It was much larger than the usual offices Chris had seen, and had a bay window with a view over some private gardens. The furniture was also different – not for Dr Stewart the functional, solid pieces that stood in other parts of the Academy. The pieces here were clearly of his own careful choosing: an old inlaid desk; some elegant lyre-back chairs placed round a table; and a handsome piano which had surely been bought as much for the breathtaking rosewood of its case as for its musical qualities. There were pictures too, mostly of renaissance angels playing lutes and organ, but there was also a fine modern drawing of a woman and two children, who were presumably Dr Stewart's wife and offspring. There was even a vase of flowers on the chimneypiece – an unheard of thing at the Academy, which confined its notions of aesthetics entirely to music.

Chris had a chance to study all this at leisure, because no sooner had she arrived than Dr Stewart had abandoned her, having to chase up some piece of business. She was not bothered by this. She had been rather anxious about this first lesson, and was anxious to postpone the moment that she must show him her attempt at orchestration. She had done her best with it, but she was not sure that she was quite at her best just then. Miranda, as well as

Antonia, had needed nursing over the last few days, and she felt drained by it all. Antonia had recovered herself a little – she had even spoken a little, and certainly cried a great deal.

'I'm sorry to keep you waiting, Miss Adam,' said Dr Stewart, breezing in. 'An unavoidable piece of bother.'

'That's quite all right. I've the work here for you,' she said, pulling it out of her music case.

'I'll look at it later,' he said, taking it and putting it on the table. 'I think we should get to know one another better before we start work. I do so hate the usual master–pupil relationship. It's so stuffy, isn't it?' He beamed at her. 'Shall we have a glass of sherry? You're not teetotal, I trust.'

'No, Dr Stewart.'

'That's good. I find some of my students are. It seems all wrong to me. Music and wine are historical bedfellows.' She laughed at that. 'It's true,' he went on, pouring out the wine. 'You'll like this. It's a very nice amontillado. Do you know about sherry?'

'Only that this is very pleasant,' she said after a sip.

'Good answer,' he said. 'I see we are going to get along famously. I learnt more from my tutor at Cambridge about sherry than I ever did about Greek civilization, you know,' he went on, pulling out a chair and sitting down at the table. He sat beside the table, rather than at it, in fact, with one elegant elbow resting on the table-top. 'I feel we sometimes neglect that side of things here.' Chris took another sip of sherry and decided she could neither nay or yea this remark. 'You'd better play for me,' he said suddenly. 'Something you've written.'

'Yes, of course,' she said, getting up. She walked to the piano feeling rather nervous. She would not have minded criticism of her orchestration, but she hated the thought of her own darlings being criticized. She hesitated for a moment, wondering what to play.

'Don't worry,' he said, coming over and sitting on the chair near the piano stool. 'I shall be kind. I never shout at my students.'

'Very well then,' she managed to smile. She was determined to try and sound confident. 'I've no name for this. It's just something . . . well . . .'

'Play,' he said and so she did.

She had chosen the piece that Angus had complimented her on, the piece he had called restless. She supposed it was restless – a rapid succession of falling arpeggios that never resolved themselves harmonically, placed over a slow, almost ponderous melody in the bass. She had deliberately left it on edge, as if to stir something very deep in the listener, something uncomfortable even. She felt it even as she played it, with satisfaction, although it was slightly unpleasant. It made her think of Antonia.

She finished, and closed her eyes. She was tired suddenly, as if the notes had her own blood in them.

'Well,' said Dr Stewart. 'That's hardly what I expected.'

She twisted round on the stool, annoyed by the tone of his voice.

'What did you expect?' she said rather more sharply than she had intended. 'Something insipid?'

'My dear Miss Adam, you will have to understand that most young ladies do not part so dramatically from conventional notions of music. I was surprised, that was all.'

'I'm sorry,' she said. 'It's just I'm rather tired of people being surprised, as if all they can imagine me doing is pressing wild flowers and playing Mendelssohn.'

'I'm sure you play Mendelssohn charmingly,' he said. 'But that's by the by, isn't it? Your sense of form interests me. You don't seem, in that at least, to feel the need for a great deal of structure.'

'I suppose not. I've never cared for it. I think a musical idea should be allowed to move and develop as it will, not according to some set of rules. That leads to music without meaning.'

'Meaning? What do you understand by that? I trust you don't have programmes to your music.'

'No, I meant that over-strict rules constrict the flow. It's like damming a burn, sending the water into neat channels instead of letting it go, like a torrent over the rocks.'

'That's an interesting analogy,' he said, getting up. He stroked his beard and looked down at her. 'You know, you really are a rather remarkable girl. I shall probably not be able to teach you much.'

He walked into the bay window.

'Oh but you will,' she said, getting up and following him. 'I know nothing about orchestration. I simply can't get down the sound in my head, the real sounds that I'm always hearing there. I don't know the language well enough yet. You'll see that when you look at that botch of Mozart I've done.'

He was smiling and shaking his head at her.

'You're so young, and so ambitious,' he said.

'Perhaps,' she said. 'But I must try, mustn't I? I may fail, but that's not the point, is it?'

'My dear,' he said, and to her surprise he touched her cheek. 'You are also very pretty when you are in a passion.'

She felt herself stiffen, for he had inched noticeably towards her. Perhaps the gesture was innocent enough, and it had only lasted a moment, but something inside her shook at it. For she had felt his fingers press into the flesh of her cheek, while all the time those unwavering eyes were looking at her with unnerving intensity.

She moved away from him and into the body of the room. She saw her orchestration lying on the table and picked it up, offering it to him, determined to get the conversation back to business.

'Perhaps you could look at this now,' she said.

'I could,' he said, following her so that he was again less than ten inches away from her. She realized she was being stalked. 'But, all work and no play does make Jack a dull boy,' he said. 'A cliché, but, like all clichés, it contains an element of truth.'

'I enjoy my work. It's quite enough for me,' Chris said moving away from him.

'Don't, please,' he said, and put a heavy hand on her forearm. 'Oh look,' he said stretching out his other arm behind her. 'There's some hair coming down here . . .'

For several agonizing seconds, she felt him twist the lock of hair in his finger.

'Thank you, I can manage that quite well myself!' she said, and this time got free of him. She stood at the fireplace, gazing into the glass, watching him in it with all the wariness of a hunted animal.

'Oh don't be a prude,' he said. 'It would be too boring.'

'A prude?' She turned and stared at him.

'It simply isn't fair of you,' he said. 'It's the least you can do, don't you think?'

Slowly she gathered his meaning.

'Do you mean because I'm studying with you . . . you expect . . .'

'Well, I am doing you a service, am I not?' he said. 'Just think about it for a moment. It makes perfect sense.'

She stood staring at him, feeling the nausea rise inside her. It seemed impossible that he could be in earnest. Well-respected, upright men, with faultless reputations, did not think, let alone do such things as that. To offer tuition and then expect such payment – it was inconceivable, really, but she knew, her own instincts told her, that was exactly what he wanted. He wanted her as a fee for his instruction, as an amusement.

'I'd rather not, thank you,' she said, diving to collect her music case. 'Not under such terms.'

'Oh don't be so hasty,' he said, catching her arm again

as she tried to pass him. 'Consider what I can do for you – how much I can help you. I know people, you know, people who could advance your career wonderfully were I to make the right noises.'

'What on earth do you take me for?' she exclaimed, wresting free of him.

'An ambitious young woman,' he said. 'And if I read you correctly, you'll realize that your moral scruples are getting in the way of what is really important.'

'What could be more important than my self-respect?' she said. 'I should have none if I agreed to what you suggest.'

'My dear,' he said, suddenly as smooth as a cat. 'I see I have shocked you. But you are an intelligent little chit, I know that, so I shall let you go and think my offer over. I shall give you a second chance,' he finished.

'How magnanimous!' she snapped, and made for the door.

'You'll be back!' she heard him call, as she stormed down the corridor.

Loitering outside the Caledonian Academy, in the dusk, Angus got a few strange glances from the rush of students who came out and quite expected the servitor in his peaked cap to come and send him on his way, but he was determined to wait for Chris. His pockets were bulging with rolled-up papers – his papers, his libretto (or at least the first two acts of it) with the ink scarcely dry upon it. He was exhausted but exhilarated and she was the only person he could think of who might understand. Besides, it was important that she see this draft if their joint venture was to succeed.

So he waited, until the stream of students dwindled into almost nothing, and he began to wonder if he had missed her entirely. Then, suddenly, the glass doors creaked open again, this time with a deal of force, as if something powerful were trying to escape the confines of the building. It was Chris, walking very briskly, with her eyes straight ahead of her, her music case again clutched to her chest in that defensive gesture he had seen the other day. Angus was sure she would have walked right past him if he had not called out her name.

She stopped, clearly startled.

'Oh it's you,' she said, lamely. In the light from the lamp which hung over the porch, her face was pale.

'Is everything all right?' he asked. He smelt distress about her. She looked about for a moment, nervously, avoiding his eyes. 'Come on. You can tell me,' he said.

'It's nothing,' she said, setting off towards the gate at the same feverish pace as before.

'Oh yes, I'm sure,' he said, catching up with her. 'Look, I came to ask you out to tea.'

'Tea?' she asked, stopping, as if he had suggested something rather strange.

'I wanted to talk to you about the opera. I've written two acts of it.' At which she grimaced. 'What is it?' he said. 'What's the matter?'

'Oh!' she exclaimed suddenly, clutching the music case to her even tighter. 'Let's get away from here, please.'

'All right,' he said. 'Where do you want to go?'

'Anywhere, but away from here,' she said glancing at the door.

'What has happened?' he said, as they walked along the street.

'Something ridiculous – something infuriating!' she said vehemently. 'You may have to wait for your opera, Angus, I've just taken five steps backwards!'

'What do you mean?'

'I don't want to talk about it. It's so horrible and stupid.'

'I think you should,' he said.

'Telling you won't change anything,' she said.

'No, probably not. But you need to rail a little, I think.'

'A little!' she said grimly. 'I could hurl curses until the buildings fell down . . .' She had begun defiantly, but ended on a choking sob.

'What has happened?' he said, stopping and putting his hands gently on her shoulders. She wrested free very quickly.

'Please!' she said, fiercely. 'I don't want another mauling, thank you very much.' She began to walk away.

'Mauling?' he said, pursuing her. 'Has some fellow done that?'

'I'm probably over-reacting,' she said, helplessly. 'But bother it, I'm not,' she exclaimed. 'He implied as much!'

'Who?' said Angus.

'I didn't think that men like that could . . .' she broke off. 'I mean, a fresh young man, but . . . This was calculated. I swear he'd been planning it.'

'Who was this?'

'You won't believe me,' she said, with a bitter laugh. 'You won't.'

'Who?'

'The assistant principal. He has a very distinguished reputation – not to mention a beautiful wife and two bonny bairns, and he writes quite lovely chamber music. So when he said he'd teach me orchestration I jumped at it, didn't I? Well, you would, wouldn't you?'

'What did he do?'

'Nothing much, I suppose, but he said that he wouldn't teach me unless I let him . . . maul me or worse. God knows what he actually intended.'

'The bastard!' Angus said.

She looked gratefully at him. 'You think so too? I'm not being a prude?'

'For God's sake, no. You can't submit to such stuff. Someone ought to knock the fellow down. I will if you like.'

'You would as well,' she said, laughing a little.

'With pleasure,' he said, and suddenly felt moved to grab her hand and clasp it between both of his. 'Look, don't misinterpret this,' he said. 'I mean this as a comrade. You shouldn't let him get to you. He's only a jealous old fool. You don't need him. You'll shine without the help of anyone. Your will, I reckon, is strong enough to do it. I know character when I see it.'

'You're very gallant,' she said.

'I don't mean it as gallantry. I hate that nonsense between men and women. I mean it honestly, as a friend.'

'As a comrade. I like that,' she said, smiling. 'So what should I do?'

'You can read my libretto, for a start,' he said. 'And see what you think of it. I'm determined we'll do this thing, and do it brilliantly.'

'Well, I suppose I've managed by teaching myself before,' she said, with a sigh. 'Oh, nothing is ever easy, is it? I suppose I should know that, being a minister's daughter, but . . . It's just, when I came here I thought everything would be solved, that everything I needed to know would be laid out for me, like a musical draper's shop. I hate to admit how disappointed I am by the Academy. There's no fire there. Everything's . . . well, second-rate.'

'Oh I understand that all right,' said Angus. 'Then we must make our own fire, without safety matches but by rubbing sticks together if necessary. It's harder, but then the thing is real. There's no real creation without sweat in it, and blood and tears. You have to fight, don't you, to make something worth while?'

'What a puritan you are,' she said.

'And so are you. We are alike, you and I. We're driven by the same terrible force. I knew it the first time I heard your music. We won't rest until . . .'

'Until we've conquered the world!' she cut in. 'Yes, I

suppose you're right!' She laughed. 'I had better have a look at this libretto then,' she added. 'And see what it sparks in me.'

Later that evening, Chris crouched by a dying fire, reading again the first two acts of *Everyman*. Angus had a true doctor's hand, and it had taken a little deciphering at first, but now she was well used to it.

'"Deprived of life, and now of love . . ."' she read, as Everyman watched his mistress finding herself another protector. '"To be dead is to be a piece of cigarette ash, flicked carelessly away by her long white hand. To be dead is to be the soiled abandoned linen of her bed."'

It was strong, sordid stuff and at first she had been shocked by it. But the power of Angus's gloomy vision was undeniable, and she found herself excited by it. There were possibilities there for such sounds – not conventional music or harmony as revered at the Academy, but new forms, which were not afraid of dissonance or garishness. Like the words, she was determined that the music should shock.

She struggled to her feet and stretched. Her legs had got stiff and painful from sitting awkwardly for so long. She had been too engrossed to notice. She wished that he had finished the third act and that she could begin work at once. Already, the germ of an overture, strident with brass and percussion, was growing in her mind.

She wanted to tell him at once – but then how could she? It was past midnight and however free their relations might be she could not quite bring herself to violate that particular taboo. The middle of the afternoon was one thing, after midnight quite another. Yet she felt as desperate to speak to him as if he were a hundred miles away and her sworn lover, rather than only on the other side of her wall. The desire was as deep, as painful and as unassuageable.

She checked herself, realizing that it was rather foolish to be obsessed by him. Yet how could she not be? He was so remarkable, so unlike anyone she had ever met before. He would say something and she would feel she was looking into a mirror. That afternoon he had been waiting for her, hadn't he? He had said to her everything that she needed to have said to her. It was a wonderful thing that he had been there, to catch her up and console her.

She decided then that her objections were stupid. Had not all her encounters with him told her that the usual rules did not apply? He would not mind and he might even be waiting for her verdict. She went out on to the landing and tapped gently on his door.

'Come in!' he called out.

She pushed the door open, and walked into a warm fug of vanilla-scented pipe-smoke. He was sitting on the bed in his shirt-sleeves, a writing case resting open on his knees, the pipe stuffed in his mouth. He waved a pencil to welcome her.

'You're not busy?'

'Just scribbling a few letters,' he said extracting the pipe. 'Come and sit down. Do you mind the pipe?'

'No, it's a nice smell,' she said, looking about her for a chair.

'Come on here, there's plenty of room,' he said, and patted the space beside him on the bed. 'The chairs are agony – believe me, I've tried them.'

She wondered vaguely if this was an overture to seduction, whether by coming there she had put herself open to that. Well, if it was, did it matter? Just seeing him had filled her with physical longing. She wanted him to kiss her. She would willingly give herself to him. It was not just her body that told her but her heart and mind as well. Not a particle of resistance remained with her. She smiled and climbed on to the bed beside him.

He laughed when she had settled herself.

'Like an old married couple, aren't we?' he exclaimed. 'Would you like a copy of the *Church Times*?'

'The *Church Times*?' she queried.

'Oh yes, my mother reads it in bed, while my father reads the *Lancet* – the marriage of science and religion.'

'Do you know, I have never seen my parents in bed,' said Chris.

'Count yourself fortunate,' said Angus. 'If you had seen mine, well, you'd shoot yourself at the prospect of it, of growing so staid and old. So,' he said, after a moment, tapping the manuscript that still lay on her lap. 'What do you think of it? Have you a stern critique for me?'

'No, no critique,' she said. 'I think it is splendid. It's so unusual – I'm sure people will hate it and be shocked by it, but they won't be able to be indifferent to it. That's what you wanted, isn't it?'

'I'm glad you saw it,' he said. 'I was beginning to worry you might not. It is, I suppose, rather graphic at times.'

'Oh, I was shocked,' she admitted. 'But I need to be. I've lived so quietly. I need waking up.' She found she had turned towards him as she spoke, and she knew what she intended by her words – that he should wake her up.

He reached out but to her disappointment it was not to touch her. Instead he took back his manuscript.

'I had better make a fair copy for you,' he said. 'Have you any ideas about the music yet?'

'Oh yes, there's plenty for me to go on there, but what I must know is what happens at the end – where it is all going.'

'Ah,' he said, getting up from the bed, and walking about. 'A very good question. I'm in several minds about it, but be assured there will not be an opportunity for an angelic chorus as Everyman sees the light of the Lord and is lifted up to heaven.'

'What a shame!' she said, managing to smile, but the distance he had put between them irritated her.

'Well, I detest happy endings,' he said. 'They are always so dishonest.'

'They happen sometimes in life,' she said, at which he scowled. 'Oh you are such a cynic!' she added.

'Have you only just realized that?' he laughed, and dropped the manuscript on to his table. 'I should make a start on this, if I'm to leave you a copy.'

'Leave' – the word sounded to her like a wrong note.

'Oh, are you going somewhere?' She tried to sound careless in her enquiry.

'Yes, down to London – or is it up to London? I never know,' he said. 'I ran into an old friend who suggested I come and stay with him for a while. He said I'd spent far too long in Edinburgh and he's probably right.'

She felt quite angry with him then. How, when that afternoon, after that wretched business with Dr Stewart when he had been so kind, so understanding, indeed so necessary to her, could he now carelessly announce he was deserting her? Of course, it was not desertion but it felt like it. He was a free man who could do as he pleased, but wretchedly she wished it had been his pleasure to stay there with her.

'A change of scene,' he went on. 'And Act Three will come bubbling out of me.'

'Of course,' she said, getting up. 'Well, I'm away to my bed.'

'I'll send it to you, the moment it's done,' he said, when she was half out of the door. 'Sleep well.'

'Thanks,' she said, and knew she would not.

18

Antonia had become communicative again, which was at least something to be cheerful about. Angus had gone now, leaving Chris with a tidy manuscript and not even a peck on the cheek to say farewell. His polite indifference had been like a kick in the stomach and she brooded on it. She was like an invalid, only concerned with her wounds – and she knew she was sick with love then. It griped at her insides in a way that was disagreeable and not the least romantic. For the first time in her life she lost her appetite – both for food and for music.

She hated her own stupidity most of all, for letting her emotions take charge of her so thoroughly. What had happened to the zealous resolution with which she had resisted Guy's onslaught? It might have been quite another person who had done it – certainly not this languishing, obsessive Chris Adam who had taken her over. She was a detestable creature who had no idea of good sense, but had permitted her head to be turned by a handsome young man who was being no more than polite and friendly. She had built a golden castle out of a few twigs. But how she longed for that castle still, no matter how much she cursed herself.

She sat with Antonia one afternoon, turning the business over again and again in her mind, unable as ever to resolve the warring sides of her self. Her sense could not be reconciled to the ranting of her emotions. While she ruminated, Antonia dozed calmly on a day-bed by her bedroom fire, bathed in its soft light. On the floor between them lay a copy of *Alice's Adventures in Wonderland* which Chris, determined to distract herself, picked up and opened at random. Lewis Carroll was a favourite with them both and Chris had been reading it to Antonia over the last few days. How comfortable one could be with Alice! She was so like them: a curious, clever girl removed suddenly from nursery certainties into a world that was in turns both wonderful and perplexing, a world in which she had to think and act entirely for herself. Those decisions about whether to eat cakes marked 'Eat me' or to drink strange potions labelled 'Drink me' seemed like powerful symbols to Chris. But how could Carroll, a bachelor don in his Christ Church seclusion, have known the confused but struggling minds of young women like Antonia and herself? Perhaps that was the mark of a truly great work of art, that it allowed all comers to find in it some shreds of their own lives.

Antonia stirred from her sleep and smiled, a broad, contented smile which would not have disgraced the Cheshire cat.

'I had,' she said, softly, 'such a lovely dream.'

'Tell me then,' said Chris. 'Or would it spoil in the telling?'

She shook her head slightly.

'I was lying in the earth – on the ground, and I thought I was dead,' she said. 'But then I opened my eyes and I was looking up into a great, green hedge, full of wild roses – and there were birds in it, and insects, and through the gaps between the leaves there was blue, intense midsummer blue sky. And then I knew I was quite alive, and quite safe.'

'It sounds quite lovely.'

'The odd thing is, I don't think I ever have lain under a hedge and looked up like that.'

'Perhaps when you were a child?'

'You've been listening to Jack. He says we remember everything. It's all printed into us somehow but we don't choose to recall it all.'

'So how do you feel?'

'Exhausted still, but it's as if I've finally climbed out of my pit. I knew I would, a few days ago, but you are never quite sure until you are out – and now, I think I am. I've been down to the bottom, and I've come up again. There's nothing to fear when you know that, when you know you can get back up. But some people I suppose never do.'

'They should have Jack to help them.'

'Yes, and friends like you.'

'Oh,' said Chris dismissively, 'I don't mind reading *Alice*. It's a treat. Now, do you want me to fetch you something to eat or drink? We are supposed to be feeding you up.'

'No, not just now. When Miranda's back. I want to think a little.'

'Well, so long as it isn't too strenuous.'

'No, it will only be about my beautiful hedge. Do you know, I'm determined now, the first breath of summer weather we have, that I shall find myself a hedge to lie under. And perhaps I will lie there the whole summer.'

'If you do, you'll probably catch pneumonia.'

'It would be worth it,' said Antonia, and closed her eyes.

'I'll leave you to it. I've got my lesson with Madame Lindstrom,' said Chris.

As she walked up to the Academy Chris found herself comparing Antonia's bravery with her own weak-mindedness over Angus. She thought of the manuscript of *Everyman* lying on her desk, which she had not touched since he had given it her. She had been afraid to, as if she might find herself reduced to some sentimental absurdity such as kissing its pages. She had felt capable of such depths recently. She decided though, as she turned into the gates of the Academy, that she would not permit any more of it. To let feelings stand in the way of her purpose was absolute folly. She had managed to overcome them with Guy and she would manage again with Angus Bretton. Not only that, she would write music for his words that would startle everyone. If Antonia could climb out of her pit, she could do that little thing. She went in to Madam Lindstrom's lesson determined to work hard.

'You see,' said Madame Lindstrom, some time later. 'Those exercises are paying off. That was so much better.'

Chris had just played her the first prelude and fugue from the *Well-Tempered Clavier*.

'After two hours a day of them, they should be,' said Chris. 'But they are good. I wish I'd known them before.'

'Much depends on the student of course,' said Madame Lindstrom. 'There has to be the will to work and improve. Without that, all exercises are pointless. You have worked hard, Christina, and you have improved.'

'I'll never be a performer.'

'Yes, this I understand. But you must be as competent as you can. It is essential if you wish to be a composer.'

At first she had found playing for Madame Lindstrom terrifying. Chris had been keenly aware of her inadequate technique, and Madame Lindstrom had very sharp ears and even sharper eyes, which were continually fixed on Chris's hands. 'Your fingering, Miss Adam,' she had said. 'It is quite . . . erratic . . . Well, we need to do some serious work.' She had produced a book of exercises, written out in a meticulous clear hand. 'I devised these myself,' she had explained. 'And if you are diligent with them, they will help you.'

It had been massively dull to do it, but Chris had persevered at them for two hours a day for almost three weeks, and now she was beginning to feel she was getting somewhere.

'In fact,' said Madame Lindstrom, 'I think you may be ready for volume two.'

'Anything for a change.'

'These are harder to master,' she said, handing her the book. 'You will curse me often, but you will feel that you have a new pair of hands at the end. Copy them out as before, with the exact fingerings, but this time every exercise is to be repeated twenty times, instead of ten.'

'Right,' said Chris, trying to sound cheerful about it. 'And the Bach?'

'Go on to number two. I'm sorry it's rather dull at this stage – exercises and only a little Bach to satisfy the soul, but we must do what we must do.'

'I know,' said Chris, taking the book of exercises and putting it in her music case. 'And I don't mind, really.'

'You're a good girl,' said Madame Lindstrom, getting up from her seat to signify the lesson was over. She rested her hand on the piano and asked, 'Now, tell me, Miss Carlingford, you and she are friends, aren't you?' asked Madame Lindstrom.

'Yes, I'm staying with her people.'

'She's a gifted child,' said Madame Lindstrom, 'but I fear she won't really make anything of herself, not in music at least.' She fixed her precise eyes on Chris for a moment. 'Oh, I know, you think I am being harsh, don't you? But I am right. She will be distracted.'

'By what?'

'By a man, what else?' smiled Madame Lindstrom. 'I imagine he will have a title and a great deal of money. She is perfect for such a life, don't you think?'

'I suppose she is,' said Chris. 'It seems a shame though. She plays so well, and her voice . . .'

'The voice, yes, it is good,' said Madame Lindstrom, with a sigh. 'Her husband will be a lucky man. Well, we shall see, shan't we?'

'I suppose so,' said Chris, rather bemused by Madame Lindstrom's frank assessment of another pupil. She wondered what she said about her to others.

Madame Lindstrom glanced at her watch. 'Four o'clock already! Mr Douglas will be waiting for his lesson. He's such a nervous person. He paces up and down outside if I run over a minute.'

Madame Lindstrom had been right – there was a young man fretting outside the door as Chris left, presumably fretting because he had not mastered the exercises. She wondered how bad they could be and decided she would spend the evening making a start on them.

She was going towards the female cloakroom when someone called out her name. She turned to see Dr Bradley.

'Miss Adam, a word, if I may?'

'Yes, of course. There's nothing wrong is there?' she asked, wondering what rule she might have unwittingly broken.

'No, Miss Adam. Perhaps if you'll step into my office for a moment. It's about the Kennedy Prize.'

'I'm sorry?' said Chris, following him into his room.

'It's a composition prize. Of course,' he went on, 'it isn't usual for first-year students to compete for it, but really the field is rather thin this year. There's no one in the advanced classes whom . . .' He broke off and considered for a moment. 'I thought you might appreciate the challenge. You most likely won't win it, you understand, but I think it would be good for you to try.'

'Of course I'll try,' said Chris. 'What are the conditions?'

'You would have to submit a piece of choral music and a piece of chamber music, by May the first next year. Do you think you could manage that?'

'Would you have asked me if you didn't think I could?' she said, irritated by the patronizing way in which he had put the question.

‘No,’ he said. ‘Unfortunately, you are one of the best students I have had for many years, Miss Adam.’

‘Why unfortunately?’

‘Because, to be frank, I do not think a well-brought-up young woman has any business pursuing the life of a composer. The creation of music is better left as a masculine endeavour, but you, Miss Adam, do seem to have more ability than many of the young men who come here to study. You strike me as a freak of nature.’

‘I beg your pardon?’

‘I am a blunt man, Miss Adam, you must forgive me, but that is the way I am.’

‘You are – very blunt,’ said Chris, feeling her temper slipping away. ‘If I were to win this prize would you be able to accept it?’

‘If you were to win the Kennedy Prize, of course, I should be bound to accept the judges’ decision.’

‘If ever I win your respect, Dr Bradley,’ said Chris, angrily, ‘then I will know I have succeeded!’

She did not stay to prolong the interview, and found she slammed the door on leaving. How dare he say such things to her – a freak of nature indeed! Then she realized, as she cooled a little, what a quandary she had managed to put the poor man into. She had upset all his prejudices about what men and women were supposed to be able to do and the only thing he could do was to be rude about it. And there had been a great deal in what he said to be very pleased about, even if it had been so gracelessly put. That he suggest she enter for the prize at all, clearly something he regarded as an entirely masculine preserve, was really quite something. He must believe she was capable, really capable.

‘Miss Adam, I see you’ve been talking to Dr Bradley.’ The voice, as smooth as Dr Bradley’s had been gruff, drifted along the corridor behind her. It was Dr Stewart. ‘Did he tell you about the Kennedy Prize?’ She had meant to walk on and ignore him, but this made her hesitate. She turned to him.

'Yes,' she said. 'What of it?'

'It's quite an honour for you to be asked to enter, you understand.'

'I understand very well. He was loath to do it.'

'He did take some persuading.'

'You mean you persuaded him?'

'Of course,' he smiled. 'I hoped you would be pleased with me.'

'Pleased with you?' she said.

'Well, after I acted so unforgivably,' he said, 'I felt I must do something, to be in favour with you again, Miss Adam. I hate to think that you despise me.'

'Do you?' she said, as coolly as she could, although she felt near to exploding.

'Yes, I do,' he said, stepping a little nearer to her. 'I really do.' There was sincerity in his voice, but she did not feel inclined to trust it. 'Please, let me talk to you for a moment. Let me explain.'

'I really don't think . . .'

'Just for a moment, that's all I ask. Please?'

There were people coming along the corridor and she did not want to be seen with Dr Stewart begging to her.

'Very well, just for a minute.'

He smiled broadly, and they went along to his office.

'Won't you sit down?' he said, offering her a chair with some show of gallantry.

'No, I'd rather not.'

'Oh, I have made you very angry, haven't I?' he said.

'Yes – are you surprised at it?' exclaimed Chris.

'No, no, not really,' he said. 'You see, I am angry at myself.'

'I'm glad to hear it. What you suggested was . . .'

'Disgusting? Unforgivable? Abhorrent?' The words, she felt, slipped too glibly from his lips for true remorse.

She stiffened and decided she would not retort but wait to hear the rest of what he had to say.

'It was all of that,' he went on, 'and a great deal more. You see, Miss Adam, men are terrible weak creatures, especially when confronted with paragons.' He indicated her with a gesture of the hand, and she felt slightly nauseated. She began to wish she had taken up Angus's suggestion to knock him down. Perhaps she should do it herself. 'I was dazzled, Miss Adam, can you understand that? You dazzled me.'

'I did nothing,' she said.

'I know, I know! I am not pushing blame on to you. You were simply being what you are – yourself, and that is something too remarkable for any man, especially for this man. I lost my head, Miss Adam.'

'You should be past the age of that,' she said.

'Love is no respecter of age,' he said.

'Love!' she exclaimed. 'I hope you are not being serious. You can't possibly . . .'

'Can't I?' he said. 'We are fellow artists, Miss Adam. I cannot help but adore your spirit.'

'Good God!' she said.

'Please don't despise me,' he said, pitifully. 'Please.'

'I . . . I really . . .'

'Just let me teach you, as we planned. Let me do that, at least. Would that be reparation?'

'It's hardly a punishment for you,' she said, 'if what you say is true. And how on earth am I to trust you?'

'Because I am being very honest with you now,' he said. 'Please believe me. And it would be a punishment. It is punishment enough to me to know I can never be yours.'

She swallowed and thought hard for a moment. She thought of the manuscript of *Everyman* lying on her desk and the difficulty of the task, and the desire she felt to do it well. She thought of the glory of winning the Kennedy Prize. She needed those lessons to do those things. Was it really wise to throw over the chance for some moral scruple? And she was in a position of power, she realized. The bargain favoured her entirely. He was crawling to her, begging her to let him teach her, for heaven's sake! Surely she ought to use the chance. She would simply have to be wary. It would be uncomfortable, but she could manage it.

'Well?' he said. 'Will you let me make it up to you?'

'All right,' she said. 'I must be mad to say so, but . . .'

'I want you to win the Kennedy Prize,' he said. 'You're the only person worthy of it. If you won it, I could arrange for you to study in Paris.'

She stared at him, blinking at the audacity of the temptations he was laying before her.

'What a devil you are,' she could not help saying.

'Only a poor fool in love,' he said. 'Now, have you time now? We could go through your orchestration of the Mozart. I was quite impressed with it, though you need to do a great deal of work.'

'Yes, I have time,' she said, taking the seat at the table he offered to her again. She could not help thinking she was sitting down in hell, with old Nick himself. But at least she knew it now.

19

The girl stood on his horizon, the sun behind her, holding out her arms so that her shawl was stretched out, forming a pair of wings. Suddenly she was mythical, a bird-woman, an angel, and Guy felt both terrified and exhilarated as he stood watching her, the sun spitting in his eyes and confusing his view of her. Miranda. Res Miranda – wonderful things!

He blinked and tried to grip on to reality, pressing his feet more firmly on to the ground. It was becoming increasingly difficult. This girl, with her scorching beauty, had been so carelessly thrown in his path that he could not quite believe in her. She was more like the hallucination of a hot night; the sort of woman one woke up to find was only a construct of wistful imagination. Yet here she was, turning what he had thought would be a tedious Christmas at Lady Seaton's into something utterly unexpected. He had come there out of nothing more than duty, after all, at his mother's request. She could not face Rankeillor. Indeed, she and Isolde had spent the months since Roddy's funeral in a succession of country-house visits, rather as if they had no place of their own to settle in. Perhaps Rankeillor was meaningless to her now.

For his part, never had the place had more meaning. He had thrown himself into the work of the estate and found that he loved it. The intricacies of dairy farming and drainage were suddenly fascinating to him. He found he was devouring books on the subject and that he bombarded anyone he came across who was more experienced with questions. The tenants, he suspected, thought him eccentric, but they seemed pleased that he listened. After all, they knew their business, when he was a mere novice. He had hated to go away then, although it was a slack time, and it was only for a week or so. Rankeillor and the routines he had made for himself there had become vital to his sanity, in making him resigned to his losses. The process was healing him, and he did not want any interruption, least of all for a house-party Christmas in Yorkshire. However, it had been impossible to dredge up any plausible excuse. The invitation had been phrased as a command.

At the first sight of Miranda Carlingford whatever deposit of calmness he had saved up over the preceding months was immediately dissipated. He had not meant it to happen. He had done his damnedest to stop himself. He had absolutely decided against any sort of romantic complication after that business with Chris. He had grown a nice image of himself as a slightly crusty yet genial bachelor who was far more interested in the progress of the home-farm piggery than in the game of love. He would not let himself slip again. Yet after a week of being thrown in Miranda's company, he knew he was thoroughly dazzled and well on the way to being obsessed.

He had come out into the gardens for a little rationalizing solitude – and there she was! She was standing at the limit of the rose-garden terrace, placing herself against the view in a manner which struck him as wilful. Of course she had her back to him, and in all likelihood she was quite unaware of the beautiful picture into which she had formed herself. Guy, though, could not rid himself of the suspicion that she had known he was heading for that particular spot. For he was always running across her in the house. It seemed impossible to avoid her for any length of time. He wondered whether he was not, like a well-trained gun dog, sniffing her out. Or perhaps it was she who was the dog, and he was merely the defenceless wounded game bird lying in the undergrowth, waiting only to be gathered into her soft jaws. He could not decide. All he knew was that Miranda was becoming inevitable.

She swung round, hearing the crunch of his boots on the gravel. Seeing him, she struck another pose. This time one arm was raised in salute, while the other was lowered, allowing the white fringed shawl to slip from being a pair of wings into the soft sculptural folds of classical drapery.

'What a glorious morning,' she said. She did not seem in the least surprised at the sight of him. Had she stood there waiting for him to come, waiting to cast her silver hook into him and reel him towards her?

'Yes, isn't it?' he said, blandly enough, but feeling that internal shaking which he now always suffered in her presence, that agitation of the gut and bowel that struck him as appallingly primitive. His body seemed to have only one response to her, as if all that was important was his own satisfaction. He craved her then as he had craved nothing else.

'Are you bunking off from your practice then, this morning?' he asked.

'Oh, I'm always bunking off!' she laughed. 'I do love it, but really, I haven't the necessary grit. I loathe the grind.'

'You mean five-finger exercises.'

She made a face, which was still enchanting. 'I suppose one has to put up with them,' she said. 'To attempt the good stuff.'

'I sometimes wonder if there is any point in that even,' he said, 'if it allows rotten amateurs like myself to foul up great pieces of music. Some things – some of the Beethoven sonatas and most of Schubert, for example – should be reserved for professionals alone.'

'Oh don't deny me Schubert, please!' she exclaimed. 'I love him the most.'

'So do I. And I fear I ruin him the most.'

'That's nonsense. You play him extremely well – with great feeling. You ought not to have given up.'

'But I'm like you, Miss Carlingford,' he said. 'I do not have the necessary grit. I couldn't sacrifice everything to the business of music.'

'You've seen quite through me,' she said, lightly. 'I only wonder when my teachers will.'

'And what will you do then?' he found himself asking, feeling it was a somewhat leading question.

'Oh I really don't know,' she said. 'What do girls like me do?'

The answer was so obvious that neither of them bothered to voice it. Besides, they had no opportunity. An interruption was bearing down on them in the strange form of Isolde almost running. Isolde would not run outright, but this hurry towards them was the nearest to running that Guy had ever seen her attempt since they were in the nursery.

'Oh Guy, here you are!' she exclaimed. 'Frank – I mean, Mr Hathersatt would like to speak to you – if you don't mind, of course.'

'Frank, eh?' said Guy laughing. 'Oh Issy, your standards are slipping.'

She blushed furiously at that, and when Miranda said, 'Oh Isolde, he hasn't, has he?' the blushes were intensified.

Guy looked from one woman to the other and pleaded male stupidity.

'What is going on?' he asked.

'I think you'll find,' said Miranda, 'that Frank Hathersatt wants to ask you for your sister's hand in marriage.'

'What?' said Guy, genuinely surprised. He had noticed that Hathersatt, a solidly built Yorkshire squire, had been dancing attendance on Isolde, but he had not thought that the thing had gone this far.

'Oh, you don't object do you?' said Isolde.

'Of course not,' said Guy. 'But what on earth is it to do with me? You and Hathersatt may do as you please, as far as I'm concerned.'

'But, Guy, you are head of the family now,' said Isolde.

'Tosh,' he said. 'Mama is, and you know it. It's she Hathersatt should be grovelling to, if grovel he must.'

'She's perfectly in favour,' said Isolde. 'Do you think I should have let things go this far if she wasn't?'

'I suppose not. But really, my consent is quite immaterial. It would be just a silly formality, a "doing the right thing".'

'Well, if I'm to be married, I want everything to be just right,' protested Isolde. 'So you'll see him and be decent, please.'

'That's more like it,' said Guy. 'I understand things better when you are ordering me about. Really, Miss Carlingford, you wouldn't guess it to look at her but my sister was a real nursery tyrant.'

'Really, Guy Lindsay, you are a great beast,' said Miranda. 'How can you say such things? Isolde only wants you to do your duty.'

'I don't see what my duty has to do with your getting married,' said Guy.

'Well, for one thing, you must give her away, mustn't he, Isolde?' Isolde nodded. 'And then, it would be considered very cheap to give anything less than two long strands of very nice pearls.'

'Not only pretty but useful!' said Guy. 'What a proper little etiquette book you are, Miss Carlingford. Or if not that, you are a terrible schemer, in league with the future Mrs Hathersatt here.'

'All women are in league with each other,' said Miranda. 'It is the only way to achieve anything.'

'That sounds like suffragettism,' said Isolde, a touch censoriously. But then, as if remembering that this was the morning she had decided to get married, she added, 'But I understand the principle very well.'

'In that case, Hathersatt and I stand no chance whatsoever,' said Guy. 'Where is he then?'

'In the library,' said Isolde. 'When you've done, bring him into the morning room and we'll tell Mama.'

'Run along then,' said Miranda.

'And be nice,' added Isolde.

In the library Guy found Frank Hathersatt, pretending to relax in a large armchair. But the drumming of his fingers on the arm betrayed him.

'I hear congratulations are in order,' said Guy, offering him his hand.

'You've no objections then?' said Hathersatt.

'No,' said Guy. 'I'm sure Isolde is perfectly capable of choosing the right spouse. After all, marriage is a private business between two people. Others oughtn't to interfere.'

'Well, I must say, I should be careful about whom my sister married.'

'But you know Isolde,' said Guy. 'How sensible she is. She always has been. She is so careful that none of us need worry.'

'She is a rather special case,' agreed Hathersatt, and sank gratefully back into his armchair. 'I suppose you want to talk about money though.'

'Must we?' said Guy.

'Well, I feel I should tell you that there'll be no need to worry on that front. She'll be well looked after.'

'It wouldn't matter if you didn't have a penny. She's plenty of capital in her own right.'

'I hope you wouldn't have let her marry a fortune

hunter,' said Hathersatt, in a style which made Guy realize how well suited to Isolde he was.

'She wouldn't have let herself,' said Guy. 'Which is why she's chosen you – an excellent fellow with a decent income.'

'I'm a very lucky man. She'll be an excellent mother,' said Hathersatt.

'So you're going to have a brood then?' said Guy, laughing. 'I thought large families were out of fashion.'

'Not amongst the Hathersatts,' said Frank proudly. He got up from his chair and strolled towards the window. From his gaze, Guy guessed he was looking down at his beloved, if that was an appropriate term. He could not quite imagine that Frank could manage such romantic heights. His view of marriage was clearly, for the most part, practical. He wondered if he lay awake, as Guy had done for the last couple of nights, aching with desire. He joined Hathersatt at his station at the window, and saw that he was watching the two women walking up and down the terrace. It struck him that Isolde and Miranda were entirely different creatures who would evoke quite different responses. One could not pant with lust for Isolde. She was too nun-like, too cool, for all her smart clothes and undeniable good looks. She seemed safe, which was exactly what Squire Hathersatt wanted in a wife. She was made like a good hunter – one knew she would not bolt in the field. But Miranda . . . She was another thing entirely, an unknown quantity.

'Perhaps there'll be more than one wedding in your family next year, Lindsay,' said Hathersatt. 'She's a pretty creature that Carlingford girl. You'll have to watch yourself or you'll get snared.'

'Considering you've just engaged yourself to my sister,' said Guy, smiling, 'I don't think snared is quite the most diplomatic word.'

'Ah, but they do snare us. That's the point,' said Frank.

'We need to be snared. What else is a good woman to do with herself than find herself a husband? It's her function in life.'

Miranda's question to him on the terrace echoed in his mind: 'What do girls like me do?' They lay snares, he thought, and realized he had stepped into one already. The question was whether he had the inclination or even the power to extricate himself.

'You'd better go and tell my mother,' said Guy. 'She'll be furious to know you've kept the news from her this long.'

The rest of the day, naturally enough, was much interrupted by talk of weddings, honeymoons, trousseaux and rings. Hathersatt stayed for lunch and then drove back to his house with Isolde to present the glad tidings to his family. With their departure Guy had thought the subject might be dropped but his mother, along with Lady Seaton, settled down to make lists.

'Lists of what?' he asked watching them. They were sitting at a round table, well equipped with paper, blotters, address books and an ink stand, and resembled, in their serious demeanour, a pair of freakishly well-dressed women clerks. 'Is a wedding really such a complicated thing?'

'My dear Guy,' said Lady Seaton, 'of course it is. But men never see that.'

'Least of all my son,' said Lady Lindsay. 'Guy, can't you find something useful to do?'

'I'll gladly stick on stamps when it comes to the invitations,' he said, flippantly.

'I suppose this is rather dull for you,' admitted Lady Seaton. 'It's a shame we've no billiard table here. I think they're always such a good idea. But my husband would never hear of it. I suspect it was because he was very bad at it.'

'Well so am I,' said Guy. 'So it's a good thing you've no

nice table for me to plough up.' The remark was wasted. Their heads were bent over their lists. 'Well, if you don't need me here,' he went on, 'I shan't bother you with any more interruptions.'

His mother dismissed him with a wave of the hand, and he left the drawing room quite glad that his help was not required after all. He could hear Miranda working at her exercises and was drawn by the sound to the library. He felt the snare wire tickling his leg, but he went all the same.

She appeared to be working earnestly at them and he stole up behind her just as he had done that morning. If then she had seemed an hallucination, now she was alarmingly real. Her slender, elegant figure, swaying about on the stool, was painfully obvious to him and tempted him to wrap his arms about it. He could study the soft and glossy darkness of her hair and see the escaped wisps of it flashing in the strong sunshine. He could even see the soft down on the back of her neck as she bent and stretched to play the summit of an arpeggio. He was certain too that he could smell her – a distant but still identifiable breath of roses and warm skin. He hovered behind her for some moments in an orgy of indecision. He wanted desperately to bury his face in her hair and kiss her neck, but some grim streak of puritan decency held him back. For God's sake, he had only known the child for a week! And she was little more than a child, he realized, hardly much past eighteen.

Suddenly she fumbled on a clutch of notes and broke off the exercise.

'Ah you see!' she exclaimed. 'I don't have it, after all.'

He was embarrassed now for those few minutes of indulgent voyeurism. She had known all the time he had been standing there gawping.

'I hope I didn't put you off,' he said, hoping to explain his creeping in as consideration for her.

'No, not in the least,' she said. 'What put me off was sheer boredom. These things are agony.' She shook her hands vigorously, and then twisted round on the stool to face him. 'Let's play some duets.'

He could hardly refuse that, and together they began to sort through the piles of music on the piano lid for something suitable.

'Ah, here we are,' she said. '"Wedding Day at Troldhausen." Very apt, don't you think?'

'Rather more rustic than the affair my mother has in mind, I think,' said Guy. 'Which hand do you usually take?'

'The right,' she said.

She sat down again on the piano bench, moving up to make space for him, but when he sat down she felt alarmingly close, as if their thighs must inevitably touch. He had practised duets with Chris in the past but that had never seemed so intimate or so dangerous. Dangerous – what nonsense is that, he asked himself, and fixed his attention on the music. It was a piece he knew well. He had played it often with Chris but Miranda was a better player. She had a real virtuoso touch, a brilliance which set him racing to respond in kind, with the best playing he could manage. How odd it was to be thinking of Chris now, and so objectively. He realized he was no longer bitter, indeed that he scarcely cared. All he cared about was playing his part as well as he could and with some of the same sparkle that seemed to come so effortlessly from Miranda.

Extraordinarily, the thing worked, and when the piece was done they stared at one another, slightly breathless with surprise that they had achieved such a sense of ensemble.

'That was rather splendid of us,' said Miranda. 'Perhaps we've been too modest. We may not be as rotten as we imagine.'

'Well, perhaps we should give ourselves a real challenge,' said Guy, reaching out and picking up the Schubert Fantasia in F minor. 'What about this?'

'Ah, yes,' she said. 'If we managed that, we should certainly deserve crowning with laurels.'

'I think they would suit you better than me,' he said, suddenly imagining her crowned with a wreath of flowers and leaves. 'The effect would be glorious,' he could not help adding.

She smiled, clearly very used to compliments, and said lightly, 'Well, I had better raid the conservatory this evening.' She stretched a little, and examined the music which Guy had set on the stand. 'Now, what do you think about tempo? I think this is generally played rather slow.'

'You're right,' said Guy, greatly pleased by her instinct for the music.

If the Grieg had required dazzle, the Schubert needed grave tenderness. This she brought out perfectly and he found himself deeply moved by it. Her phrasing seemed as faultless as the lines of her face.

'Oh that was good!' she exclaimed when they had finished. 'We do play well together, don't we? And I so much prefer this to working alone.'

'Well, we must do it more often.'

'But I shan't see you after Boxing Day,' she said, and there was a touch of tender regret in her voice that annihilated him. Like her playing, she was exquisitely expressive.

'I could come and see you in Edinburgh,' he ventured. 'If you like. If you don't mind . . .'

'Of course I shouldn't mind. In fact, I should be quite annoyed if you didn't. My sister and I like as many visitors as possible.'

'Then I'll hold you to that.'

'I shall expect you to practise,' she said. 'And you mustn't let me be such a prima donna. You were holding back on account of me, I could tell.' She flicked through the copy. 'Here, for example. The bass part should really come out here.'

'Fortissimo, yes, I see,' said Guy, but he knew then it was impossible to let her be anything but a prima donna. She was made to be the centre of attention, alone in the intense light of acclaim and adoration, with flowers being heaped at her feet. And he knew he would throw flowers until she was waist-deep in them.

20

There was an element of novelty in giving a party on New Year's Eve when most Edinburgh folk were stuck fast in the bosoms of their families. However, Jack and Antonia had declared open house and had even ordered a lavish cold supper and quantities of champagne. After all, they had something to celebrate: Antonia's recovery. She was looking well with it. She had the glow and energy that come after recovering from a serious illness.

Presented with Jack and Antonia's obvious happiness Chris felt pleased for them, but not with them. She was hollow inside just then. Christmas at Rankeillor had been a trial and she had left early, feeling guiltily aware that she had been very difficult. She had hoped that Edinburgh would restore her spirits and give her a sense of belonging but here even with her friends, she felt the same dislocation, the same emptiness. She had come into her room and remembered Angus lying on the bed, a sleeping warrior. She had wanted more than anything to find him there again, awake this time though, and waiting for her, just as she had found herself waiting for him, or at least some small sign of him. A few words on a postcard would have been enough. It did not put her much in the mood for a party.

She was not allowed to brood, however, for Miranda insisted she come downstairs and help her choose a dress for the evening. She was in a state of high excitement, having hinted that during her holiday at her great-aunt's she had begun some exciting romantic involvement. It was making her somewhat skittish.

'No,' said Miranda, holding up yet another dress against her, 'that won't do either.' With wonderful profligacy she tossed it on to the growing heap of gauze, silk and ribbons on the foot of her bed. 'If only there'd been time to order something new. That's always the thing, isn't it? You think you have something and you don't bother about it, and then it comes to it and they're all dowdy or tired or simply not right.'

Chris, who was sitting on the bed, her territory a little encroached by all that finery, thought Miranda was making a great fuss about nothing. If she had half the number of evening dresses to choose from she would have been ecstatic – not that it mattered of course that she had only one. There was no point in her decking herself out particularly, except to aid the party. Unlike Miranda, she did not have some mysterious man to dress for.

'What about the pink and white?' said Miranda, reviewing her options, and pulling out a dress from the pile. 'It's quite the newest, but it's a bit jeune-fille don't you think?'

'Isn't that what you are?' said Chris.

'Yes, but I wish I wasn't. I want to be sophisticated.'

'Then that bronzy one, with the embroidered gauze,' said Chris. This dress had particularly caught her eye.

'The colour's awful on me,' said Miranda. 'It was a dreadful mistake.' She looked at her. 'It would suit you better. That's why you liked it. You can borrow it if you like.'

'Oh I don't know . . .'

'Go on,' said Miranda. 'It will only rot in the press otherwise. But on one condition.'

'Yes?'

'You help me choose one of these. I can't possibly.'

'All right,' said Chris. 'Thank you.' She got up from the bed and walked round to confront the heap properly. 'Now let's see – this one is awfully pretty,' she said, fingering the pale pink chiffon overskirt of the dress Miranda had rejected as 'jeune-fille'. 'You just need some matching ribbon for your hair and you'd look very Empire.'

'You're very well informed,' laughed Miranda. 'I thought you didn't care about clothes.'

'I don't really. No, it's my sister May's fault – she studies these things very thoroughly. After a week at home, I'm in that way of thinking again. The Empire line is "it", I'm told.'

'Quite so,' said Miranda. 'Yes, it is the best of them. It's just a pity, though, he's seen it before . . .'

'Ah, the mysterious fellow. Why won't you say who he is?'

'Because I'm perverse,' smiled Miranda. 'And he is so perfect, I want to keep my absolute and wonderful secret.'

'If he comes tonight it won't be a secret any more.'

'I'm not sure he will. People are funny about New Year's Eve – they like to stay at their own hearths. But I sent him a card, just in case he's desperate for an excuse to see me.'

'Do you think he might be?'

'Hmmm, well,' said Miranda, laughing, 'there's quite a possibility of it.'

'You're quite taken, aren't you?'

'And why not? I tell you, he's perfect. I couldn't have created a more blissful person. He has everything – absolutely everything. You see, I always dreamt of someone with a lovely house in the country,' she said, grinning. 'But he'd have to be able to leave it. I'd love nothing better than to spend half the year on the continent and half in some wonderful house with peacocks and tapestries and goodness knows what!'

'And he has all that?'

'I believe so. The peacocks certainly.'

'I can't think what you'd want with peacocks. They're dreadful things. There are peacocks enough at Rankeillor – you can hear them right through the village. Everyone wishes the Lindsays would get rid of them . . .'

'Are there a lot of Lindsays in Forfarshire?' asked Miranda suddenly.

'Well,' said Chris, a little confused by the question, 'I don't know. I mean, they're quite a family in county terms.'

'There can't be many Lindsays with peacocks, though, can there? Which ones do you know? I'm surprised you haven't mentioned it.'

'It didn't seem important. Is it?'

'Well, I think you might know him, my beau-ideal, that is. He's frightfully musical.'

Chris took stock for a moment, the cogs of her mind whirring to the inevitable conclusion.

'It's Guy, isn't it?' she said, timidly.

'Guy Lindsay – yes! You do know him then – what a marvellous thing. Why ever didn't I realize it before? I mean, he kept talking about Forfarshire and the house, but I never thought . . . Well, I never made the connection,' she said. 'Silly me. So, how long have you known him?'

'Since I was a child,' said Chris, trying to sound normal.

'Isn't he divine?' Miranda said, sitting down on the bed, suddenly, breathless at the thought of being able to discuss the beloved with someone else. 'He's simply splendid.'

'Well I suppose . . .' Chris wondered what she should say. She felt rather stupidly angry at Guy for making Miranda fall in love with him, although it was none of her business. That connection was quite severed, and she had no right to think of him so proprietorially. Yet she found she was piqued all the same. After all those protestations of love, it seemed ridiculous that three months later he was apparently, to use her father's expression, keen on Miranda. It suggested a fickleness in him, a thing she would never have suspected of him. Yet Miranda was a powerful medicine. She knew very well for herself that her charm was difficult to resist.

'What was he like when he was younger?' asked Miranda.

'He was away at school, I don't really remember,' she said.

'But the holidays – you must have seen him about?'

'Oh well, sometimes – but, Miranda, a village like Rankeillor, it's very stuffy. Everyone keeps in their place. We didn't really have that much to do with each other.'

What rubbish that was! What about those lovely picnics in the braes, and the expeditions to the seaside, to which the Manse children were always kindly invited? What about those long sessions of piano duets at the Castle, supervised by Isolde's German governess, who would complain bitterly about all the wrong notes? Or those wonderful times, with a red kite, on Rankeillor Hill? The memories came back in a painful rush, for on breaking with Guy she had mentally sealed them in a box, like old letters and photographs, so that they should not disturb her.

'Oh,' said Miranda, somewhat disappointed, it was clear. 'Well, it'll be nice for you to see him again, I suppose.'

Chris realized she had been rather ungracious.

'Everyone thinks he's a terribly good person, though,' she said. 'I know it for a fact.'

Miranda broke into an intoxicated smile at that.

'Oh yes, you can tell,' she said.

'We'd better get ready,' said Chris, wishing rather she

could lock herself in her room all evening and work on *Everyman*. She went to the door.

'Don't forget this,' said Miranda, holding out the dress. 'I think you'll look beautiful in it.'

Chris took it gratefully. She felt she needed a little armour to face Guy.

She laid it out on her bed, and was about to get on with the business of bathing and dressing when the sheaf of notes for *Everyman* which she had been doggedly compiling since Angus had left caught her eye. She flicked through them in annoyance. There had not seemed much point working them up into real music, when he was not there to consult with. She was not sure she had interpreted everything correctly.

She put the notes aside, realizing she was making excuses. She did not want to see Angus to discuss the progress of the opera. She wanted to see him in the same way Miranda wanted to see Guy, and was in truth, in the same infatuated, unreasonable state. How galling it was going to be to see Guy, and know that despite all her brave protestations of independence she had allowed herself to become entangled! She felt like a fool, but she could not help herself.

Miranda was like a beautiful, sea-washed pebble, so smooth and perfect did she seem, and so desirable. She was the odd rose-coloured stone amongst the other grey rubble of the beach, the one which must be picked up and kept as a treasure. She sat languidly on the sofa, almost placidly in fact, as if she were only waiting for him to pick her up and put her in his pocket.

Guy was gratified, and yet unnerved. The same creeping sense of inevitability he had felt at Lady Seaton's began to afflict him as he stood in front of her and handed her the glass of champagne he had fetched for her. He felt that a plot had been laid in which he was the prime victim and that nothing he did in relation to her was actually the result of his own will. It was like being pushed into a maze, his vision bounded always by high green hedges so that he could only blunder towards the centre, where the prize lay. He could not rid himself of this sense of manipulation – though, in truth, what was there manipulative about her sending him a card for her sister's 'At Home' with 'Do come, please' inscribed in a charmingly childish hand on the back? It had only been a request, after all, but it had made the nerves twitch in him when his mother had seen it, smiled, and said, 'Yes, you should, you know. I'll manage things here.' He had never been away from Rankeillor at Hogmanay before. It had seemed a heresy to him, especially now he was the Laird, with all the tenants to entertain. But his mother, who would usually have hated such responsibility alone, seemed to think nothing off it. 'You go and enjoy yourself for once,' she had added. So he had found himself in Edinburgh, on a freezing night, with a breath of snow in the air, and he realized there was a sort of relief in having been propelled there. If he had stayed at Rankeillor he would have been sure to run into Chris, which would have been awkward.

He settled himself on the sofa at what he hoped was a decent distance from Miranda, although it felt disturbingly close, and watched her take a small, delicate mouthful of champagne.

'Ooh, but that's dry,' she said, with a surprised shiver.

Guy took a much larger mouthful from his own glass.

'Mmm, yes,' he agreed, 'but it's very good. Your brother-in-law has good taste.'

'So he should,' said Miranda. 'His father's a wine-merchant.'

'So was Ruskin's,' said Guy, with a shrug.

'You're not shocked then?'

'That your sister should marry a wine-merchant's son? No, should I be? I mean, did you think I might be?'

'I simply wondered,' she said, after another elegant little mouthful of wine. 'People are sometimes . . . Well, you know . . . My great-aunt, for example. She's a darling, as well you know, but she's been rather horrid about Antonia marrying Jack. She called it sheer perversity.'

'I'm sure she'll come round eventually. When he's appointed to something distinguished – I don't know what – what is it doctors aspire to? The medical equivalent of Admiral of the Fleet.'

'Physician to the King, perhaps?' said Miranda. 'I don't think that would suit Jack.' Guy, who had spoken with Jack Rosenberg briefly when he arrived, had seen enough to nod with agreement. 'He's far too clever for that,' she went on. 'Did you like him then?'

'Yes, what I saw of him – I only spoke to him for a few minutes. I shall make a point of searching him out later though. He is rather intriguing.'

'Oh will you?' she said, with a smile. 'I'm sure you'd get on famously. It would be good if you were friends.'

'Because Lady Seaton might be better disposed towards him if I were his friend?' he asked.

'It couldn't do any harm,' she said. 'She thinks a great deal of you, you know. And I do think you would like one another tremendously. Clever men usually get along, don't they?'

'I don't think I'm quite in his league,' said Guy. 'I'm just a simple farmer . . .'

'What rot!' she laughed. 'How you do love to play that silly game. You're like Marie Antoinette, milking cows into Sèvres buckets. You'll get tired of this farming fad soon enough, and you'll have to find something really solid to occupy your mind.'

'Aren't piggeries solid enough?' he said.

'No, not for you, not for ever, at least. I'm sure of it.'

'So,' he said, highly amused by her conviction. 'What do you think I should be doing?'

'I could quite easily imagine you in the Cabinet,' she said.

'You are an appalling sop for my vanity,' he said, and she laughed deliciously, and he realized, for her laughter tempted him dreadfully, that they were almost alone in that back drawing room. The other guests had drifted towards the double doors and into the large drawing room beyond. Someone was tuning up a violin. He paid little attention. The fact of being, for all intents and purposes, alone with her was too exciting. It would perhaps only be a moment's intimacy and he decided he would grab it. There could not be, he was certain, a better chance to kiss her as she sat there, the very lines of her body singing of her willingness to yield.

'Shouldn't I be?' she said. 'Aren't I allowed to encourage you?'

'You're perfectly allowed,' he said, and stretched out his hand and cupped her cheek in it, drawing her head a little towards him. 'If you were to let me kiss you, I'd be very encouraged.'

'Hum.' She giggled delicately, and with the slippery ease of a cat, she twisted herself round and lay, suddenly, with her head in his lap, gazing up at him, smiling. 'There, will that do?'

It seemed senseless to say anything else, so instead he bent and kissed her, gently and almost diffidently at first. Yet he soon realized that she was sparking in response, that her submission came from her own eagerness to please herself rather than him. Her feeling, so hot-breathed, so fierce, swept away any last vestiges of his own reserve. He scooped her up from his lap, so she sat upright in his arms, and kissed her properly, holding her tight with one hand clamped over one of her breasts and another on the warm flesh of her shoulder, as if she were some machine he was driving, who would get out of control if he did not hold fast and master her.

And then the music began. At first he scarcely heard it, that simple thread of melody, played quietly on the flute, for he was too drunk with the smell and feel of Miranda to hear anything. But the painful beauty of it began to touch him. He felt a shudder of recognition, and raised his head a little from Miranda's neck. The violin had come in, a little lower, sweetly but plaintively answering the flute.

'God . . .' he said. 'I know this . . .'

'Of course,' said Miranda. 'You would, wouldn't you? I quite forgot to say. We've an acquaintance in common, you know. Odd we didn't find it earlier. Chris is a dear friend of mine. And this, it's ravishing, isn't it?'

It seemed so obvious then. Miranda had said she was studying music, but not at the Academy. It had occurred to Guy that she might have been, but with some private teacher. She had probably been drilled by Lady Seaton not to say she was at the Academy lest he be put off. Men were not supposed to like women students. But her music now struck him as so intensely professional that she could only be the product of such a place, and then of course she would know Chris. These thoughts rushed through his mind in an attempt to stem his own surprise at hearing her music. He did not want to feel upset or in any way bothered by it. He wanted to accept it as quite a logical thing, which meant that he could simply smile and say, 'Oh yes, Chris Adam,' as if the name meant very little to him.

Yet he did feel shaken. Miranda was lying again in his lap, her eyes closed, caught just as he was by the beauty of that little trio. He felt invaded by it, destroyed even, as if he could never escape her, never avoid the pain of not being able to have her, even now, when this exquisite, submissive creature lay in his lap, her soft hand twisted up in his. He stroked her forehead, ineffectually he thought, but she opened her eyes and smiled up at him.

'So lovely,' she said.

'Yes, you are,' he said, consciously blocking his ears to the music. 'Look, let's get away, shall we? I'd like to be alone with you, properly alone . . .'

'Yes, oh, yes,' she said, sitting up. 'I should like that too, very much. We'll go upstairs, shall we?'

'Upstairs?' he said. 'Are you sure?'

'Yes,' she said. 'You're not shocked are you?'

'Just surprised,' he said.

'Oh good. I knew you'd understand,' she said, and stood up, holding out her hand to him.

She led him upstairs. As they went up the music faded a little and it was as if Chris's hold over him were diminishing too. There was a certain relief in it, for as he stood on the threshold of Miranda's bedroom, and watched her stretch herself out on the bed, he perceived that this was the reality of his future now. Chris was a past dream, like that distant music, rising faintly up the stairwell.

Miranda said, 'Close the door,' and opened her arms to him.

The New Year arrived at 15 Royal Circus with an impromptu and ragged performance of the 'Ode to Joy' from Beethoven's Ninth, which merged imperceptibly into the more sentimental and traditional 'Auld Lang Syne' when it was realized that the clocks had struck midnight.

Chris by then was enjoying herself. She had missed the painful beginnings of a party by working on the opera for a couple of hours and had come down to find the rooms buzzing. She had looked anxiously around for Guy, having carefully composed a speech for him, but there was no sign of him, and fortunately she had no chance to look for him, because Jimmy Black from the Academy marched her off to play her trio. He had come with his sister who played the flute and they played her music with real appreciation and enthusiasm, after which she forgot her troubles and threw herself into the fun.

Jimmy proved himself as adept at playing reels as Bach on his violin, and she danced whenever she was asked, with a succession of young doctors, scholars, lawyers and other, less definable but very interesting oddities that Antonia and Jack had contrived to invite. At supper, Jimmy took her down and flirted outrageously with her, as he flirted with every woman. Miranda was his usual prey at the Academy, but she, like Guy, was elusive. Chris wondered vaguely what might have become of them, and then decided it was their own private business, which she had no right to know about. Besides, after so much champagne she scarcely cared. All that mattered was that the opera was under way and she had her own silly weakness under control.

After 'Auld Lang Syne' had died away, the front bell was heard to jangle and there was an enthusiastic rush downstairs to greet the first footer. Chris stood in the crowd on the stairs as Antonia opened the door to reveal a street that had been transformed by fresh-fallen snow. And standing there, hatless, his hair matted with snow, with a loaf of bread, a piece of coal and bottle of whisky, was Angus. She found she gave a little involuntary cry at the sight of him, and it seemed he noticed, for he looked up and their eyes met. It seemed too wonderful to be true.

'You're not a stranger!' exclaimed Antonia, with the pedantry of a true scholar.

'I've been away for a month! Doesn't that make me one?' he protested. 'Let me in.'

'Of course,' she laughed, and took the loaf of bread from him. 'A dram?'

'Please. It is perishing out there!'

The door was hastily closed and everyone went into the dining room for black bun, shortbread and whisky. Angus stood with Antonia at the doorway, shaking hands and exchanging greetings. As a first footer, bringing in the New Year, he had a ceremonial role to discharge. Chris lingered at the back of the crowd, wishing she had a speech for him, like the one she had prepared for Guy. But she was simply speechless. His arrival, on the cusp of the year like that, seemed portentous. He had planned it, of course, for he had the props, she realized that, but he was there at the start of 1913, stepping in from a world transformed by white, obscuring snow. It was a fresh start, she was certain of it.

Now she was in front of him, and to her surprise he grabbed both her hands and kissed her on each cheek in turn. It took all her restraint then to stop herself flinging her arms about him. Instead she returned his kiss.

'I've something for you. You may not like it.'

'Oh no?' she said.

He was digging inside his overcoat. 'Here.' He handed her a solid baton of rolled-up paper, tied together with string. 'It's two more acts. It's finished now.'

'Two more? It's a good thing I've plenty of ideas. There's lots to discuss, you know.'

'That's why I'm back,' he said, taking her arm and leading her into the dining room. 'I feel conscious I abandoned you slightly.'

'Oh, no you didn't,' she found herself saying. 'You needed to go somewhere to do the work. I do understand.' For now, she felt capable of forgiving him anything.

Jack came up with two glasses of whisky for them.

'Both for me?' said Angus, taking them. 'Here,' he handed one to Chris, after making some pretence of checking which was the larger. He swallowed his in one go, but Chris could only manage a sip. The fiery liquid was just touching her throat when she heard Miranda say behind her, 'Ah it was you! We'd given you up for dead, you know, Angus!'

She swept into the room, and in her wake, Chris turned and saw, there was Guy, holding back somewhat and looking sheepish. Both of them, she noticed, had a high colour in their cheeks, and Guy passed a quick, surreptitious hand over his hair, as if he were sure it needed smoothing.

'Happy New Year, Chris!' said Miranda with huge enthusiasm and kissed her, and then walked on past to greet the others.

Guy made her a slight bow, and said, 'Chris, it's good to see you. I'd no idea you knew Miranda.' He seemed a trifle stiff, quite out of his depth, and Chris could not help smiling.

'How is everything?' she asked.

'Oh fine, fine,' he said. 'And with you?'

'Fine,' she said, with certainty.

'Good,' he said. 'Well, Happy New Year,' he added, and put out his hand.

They shook hands and he moved on in Miranda's wake, quite like a stranger. She had never had such a formal conversation with him before.

'Who was that?' asked Angus.

'Oh, just an old neighbour of mine,' she said, offhandedly, turning to him.

He grinned, and to her surprise slipped his hand around her waist.

'I missed you, you know,' he said.

'You did?'

'I did,' he said. 'And I'm looking forward to all this,' he added, tapping his roll of manuscript.

'So am I!' she laughed. 'It will be a wonderful thing, I'm sure of it!'

He pulled her a little closer, squeezing his hand gently on her hip. She felt a prickle of excitement run down her back. She noticed that Guy had glanced back at them then, though only for a moment, for he turned away, having seen their closeness, and took Miranda's hand.

'They'll suit well,' said Angus, noticing it too.

'How do you know?' she asked.

'They're like a pair of race-horses,' he said. 'No doubt she'll breed well.'

'You're most unkind,' she said.

'I know,' he said. 'Come on, I want some black bun. I'm famished. And then you can play me all you've written so far.'

21

'No, but you see my point, don't you?' said Chris. 'No one could possibly sing that and make sense of it to the audience. All those s's . . . it would sound like a hiss, and nothing else.'

'But it's a good bit and it's important,' said Angus. He saw her point, but he was not going to relinquish the passage without a small fight. That was part of the pleasure of the thing, after all, these struggles between them. 'Perhaps if the music were slower.'

'That would be daft,' she said. 'The character's in a fury. Fury should be fast, as fast as possible. Presto Allegro!'

'That's simply a cliché,' he said. 'Anger can be any speed. It could be jolly slow, seething, like a great pot of syrup, just about to boil.'

'I suppose . . .' she said. 'Oh, I don't know. Leave that with me. What's next?' She flipped over the page of her score and sighed. 'Do you know, I'm tired?' she said suddenly.

'It's hardly surprising. You've been at this like a slave.'

She got up and stretched. They had been sitting, heads together, in front of the drawing-room fire, having their *Everyman* conference on the hearth rug.

'Time to light the lamps,' she said, looking about her.

The room was dark except for the light of the fire and the harsh, bright light of the frosty street outside.

'No don't,' he said. He liked to see her in this austere

half-light. It reassured him, like a nursery comfort, for she looked very beautiful in it. He relished it, as the fire lit up her fair hair and skin, as she stood over him. He had not, until he came back, realized how much it affected him. He had believed that he was immune. Hugo had told him constantly he was immune, that one could be only fish or fowl, but he knew looking at her then that it was altogether more complicated. Why else had he come back, when Hugo had offered him indefinite, elegant and luxurious shelter? Because of her, the creature that he was not supposed to have any feelings for?

Hugo had it wrong. He had a great many things wrong, and Angus felt guilty now at every one of them. All those nights he had spent with Hugo, so thoughtlessly, now haunted him. He wanted to destroy the memory of them utterly, and destroy in himself that thing, that terrible unnatural urge which had made him do it. He wanted to wash himself clean of it. And Chris was clean. She was as straight and true and clean a thing as he could imagine, like a pine tree in a northern forest, supple yet strong, simple and yet a marvel of complicated nature. She looked, indeed, to him, like redemption itself.

She moved away and sat down at the piano. There were often these comfortable silences between them, when they were not arguing over scenes and styles. In these interludes he felt all their significance lay. It was the nearest to serenity he had ever known.

She began to pick out a melody; a slow, unstructured thing, which had a hint of Gael about it.

'What's that?' he asked.

'The final music,' she said. 'For your madhouse scene. For that girl. She should be a highlander I think – an exile from the islands. She sings about her birthplace doesn't she?'

'You're right,' he said. 'I'll make it clear, if you like. That tune, it sounds like those Gaelic songs.'

'You know them?'

'I heard them one summer, in Lewis.' He was marvelling at her perception. Yes, this thing was right, as right as it could be. He got up and took the manuscript over to the piano, trying to find the place. 'That will be a splendid end.'

'Not a dry eye in the house,' she said with surprising levity.

'We'll cut Everyman's last peroration, I think,' he said, glancing at what he had written. 'With that it's superfluous.'

'But he should do something.'

'Yes but what? Take his place with them?'

'He could greet them like his family then,' she said.

He exhaled sharply, realizing that that was exactly right.

'Chris, that's quite perfect,' he said, and reached out and grabbed her hand and squashed it hard in his own. 'I don't know how you do it.'

'We do it together, I think,' she said, and placed her hand over his. He wondered if he should kiss her then, wondered how she might react. In truth he was afraid too, in case he ruined this harmony between them. His hesitation was fatal, for a moment later Antonia came in.

'You don't mind if I bring a visitor in?' she asked. 'We've been sitting downstairs in the study, but it's too cold.'

'Of course not,' said Chris. 'It is your drawing-room.'

'Yes, but you've been working so hard. I hate to interrupt artistic endeavour.'

'We've done enough for now,' said Angus.

'Good, so you'll have some tea with us? It's Guy Lindsay, by the way, Chris, in case your ears were burning. We've been talking about you. He's so pleased about the opera.'

'He must be disappointed Miranda's out,' said Chris.

'She'll be back soon. We shall just have to distract him until then,' said Antonia. 'I'll go and get him.'

'Is that the fellow who was with her at the party? Your old neighbour?' Angus asked, when Antonia was gone.

'Yes,' she said, and he thought he detected a note of annoyance in her voice. He wondered if, like him, she did not really like the thought of being interrupted just then.

'Do you not like him?' he asked.

'No,' she said. 'What gave you that idea?'

'You didn't seem too pleased that it was him.'

'Well, it might be slightly awkward, that's all,' she said, going back to the fire and gathering up the papers which they had spread all over the floor.

'Why?'

'I'll tell you some other time,' she said. 'Now, which of these are we keeping and which not?' she added, gesturing towards him with a piece of paper. It was hardly a necessary question – the piles had been sorted as they went – but rather a definite command to him that the subject was quite closed.

Antonia reappeared with Guy Lindsay, who turned out to be Sir Guy, which did not surprise Angus a great deal. There was something about the man which spoke of the landed gentry, something in the old-fashioned cut of his suit and its cloth that gave a whiff of both the stable and inherited privilege. Angus wondered if, like many Scottish landowners, he had the name of his demesne tagged on to his own name to emphasize (as if that were needed) his proprietorship, and decided that Sir Guy Lindsay would certainly be 'of' somewhere. And of course he did not sound like a Scotsman.

The situation was, as Chris had predicted, awkward. He sensed her own lack of ease, and it infected him. He felt hostile to the man, because she was rattled. He realized he did not like it that she should be upset, and he found himself sitting protectively close to her on the sofa.

'So when can we expect to see this opera?' Lindsay asked, after the introductions had been got through. 'This all looks impressive,' he added, indicating the pile of papers.

'That's mostly waste paper, actually,' said Chris. 'But it's coming along. A few months perhaps?' She glanced at Angus.

'I think so.'

'Well, you must let me know,' said Lindsay. 'I couldn't miss it, could I?'

'Not with Miranda taking a lead part, no,' said Chris.

'She'll be singing in it? Oh good,' he said, with an enthusiasm which betrayed him. 'And you, what will you do?'

'Conduct, I suppose.'

'How splendid,' said Lindsay, leaning back in his seat. 'Well, you always did threaten to do wonderful things.'

'You'll have to judge when you hear it,' said Chris, 'whether you think it's wonderful or not.'

'It's very uncompromising,' said Angus, who suspected that Lindsay would have conventional tastes.

'Well, Chris is the last person to compromise,' said Lindsay. 'You must know that by now.'

Angus had the sense he was being prodded in the ribs with a lordly stick. Lindsay's words smacked of paternalism, as if Chris were a charge of his, to whom he had behaved beneficently. He looked almost as if he expected gratitude from her.

'Of course,' said Angus. 'Working with her is almost painful because of it. She rips my verse to pieces for the sake of the music.'

'I do not!' said Chris, with mild annoyance. She jumped up from the sofa and went to stand by the fire. Angus wondered if his closeness had driven her away. Perhaps in front of the Laird she wished to appear quite independent.

'*Pace*,' he said, and held up his hands.

'So much for harmonious collaboration,' said Antonia. 'Do you think Mozart and Da Ponte were like this?'

'How's everything at Rankeillor then?' said Chris, ignoring this.

'Oh, quite as ever. I'm rebuilding the Home Farm. We are going into pigs, in a large way.'

'Pigs . . .' said Chris. 'Well, you surprise me.'

'I surprise myself. It's fascinating really, farming.'

'So you don't play any more?'

'A little – but I'm horribly rusty. You should have heard me at Christmas. It must have been excruciating for Miranda. You're probably better than I am now.'

'I doubt it,' said Chris. 'You always were better than you ever said you were. Miranda said it was wonderful playing with you. Perhaps you have an affinity, since you are such friends. Shall I write something for you?'

'Yes, do that. We should be honoured. Make it good and difficult, though, so I have to get some practice in.'

'Won't the pigs get neglected?' said Chris.

'I doubt it. I've got Sandy Tulloch looking after them.'

'Is that wise?' laughed Chris. 'Sandy,' she explained, 'is something of a Rankeillor character.'

'I doubt he'd waste much of his whisky on them,' said Guy.

'You might find the village overrun with pigs, though.'

'The joys of country life,' said Lindsay philosophically. 'Besides, I resent your assertion. My pigs are very well mannered.'

'This village sounds enchanting!' declared Antonia.

'Then,' said Guy, 'perhaps you'd honour us with a visit. My mother was suggesting it actually. She was most taken with Miranda.'

Angus wanted to laugh at the obliqueness of this. It was obvious that it was Lindsay who was taken with her. Anyone who had seen them together at Hogmanay would have seen it. However, if that were not proof enough, the fellow's face when Miranda finally came in, a few moments later, was. He might have been presenting a dozen bunches of flowers in his greeting. She, in her turn, kissed him on the cheek, to make the point quite clear. Angus wondered how long it would be before the engagement was announced in the *Morning Post*.

When Miranda at last arrived Guy's instinct was to hurry her away. He had come there with the intention of taking her out – he had hired a motor for the purpose, hoping for a leisurely drive out to Gullane for tea. He had somehow imagined she would have been at home, with the whole afternoon at her disposal for him. Instead he had only found her apologetic and charming sister and then, more terrifyingly, Chris. Terrifying, because, as at Hogmanay she had seemed to look at him sharply, with a sort of scorn at his changefulness. It was hardly fair of her though, he thought with increasing annoyance, as she sat on the sofa with Angus Bretton. She was clearly deep into something there, which made all her protests about needing to fly alone sound strikingly hollow. Of course, he did not know what might be going on between them, but the man had a protective, lover-like air about him. He had seen him the other night with his arm about her waist, for goodness sake. So much for all that passionate idealism, he thought, and put her character down on a distinctly lower peg in his estimation. There was a great deal of comfort in doing so. He felt he had finally conquered her, or rather had finally conquered his obsession with her. He had reduced her again to simple, depressingly fallible humanity, while Miranda soared, still angel-like, into the skies for his ready adoration.

And that afternoon, for all her lateness (which was of course hardly intentional), she was adorable. She was wearing a Russian-style fur hat and a broad fur collar, and had for him the air of a luxurious parcel delivered from an expensive shop. With her kiss, it was as if it were addressed to him alone. She agreed at once to go out to tea with him, and they left in the same sort of excited flurry to be alone with which they had gone up to her room on the night of the party. The broad-seated, comfortable privacy of the back of an expensive hired Lanchester, with a curtain drawn across the glass which separated the driver from them, provided the same opportunities for the dangerous intimacy which they had practised that night. It was a game, made exciting by the nearness with which they had approached the threshold of acceptability: a tangling of arms and legs, a furious exchange of hot-blooded kisses, and underlying it all the sense that this was only a smoking fuse compared to what might follow.

The motor turned a sharp bend and the swerve threw Guy away from her. It made him catch his breath, and realize what he had been doing. He stared across at her as she sat, half reclined, wedged in the corner of the seat, breathing hard. Dizzy, he watched as she licked her lips swiftly and tweaked an earring which he had forced awry. The motor seemed to be going as fast as they were and he felt obliged to grab the leather strap by the door.

'Guy?' she said.

'Perhaps we should be serious for a minute,' he said. 'I feel . . . all at sea.'

'Oh,' she said, and pouted very slightly. 'Oh, I haven't shocked you have I?'

'No, no,' he said, grabbing her hand. 'Of course you haven't. You know you haven't. I think I simply shocked myself.'

'How funny you are,' she said, and, repeating the gesture of the other night, slithered again, so that her head lay in his lap. 'Very well, let's be serious,' she said, gazing up at him, with candid eyes.

'Well, where do you think we're going?'

'Going?' she said, laughing. 'Gullane?'

'No, not now, I mean us, generally.'

'Oh I see,' she said, and thought for a moment. Then she giggled and said, 'For a nice long honeymoon in Venice, I hope.'

He blinked, taken aback with her boldness.

'Are you being serious?' he found himself asking.

'It's what you wanted, isn't it?' she smiled. 'Seriousness. Of course I am. Isn't that what you want?'

'It's a delicious thought,' he said. 'Certainly.' He stroked her forehead. 'But are you quite sure?'

'Of course I am. I was sure the moment I laid eyes on you. I saw you and I thought, "A palazzo in Venice".' She laughed again. 'Oh dear, that sounds dreadful, doesn't it?'

'No, not at all. In fact, I'm terribly flattered, if it's true.'

'How dare you say it isn't!' she exclaimed, with mock outrage. 'Really, you are a dullard about proposing, Guy. Still, I don't suppose you've ever done it before. That's what I find delicious about you. There's nothing of the common or garden flirt about you. You're almost an innocent, I think.'

'I'll take that as a compliment,' he said, and bent to kiss her but she pushed him away and sat up again.

'I shan't let you off that lightly,' she said. 'Dullard. You have to do the thing properly.'

'What, go and ask your father what your dowry is and haggle over the settlements?' he said. 'I can't do that, can I?' he said, being deliberately oblique.

'No, you must ask me properly,' she said, suddenly as demure as a child in the school room. 'Or I might not say yes,' she added.

'You've already said yes.'

'Not properly!' she said.

'Oh very well,' he said, and took her hands. The words would have slipped out glibly enough, but something about the solemnity of the business made him hesitate. He was seized with silent fear that she might indeed only have been teasing him, that rejection lay at the end of his question. It was a thought he could not quite bear, when his mind had already in the very few moments since she had said the word 'Venice' constructed a solid fantasy about this particular event. He did not want to have to face the destruction of his hopes again. He needed to be sure.

'Guy?' she said. She was prompting him, he understood at once, and found his heart was pounding with relief.

'You'll have to forgive me,' he said. 'You were quite right. I haven't had a great deal of practice.'

'Don't worry,' she said, reassuring. 'It will be fine.'

'Will it be?' he said. 'You're sure?'

'Just ask me,' she said. 'Just do it.'

So he did, in words which had a mannered, measured sound to them and would not have disgraced an early Victorian novel, in words of which he felt his father might have approved or even used to secure his own exotic choice of a wife. There seemed something inevitable and traditional about it, as inevitable and traditional as the fact that Miranda would wear white on their wedding day.

He finished and there was a heart-stopping little pause from Miranda. Then she clasped his hands and said, 'Oh yes, yes, yes!'

Three times she said it, just as Chris had said, three times: 'I don't! I can't! I won't!' God, why did he think of that then, with Miranda, sitting so eager and compliant beside him, her hands wrapped about his, her face bright with happiness? Why did he have to be haunted by that now?

He bent over her hands and kissed them, furiously slamming that door in his mind. This was his future now. That path could not have been taken, but this one was right. It was a straight, well-paved path, easy to walk, and the sun would shine on it, he was certain.

They reached Gullane in time for a very late tea, in an

almost deserted tea room, which suited them well for all the talk of plans which they had.

'It had better be April,' said Miranda, digging her fork into an eclair. She had insisted on cream cakes, as if she were being taken on a holiday treat. 'For Venice, but I'd rather not announce it just yet.'

'Why not?'

'Well, people make such a fuss. Not that I shouldn't enjoy the fuss, but I should rather go on as we are for a little while. It would be so much more fun. It would simply be our secret for a while and then we can choose a moment to announce it that will be theatrical.'

'I'd no idea you had pretensions to drama,' he smiled.

'I haven't, but I should like it to make an impact. It's an important thing, after all,' she said, with a touch of gravity that amused him. She took a mouthful of eclair and appeared to considering deeply as she ate. 'Besides, if we leave it a little while, we won't seem so indecently hasty. I should hate anyone to say we were being rash, wouldn't you?'

22

Chris felt a sudden hand on her shoulder, a man's hand, from the weight of it. She jumped at it, raising her head, and realized she had fallen asleep on her folded arms. She stared round her, remembering vaguely that she was in the Academy Library when she saw the green-shaded desk lamp in front of her. She straightened up and looked round.

'Oh Dr Stewart . . .' she said. He did not take his hand away.

'My dear, are you all right?' he said.

'I simply fell asleep . . . how stupid of me.'

'It's well past nine. There's only you and I left here.'

'Oh . . .'

'Don't worry,' he said, finally taking his hand away. 'What were you working so hard on?'

'Oh, just something,' she said, gathering her wits and closing the notebooks. She did not wish to reveal to him that she had committed the pretentious act of writing an opera.

'It looks quite substantial to me,' he said. 'Clearly something very tiring.'

'I've just had some rather late nights.'

That was a slight understatement. She had been up until the small hours every night of the last week, working on the score. There had been such a tide of music in her that she could not stop, painful and exhausting though the struggle of it was. But the growing pages of orchestrated score were the carrot which she dangled in front of her each time she sat down again to work. She had sat down in the library that afternoon with the same intention, but instcad she had fallen asleep. She felt extremely annoyed with herself.

'I ought to get home,' she said, stuffing her papers into the music case. She stood up and realized her knees were shaking. She swayed for a moment, and grabbed the table edge.

'Miss Adam, I think you'll faint if you're not careful,' said Dr Stewart. He was supporting her now, and although she might wish to break free of him, she knew she had not the strength to do it. 'Sit down again,' he said, easing her like an invalid back into her chair. 'I'll fetch you some brandy – or tea? Perhaps that would be more the thing. The servitor's wife usually keeps a pot brewing. I shall be back in a moment.'

She sat alone, feeling useless. Of all the people who had to find her it would have to be Stewart! She would not have minded Bradley even seeing her at this moment of quintessential feminine weakness. She could have taken his straightforward scorn about women and brain work, but Dr Stewart's kindness she did not want. She did not wish above all to be obliged to him, but it seemed as though she would have to be.

She wondered if she had caught 'flu. It was that time of year, after all, and her head was pounding and her throat was dry. It would be maddening if she had caught it, when she was so near to finishing the opera.

Dr Stewart returned after a few minutes, carrying a tray of tea. He sat down beside her and poured out.

'Sugar I think,' he said, reaching for the bowl.

'I don't take sugar,' she protested.

'I think you should. You need energy. You see, I know what it is to do that sort of work – not study, but real work, creative work. One needs a little extra something. My vice when I'm composing is honey.'

She could not help laughing at the image this presented. Dr Stewart dipping into a honey pot seemed unimaginable. She wondered whether he used a spoon or simply his fingers.

'That's better,' he said, handing her the tea. 'Drink that now. You see, I do understand.'

'Do you?' she asked, feeling perhaps he might, but unwilling to admit it.

'Yes. It's the fellowship of artists. No one else understands us because they don't know, they cannot know, what it is to do such work.' She found herself nodding and then was annoyed that she had, for he smiled significantly and said, 'That is why I wish you would overcome your reluctance about me, Miss Adam, so that we can be friends. I can help you more than you can possibly imagine.'

She sipped her tea and wished quietly that she were not there, but safely back at Royal Circus. His earnestness was unsettling, an additional burden to carry with her exhaustion. Why could this man never behave normally?

'It isn't fair to press you now,' he said, as if reading her mind. 'I don't think you can be well.' He put out his hand to test the temperature of her forehead, from which she instinctively recoiled. But he persisted, saying, 'Trust me,' in a manner that struck her as most untrustworthy. 'Ah, as I thought. You're blazing hot.'

'Then I'd better go home,' she said, putting down her tea-cup and girding herself for the effort of it. 'Hadn't I?' She struggled up from her chair again.

'I'll take you,' he said, rising also.

'No,' she said. 'No, I'm quite able to walk back.'

'I insist. We'll take a cab, in fact.'

'That isn't necessary,' she said. 'I shall be quite all

right.' In fact she was not at all sure that she would be, but she was prepared, if necessary, to go on hands and knees back to Royal Circus rather than suffocate in a cab with Dr Stewart in this present solicitous mood.

'I'm not prepared to let you risk that,' he said, and put a ponderous hand on her forearm. She tried to flick it off, but he held fast, almost gripping it. Nausea rose in her stomach.

'My poor little girl,' he said. 'You shouldn't be so fierce and proud. Why won't you let me help you?' and he stretched out and put his other hand on her shoulder.

'Because . . .' She wished she could move, she wished she could at least wrest herself out of his control, but she seemed fixed there, not by the strength of his holding her, that pressure was slight enough, but by her own fear, that of an animal gone rigid in the sight of the hunter's lantern. She could not even manage to say more than that pathetic 'because'.

'Because there are no good reasons,' he said. 'You know that, Christina, you're just afraid to admit it. No good reasons at all. You feel exactly as I do, in your heart, I know it. I can see that in your pretty eyes, that you too believe there could be something quite magnificent between us.'

'Such as taking advantage of me in an empty library?' She found her voice and her strength at the same time. She pushed him away. 'Yes, that would be magnificent!'

'Yes it would!' he shouted, and grabbed her back, this time with real force so that she was locked there with him breathing hard on her face. 'And you know it, don't you? Don't you?'

He did not let her answer but began to kiss her, cramming his mouth over hers, grinding his face against her, so that the hair of his beard and moustache felt like wire wool scrubbing at a stain. She struggled desperately but he had her fixed there, entirely.

'You like that don't you?' he whispered. 'Come on, admit it.'

'No!' she shouted and managed to break free, but it was only for a moment. She had backed away from him a single pace before he had grabbed her again. Now he shook her violently and said, 'I'll prove it. I'll make you beg for me. I'll have you and then you'll see!'

'I'm damned if you will,' she screamed, fighting him as best she could. But he was strong, horribly strong, and she found she was being forced towards the floor. Her legs had no resistance, and before she knew how she was lying there, pinned down by him on the dusty parquet floor. She began to cry out, but his hand clapped over her mouth. He sat down on her stomach, so that she could not roll away to freedom. She could hardly breathe with his hand covering both her face and nose.

'There, that's better,' he said. 'Now, my dearest, don't be afraid of me. The first time is always a little painful, but you'll get to enjoy it, I promise you.'

She turned her head to look away, but he forced it back so she must look as he fumbled open his flies with his other hand. She closed her eyes tightly, and heard him laugh at it. She tried to find some strategy for dealing with it, but she could not think how she could get loose. She tried kicking and flailing with her legs, but he only moved further down to sit on them. But that at least released her arms. She tried to push him off her, to hit him, to do something at least to free herself, but he shouted, 'Keep still!' at her and suddenly threw the whole length and weight of his body on top of her. His face was pressed against hers again. 'I could kill you know,' he said. 'It wouldn't be difficult. Remember that and do as you're told!'

I might as well die, she thought, screwing up her face, longing for oblivion. Death seemed simple and welcoming compared to this. She felt she must die, for there seemed no air left in her lungs, that the weight of his chest on hers had knocked it all out. She knew her danger but could not think clearly enough how to avoid it. She felt utterly out of control, as if he had invaded her mind already, a worse thing by far than his threatened invasion of her body. He had squashed her spirit and she was now only this dreadful, supine lump under him which could do nothing, which could not fight his attack and which would be forced to submit to this appalling thing.

'I will have you,' he said. 'I will. You can't do anything about it.'

She felt him pulling roughly at her skirts, felt him jerk up her leg and fumble with the cloth of her drawers. Suddenly there was a tearing of cotton and she felt his fingers on her thigh.

'No, you shan't!' she shrieked out, and began to struggle again with all the strength she had. That touch, that horrid groping of fingers, found her resistance. She had to fight again – it was as if her body had only now fully realized the threat to it. It was like the smell of smoke in a burning house. She fought and fought, for ever it seemed, but it angered and distracted him and he began to slap her about the face, with bruising thoroughness. He half knelt to do it, and at last she saw an opportunity. Her legs were free and she could kick. She managed to knock him in the groin, with all the force that her booted foot could muster. He fell back, yelping, and she was free. As quickly as she could, she struggled to her feet and ran.

She lay rigid in the darkness, desperate for sleep, but her body would not permit it. Her body insisted on vigilance, like some soldier on the battlements convinced that the enemy would try again to attack. She was alert to every sound, construing something dangerous in every innocent creak of the building. She could not rid herself of the idea that he was still pursuing her. As she had run down the hill to Royal Circus she had not even dared look back, in case she lost the advantage of time, sure that he followed close on her heels to finish what he had determinedly begun. She had got inside and run straight upstairs and locked the door of her room. Only then had she felt slightly safe.

But now, in bed, in the darkness, she felt like a child, tormented by imaginary monsters. She knew it was irrational now to be afraid, but she was. Images of axes hacking down her door filled her mind, and she wished she had not bothered to undress and that she did not lie defencelessly under the covers in only her nightdress. Yet she had felt she had to get out of her clothes. She had felt so tainted, so filthy, as if his hands had been covered in excrement, that she had struggled out of them, and scrubbed painfully over herself with a damp towel. The white neatness of the bed seemed like a sanctuary, and she had hoped for oblivion between the smooth sheets.

Yet she hardly needed to fear his coming. He was still there with her, a stench on her fingers, ineradicable, like wild garlic. She could remember it all too vividly, as if she were reliving the moment. She felt his weight still pressing down on her and the terrible choking fear of it, like being buried under a cartload of muck, muck that was crawling with gross, writhing things. She sat up sharply, trying to force back the tide of nausea that rose inside her. She felt the sweat flashing over her body and her head throbbing until it might explode. Oh that it might! she prayed, and I could know nothing! Nothing!

I'd kill him. If I could, I would kill him. The thought came into her mind, like a blazing torch, and kindled her anger. She refused to feel afraid. To be afraid was to let him succeed and she would never do that. She got out of bed and lit the gas. She began to pace about the room, feeling the surge of fury take control of her. There was a tremendous relief in that. She was sure now she was not broken. She had nothing to feel ashamed about. The fault was his entirely and she would make him pay for it. She rose higher and higher on a private wave of coloratura righteousness. If there was any justice in life he should pay for it.

She stopped short. If there was any justice in life, this would not have happened. Indeed, who would believe her that it had happened? Dr Stewart's reputation was unassailable, like the steep, white, snowy face of a mountain. She pictured herself explaining to Dr Bradley, or even to the Principal, what he had done, and she saw that they would look with blank incomprehension at her. How could this young woman possibly be telling the truth about the charming, well-educated, companionable Dr Stewart, the ornament of the Caledonian Academy? They would call her hysterical and wonder why they had ever consented to admit women. There was, she saw, in a plunging spiral of despair, no hope of his being disgraced, no hope of his feeling as she had felt, shamed and dirty for what he had done.

There was only one possible revenge – through her music. She would have to prove herself better than him. She would have to succeed on a level that he had not. She would have to work until she was remembered, when he was forgotten. And she would have to do it alone, learning for herself how to do things, just as she had always done. Working on *Everyman* had taught her more than any class offered by the Academy.

Everyman . . . She thought at once of the score, almost complete now, in her music case that was lying in the library at the Academy. She would have to go back and get it, and she was terrified again. She did not want ever to set foot in the place, or ever to tangle with him again, but she would have to go back, like a mother going back into a burning building to fetch out her child from danger. For danger there was, she had a sick certainty of it. She remembered how interested he had been in her manuscript, peering over her shoulder to look at it. She hoped to God he had forgotten it was there.

She sat down on the bed, breathing hard, trying to steady herself. She would have liked to have gone there at once to retrieve it, but the building would be locked by now, and she was sure it would not be in the library. Stewart would have taken it home with him. It was entirely in character for him to do so. The thought of his looking through it, defiling the pages with his filthy hands, frightened her. If he had no scruples with a defenceless woman, what might he do with her precious opera? Burn it?

For the first time that night, she cried.

23

The Academy looked as it always did: stony and gothic and respectable. The bicycles outside were neatly tethered in their racks, and as she went in to the students' entrance, one of the daily maids was polishing the brass door handles. She remembered the ecstasy with which she had gone in on her first day, accompanied by an equally excited Miranda. What hopes they had had then! The place had seemed sacred almost, containing the mystical keys to something higher and more mysterious than they could possibly unlock alone. Five months later and it took all the courage she had in the world to march through those doors with her usual daily confidence.

She went first to the servitor's room, determined that her music case would be there, handed in by the diligent librarian Mr Malcolm. But he shook his head. No, there was nothing. Soothing her wildly flapping nerves, she told herself sternly then it would still be in the library, lying just where she had left it. All her fears about burning and destruction were simply bogies of the night. Dr Stewart had probably gone straight home without noticing it.

'Ah, Miss Adam,' said Mr Malcolm, greeting her cheerfully as she went into the library. She sighed – he must have it, tucked behind the desk.

'Have you got it?' she blurted out.

'The Mahler score, yes,' said Mr Malcolm. 'Mr Reid brought it back this morning.'

'Oh, that,' she said lamely, remembering how she had

ordered the score a few weeks ago. 'Thank you. I was looking for my music case actually. I left it here last night, I think . . .'

'Is this it?' he said, reaching down and bringing it out.

'Oh yes, thank you, it is.' She took it gratefully, and then realized it felt oddly light. She flipped it open and looked inside. There was no score. Just her class notebooks and a harmony book. 'Nothing's fallen out?' she asked, as brightly as she could.

'No, it was just lying like that on the table over there. If there was anything else, I would have noticed, I promise.'

'Yes, of course,' she said. 'Thank you.'

She turned quickly and bit her lip to stop herself screaming out with agonized rage. He had stolen it, just as she had feared! Was there no end to this man's wish to hurt her? What had she done to unleash this demon on her?

She hurled herself in the direction of his room. She was determined to have it back, no matter what it might cost her. Even if she had to beg him, she would get it back. It was too important a thing to her, to let fear or pride get in the way. *Everyman* was all that mattered in that moment, and she would get it back.

She was at his door now, and rapped on it, without even taking a minute to gather her courage. She did not need to. The hot white coals of anger were driving her now.

There was no answer, no 'Enter' shouted out airily, and she realized he was not there. Well, it was a risk, but she would take it. She needed to take it. There was a good chance she would find *Everyman* there somewhere.

She found her hands were shaking though, as she rifled through the piles of paper on the desk and on the piano. It was sickening to be reduced to such behaviour. She had to swallow hard as she pulled open the first drawer of the desk. As she looked in, she heard the door open, and froze where she was, wondering if she might vomit straight into the drawer in sheer terror.

'Aahha . . . Well, well, what a surprise!' he said.

His voice affected her physically, it seemed to strike like a cut from a whip across her back. But she had to hold on to her courage. It was all she had left. She straightened quickly and turned.

'Where is it?' she demanded, with all the authority she could manage.

'Where is what?'

'You know quite well – where is it?' she asked again.

'My dear, I think you may be a little confused. Certainly you must be. I didn't think nice girls went through other people's papers. It's not good manners, you know.'

'Where is it?' She shouted this time.

'I have no idea what you are talking about,' he said. 'This is rather distressing to find you like this. I'm expecting a visit from the Principal in a moment and I shall feel it's my duty to explain I found one of the students breaking into my desk. A serious thing, wouldn't you say?'

'If you tell him, I shall tell him about last night,' she said.

'Oh, and do you think he'd believe you?' he said. 'Besides, you know I've taken a little insurance against your blabbing, Miss Adam. A small folio of musical manuscript, you understand?' He strolled over to the piano and began to pick out the theme from the overture. 'A fanciful conceit, the whole affair. It would be best put on the fire, but I find it useful to keep it, in case . . .'

'I will tell Sir Henry,' she said.

'Will you? Well, I shall burn it then. And don't think you'll find it here. I've put it somewhere quite safe.'

'How dare you steal it! How dare you!' she exclaimed. 'You are the most despicable, evil person I have ever . . .'

'I didn't steal it,' he said. 'I protest at that. I simply

found it. You were careless enough to leave it lying there, weren't you? You are a very careless person altogether. You put yourself in dangerous situations. Like this, for example.'

'Careless?' she said, incredulous. 'Careless?'

'Yes, I shall have to tell Sir Henry about this. A very serious offence. You might be expelled for all I know. That would end your career, pretty promptly.'

'Why do you hate me so?' she exploded. 'What have I ever done to you? Why? Tell me that?'

'You tempted me,' he said simply. 'You were provocative.'

'I was nothing of the sort. You know that. You simply loathe me for twisted reasons of your own. I am innocent of all this. You have driven me into your filthy corner and made me stink with your own bad deeds. Well, I shan't let you. I shan't let you get away with this. You deserve to be ruined for this, because that's what you tried to do to me. God, if there's any justice in this world, then I shall bring it down on you, if I do nothing else! What you did to me last night, what you tried . . .' She lost the use of words, as he stood there, his arms folded, his expression one of indifference. She could not restrain herself any longer. Curses were not enough. She struck him hard across the face, and then again, even though it hurt her own hand to do it. She saw his face flash livid with anger suddenly, and brought across another quick blow, delighted and reckless at the satisfaction this brought her.

Then she realized that the door had opened, and they had a witness, none other than Sir Henry Mackenzie.

'Ah,' whispered Dr Stewart. 'Here's justice, miss!' He stepped away from her and coughed, as if he were about to make some grave speech. 'I'm afraid, Principal, I've to inform you of a serious breach of college discipline.'

In retrospect, it seemed extraordinary to her how easily she let the thing slip away from her, that thing which she had once desired above everything: the chance to study at the Academy. The appearance of Sir Henry numbed the feeling out of her. She stood and let Dr Stewart slander her and watched as the Principal's expression set itself in an even grimmer mask of disapproval. She felt paralysed and powerless. The heat of her anger had been replaced by cold, sick fear.

'Is this true?' he asked, when Dr Stewart charged her with rifling through his desk, and she said 'Yes' in a thin, timid, girlish way which she found disgusting.

'And I saw you hit Dr Stewart with my own eyes,' he went on. 'Can you offer any explanation for that, Miss Adam?'

She hesitated for a moment and then said meekly, 'No.' In her mind she could see Dr Stewart dropping page after page of *Everyman* into the fire.

'None?'

'None,' she affirmed.

Sir Henry shook his head, stroked his whiskers and there was a long, ponderous pause, in which it seemed to Chris that the silence shook with mocking laughter.

'Miss Adam,' said Sir Henry, 'you realize, I trust, how difficult it will be for me to let you continue as a student here. I shall be forced to institute disciplinary proceedings to remove you, unless, of course, you are willing to leave of your own accord. That would be a far preferable state of affairs, I think.'

'Yes, yes,' said Dr Stewart. 'If you were to do that, this unfortunate business need go no further.'

She looked from one man to the other, wishing she could find some reserve of strength to protest that she would not go on such terms, that she would fight any disciplinary board tooth and nail to vindicate herself, that she would clear her name and blacken his! But she could not find the strength. She felt exhausted already, and had no stomach for a fight which she stood only to lose. She felt such a humiliation might destroy her altogether. She knew she had no real choice in the matter.

'I think you may be unsuited to higher studies,' said Sir Henry. 'That you might be happier at home.' It was as if he were squashing a large silk cushion into her face, determined that she should choke to death on domesticity. She knew how unbearable it would be to return to the Manse, but really, what else could she do?

'Very well,' she managed to say, and made for the door, feeling the harshness of their eyes upon her.

'Unfortunate girl,' she heard Sir Henry mutter, when the door was not yet shut. 'Hysterical, I suppose?'

She stood in the passageway, clenching and unclenching her fists, whipping up all her anger to keep her from despair. She would not break now. She was determined not to. If she did, he would have won another victory over her. No, he had had his pound of flesh from her. She would not give him any more satisfaction than that. She would still get *Everyman* back. If she could do that, she would at least have salvaged something.

She was surprised at her own quick deviousness as a plan formed in her mind. She went to the servitor's room and spent a few minutes consulting the post-office directory to discover that Dr Stewart lived in Ann Street.

The house had the same elegant air as his office. A pretty housemaid opened the door to her and Chris wondered if he had persecuted her as well.

'Is Mrs Stewart at home?'

'Whom shall I say is calling?'

'Miss Adam, one of Dr Stewart's students. I've come to fetch some papers for him.' It had seemed plausible enough when she had rehearsed it in her mind, but saying it she was sure it had the suspicious timbre of a lie. Perhaps Dr Stewart never sent anyone on such errands and Mrs Stewart would be instantly suspicious. She fretted on this as she waited in the hall, and on the vast risk she had taken in going there. Dr Stewart could come back to his house at any moment, just as he had come back to his office. He probably would. She was convinced now that he had some supernatural knowledge of her actions. She wondered if she ought to bolt, but Mrs Stewart appeared.

She was as lovely as her picture – a slender, willowy woman, dressed in soft, very feminine clothes. There was not a ruffle crushed, or a hair out of place. She seemed highly decorative, like a fragile ornament, that did nothing of any use.

'Papers, Miss Adam?' she asked. 'Well, it isn't like my husband to forget things, but we all do have our moments, don't we?' she added, as if she were always forgetting things. 'I think they should be in here,' she went on, opening a door. 'Though I don't know for sure. I'm not really allowed in here – it's his growlery, you see.'

She went in diffidently, and Chris followed.

'You see,' said Mrs Stewart, gesturing about her, 'lots of papers! Now, what precisely are we looking for?'

'A score,' said Chris. 'An opera – hand-written still.'

'In my husband's hand?' said Mrs Stewart, looking on top of the piano.

'No, no, it's mine. Something I've been writing.'

'You're writing an opera? Goodness – how clever you must be,' said Mrs Stewart. 'I wish I could do such things.'

'I'm sure you can,' said Chris

'Oh, I don't think so,' said Mrs Stewart. 'I'm very silly. My poor husband – he's so used to clever people. Is he helping you with it, then?'

'Helping . . .' Chris could not find an answer for that but Mrs Stewart was opening the piano stool and she glimpsed *Everyman* lying inside. 'Ah, there it is,' she said.

'Really?' said Mrs Stewart. 'What a funny place for him to put it. Here you are.' She handed the score to Chris, who at once held it to her, like a baby at her breast. 'But he's been working so hard lately, I expect he's a little distracted,' she went on. 'Do you know, he didn't get back until ten last night?'

The urge to speak then was overpowering. Chris swallowed back the truth though, for what good could come of it? This poor sweet creature did not deserve to be deceived, but on the other hand, could she bear the truth? Might she not shatter into a hundred pieces to find that the man she adored was a monster? Or perhaps she already knew, although she would never admit it, even to herself. Perhaps she had suffered far more from him than Chris could ever imagine.

'That's clearly terribly precious to you,' observed Mrs Stewart.

'Yes, it is rather,' admitted Chris.

'Stay and have some tea, won't you? I usually have a cup just now,' said Mrs Stewart.

'I should like to,' said Chris, 'but I'm expected back.'

'Of course you are,' she smiled. 'Another time perhaps. I so rarely meet new people, you know, though I'm always suggesting to my husband he brings his students home. I'm quite surprised he sent you today – though I'm glad he did. You must be quite a favourite with him, I think, Miss Adam. You will call again, won't you?'

They shook hands and her thin little hand struck Chris as horribly cold, as if it needed someone to rub the life back into it Her loneliness seemed almost tangible and Chris wanted to hold her in her arms and offer her a little warmth. Yet that would have been impossible – it would have opened the floodgates of her own misery.

So she walked back to Royal Circus, still clutching *Everyman* to her, the only piece of armour she had left.

24

Angus glanced in at the open door of the dining room and saw that Miranda had turned it into a flower shop. The smell of hot house freesias and lilies, sweet and expensive, filled his nostrils and for a moment he felt dizzy.

'What's up?' he asked. She was fiddling nervously with more flowers at a side table, just as he had often seen his mother playing with them before an important guest. 'I mean, whom are you expecting?'

'Lady Lindsay,' said Miranda.

'Ah, I see . . .' he said, noticing now that, under the burden of flowers, the table was dressed to the nines with china and glass he had not seen before. 'She should be impressed.'

'I hope so,' said Miranda. 'Antonia's been so difficult about this. She didn't see why we couldn't have an ordinary luncheon!'

'I think she was only teasing you,' said Angus. Lunch, on weekdays at Royal Circus, was usually a rather perfunctory, unceremonious meal, available for those who were there and wanted it and generally made up of something plain and nursery-like, such as shepherd's pie or cauliflower cheese. At lunch no one was expected to be sociable – if one was deep in a good book, there was no need to stop reading it.

'I know, but that's not the point, is it? I mean, this is important, really important, and all Antonia can say is she doesn't see the need for fuss. This isn't fuss. This is quite necessary.'

'Yes, quite,' said Angus, repressing the urge to laugh himself. The amount of fuss that Miranda had indulged in was quite extraordinary, in fact – even the ribbons on her dress matched the flowers. 'And everything looks . . . magnificent.'

She smiled broadly, and said, with a little wriggle of her shoulders that shook her flounces, 'Yes, it does, doesn't it?'

'I suppose I should go and lunch somewhere else then,' he said. 'I'd hate to lower the tone.'

'You're welcome to stay,' said Miranda. 'I'm sure you can behave. And if you can get Chris out of her eyrie for me, you'll be my saviour. I've knocked several times, but she's just told me to go away. It's all your wretched opera you know – she's no sense of anything else just now. Go and tell her I need her, will you? She'll listen to you.'

It was pleasant to have a good excuse to go and search her out. So often he found himself filled with diffidence about her, holding back out of fear. Fear of what exactly, he was not sure, but fear there was, always quietly there, as if to take their friendship any further might be very dangerous. He had always imagined himself reckless, but with Chris he felt he behaved unnaturally, when he wanted above all else to be natural and let himself go, to show her his feelings, to make her understand that she affected him so deeply. Why could he not do it?

He tapped on her door, and heard her say, 'Yes?' Only a single word, but it struck a sharp note, full of fear and suspicion.

'It's me,' he said. 'Are you all right?'

There was a long pause, and then she said, 'Come in.'

He pushed open the door and went in. The room struck him as cold and driech, as if the weather in the street had come in through an open window. There was no fire lit, or any lamp, and Chris herself sat in the middle of the room, on the floor, her knees drawn up under her chin, her arms clasped around her legs. She smiled up at him wanly, and said, 'I'm glad it's you.'

'What's wrong?' he said, going at once and crouching beside her. Her saw her eyes were red with crying. 'What's happened?'

She took a deep gulp and looked away from him.

'Chris, what's going on?' he said, and put his hand on to her shoulder. 'What has happened?'

She drew up her hands to cover her mouth and sighed into them.

'I don't know where to start,' she said, in a dry thin voice. 'I mean, I've just ruined everything . . . and . . .' She looked at him intently, as if he were a priest she was confessing to. 'I've been so stupid!'

She looked away from him again.

'I'm sure you haven't,' he said.

'Haven't I?' she said. 'I wasn't sensible about it. If I'd been sensible about it I would have . . . but I was so angry I had to do something and now . . .' She broke down now and began to sob. Angus put his arms round her and she seemed to fall against him, clinging to him, her arms like briars.

'What's happened?'

'I don't want to tell you,' she said. 'I don't want anyone to know – it's too . . .'

'You must tell me,' he said. 'I can't bear to see you like this. I want to help you. Tell me.'

She let go of him, and straightened herself a little, wiping her eyes with the handkerchief he offered.

'It's sickening,' she said.

'Tell me.'

'Remember Dr Stewart?' she said.

'How could I forget?'

'Last night,' she said, taking a deep breath, 'he tried to

rape me.' The words were indistinct but Angus felt as if a hot poker had been laid on the flesh of his stomach.

'What?' he said, and then more forcefully, 'What?'

'You do believe me, don't you?' she said, earnestly. 'You do?'

'Of course I do. I . . .' He broke off. He could find no words, feeling a vile mixture of anger and nausea brewing inside him. He looked at her sitting there, so pale, so red-eyed, so consumed with misery that he thought he might shout out with the pain of it. 'How dare he?'

'God knows!' she exclaimed, with sudden sharpness. 'But he did!'

'I'll get him for this,' he said. 'I promise you I will. I'll do him such harm that . . .'

'And what would be the point of that?' she cut in fiercely. 'He'd only destroy you as well. The man's evil, Angus, I'm telling you. I'm better cutting my losses.'

'You can't just let this thing go. You'll have to tell the police.'

'Oh God no!' she said. 'They'd never believe me. It's his word against mine, and who do you think they'd believe?'

'I believe you. I'm an ordinary man, I believe you.'

'You're not ordinary, Angus,' she said. 'You're not like other men. You don't have their notions about things, about how women should be. You'd believe me, yes, but would your father – would mine, for that matter?'

'I won't let this drop, Chris. This is why we have courts and judges.'

'It's too late,' she said. 'Any chance I had, I've ruined.'

'How?'

'He stole *Everyman*. Well, he didn't steal it so much as appropriated it. I left it last night, in the library. I had to run to get away, and when I went back this morning to get it, it had gone. I knew he'd taken it. So I went to his office to get it back. He wasn't there at first, so I had a look around, like the idiot I was, and in he comes, to find me looking through his desk. Can you imagine how that would sound in court?'

'I would have done exactly the same,' he said.

'You wouldn't have been so stupid as to get caught,' she said, bitterly. 'Well, he guessed what I was looking for and he told me he'd got it somewhere safe, as insurance, and that if I told, he'd burn it.'

'What . . .'

'He's evil,' said Chris. 'And so I lost my temper. I tried, but I couldn't hold out any longer. That work, it's like a bairn to me, Angus, I couldn't bear the thought of him doing something to it. I didn't care what he did to me. I mean, that doesn't matter, but the work does. That's my soul and he was threatening to do who knows what to it, if I said anything. So I hit him. I hit him three times actually, but the Principal walked in. God, you should have seen Stewart's face – he looked so damned pleased!' She growled then and he saw her bite at her knuckles. 'So I was sunk, and I didn't put up a word to defend myself. I was told to go, or they'd publicly humiliate me, so, like the coward I am, I went, like a meek little lamb! It was pathetic! But I did get *Everyman* back, you'll be pleased to hear,' she added with a touch of defiance.

'How?'

'I went to Stewart's house and told his wife that I was fetching some papers for him. It was ridiculously easy, actually. If only I'd done that in the first place I might have a place at the Academy still.'

He leant back on his heels, letting the details of her narrative sink in.

'Do you know, I think you're the most remarkable person I've ever met,' he said.

'I don't feel very remarkable,' she said.

'But you are. To manage to do that, after all you'd been through. You're a lion, woman!'

'I was desperate,' she said. 'I needed to salvage something. What if we'd lost it? What if he had burnt it? I shouldn't be able to cope then. At least I've something left. Oh but, what will I tell people?' she appealed to him, suddenly. 'How will I look them in the face when I go home? That's what I can't bear. You've no idea how I had to fight to get this far, what I had to give up, and the thought of going back with my tail between my legs is just too horrible to contemplate.'

'Then fight Stewart. I'm sure you're capable of it. Get yourself justice.'

She shook her head. 'And exhaust myself on a battle that isn't worth fighting, that I can't possibly win?'

'I know it seems like that, but I'm sure you could. I'd help you.'

'But is there any point? What would it gain me? I don't want a crusade, Angus. If I wanted a crusade I'd join up with Mrs Pankhurst, wouldn't I? All I want is the chance to write my music, to work. Fighting Stewart would be a distraction from that. It would be giving in to him. He'd have won because I'd be silenced. Do you understand that?'

'Yes, I think so, though I hate the thought of it – this cloud over your name. It's so unjust that you are suffering when he should be.'

'Real life isn't just,' she said, getting up. 'That's something I shall learn.' She stretched and looked about her. 'At least *Everyman* will be finished. It may take longer though. My mother likes to load me with domestic duties.'

'So you'll go home then?' he asked, clambering to his feet also.

'What choice do I have? The money my aunt gives me is for studying. She expects me to do brilliantly – not come back a failure, after only two terms. I can't cheat her of her investment. I couldn't accept any more from her.'

'You don't have to go home, I suppose. If you got some sort of job . . .'

'Such as? I wasn't sensible enough to learn typewriting. All I'm good for is composition or plain sewing. Oh, and I can cook. You see, I'm quite hopeless. I built myself a dream, and now . . .' Suddenly she laughed, not comfortably but with a touch of hysteria. 'Have you seen Miranda today?'

'Yes, she's turned the dining room into a bower of flowers to impress that fellow's mother. Why do you ask?'

'Well, it's all so ironic really. I suspect they're going to announce their engagement today.'

'It looks like that sort of thing. There was a distinctly bridal air about her.'

'Oh yes. She's been very sensible,' said Chris with a sort of bitter calm. 'That's what my mother would say. And she'll throw that at me, time and time again, that I was a fool to turn him down.'

Angus stared at her, struggling to understand.

'You mean that Lindsay asked you . . . ?' he began.

'To marry him? Yes,' she cut in. 'Just think of it, I could have been a baronet's wife. It was very tempting but I resisted for the sake of my brilliant future. Very brilliant, eh?'

'Did you love him then?' he found he must ask, feeling something very cold creeping over him.

'Oh no, no, I didn't,' she said, and he felt an exquisite sense of relief. 'All I was in love with then was the thought of my career. Now people will have a splendid time telling me what an idiot I was, telling me I should have done the sensible thing, the accepted thing, instead of building myself a temple out of my own misguided sense of worth. Well, the temple's fallen down now, hasn't it?'

'No it hasn't,' he said. 'I won't let you talk like this. You are as marvellous as ever, Chris, no matter what people do or say to you. Just remember that.' And he found it easy to put his arms about her and press his lips to hers. 'There,' he said, moving only a tiny distance from her. 'Does that prove it?'

'Oh . . . oh, Angus . . .' she whispered and he saw the tears starting in the corners of her eye.

'Don't cry,' he said, urgently. 'I didn't mean you to cry.'

'I can't help it,' she said, and returned his kiss, so that he felt the warm salt of her tears lick his face, as if they were his own tears.

He felt strong then, and whole, as if someone had put fresh, clean blood into his veins. Her kissing him was a sort of liberation, that she, this marvellous, true creature, could choose him out of all others, made him decisive.

'I can help you, you know,' he said, giddy with the intensity of it. 'We can help each other.'

'How?' she said.

'We'll run away together,' he said, and then laughed. 'How good that sounds – as if we'd need a pair of fast horses and pistols stuck in our belts for that. What I mean is, we could go somewhere together, get away from here, and I could pay for everything. I've plenty of money. It would be sensible really.'

'I couldn't accept money from you,' she said, moving away from him a little.

He grabbed her back.

'Yes you could, and you must. I need you, Chris. I need to help you. It wouldn't be charity for me, it would be necessary. If I didn't help you, I should be destroying myself. You mean that much to me. You've turned me upside down, Chris. You've made me make sense of myself.'

'I don't understand . . .' she said.

'Oh neither do I,' he said. 'But we shouldn't understand the really great mysteries in life, but just accept that they are. Just accept that I love you. You can understand that, I think.'

'You do?'

'Yes, yes, I do.'

'My God . . .' she said, softly, and touched his cheek with her finger. 'Then they're true, all those feelings I've had, they're true. I didn't think it was possible, but it was all so strong, like a fire inside me and . . .' She shook her head and rested her cheek against his. 'I love you too, you see.'

He clung to her then, laughing with joy at her declaration. He lifted her and swung her round.

'Then we'll go away together?' he said, putting her down again.

'It seems like madness,' she said laughing, 'but I'd follow you to the ends of the earth, even if you didn't want me.'

'But I do,' he said, grave again, looking hard into her eyes. 'I want you more than anything,' and he kissed her again.

'Where shall we go then?' she said.

'Somewhere where we'll find you the best teacher you can get. No provincial academies for you any more, Miss Adam, but real musicians with real reputations.'

'Really?' she said.

'Yes, really,' he said. 'Now, who is that fellow you are always talking about – the Frenchman?'

'St Juste?' she said.

'That's the one. Where does he live then? We'll go to him.'

'Paris I suppose. Angus, do you honestly think I could?'

'I don't see why not. You're competent, aren't you?'

'Competent,' she smiled. 'I think I'm more than that.'

'That's the spirit,' he said. 'Then Paris it is!'

Chris washed her face and put on a fresh blouse: a frilly, open-neck, spotted muslin affair that had been a Christmas present from Annie, a blouse that had a touch of flippancy and defiance about it. She examined herself in the looking glass, gazing at her cheeks which had flushed pink with elation at Angus's unexpected declaration. Her skin seemed to understand his words better than her mind did. She felt a little dense, in fact, like a child unable to grasp the solution to an arithmetic problem although the dominie had explained it several times. Angus had solved her problem but with a suggestion that was so audacious it took her breath away. He had told her he loved her and would take her away somewhere she could study all she needed to. It was too wonderful a thing he had said, too much of a miracle for her poor bleeding battered brain to accept in an instant.

Yet, as she dabbed cologne on her wrists, searched for a handkerchief and tidied her hair, she felt the soft white bandages of his words wrap about the slash of gore which lay inside her. He had cleaned the wound with careful hands and now it was safe. She still felt the deep, throbbing, burning pain of it, but there was no longer the fear of it spreading and destroying her. She would heal.

They went downstairs together and into the drawing room which Miranda had made giddy with the scent of hyacinths. Their sweet, pungent smell struck her as unreal, just as everything seemed unreal just then, as if morphine were acting on her brain. In the centre of the room, sitting in a thick wash of sunlight, was Lady Lindsay, spectacular in the dark elegance of her town clothes. With mannered grace she greeted Chris and demanded, with all the peculiar languor of her American accent, that she kiss her. As she bent to touch her cheek with her lips, Chris felt a little like a pilgrim kissing a sacred statue. Lady Lindsay had never been so condescending before.

'It's so charming that you and Miranda should be friends,' she said. 'We never could have guessed!'

Chris's being at Royal Circus clearly gave her status.

She noticed, with amusement, that Guy looked embarrassed.

'May I introduce Mr Bretton to you, Lady Lindsay?' said Chris. Lady Lindsay inclined her head a little, and put out her hand to Angus, who kissed it with a grace that she clearly appreciated.

'The poet?' she said. 'Miranda has been telling me all about you. A poet and a composer . . .' She looked Chris and Angus over carefully. 'Well, Mrs Rosenberg, how bohemian you all are.'

'We do our best,' said Antonia, smiling. 'Shall we go into luncheon then?'

Chris watched Guy offer Miranda his arm, and the closeness with which she leant on him, when she took it, as if she were so frail she would fall without him. She felt a prickle of annoyance at it, at Guy's clear pleasure at it. She saw him look down at Miranda with a sort of idiotic raptness, while she whispered to him about something as if they were taking part in amateur theatricals and playing as best they could the sentimental young lovers. She turned away, a little disgusted by it, and met with a grin from Angus.

'Just before we do,' said Guy, 'I think there's something we ought to tell everyone, isn't there, darling?'

At last she was alone with Angus again. Miranda, Guy and Lady Lindsay had gone on somewhere else, and Antonia declared that after all that she wanted to do nothing but sit quietly and read for the rest of the afternoon. 'No interruptions!' she said. 'I beg you.'

They sat still in the dining room, looking across the table at each other, over the vast bowls of flowers. There was most of a bottle of sweet champagne left for them to drink and half a meringue cake filled with brandied strawberries to eat. Angus cut himself a large slice and settled down with it.

'I bet you're glad that's over,' he said, digging in his fork.

'Rather,' she said, and picked up her glass and studied the bubbles rising to the surface.

'I was thinking,' he said. 'About what I said earlier . . .' He broke off to eat some cake.

'What?' she said, finding the word came out loaded with suspicion. She felt cold suddenly, as if the sun had just been hidden by a cloud. 'You don't regret what you said, do you?'

'No!' he said, his mouth full. 'Of course not. It's just that . . . with all this . . .' he gestured with his fork. 'Well, it made me think.'

'That it isn't such a good idea?' she found herself saying. 'Oh . . .'

'Well to tell you the truth, I hate the idea of the shabbiness of it. Not for myself, but for you. I know what people would say – your family, for instance. It wouldn't matter to me, but I don't like the idea of your being made to feel . . . Oh dear, I'm not being very clear . . .'

'Do you mean,' she said, carefully, wondering if she could bear the truth of what he seemed to be suggesting, 'that we shouldn't go, that we shouldn't be together? Oh for heaven's sake, Angus, no, don't say that . . . I don't think I could stand it.' She stretched her hands out to him across the table, but it was too wide to reach him. She felt an impossible gulf between them opening up. 'I don't care what people think. I really don't.'

'But I do,' he said. 'Despite myself I do. I don't want people sniping at you. You're too damn good for that.'

'I don't care,' she said, again.

'You don't have to. I mean you wouldn't, not if we did the thing properly.'

She stared at him.

'What do you mean?'

'If we got married. No one would bat an eyelid then. Our families might even like us for it.'

'Married . . .' she said. 'You want me to marry you?'

'Is it such a repulsive idea?' he said, getting up and running round the table to her. 'I didn't mean it to be . . .'

'No, no,' she said, and wished there were not tears springing in her eyes. It felt so weak, and yet she could not help it. 'No, it's quite wonderful.' He was squatting beside her now, and had taken her hands. 'Of course I'll marry you. Of course!'

Part Two
Paris, March 1913

[illegible]

[illegible]

[illegible] deep after [illegible]

champagne [illegible] same [illegible]

[illegible] experience [illegible]

[illegible] They had been travelling [illegible] the two nights since the wedding.

It seemed [illegible] now how [illegible] ring had been managed [illegible] the [illegible] had arranged everything. He [illegible] even [illegible] his parents. He had felt [illegible] tell them of his [illegible] and had

25

'This bag is full of rice!' said Chris, shaking out a nightdress so that a shower of rice clattered on to the wooden floor.

'Enough for a rice pudding?' asked Angus.

'You don't come to Paris to eat rice pudding,' she said, laughing.

'I like rice pudding,' he said.

'Is that a husbandly request then?' she smiled. 'Will you expect me to make it for you once or twice a week?'

'Oh, at least three times.'

'Well there's enough here for that,' she said, tipping out a slipper. 'May must have been reading your mind rather than playing a silly prank on me.'

Angus found himself looking at the white expanse of her nightdress lying on the bed and at the other tokens of her private life which she had already scattered about the bedroom; tokens which were now part of his own private life. His wife's hairbrushes, his wife's slippers, tucked under the bed, his wife's nightdress lying on their bed. His eyes fell back on it, taking in every detail, every soft ruffle and lace edge of it. He would see her in it that evening when they would share the bed for the first time. They had been travelling for the two nights since the wedding.

It seemed extraordinary now how simply the thing had been managed. In the space of a month they had arranged everything. He had even mended the rift with his parents. He had felt he must tell them of his plans and had expected them to be angry at it. To his surprise they had been delighted, taking it as a proof of his rightness at heart. His mother had even cried, and when she had met Chris her joy had been unbounded to find her a nice solid girl from a nice solid family. A daughter of the Manse herself, she could not help but approve his choice. Dr Bretton had been less effusive but on the morning of the wedding, just as they were about to leave for Royal Circus, he had pressed a folded cheque into his hand and told him gruffly that he had better make something decent of himself in Paris so as not to let Christina down. And then, in the Rosenbergs' drawing room, in front of only a handful of people, ten minutes of quiet words, mostly uttered by Mr Adam who officiated, had been enough to accomplish the thing. Their separate lives were over and the proper common life would now begin, in this little flat in Paris.

His own luggage had not been opened and he felt too dazed to begin unpacking it. Chris had wanted to wash and change after the journey and he supposed he should too. She sat down on the bed and began to unlace her shoes. There was a small pile of underwear beside her, which she was presumably about to change into. He suddenly felt like an intruder, and hastily sloughed off his jacket and went into the bathroom which lay directly off the bedroom.

It was a tiny square room, papered with faded roses and smelling faintly of drains. He pushed open the window and looked down into the courtyard the flat overlooked. Their flat, comprising a bedroom, a kitchen, a bathroom, a living room and a dining room was wedged into the steep mansard roof of one of the wings of the Hôtel Chambertin in the rue du Bac. The view, therefore, was a pretty one, of the façade of the main house occupied by the Comte and Comtesse Chambertin, with tall casement windows and white painted balconies. On steps leading to the front door were a pair of bay trees, neatly cropped into globes, with bright ribbons tied about their trunks, fluttering in the stiff spring breeze.

There was a tentative tap on the door behind him.

'Angus?' she said. 'I wondered, are there any towels?'

He looked around him.

'No,' he said.

'My mother was right,' she said. 'May I come in?'

That she asked, pleased him. If she felt diffident and awkward then he could also.

'Yes, of course.'

'Here,' she said, holding out a pile of white linen. 'Mother made me put them near the top. I don't think she believes that the French have such things.' She put them down on the window sill and stopped herself to admire the view.

'Do you like it then?' he asked, turning on the tap, but no water came out.

'It's wonderful,' she said. 'Even if the plumbing isn't . . .' The tap began to clank and creak and a dribble of water at last appeared.

'What can you expect for two hundred francs a month in the rue du Bac?' said Angus. 'A good address but no running water.'

As if responding to his words the tap suddenly gushed vigorously and sprayed water out across his waistcoat front. They both laughed and Chris bent down and splashed her face in the water.

'That's better,' she said, rubbing her face. 'I felt so grubby.'

She straightened up, her face still beaded with water, and smiled at him. It was easy for him to kiss her and her face felt cool and fresh. All his little fears melted away. It would be all right.

'You need to shave,' she said, with a giggle when he released her. He rubbed his chin and agreed.

He followed her back into the bedroom and hunted out his shaving kit. As he did so, he noticed she was undoing her blouse. She had turned away from him a little to do it, naturally modest, he supposed, but seeing him watching, she turned to face him properly. He tried to think what he should feel at the sight of her undressing, at the sight of her thin chemise and bare, pale arms. Should he feel excited? Was that awful nervousness, that had been continually jumping up inside him, excitement, was it actually desire for her, for her body?

She stood holding her discarded blouse and gave him a questioning look.

'Do you want . . .' she began. 'I mean now . . .?'

He could not speak, knowing perfectly well what was expected of him. How could he feel so much for her and yet feel so little when she stood offering herself to him? It ought to have been a magnificent moment when he stepped forward and took her in his arms again, filled with animal hunger, filled with proper passion. But he did not. Instead he stood there gripping at his shaving kit.

'Do you know, I'm awfully hungry,' he found himself saying. 'Really starving . . .'

'Well let's go and have lunch then,' she said, quickly, with a touch of embarrassment as if she had made an improper suggestion which he had been obliged to squash. He felt ashamed of making her feel so, when she had been only acting out of instinct. After all, what was more natural than to expect him to want to make love to her at the first opportunity they had?

He dashed back into the bathroom and shaved himself, with shaking hands. He was determined though that, after a good lunch and a fair amount of wine, he would feel right about it, that he could manage it. They had had a long journey, after all, and he could be excused his nervousness, surely? Later it would be all right.

* * *

They went to eat in a large modern restaurant in the Boulevard St Germain, a place which Angus remembered from a previous trip to Paris. It was vast and very noisy for it was packed with people. The waiters, in long white aprons, dashed about with large trays balanced on raised hands, like circus acrobats. The air was full of cigarette smoke and all the people there seemed colourful, as people in Edinburgh never were. The scene was almost oriental for the women were wearing the bold, rich colours of the moment, and were so highly decorated with contrasting fringes and scarves and feathers that they appeared to be in fancy dress. From their table in a corner, Chris could see only the reflections of these women in the large gilt-framed looking glasses that hung everywhere, multiplying and confusing a scene that was already dazzling enough. She rested her chin on her folded hands, while Angus studied the menu, and gazed at the patterns in the glass as if they were coloured versions of the cinematograph. Certainly they seemed as unreal.

'Isn't it funny,' she remarked, 'that we always seem to be eating together?' She meant at significant moments, such as that night in the fish restaurant in Leith, when she had first understood her desire for him. And here they were again, about to eat in a very different sort of place, at another significant moment: the first real day of their marriage.

'That's because food is important,' said Angus. 'Symbolically, as well as physically. We have to eat to live, but it takes on all sorts of other connotations. Meals can be sacraments. It's no coincidence that the mass involves eating. Communion with God through food. Perhaps it's like that with us.'

She found herself smiling, feeling a warmth deep inside her that he had understood her.

'Perhaps we'll come here again in twenty years, and remember today,' she said.

'Why not?' he said. 'And we'll eat the same things. There, we've made a ritual already. So I had better order something good, hadn't I? Have you any preferences?'

'No, you choose,' she said. 'There, what a submissive wife I am.'

'Don't make a habit of it,' he said. 'Please.'

While he gave their order to the waiter, Chris felt the comfortable certainty of having done the right thing. Marrying Angus was not like marrying Guy would have been. For one thing she loved him – and of that she was marvellously sure. She did not think she had ever felt so happy as she did then. It was as if she had lived only half a life before this, before this knowing that he loved her in return. And marriage to him was an adventure. There was no prospect of fifty dreary years at Rankeillor, presiding over the dinner table and the nursery. Who could say what they might do together, or where they might go? Paris, she was sure, was just the beginning of it. Tomorrow, after all, she had an appointment with M. St Juste.

The waiter brought a bottle of wine in an ice bucket and dumped it down on the table with little ceremony, before dashing off to another table.

'Well, I can't stand fussy waiters,' said Angus, pouring out a glass of wine. 'Muscadet. You never find this at home.'

It was dry and cold, a little like drinking from a mountain burn. Chris sipped at hers gently, but Angus swallowed down a glass at once, as if it were water.

'That's better,' he said. 'I needed that. It's been hard work, getting married, wouldn't you say?'

'But fun,' she said. 'Wouldn't you say?'

'Of course,' he said, grabbing her hand and squeezing it. 'I haven't any regrets. I'm just a little edgy. It's missing two nights' sleep, I think. You were lucky – you managed to sleep on that damned train. How did you do it?'

'I couldn't help it. I was so tired.'

'You looked beautiful you know, when you were asleep,' he said, refilling his glass.

'I'm surprised I didn't have my mouth open.'

'No, you didn't,' he said. 'I kept looking at you and thinking – you're mine now, my wife – and I couldn't quite believe it. I don't quite now.'

'Believe it,' she said.

'I will,' he said. 'In time.'

They ate their way happily through the meal that Angus had ordered; through a heap of langoustines (which made a great deal of mess) and a plate of roast lamb, surrounded by garlicky green haricot beans. They drank all the Muscadet, and then a bottle of claret, so that by the time the waiter put a dish of crème caramel in front of her, Chris found her head was swimming pleasantly, and that the images in the mirrors swam also. Yet all the time, as they ate and drank, and laughed so deeply, she felt an itch of excitement growing inside her, something that was acute and focused, that began to drive her. She was thinking, almost constantly, that soon she would be alone with him, and that the final barrier between them would be overturned.

They stood outside the restaurant at last, blinking in the bright spring sunshine. Angus took her hand, and clapped his over it.

'Let's go home,' he said.

The stairs to the flat seemed steeper and more twisted after a bottle of wine, but they climbed them cheerfully, Angus pressing his hand into the small of her back as if he were shoving her up them. His touch seemed amplified to her, as if the nerves beneath her skin had suddenly doubled in quantity.

The bedroom was warm, and stuffy smelling, with the sunlight hanging thickly in the still air. Chris flung herself on to the bed and said, 'Well, now what happens?' She was amused by her own tone of voice, as if she were playing a soubrette.

'Well,' said Angus, who was standing by the window. 'I suppose we ... consummate the thing.' He began to wrestle with his collar and tie.

'What a horrid word that is,' she said, getting up from the bed, adding, 'let me do that,' and she pulled off his tie and threw it across the room.

'Careful,' he said, 'that cost me six bob.'

'Phuhhh...' she said, and could not resist pressing herself against him. The nearness of him was overwhelming. 'Oh Angus ... I want you so much...' she said. She would have thought it might be difficult to say that, but it was easy now. Her desire for him, for the physical him inside her, was ruling everything. She wanted nothing else but to lie with him and give up the last shred of her old life.

'Let's get undressed shall we?' he said, pushing her very slightly away from him.

'Yes,' she said, trying not feel that there was anything of a rebuff in this. She had wanted him to kiss her just then. Still, there would be plenty of that to come. It was just like Angus to want to go straight to the heart of the thing and strip down to necessities.

As she fumbled with her own clothes, she watched him undressing. She had seen him undressed before, of course, wrapped only in a bath towel and dripping with water. Today though, he seemed more inhibited, as if he were hiding himself slightly, for he turned away as he removed his underclothes. She sensed his nervousness suddenly – it was as if she could smell it, a sharp, unpleasant smell of fear.

She went at once and put her arms round him, pressing

her own now naked flesh against his. His back was to her and she felt him stiffen a little where she had expected him to yield.

'Angus,' she said. 'You mustn't be afraid of hurting me. I know you might be. I know it will hurt, but I'm not . . .'

Gently he unprised the arms she had clasped around his chest.

'I'm not afraid of that,' he said.

'Then what? What are you afraid of? I can feel you're afraid.'

Still he did not turn, and she moved round so he must face her. But he did not look at her, but at his feet.

'Angus, what is it?' she said again.

Now he did look at her, or rather looked over her. She felt his eyes run from her face, down across her bare breasts and stomach, at her hips and then at the small triangle of hair on her pelvis. It was the oddest sort of looking, though, with something objective in it, as if she were a corpse lying on the dissecting table. Perhaps that was when he had last seen a naked woman.

Slowly he lifted his hand and touched her left breast. She could not help gasping, for he ran his finger around the already stiff nipple. She threw back her head involuntarily and closed her eyes, wondering how there could be so much pleasure in so small a thing. Then he stopped, and automatically she reached out and tried to catch his hand and draw it back to her breast. He eluded her, folding instead his arms across his chest, gripping his shoulder, holding himself in a desperate, self-comforting embrace. He turned away, and as he did she saw his face contort into a great scowl of pain.

'There's no point,' he said, as if between gritted teeth. 'Get dressed, for God's sake.'

'What do you mean?' said Chris, coming close to him and trying to hold him. But he pushed her away. 'What's the matter? Are you afraid . . . Do you think it's wrong? What? Please, Angus, tell me. If you tell me . . .'

'That'll solve everything? I don't think so.' he said. 'Get dressed. You'll catch cold.'

'I won't,' she said. 'Angus, I want you, don't you understand? I want you to take me. Please . . .'

'I can't,' he said sharply, grabbing his shirt and pulling it on. 'Do you understand that?'

'No, of course I don't! I've no idea what's going on here. You say you love me and yet you can't . . . It isn't wicked, Angus, no matter what they told you when you were little. I had all that told to me, but I can see it's cant. I know what's right, and that's you and me, together.'

'No!' he said. 'It won't work. I can't do it. I thought I could, that I might be able to, but I can't. I look at you' – he paused, shaking his head, looking at her again – 'and I feel, nothing. Absolutely nothing.'

'Nothing?' she said. The word felt like a slap in the face. 'Nothing? How can you feel nothing? You say you love me and yet . . .'

'I do love you,' he cut in. 'That's the worst of it. I have never felt for anyone what I feel for you. And I thought that would change it, that it would change me, that feeling, that thing that's so strong. I thought it would cure me, make me right, but . . . it's the same, just the bloody same. I don't have it in me, Chris, to do it. I can't sleep with you. I can't make you my wife.'

She sat down on the bed, and stared at him. He was standing in the corner, looking like a man on a scaffold, his shoulders bent horribly.

'I really don't understand. If you love me . . . well, it follows. It's natural.'

'I'm not natural,' he said. 'That's it.'

'What do you mean? You're talking in riddles, Angus, and I don't understand.'

'Well how could you?' he barked. 'Normal people don't understand. They can't. It's not something you can understand – for God's sake, I don't even understand it myself! You'll just have to accept it, that's all.'

'And if I can't?' she ventured to ask.

'Then ... then ... Oh I don't know,' he said, and sat down, despairing, on the other side of the bed, so that they were back to back. 'Look, let's sleep now, shall we? We can talk later, when we're less tired.'

'I'm not sure I could sleep,' she said. She felt a terrible tension in herself, as if someone had fixed each joint with iron brackets.

'Well, try to,' he said, and handed her the nightdress that was lying on the bed. It was a new one, chosen especially for the wedding night, a far more frivolous item than she usually wore. She sat with it on her knees, and watched as he blundered about the room looking for his pyjamas. He found them, put them on, and then drew the curtains, jerking them shut. It was as if with that the subject was closed.

She pulled the nightdress over her head, and pushed her arms through the short, lace-edged sleeves, but still sat there, feeling cold and helpless. Angus was turning back the sheets and getting into the bed. It was a small bed. It would be hard to avoid touching each other. She wondered if she could bear to be so close to him and yet know that nothing would come of it.

'Come on,' he said, and patted the pillow beside him.

She grimaced at the gesture. It smacked of seduction. But what else could she do but respond to it? She was tired, her body ached for oblivion. She got into the bed and lay stiffly beside him, staring up at the ceiling.

'I wish I could understand,' she said, softly. 'I feel . . . I feel you don't want me.'

'I do,' he said. 'That's the worst of it.'

She rolled on to her side and stared into his eyes. How

close they were, under the embrace of the smooth, clean sheets. His blue eyes shone out even in the half-light.

'Then why . . . ?' It came out as a plea, and it seemed to speak for every nerve in her body, which was singing with its desire for him.

'If I knew that . . .' he said. 'Oh look, it may happen. It may still happen, some time or other.'

'Do you think?' She snatched at this idea. It was like a bucket of water thrown over the smouldering fire of her disappointment.

'I can't promise anything,' he said. 'But I can try.'

She exhaled, suddenly exhausted with relief. She could wait. She had waited enough already. What difference would a few days, or weeks make?

'Besides,' he went on, 'to be brutally practical, it's almost a good thing. You don't want children do you?'

'No,' she admitted, 'I don't. But Angus . . .' She paused, and then found her courage. 'You do love me, don't you?'

'Of course I do,' he said. 'I can't prove it in the ordinary way, but I do. Desperately. I shouldn't have told you all this, if I didn't. I should have just made some excuse. Believe me, I'm as disappointed as you are. I wanted this to work.'

She reached out and touched his cheek.

'It will work,' she said, and she felt him relax.

'You are wonderful you know,' he said, and propped himself up on his elbow to kiss her forehead. Then he swept his hand gently over her eyes to close them. 'Sleep now. We'll feel better for some sleep.'

26

It was not as if it mattered, really, Chris told herself. It had been only one night, after all. Perhaps Angus had been just so tired that it had made him fatalistic. With resolution she pushed all his doom-laden declarations out of her mind. Things would work out. She was determined that they would.

Yet the business still nagged at her when she would rather not think of it. She had better things to worry about as she sat waiting to see Edouard St Juste, in his rather impressive circular drawing room. The prospect of a stinging rebuff was all too likely, but she found she was not concentrating on the most effective way to argue her case. Rather she was thinking of Angus's incomprehensible words, how he had spoken of being unnatural, of wanting a cure. She could not make sense of them, and he had said nothing more on the matter that morning. He had been instead delightfully cheerful and had left her to sleep while he fetched some food for their breakfast. It had been amusing to watch him clumsily attempting to make coffee and fry eggs in the little slit of a kitchen, and for a while she had been able to forget the day before. It was just how she had hoped it might be except for that. Was it really worth agonizing over?

'Madame Bretton?' said a woman coming into the room. Her hair was half up and half down, and she wore a long loose black and white wrapper that looked Japanese.

Chris started a little. She was not used to being addressed so.

'You must excuse us for keeping you waiting,' said the woman in French. 'My husband won't be a moment,' she added, putting her hand out to Chris. 'I am Blanche St Juste. I have been looking forward to meeting you. We think your trio is charming.'

'Oh, you do?' said Chris, surprised at this immediate endorsement. 'I mean, thank you.'

'Come and have some coffee,' she said, and took her through to what was clearly the dining room, a room which, despite the obvious grandeur of its size and furnishing, had an air of cheerful domesticity about it. There were two small children sitting at the table, which had been prudently covered with a vivid piece of yellow oil cloth, for a drawing session was clearly in progress, with crayons and pencils lying all about. At one end, by contrast, were the coffee things, sanctified by a small white cloth under them.

One of the children looked at Chris with curiosity, the other continued scribbling with fierce concentration.

'Pascal, Albertine, come and shake hands with Madame Bretton,' said Mme St Juste. Chris decided she liked the French pronunciation of Angus's name – it had the advantage of making her feel less of a stranger. If one's name was pronounceable, one was much more likely to be accepted. Yet, it felt she had already been accepted as the children came and shook her hand and said hello in charming, fractured English. Mme St Juste smiled, clearly delighted at her darlings' performance.

'What do you play?' asked Pascal, reverting to French. Clearly everyone who came to the house was a musician.

'Well . . .' began Chris, and was grateful that Mme St Juste stepped in and fielded the question.

'Madame writes music, chéri,' she explained. 'She might be studying with Papa . . .'

At that moment the man himself came in, pulling on his jacket and apologizing profusely. He was not a large man, but his presence filled the room, like a rush of spring air through an open window. He kissed Chris's hand with swift elegance and began to explain himself in such rapid French that Chris only just managed to follow.

'I was on the telephone and I could not get away. That machine is an appalling intrusion, is it not? I can't think why I allowed one to be installed. What is wrong with writing letters? If we are not careful we will lose that art and then where will we be? Some of the greatest literature in my language is in the form of letters . . . But now we have the horrible telephone which keeps me from those I should be seeing. Madame, I apologize again.'

'There's nothing to apologize for,' she said. 'I've been very well entertained.'

'Elle est si gracieuse!' he smiled to his wife. 'And your French is very good, madame.'

She was glad then that the rather grim Mademoiselle at school had been such a hard taskmaster. Everything here would have been spoilt if she were floundering always for words.

'Time for your walk, mes enfants,' said Mme St Juste, gathering her charges. 'We will see you later no doubt, madame.'

Alone then, M. St Juste poured out coffee and sat down opposite her. Chris braced herself for a serious cross-examination.

'So, what do you think of Paris?' he asked, rather surprisingly.

'Well, I can scarcely judge yet . . .' she said. 'But I think I shall like it.'

'Good. That's important, because if you come to me I shall expect it to be for at least three months. If you were to get homesick suddenly . . .'

'No, no, I shan't feel like that,' said Chris. 'There's nothing really at home for me to miss.'

'A happy exile? Good,' he said. 'And your husband, he will not want to drag you home?'

'He's like me,' she said simply. 'There's nothing in Scotland for him either.'

'And what will he be doing here? I don't mean to sound impertinent, but I would keep you extremely busy here, madame, and he might be jealous. He might want you dancing attendance on him. Have you considered that?'

'He wants to write a novel,' said Chris. 'It's probably better that I'm out of the way.'

'What a paragon! Tell me, are all Scotsmen so reasonable?'

'Hardly,' she laughed. Yes, she decided, Angus was a paragon. Thinking of it in such terms made the disappointment of yesterday fade away. She would not let it be important.

'Now there is one matter we haven't touched on,' said M. St Juste. 'The question of payment. I hate talking about money don't you?'

She smiled, and wondered what enormous sum he was about to request. Still, Angus had said he did not mind paying.

'So I've decided we shall make another sort of arrangement,' he went on.

'Oh,' she found herself saying heavily. 'What did you have in mind?'

'Oh, mon Dieu!' he said, 'that sounds terrible. Of course I did not mean anything like that. Actually, it was my wife's idea that you might like to teach the children English in return.'

'English lessons – Oh,' she smiled. 'Is that all?'

'You would not mind? You would not think it beneath you?'

'No, no, of course not. They're clearly lovely children. It would be a pleasure.'

'We were going to look for a governess, but we really did not know where to start, and then your letter arrived. And we thought that you might agree to this. Young musicians do not usually have much money, do they? Besides, a musician will fit better in a musician's house, you will understand us because you are one of us.' He smiled. 'It would only be an hour or two a day. They could not concentrate for longer.'

'I would be happy too, if that's all you want, and if you're sure you want to teach me.'

'I was sure the moment I read through your Rhapsody. I like to teach, Madame, ours is a generous art. We should share it. By the way, I took the liberty of showing it to my publisher, Monsieur Thiebault – you know him? Well, he would like to meet you also. He's coming to lunch with us, you had better stay, had you not? I hope you have not sent it elsewhere?'

'No, I hadn't thought . . .' She broke off, shaking her head. 'A publisher? You really are so kind, Monsieur.'

He shrugged his shoulders, and said, 'It's nothing. Now, tell me about this opera that you and your husband have written. You should have brought him today. You'll bring him tomorrow, then?'

Chris could only nod. She felt her face must be fixed in a silly grin, like a clown mask, but she could not stop smiling.

'Would you like to see the score?' she managed to say.

'Well yes,' he said, getting up and going to the piano. 'What are we waiting for?'

The moment still tormented him, when he had turned and saw her standing quite naked before him. Slowly he had looked at her, trying to find some element to which to respond. He had touched her breast, hoping it might awake his senses, but there had been nothing. Then, when she slept, he had looked at her again, looked at her hair. If he had been a decent, honourable, normal man he could have loved that spread of her hair that covered the pillow. With unselfconscious, happy lips he might have kissed it and caught its fragrance. But there had been only the disinterested aesthetic pleasure of it for him, the noting with his poetic eye, that in the wan Paris moonlight the colour of it was washed quite away and that the curling tendrils made him think of seaweed. Poor child – at least she had managed to sleep, though God only knew what she might have dreamt of. Of him perhaps, loving her as she expected. He had seen the disappointment in her face, however bravely she had taken it, heard the quiet pain in her voice.

He swallowed down his cognac and ordered another. There was something to be said for the life of the *flâneur* in such circumstances. Cognac and strong black coffee in large enough quantities might blow the memory of it all quite away. Wasn't that what they had decided to do anyway? Tacitly, of course, in the morning, in the brisk, cheerful way they had made breakfast, as if everything was quite as splendid as before, that this thing was nothing more than a slight setback, a little piece of mess that was easily swept away? Perhaps Chris believed that, perhaps he even believed it himself, that everything might still work. He certainly wanted to believe it. He did not want to be responsible for making a disaster rather than a marriage.

'Excuse me – it is Mr Bretton, isn't it?' The small, dapperly dressed man with a moustache who had been standing gazing over the café tables had suddenly stepped forward and addressed him, in a strong Glaswegian accent. 'Well, it is! I was standing there wondering if it was you, I couldn't quite make up my mind.'

'Well, I'm certainly he, but . . . I'm sorry . . . you are?'

Angus was searching his memory for a name for this dimly familiar face.

'Neill,' he said, 'Davie Neill. You were good enough to buy one of my paintings.'

'Oh yes, the bowl of fruit! I ought to have remembered you. That's the only picture I've ever bought!' He jumped up and shook his hand. 'Will you join me?'

'If you don't mind,' said Neill. 'So, what brings you to Paris? Are you on holiday from the doctoring? You must be qualified by now.'

Angus was always astonished at how people remembered a great deal about him, when he, most impolitely, seemed to have forgotten everything he might ever have known about them. Such was the case with Neill, although the picture was vivid in his memory – a dish of oranges, so solidly painted it seemed one might reach out and take one.

'I've thrown all that in,' he said. 'It wasn't for me. I'm trying to write now.'

'So I shan't be able to sell you any more pictures,' grinned Neill. 'Now you've joined the ranks of impoverished artists. Are you living here then?'

'Just arrived yesterday – with my wife.'

'Congratulations,' said Neill. 'Is that recent then?'

'Three days,' said Angus. Neill looked a trifle surprised that a newly married man could let a wife out of his sight in the first week. 'She's gone to see St Juste – the composer, you know? She's going to study composition with him.'

'Oh,' said Neill. 'She must be quite talented.'

'She is, very,' said Angus, rather enjoying saying that.

The waiter brought a tall, sparkling glass of *Bière blonde* which Neill sipped appreciatively. 'Well, you had both better come and see us,' he said. 'There's quite a crowd of Scots here at the moment. You'll probably know some of them already. Funny though, isn't it, how we all have to get away from the old place, to do anything properly? I couldn't bear it in Glasgow, with all my relatives sniffing every time I painted a nude.'

'The place is trapped in a Calvinist straitjacket,' said Angus. 'I mean, where in Scotland could we sit on the pavement drinking like this?' He made a gesture which seemed to include the whole boulevard, and all the fascinating life it demonstrated beneath the canopy of its fresh-leafed trees. 'The trouble is, though, it's too distracting, too civilized. I wonder if I'll actually get any work done on this novel I'm planning.'

'You will,' said Neill. 'I've done far more, and far better work here. It's being with like-minded people. So, what's this novel to be about then?'

'Scotland,' said Angus, and then laughed. 'Aye, that's the rub, isn't it?'

27

Davie Neill had his studio in the rue d'Assas which skirted the Luxembourg gardens, so Chris and Angus, being early for his party, took a leisurely, circuitous stroll about the gardens. It was about seven o'clock and twilight was just coming on after a long day of spring sunshine. Now it was cool, but not unpleasantly so, and the gardens were almost deserted. The nursemaids and their charges had all gone home, leaving only the pattern of their visits in the odd groupings of the green wrought-iron chairs and in the tracks of perambulators in the gravel walks. The people who remained were like themselves engaged in slow, quiet strolls, or sitting poring over the last few pages of a book while enough light remained to see by. The great Carpeaux fountain was not playing, indeed its waters seemed so still that it might never have played. The whole place was caught in a trance of muted light, making coloured shadows of everything. The only thing of distinctness was the noise of the birds in the trees, making the usual furious spring twittering.

They said little as they walked, and at one moment Angus wandered away from her to plunge his hand into the fountain and ruffle its waters. She watched him and wondered how she continued to silence her desire for him. He was so beautiful then, stretched out over the water, as beautiful as the prancing horses and the nymphs who rose up from the centre of the pool. He was also as unobtainable. He turned to her smiling, lifting his hand slowly from the water, and she saw the shower of drips falling from it, sparkling gently in the silvery light of dusk.

'What did you do that for?' she asked.

'Because water should move,' he said. 'It's not a dead thing. Still water is stagnant.'

She nodded, and felt again the stab of anguish at her situation. It was not his body which tempted her but his mind. They had been married two weeks now and he grew more and more delightful to her. His ideas seemed to set lighted candles in the dark places of her mind. With him, she was inspired. Just seeing the water crack into movement inspired her. There was music in such a thing – a still pool of ponderous chords and then – movement, in a brilliant, rapid succession of echoing phrases, bursting out like the ripples that rushed across the water, ripples made by his strong, inventive hand.

How impossible it all was to bear! To love him so deeply and live so closely with him and yet find always that final door that could not be unlocked, that he would not unlock to her. She wished she could be content with what they had, but she could not be. She was beginning to feel like a starved animal, a lioness hungry for red meat. It was not always pain she felt now, but anger, for her desire was beginning to conquer her. Sometimes, at night, it was unbearable and she wanted to beat her fists against his sleeping back, to wound him for his negligence. And now, in the peaceful beauty of those gardens, she felt it and it made her want to roar.

'We'd better be going,' said Angus consulting his watch. Chris was glad enough to go. The distraction of a party was exactly what she needed. There was too much room here for agonized rumination.

After dinner, it seemed Davie Neill had declared open house and the place began to fill up. A violinist unpacked his fiddle and played a sonata by St Juste, and Angus, sitting next to Chris on a sofa to listen to the music, felt a wonderful sense of contentment. To watch her pleasure at the music was more of a pleasure to him than the music itself. She sat with her chin resting on her folded hands, her eyes slightly closed, almost as if she were praying. The atmosphere in the room was heady with scent and with the swelling then falling melodies of the sonata and seeing her, in that bronze-coloured silk dress, with wisps of gauze falling over her bare shoulders, Angus felt some distant longing tremble inside him. Could it be possible that tonight, he might . . . ?

The sonata came to an end and the audience clapped furiously. She turned to him and he saw a slight tear in her eye.

'That's so . . .' she said. 'Don't you think?'

'Beautiful, yes,' he said, though he felt he was complimenting her as much as the music.

'Do you think I'll ever manage to write anything as good as that? With such . . . oh . . . passion in it? And the craftsmanship of it . . .'

'You know I think you will,' he said, squeezing her hand.

'Yes, it's wonderful that you do,' she said and kissed him briefly on the cheek. He felt the quiet forgiveness in this gesture and it made him feel ashamed again. 'Now, I must go and congratulate that fiddle player. Will you come?'

'No, I'll sit here a minute and watch folk. Is that all right?'

'Of course,' she said laughing. 'I know you find music talk a little wearing,' and she kissed him again.

He watched her walk away, and saw how quite a few men threw an admiring glance in her direction. They, he supposed, would have no difficulty at all making love to her.

'What an affecting scene . . .' said a voice behind him. Hearing it, Angus felt his skin prickle as if he had just walked through a bed of nettles.

'What the hell are you doing here?' he said, turning in his seat.

There, looming above him, a massive expanse of immaculate white shirt front and waistcoat, with a lily in his button-hole, was Hugo Doyle.

'And what sort of a way is that to greet an old, dear friend?' said Hugo. 'Aren't you pleased to see me? I think this is rather a delightful coincidence.'

'Very,' said Angus without enthusiasm.

Hugo raised an eyebrow and sipped his wine.

'I thought we were friends,' he said, taking Chris's place on the sofa.

'That's not possible now, I'm afraid,' said Angus, and swallowed down his own glass of Chartreuse rapidly. At once he wished he might have another to follow it. 'How come you're here then?'

'You've clearly forgotten. I introduced you to Davie Neill. He was so glad to run across you like that. He's always rather admired you.'

'Oh for God's sake . . .' Angus muttered and was about to get up from the sofa. But Hugo grabbed his arm and forced him to remain.

'You abandoned me,' he said sharply. 'Do you think I like that?'

'I did not abandon you,' said Angus.

'We were lovers. Didn't that mean anything to you?'

'No, it was extremely sordid. I was glad to leave.'

'I don't believe you.'

'Then you had better try to, Doyle, and stop acting like a damnable cast-off mistress.'

'Why should I?' he said. 'That's exactly what I am. Your cast-off mistress. I've been watching my letterbox for months, waiting for a word from you.'

'God in heaven, what did you want? Violet-coloured letters smelling of patchouli? That would be just your style.'

'And yours too, though you won't admit it.'

'No, I shall not. As far as I am concerned that's all over. It's part of my life that I would rather forget, thank you.'

'But you can't,' said Doyle. 'Not for all the pretty little wifies in the world.'

He gestured to the corner of the room and Angus turned slightly to follow the gesture. He saw Chris talking with the violinist. She caught his eye, smiled and gave a slight wave of acknowledgement.

'For God's sake, Angus,' said Doyle, pressing his hand more heavily on Angus's arm. 'Own up to yourself. Admit what you are.'

'I am a married man,' Angus managed to say. 'And I chose that.'

'I don't believe you could even lay a finger on her,' said Doyle softly. 'Could you, Angus? Have you? Doesn't she repulse you?'

'Leave me alone,' Angus spluttered, wresting free his arm and getting up.

'I will not,' he heard him say when he had turned his back on him. Quickly, Angus slipped into the crowd, wanting a shield of people between him and Hugo.

His first instinct was to find Chris and tell her they must go home. He could not stay there with Hugo. He already felt as if his brain had been set in a vice and the handle turned to crush it. He struggled through the crowd which now seemed to have filled the rooms to bursting point. A couple waylaid him; vague recent acquaintances who were determined to sit down and have a good talk with him. He managed to excuse himself as quickly as he could, and reached the corner where she had been standing, only to find she had gone.

Desperate for air he retreated on to the balcony, and

leant on a wrought-iron railing there as if it were his only support. He felt weak and sick, as if Hugo were a sudden fever running over him, destroying him with uncertainty. Before, he had been certain, or at least hopeful of certainty. He looked up and saw he was looking over the Luxembourg gardens, a deep patch of velvet darkness now. He thought of himself dipping his hand into the fountain, feeling the clear cool of it on his skin and being alone with Chris. He wished he were there still, that they had simply stayed there all evening instead of coming to this damned party. Why the devil had he not remembered that Hugo had introduced him to Davie Neill? He had probably been drunk at the time, he concluded ruefully, and sank his forehead on to his clasped hands, closing his eyes to the silent beauty of the night-shrouded tree-tops. In his ears Hugo's words stung, even as echoes: 'Own up to yourself. Admit what you are.'

'Mrs Bretton?' She looked up and saw the man she had noticed talking to Angus earlier, that tall, impossibly elegant man with fair hair slicked back from his forehead. 'You don't know me of course. I'm an old friend of your husband's. Hugo Doyle.'

He put out a languid hand to her so she supposed she must shake it. She tried, ineffectually, to recall if Angus had ever mentioned him.

'How do you do? Christina Bretton,' she said.

He indicated two empty chairs.

'Shall we sit down?' he said. 'Are you enjoying yourself?'

'Oh yes. It's always so interesting to watch people in Paris. They're so unlike the people at home.'

'And where is home – where in Scotland I mean?'

'A little place in Forfarshire.'

'Oh, Forfarshire . . .' He said it a doom-laden way which made her smile.

'So how do you know Angus?'

'We were at Glenalmond together.'

'What was he like at school?'

'A very pretty boy,' he said. 'Of course, he still is, you must find.'

It was an odd response. She had expected him to say that he was always in trouble or good at rugby.

'Well, I suppose so,' she answered. 'My sister was very jealous to find I was marrying such a braw fellow.'

'Ah, she's not the only broken heart,' said Doyle.

'I'm sorry?' said Chris.

'My dear, surely he's told you,' said Doyle.

'Told me what?' said Chris feeling her back stiffen.

'He's always been so honest . . .' Doyle went on with a sigh.

'He is, yes,' said Chris.

'Well, perhaps I shouldn't say anything.'

She felt annoyed at that. The phrase sounded like that of an old gossip only pretending to be discreet.

'Perhaps you shouldn't,' she said and got up from her seat. 'If you'll excuse me.'

'I think you should know,' he said, getting up also. 'A clear-eyed Scotswoman would prefer the truth, I'm sure.'

'If it is truth and not slander,' she said.

'God's own truth,' said Doyle and indicated the empty seat. 'Do sit down again, Mrs Bretton.'

She did so with extreme reluctance. She was wary of him There was something malevolent in his glib, grave sincerity.

'That's better,' he said. 'Oh, how I hate to begin.'

She said nothing, feeling the dry tightening in the back of her throat. She decided she was being very silly though and that all he was going to give her was some silly piece of slander concerning another girl, long ago. Doyle looked like the sort who would make much of such trifles.

'Carry on, Mr Doyle,' she said as brightly as she could.

'I think you are only trying to scare me and I am not easily scared. I know Angus a great deal better than you imagine.' There was a touch of bravado in this. Often she had felt she did not know him at all.

'Perhaps,' said Doyle. 'Perhaps not.'

'You are rather pointed, you know,' she said.

'Yes, I have a right to be, Mrs Bretton. You and I are rivals, you see.'

'Rivals? What are you talking about?'

'Your husband and I have been lovers,' he said. 'There, am I clear enough for you?'

'I'm sorry but . . .'

'Oh dear, clearly a sheltered young woman,' said Doyle. 'Perhaps you are not familiar with the situation. It is possible, Mrs Bretton, hard though it may be for you to believe, that men can love men, that men, indeed, do love men.'

She found she was shaking her head.

'Believe me, they do,' said Doyle. 'Your husband – well, husband is hardly an accurate description, is it? You are hardly married, are you? At least in the strict legal definition of the term you are not. I don't suppose he has done his . . . er . . . conjugal duty towards you, has he?' He paused for a moment, giving her an enquiring look. She could find no words to answer. 'As I thought. Silence means consent.'

'I'm not naying or yeaing you, Mr Doyle,' she managed to say. 'I'm only stupefied at your rudeness.' She got up from her chair.

'Are you?' he said, with a slight smile. She did not wait to give an answer but bolted, looking desperately about for Angus.

She found him, after an eternity, on the balcony. He was sitting on the floor, his back pressed against the railings.

'What are you doing out here?' she blurted out. 'I've

been looking for you everywhere. There's this dreadful man who says he knows you and he's said the most . . .'

'Hugo Doyle,' said Angus.

'Yes, who is he? He said . . .'

'He told you then?' he said, getting up.

'He told me a lot of sickening nonsense.'

'It isn't nonsense.'

'What? I don't understand.' It sounded feeble to say it. It came out as a sort of wail of which she was ashamed, but confusion was ruling her now, like a fever, eating her up.

'Let's go home. I'll explain when we get home.'

She was glad to agree. They walked home in silence but it was not the comfortable, companionable silence of earlier. It was a silence she wanted to break, but Angus, with his hands stuffed deeply into his pockets and his aggressive pace, deterred her. Or perhaps it was her own fear that stopped her tongue. She would gladly have deferred any explanation until the end of time itself. She would rather wipe the whole thing from her memory than have to face what might lie in that ominous word 'explanation'.

When they reached their front door she was seized by the desire to go on walking in that silence, uncomfortable though it might be, pushing forward for ever, without any need for the truth to tear them apart. For that was what she had begun to be afraid of, as she followed Angus up the stairs.

They went into the drawing room and lit the lamps, and then in a parody of happy domesticity sat down in the chairs which in the two weeks they had been there each had marked as their own: Chris in the large chair by the fireplace, and Angus at the table which he had already covered with his books and papers. Chris found herself drawing her legs up under her, so that she was deep in the defences of the chair, as if its padded wings would protect her from whatever she might have to hear.

'What did he say to you then?' said Angus breaking the silence.

'He said ... He said that you'd been lovers ...' She could not help the note of incomprehension in her voice. 'That's not true, is it?'

'What would you say if it was?'

'I don't know. Is it true?'

He grimaced and said, 'Yes.'

'But he's a man ...' she said.

'Yes.'

'But ...'

'It happens, Chris,' he said. 'Unfortunately.' She pressed her head against the chair back and closed her eyes tightly for a moment. She felt faintly sick.

'How? I can't see how.' She forced out the words.

'You can't understand. You wouldn't – you're normal.'

'Make me understand,' she said sharply.

'How can I? You can't have the least idea. You're so ...' He broke off and stared at his hands. 'So straight and good, and clean and perfect. How can I make you understand what it is to be diseased? Think of me as a cripple if you like.'

'A cripple?'

'Yes. A cripple can't walk, but he'd damn well like to, and he loathes his mangled limbs for it. Well, my limbs are mangled. They can't do what they are supposed to do. That's what it's like. That's how loathsome it is.'

'But why, why are you like that?' she asked, desperately. 'I mean, it's not something ... I mean, a cripple loses his legs or something but this is ...'

'It's just the same. It's an accident of nature.'

'But can't you change?'

'I thought I could. Why else do you think I married you? I thought, I hoped, you see, that it would be all right, that the thing in me would go. That I'd be whole and able again. That I'd be normal, like you.'

'So that's why you can't . . .' She broke off, stifling the sob that had risen in her throat. 'I suppose this means,' she managed to say, 'that you don't love me.'

'I do.'

'And how am I supposed to believe that?' she burst out. 'When you say you married me to cure yourself? I feel like nothing more than a dose of medicine.'

'I do love you,' he said, jumping up. 'I feel just as you do.'

'Then why can't you show it? If you really loved me, you'd want me, want all of me, not a cure for your own sickness! I suppose if I were a man you'd want me soon enough, properly I mean, if what men do together can be proper. I'm your wife, Angus, does that mean anything to you, really?'

'It means everything in the world to me. I wanted this to work. I still do. I want to make love to you, Chris, I honestly do but . . .' He crouched down beside her chair.

'No, you don't!' she exclaimed, pushing him away. 'You're simply pretending. It's all in your head, isn't it, your love? It isn't here, where it matters, here!' She slapped her hand on her chest. 'Here! Love isn't just in the head. It should be in every bone, in every nerve, in the pit of your stomach. That's where I feel it. That's where I feel I want you. I'm hungry, and you're not, are you?'

He shook his head slowly.

'But I do feel for you, Chris. I shouldn't have married anyone else. You move me more than anyone but . . .'

'But it's the wrong sort of love.'

'Is there a wrong and right sort?' he said. 'Isn't love enough?'

'I don't know. I only know what I feel. Oh, I suppose I'm cheap for feeling so frankly about it. My mother rather implied that the marital bed was a chore, but I can't agree with that. I am what I am and I want you. I wish – oh, but it isn't any good, is it?'

He said nothing but sank down on to his haunches beside her. There was a long silence between them, as taut and as dry as a string about to break.

'I don't want Hugo any more,' he said. 'Please understand that. I never felt for him one tenth, no, one hundredth of what I feel for you. Despite everything, there is meaning in this for me. Can you believe that?' His voice was full of supplication.

She looked down at him as he sat at her feet.

'I think so,' she managed to say, and leant forward to put her arms about his shoulders, drawing him forward so that his head lay buried in her lap, like that of a child. She felt his arms clutch about her legs and his body shook with its own private pain. She realized he was crying and then discovered she was too.

28

Guy and Miranda had found they did not like Florence, or to be strictly truthful, Guy had found he did not like it. He had found it a treeless, dirty city, with none of the charm everyone had promised. Even the picture galleries and churches, of which they saw far too many, failed to mitigate his disappointment. Miranda had not declared for the place either way, but had agreed at once with his suggestion they go to Paris earlier than they had at first planned. She was eager, he knew, to get some dresses made before they went to Venice and the paintings had probably bored her dreadfully. But she had been gracious enough not to say anything. In return, he was determined to give her a good run at Paris which he knew would be far more to her taste. And on the train they had decided it had been a very good idea altogether, as Florence had been an impossible place, too full of aunt-like spinsters and English clergymen being pompous to afford any real amusement. For amusement was what, Miranda declared, she wanted above everything else on this holiday of theirs. 'I simply don't care if I never see another decent painting,' she said. 'But I should like to see some interesting people. At least one can talk to people.'

'Well, there'll be no difficulty of that. There are plenty of people we can call on,' said Guy. 'My mother has an army of friends in Paris.'

'Then I shall have to spend a horrible amount on

dresses,' she had said. 'If we're to go anywhere decent. You don't mind, do you, Guy?'

'Of course not,' he had said, kissing her. There was, he had found, something thrilling about kissing her on a train. He felt at that moment he would travel for the pleasure of that alone. In fact he kissed her so long and so hard that he was stirred up enough to want her there and then, and contemplated locking the compartment door and drawing down the blinds. Miranda calmly pointed out that he had better stop disarranging her hair and clothes so, as it was nearly time for them to go down to the restaurant car for lunch. He tried to swallow his disappointment by telling himself she was only being pragmatic.

Yet the disappointment had lingered. It was the first time she had denied him, and although he knew it was a sensible enough thing to have done, he still felt piqued, as if she had been more concerned about her hair and clothes than she had been with his feelings. That, of course, was ridiculous, but he could not help thinking of it, while he sat, very much the redundant male, in a showroom chez Poiret.

Miranda had approached the visit to Poiret with something of the ardour of a Roman Catholic granted an audience with the Pope. Guy had the impression that it was perhaps easier to see the Holy Father than to see Poiret in person. It took her an hour or so to decide what to wear, and then she was tormented by the choice of a hat.

'Anything looks splendid on you,' he said.

'You haven't the least idea,' she said, and then, suddenly noticing his silk hat, which was lying ready for him to put on, exclaimed, 'There's no shine to this at all. Doesn't Johnny know what to do?'

'What does the shine on my hat matter?'

'You know it matters,' she said.

'My father told me that too much shine on a silk hat suggests a cad.'

'That was years ago. Now they have to be shiny,' said Miranda. 'It's fashionable.'

'I am not fashionable,' said Guy. 'I refuse to be.'

'You will, if I have anything to do with it,' she said, flicking her hands deftly across his lapels. 'Really, this coat is positively shabby.'

'It's well broken in, that's all. If I have to wear a morning coat, at least let it be a comfortable one. Though heaven knows why I must. He's only a dressmaker.'

'He is not, he's an artist.'

'How can fashion be to do with art?' said Guy. 'Art is enduring. Fashion is the complete opposite – a dress is thrown away when it's out of date.'

'You are being very grumpy,' said Miranda. 'It isn't fair of you at all. You said I could buy all the clothes I liked.'

'Of course you can,' he said, 'but it's such a fuss. I don't understand it. When I go to my tailor . . .'

'When you go to your tailor, you simply ask for the same dull things. That's all right for a man, but you see I must do the thing properly. I'm your wife. People will expect me to be well dressed.'

'You hardly do it out of duty,' he laughed, catching her in his arms, 'my little bird of paradise.'

'We really ought to go,' she said, slipping out of his arms again.

If the paintings in Florence had not captured Miranda's imagination, Poiret's clothes did. She sat on the edge of her little empire chair in the salon, while a succession of girls in exotic clothes came sweeping in. It was a pretty enough sight: the bright stuffs, with embroidery and beadings, against the pale grey violet of the walls, the girls themselves, all tall and thin, with elegant carriage, and he tried to enjoy it, as she enjoyed it. However, it irritated him. Her rapture was too complete, her little exclamations too full of pleasure. He could not help but think of the noises she gave out when he made love to her. They had never seemed as joyous as these.

'Oh, but that's charming!' she said. 'Look, Guy, look!'

He found he had been staring down into the rim on his hat.

'Yes, charming,' he said, looking up. A girl in a diaphanous dress had struck a pose in front of him, and stared him straight in the eyes. She did not smile, but there was something in the passive beauty of her face which disturbed him. Like Miranda she was very lovely, but the beauty was a blank and flawless mask presented to him, carefully cultivated to please him, or any man who happened to sit there. He wished the girl would laugh or wrinkle up her face in disdain rather than stand there, her arm outstretched, as if she could be bought as well as the dress.

'I shall have that, certainly,' said Miranda, and Guy could all too easily picture her head and fine shoulders rising out of that low, gauze-covered collar. Miranda could have been a mannequin, just like this one, selling her own face as much as the clothes. Perhaps she had already done that, with him. He thought of her standing on the terrace at Lady Seaton's, composed into a picture to capture him, to make herself irresistible. What was the difference between that girl and his wife? Perhaps it was that Miranda had not been selling an evening dress, but herself.

He began to wonder if she did love him. He did not want to think of it at all, but his uncertainty began to grip him. He had hardly been plagued by adoring women in his life. Chris had not loved him, after all, then why should Miranda? Perhaps she had only convinced herself of her love, a sort of receipt for all the things she would gain from him, all the things which he knew she wanted. He had seen her excitement in looking over the family jewel cases – she had been like a child in a sweet shop. He glanced at her, and felt that for the last three weeks he had been intimate with a stranger. He knew no more of her heart than he had on the first day he had met her.

He wished he could ask her at once, demand that she be perfectly frank. He wished it because he felt a few sweet words from her would cut the canker of this uncertainty out of his mind. He wondered what it was in him that was causing this ridiculous piece of self-torture. How was his mind able to conjure up such spectres?

He felt hot and slightly sick, and as if his collar had just been tightened. The air in the room seemed heavy with scent and he wondered if he might pass out from lack of air. If he could get into the street, then . . .

He leant across to Miranda.

'Will you be long?'

'A while,' she said. 'Oh you don't want to go now, do you, darling?'

'No, I just need some air. I'll be back in ten minutes.'

'All right,' she said, and at once returned her attention to the dresses.

Guy got up and went to the door.

'Oh, c'est de trop pour Monsieur?' enquired the vendeuse.

'Un peu,' he muttered and went out.

The air outside was instantly refreshing. It did not smell of women. He spotted a café across the street and headed for it. He settled there, like a real *flâneur*, and ordered a grenadine, a childish drink he knew, but which he had always liked.

The grenadine arrived in its customary tall glass, with a long spoon, the sirop itself trickling down over the pile of crushed ice. He poured on some soda water, and stirred it until it was an even, deep, pink. He sipped it, and wondered how large a bill Miranda would run up in there, and whether this business of getting clothes would be an annual event in their life. Perhaps in future he would not go. It had made him too uncomfortable. Even here, in the anonymity of this café, he felt something of an organ grinder's monkey. He wished for a long moment he were back at Rankeillor, where the daffodils would be out now, and he would have something to do rather than fret about Miranda. He thought of the summer they had planned – Venice for a month, and then Switzerland, for July, perhaps Lucerne. Then finally to Bayreuth, for a fortnight of Wagner. He had agreed to it without a thought, but now he could not bear the idea. He decided he would ask her if they could go home early.

He finished his drink and paid for it and, hands in pockets, stalked back to the Maison Poiret. He had only crossed the black and white tiled entrance hall when he saw Miranda coming down the stairs.

'Was I so long?' he said. 'I'm sorry.'

'No, I'd seen enough,' she said. 'Well, I think I was being beastly. It was terribly dull for you. I shan't be so long again.'

'Perhaps you're better going alone,' he said. 'Then I'll be pleasantly surprised by whatever you choose.'

'You are nice,' she said, touching his cheek with her gloved fingers. 'Some men, you know, would be beastly about all this.'

'Well, my mother brought me up properly, didn't she?' he said.

'I'm glad to hear it,' she smiled. 'The vendeuse told me about a marvellous place for hats – I'm anxious to have a look.'

'Then I shall go to the Louvre,' said Guy. 'Unless you want me . . .'

'Of course I want you,' she said with infinite sweetness, 'but it isn't fair. You go to the Louvre.'

'Are you sure?'

'Quite!' she laughed. 'Please, Guy, don't worry about me. I shall be perfectly happy. Now where shall we lunch?' she added, taking his arm.

He knew then, he could not possibly ask her to go home early. It would be like taking a favourite toy from a child.

In the Louvre, Chris looked up at Manet's *Olympia*, and the painted eyes looked down at Chris, with a frank, unsettling stare that suggested she knew far more than the canvas and paint world she occupied. The stare was uncanny, and so compelling that the nakedness of the girl seemed irrelevant. She was not simply a display of prime female flesh, like the Ingres *Grande Odalisque* that hung nearby. No, this girl was a whole being: a mind as well as a body, with character as well as a pretty face. She lay there, starkly white, on still whiter sheets, making only a gesture towards modesty with her crossed legs and discreetly placed hand. She was supposed to be a whore and the picture was regarded by many as shocking. Rankeillor, Chris was sure, would find it so, and find it shocking too that she should stand there looking at it for so long. Yet she could not tear herself away from it. She found she could imagine herself lying there, on those crumpled white sheets, propped up on one elbow, assertively offering herself, failing to conceal her hunger. For that body bluntly accepted its own physical need. Olympia might trade in that, but Chris felt she still must enjoy it, to lie there so openly naked, without any sort of languid coyness about her. For there was an appetite for that sort of intimacy, she knew that now. It was not respectable, of course, in the same way it was not respectable for women to show they were hungry for food or for intellectual stimulation. She felt resentful of Angus for not feeding her. She wished she could forget it, and live, comrade-like, with him, able to enjoy being with him without being constantly haunted. It made her ashamed to be always stumbling over her own weakness. She was in Paris, after all, being taught by one of the greatest musicians alive and living closely with a man she loved. Could that not be enough for her? She had been trained in self-denial after all. The whole creed of the Manse should have made it second nature to her to accept the shortcomings of her situation. Yet it had never stopped her feeling and wanting the things that were denied to her, though she felt half crucified for wanting what it had always been said she should not want.

She wished and wished, of course, that she would not feel it and that this thing would not constantly sit on her shoulder like a demon, whispering always that she must feel hungry. Why did she have to have to suffer this tormenting greed which made her feel like a whore, a horrid, corporeal thing incapable of redemption? Sometimes, she felt little better than Dr Stewart.

The worst of it was it bred bitterness. Try as she might, she could not look at Angus without feeling she had been duped by him, without being certain that everything had been destroyed between them. Of course, they went on with the charade of being a happy couple. Indeed often they were happy. Angus would say something and helpless laughter would consume them, and then, as sobriety returned, she always found herself remembering how things really were or imagining how, in different circumstances, they might be. Yet mostly, they kept carefully separate of each other. Angus had found a café to haunt where he could write so that she had the run of the flat and its piano. It was all rather too civilized. She wondered when her patience with it would give out. That would require courage though, and there would be the possibility of losing him altogether, the thought of which she could not bear.

She turned from her vigil beneath *Olympia* and glanced

around the great gallery, at the vast pictures of the last century which seemed dull and brown after *Olympia*, and at the people who were studying them earnestly, often as not with an open guide book in hand. She watched to see how they reacted to *Olympia*, and saw one woman purse her lips in disapproval and pass on quickly to the next painting. She felt a sudden pang of sympathy for the painter. The thought of having one's work rejected so glibly, with such a sour look of disapproval, when it had clearly cost much effort, appalled her. Who was to know it would not happen to her? M. St Juste's publisher had been very enthusiastic about her Rhapsody, and had asked her to write some salon piano pieces. She had written one already, but she wondered if it were not too stark and strange to agree with general taste. That was the great difficulty of such things – to write something new, which satisfied her own craving to experiment, but which was also comprehensible to people. To attempt that, M. St Juste had told her, was a better exercise than any he might set her. She looked again at *Olympia* and found herself thinking of a slow waltz theme, in a minor key, an ironic waltz, that twisted the usual romantic sentimentality into something quite different. It would be the simplest thing, or at least it would pretend to be simple, as those little pieces of Schumann so often did, with the harmony really very cleverly thought out. She would make it easy too, so that it fell comfortably under the hands of an amateur, and yet made them feel they were playing something quite complicated. She found she smiled at the thought of it, and thanked heaven again that she had the refuge of her work. To throw herself into her writing was to crawl into a warm, dry cave during a storm.

She decided she would go home and start work on it. But as she turned to follow the signs to the Sortie, she noticed a familiar figure standing in front of *Madame Recamier* by David. It startled her and she half wondered whether to scurry away without acknowledging him. But that would have been unthinkably rude, a violation of the most primitive laws of Rankeillor.

She went up to him slowly, wondering if indeed this was Guy. It was his face, although she could only see it in profile, and it was certainly his height and breadth of shoulder, but it did not seem like Guy at all, in the dark elegance of that cut-away coat and a silk hat. He even carried a stick, and the obligatory pair of crumpled leather gloves. She found she was looking about for Miranda, but there was no sign of her.

She plunged in: 'Hello, how nice to see you . . .' She saw him start a little, and then he turned, sweeping off his hat, and put out his hand to her.

'Goodness – well, yes. What a small town Paris must be. Hello!'

The old warmth was in his voice and the vigour of his handshake. The awkwardness of the past seemed to melt away. He was simply an old friend.

'I thought you were supposed to be in Italy.'

'We left early – I'm afraid I didn't like Florence and Miranda wanted to get her clothes sorted out. So, here we are.'

'Is she here just now?'

'No, she's at some milliners. I couldn't face that, after a morning at Poiret.'

'Poiret – well, she will be smart.'

'I suppose so – but it does take time, doesn't it?'

'Well, I wouldn't know about Poiret . . .' she said.

'You look very nice, whoever you go to,' he said. 'Marriage seems to suit you.' He phrased it almost as a question.

'I suppose it does,' she managed to say brightly, but was appalled at herself. She wished she could tell him everything, but instead she asked herself, 'And you?'

'Oh very well,' he said, and then smiled and added, 'but

to tell you the truth, I'm slightly homesick. This is all very well' – he said, gesturing about with his hat – 'but it isn't Rankeillor, is it?'

'No, no, certainly it's not.' She could not prevent herself laughing. 'Oh, I'm sorry, it's simply I find it quite hard to imagine missing the place.' He looked slightly dismayed at that, so she added, 'But in your case, I suppose . . . well, you are Rankeillor, aren't you?'

He smiled briefly and said, 'I ought not to miss it. It feels very childish of me. But at least there I feel useful . . . Well . . .' He broke off and turned to look up at *Madame Recamier* again. 'She's very lovely, isn't she?'

Chris studied the picture. She had not noticed it before, but this woman, like *Olympia*, looked down at her with equally sharp eyes.

'Aren't the feet well done?' Guy went on, stepping forward to examine properly where Madame Recamier's bare feet emerged from the hem of her white muslin dress. 'They're so real, you feel you could touch them.'

Chris has a sudden vision of him examining Miranda's feet with the same admiring care, as she sat on a similar couch in her wrapper. Indeed, she could quite imagine him kissing them. She had the impression that he was looking at Madame Recamier not as a paint on canvas but as a woman who could be undressed and made love to. His straightforward maleness struck her: she almost smelt it, a good smell to her, like bread baking or damp tweed. And then she remembered lying under him, crushed by him, on the cold grass at the Castle gates. She felt it with all the vividness of a moment ago, as if the bruising passion of his lips on her neck and breast and the warm touch of his fingers were still fresh upon her. Most of all she remembered her own desire; that sensation of falling and falling away from civility and restraint into a darker, deeper, primitive place where she might have felt something so strong that . . . Well, that she did not know, could not know. Angus had never kissed her like that, though she prayed then he might, that he might only look, as Guy was looking at a mere painting, and feel the blood stirring in his veins. Why could he not, like every other normal young man, see a pretty woman and want her, however fleetingly? Why could he not do it? Why could not the man she loved, love her, love her with every inch of his skin and every drop of his blood?

'She looks rather like you,' said Guy suddenly. 'Don't you think?'

She was aware of his eyes on her.

'Oh I really don't think so...'

'I don't suppose you'd see it,' he said. 'You're not vain enough for that sort of thing, are you? But if I were your husband, I should have you painted just like that, with bare feet and black ribbon in your hair.'

'Guy...' she began, but he interrupted her.

'Oh don't worry, I was only speaking academically,' he said. 'No regrets.'

She smiled but did not feel the conviction of the smile. She did not quite believe him, and then wondered if she were only reading into his voice the signals of her own discontent. If she had taken that other path and said yes to him, after all, might she not be standing there, fulfilled, leaning perhaps on his arm, a happier, more innocent Chris?

The moment he said he regretted nothing, he began to wonder whether he did. He remembered the panic he had felt that morning, his creeping conviction that Miranda did not love him, and found another fear: that he did not properly love her. For seeing Chris touched something in him which he had forgotten, or perhaps suppressed. It was like being woken up from a fitful, confused sleep into a bright, sunny room, with white walls. There was no artifice about her. Her clothes had no touch of Paris about them. She was just as she had been when he had fallen in love with her, with that touch of colour in her high cheekbones and those clear, honest eyes. Angus Bretton was a lucky man to get her, in fact, he reasoned, he must be exceptional. How happy they must be, he thought, and remembered the beautiful enigma he found in his bed each morning, the creature who was his wife, and yet to whom he felt attached only by the slenderest threads of feeling. It was true he loved her body and her perfect face, he worshipped them, indeed, but how could he love her mind or her soul when they were so opaque to him, and beyond his understanding? Chris he could understand. He had been able to give her up, because he could understand.

'I should be getting along,' she said. 'I've work to do.'

'How is the work? What are you writing?'

He began to walk with her, in the direction of the Sortie.

'Oh piano pieces at the moment. Apparently that's the best way to get known. I've a publisher interested, anyway.'

'That's splendid. I shall buy it all, of course.'

'That would be very kind.'

'I shall want a first edition,' he said. 'Signed, for the library at Rankeillor. You'll be a famous daughter of the place, the only famous daughter, I imagine.'

'I'm not sure about that,' said Chris. 'One can never take anything for granted. Sometimes things seem precarious to me . . .'

'I'm sure they won't be,' said Guy. 'After all, you've someone to look after your interests now.'

'Angus you mean?' she said. 'Yes, he has been very good.'

'Well, I should have done the same for you,' Guy found himself saying. 'I mean, should we have decided . . .' He broke off and looked away.

'No regrets?' she said, after a little pause. He wanted then to say yes, and to tell her that it was impossible not to regret losing her. But he had no right. She had her happiness, and it was ill mannered to upset that with his own silly confusions. He did not want to make her feel guilty when the fault was not hers. She had never loved him. She had been perfectly straight. He had only imagined her love, whipped it up in his own desperation, much as he had probably imagined Miranda's affection . . .

'I'm sorry,' she said, suddenly. 'That was most unfair.'

'No, no it wasn't,' he said. 'Heavens, things are bound to be a little awkward between us. We've history behind us.'

'It would be nice to be able to forget that, and be friends as we always were,' she said.

'There's no reason why not.'

'No of course not,' she said, and then, having thought for a moment, smiled and went on. 'You know, I should invite you both to dinner. We've a wonderful cook called Célestine – her food is as lovely as her name.'

'Does she cook as well as Phemie, though?'

'Oh Guy!' she laughed. 'You have got a bad case if you can miss that. No, I promise you, there will be no mutton broth and certainly no boiled haddock.'

'Then we'll certainly accept.'

They had reached the foot of the great staircase, with the *Winged Victory* hovering at the top of it. Guy could not help turning to look up at it. She did too, and for some moments they stood in silence, examining it.

'You see something so ancient and yet so perfect,' said Chris, 'and you wonder why struggle on, why try and do more? It would be hard to surpass that.'

'That doesn't sound like you,' said Guy.

'Oh, I doubt myself all the time, now,' she said. 'That's part of understanding life, that it seems more and more complicated, more challenging, than you first imagined. I mean it would be arrogant now to think that anything was simple.'

'Yes, but I wish things could be, don't you?'

'Perhaps, perhaps not,' she said. 'Give my love to Miranda, won't you? I'll be in touch very soon. What's the name of your hotel?'

'The Bristol, in the Place Vendôme.'

'Of course,' she said, smiling. 'Well, I'd better go.'

He watched her walk away, and vanish suddenly in the crowd, as a large party came along the gallery. He pulled out his watch – it was a little after three, and he imagined that Miranda would still be deep in hat shops. He turned and went back up the stairs. He could waste another hour with the Chardins – and he did not think he would be missed. There was some comfort in that.

29

Chris was sitting at the dressing table arranging her hair. It was a scene he had become quite used to – not because she was a coquette who spent an excessive time in front of the glass, but because he had found himself the close observer of all her small domestic actions. He knew her routines inside out now, from the way she cleaned her teeth to the way she set about her piano practice. Watching her now, from his observation post on the bed, it seemed to him that he had caught her there in that little flat, simply to observe her. She was like a laboratory animal, in a too small cage, attempting to behave quite ordinarily, although everything was quite abnormal. He remembered the white mice leading purposeless little lives in boxes in the medical school labs, and how he had pitied them, and longed to set them free. He had despised the exploiters of those mice, for their cold use of the poor animals for so called 'greater' ends, to look for cures and explanations. Now he knew he was one of them. He had caught her there for an experiment, an experiment which had failed. Ought he really to go on with it?

They were giving a dinner that evening, which felt to him like an obscene piece of play-acting, for it was exactly what married couples were supposed to do. Chris had organized the thing with a sort of manic thoroughness. He had hardly expected she would care so much for conventionalities, but he suspected he had driven her to it, and that she was trying to prove something, as she wrote out place names for the table, and arranged armfuls of spring flowers. She was trying to prove exactly what could not be proved, that everything between them was just as it should be and that they were quite blissfully happy.

She was clipping to her ears the drop pearl earrings he had given her as a wedding present, along with a string of pearls. God, how carefully he had gone about all the details then! He had acted upon every piece of received wedding wisdom, determined that nothing should be left to chance. Like a superstitious old crone casting a spell, he had gone through it all down to the last sprig of white heather. He might as well not have bothered. All the glib convention in the world was not going to put him right.

She got up from the stool and stood smoothing the folds of her white silk dress.

'How do I do?' she said, turning round.

He was sure she was pretty and desirable. He was certain of it, but only in his mind. He couldn't feel it deep inside him. Should he make some fatuous compliment which she would know was hollow?

'You'll do,' he said. 'Very well, I imagine.'

He saw the faint flicker of annoyed disappointment cross her face and wondered if he should not have given her a piece of silly gallantry after all. He realized, though, he could do little right.

She came up to him, and fiddled with his tie slightly.

'There,' she said, 'you'll do too.'

He could smell the lavender water on her skin as she did this, and he wished he might pull her suddenly into his arms and kiss her passionately, or rather, he wished he might want to. He brushed his hand across her forehead instead, and said, 'Oh Chris, I wish . . .'

'Let's not worry now,' she said, moving away from him. 'There's no point agonizing just now, in fact there's no point agonizing at all. We just have to carry on, don't we?'

'I suppose so,' he said, getting up from the bed and picking up his evening coat. 'Well, I could do with a drink.'

'They'll be here soon.'

He followed her into the little drawing room, which had been cleared of its usual debris and seemed unnaturally tidy. When it came to papers and books, they at least had it in common in being quite unable to keep them in order. Chris declined the offer of a dram, but he did not feel he could face the evening without one.

'It's bound to be awkward,' he said, swallowing down his whisky.

'Oh, I don't know,' said Chris, who sounded as if she were swallowing down her nerves. 'Guy and I have quite sorted things out.'

'Do you think he's told Miranda, though?'

'I've no idea. I can imagine he would have. He's a terribly honest person.'

'Oh,' said Angus, and refilled his glass. It sounded like a reproach, as if he were not, which was quite true. He wondered for a moment whether inviting Lindsay and Miranda was on Chris's part a piece of puritan zeal, a punishment for herself as well as for him. 'Well this will be fun, then.'

'You thought it was a perfectly good idea a few days ago,' she said.

'I wasn't thinking straight. I mean, it's ridiculous, to invite your former lover . . .'

'He was not my lover!' she exclaimed. 'He asked me to marry him, that's all.'

'Oh, for heaven's sake, Chris, you don't ask someone to marry you unless . . .' He broke off, realizing the trap he had walked into.

'You would have made a very poor lawyer, Angus,' said Chris.

'Why did you invite him?' he persisted.

'Because I like him. He's a friend – and he's married to a friend. What better reason could there be?'

'I just hope to God he doesn't talk about pig farming,' he said.

'He won't,' she said. 'Goodness, you're sour tonight.'

'Well, what do you expect me to be?'

'Civil, charming, you know, the usual thing.'

'I don't feel like play-acting tonight.'

'And what else should we do, please?' she retorted. 'All we can do is make the best of things. You know that as well as I do.'

'Spare me the kail-yard philosophy, Chris!' he exclaimed. 'As far as I'm concerned I don't know what the hell we are doing here! And if you managed to be honest, for one minute, you'd admit the same.'

'You want me to be honest?' she said. 'You make it sound as if this was all my fault, that I trapped you under false pretences . . .'

'Look, I know it's my fault. How do you think I can escape that? I can't ever forget it can I? All I am asking from you is that you start thinking how we might solve things, instead of this nonsense . . .' He gestured around him. 'I mean, this is absurd! A bloody doll's tea party!'

'Well, it's too late to change this now,' she said, crisply. 'So you had better wear it, hadn't you? You might even enjoy yourself,' she finished bitterly.

The bell was jangling, and a moment later Françoise, the little maid servant, was bringing in the first guests.

The dinner, Chris supposed, was a success. The guests ate their food, drank their wine and there were no awful gaps in the conversation. Miranda was decorative in a new dress from Poiret, M. St Juste was expansive and whimsical as ever, while Davie Neill put in the odd sharp remark which amused them all. However, she could not say she enjoyed it. All the time she found she was watching

Angus, his words still stinging in her ears: 'a bloody doll's tea party!' and her annoyance at them grew and grew, as they passed from fish to meat, and then to the dessert. How could they do anything else but play such games, if games they really were? Surely it was necessary to go on as if nothing were wrong. One did not admit publicly to failure. For her part she had hoped to enjoy the dinner a great deal more. The thought of a civilized evening with her friends had been a comfort to her, a balm, and he had ruined it with just a few words. Well, damn you, Angus, she decided, and gladly accepted a second glass of Sauternes to go with Céleste's exquisite marquise au chocolat. There was an irony in that – she had chosen it especially to please Angus, who was inordinately fond of chocolate. She smiled at him across the table, with all the sweetness she could manage, and he was naturally forced to smile back. She saw that Blanche St Juste noted this exchange of smiles approvingly. So, their play-acting could convince someone.

Yet, although she had meant it in a defiant spirit, she could not help wanting it to mean something, that smile of hers, that it might suddenly touch him and change him. She could not give up hope yet, could she, after only a month together? She had felt something cold and ominous inside her when he had talked of 'sorting out the mess' and wondered what drastic solutions he might have in mind. No, she told herself, she would not think like that, not now, not at least while the candles were burning at their first dinner. She would not be fatalistic.

After dinner, the St Justes announced they had a box for the Ballets Russes which they could not use that night, as they had to go on somewhere else. They offered it to Chris and Angus instead. She glanced at Angus, rather fearful he would want to stay and talk bitterly on, but he accepted at once. Perhaps he too was beginning to find the value of distraction.

'You'll come too?' he said, rather surprisingly, to Guy and Miranda.

'They're giving something new,' said St Juste. 'With a score by Monsieur Stravinsky.'

'The *Firebird* man,' said Guy. 'I should think so, don't you, Miranda?'

'Of course. I love the Ballets Russes,' she said.

'Nijinsky, certainly, is extraordinary,' said Angus. 'I saw him as the Faun. You'll be astonished, Chris. I can promise you that.'

It was as if he had thrown his arm around her shoulder. She felt herself relax at once, and threw herself into the exciting prospect of finally seeing the Ballets Russes.

The theatre was packed, and from their box, which was a good one, they had a good view of the whole crowd. Miranda and Chris sat with their elbows on the parapet, looking over it, alone for a few moments while Guy and Angus finished their cigars in the passageway outside.

'Who'd have imagined this, six months ago?' said Miranda, with a giggle. 'Isn't it wonderful, being married?'

'Well, I suppose it is . . .' said Chris.

'You suppose?' laughed Miranda. 'Ah look, there's Madame La Baronne de Hulbert.' She gave a little wave of her fan to the lady sitting down in a box across the theatre. 'She's been so nice. I'll present you if you like. She's a great friend of Lady Lindsay's and since you know her . . .'

'Oh I don't know . . .'

'But it would be amusing. She has a salon, you know.'

'I don't think I'm quite ready for society,' said Chris. 'I've too much to do, really.'

'Oh, you shouldn't be so serious about that now,' said Miranda. 'It isn't important, is it?'

'It is to me, yes – you know that,' said Chris, rather put out by this.

'Yes, yes, but one shouldn't be so open about it. Now, if you were to be seen helping Angus, well that would be quite something else, wouldn't it? If he's to be a great man of letters . . . Literary men have quite an entrée in Paris, you know.'

'You'll have to ask him about that,' said Chris, watching the orchestra dribbling one by one into the pit, and noting the size of the forces.

'But you want to help him, don't you?' she said.

'Of course, but . . .'

'It's your duty,' said Miranda.

Chris could not help laughing.

'My duty? Miranda, the Lindsays have quite ruined you.'

'It's true,' she said pouting. 'I mean to make Guy make something of himself – in politics, for instance.'

'He won't like that,' said Chris.

'Oh?' said Miranda. 'Why not?'

'Well, you know how he is, surely? He's no more interested in politics than he is in the moon! Besides, he would hate being away from Rankeillor.'

'Oh Rankeillor,' said Miranda, flatly. 'Well, he may have to be weaned off that particular wet-nurse. I am certainly not going to live in the country all year.'

'It's a lovely house . . .'

'It's nowhere,' said Miranda. 'You've said as much yourself.'

'Yes, but there can't be a Guy without Rankeillor. You take that on with him.' She did not add that it was one of the reasons she had turned him down.

'It's all so appallingly feudal,' said Miranda. 'I won't have it, not all year. What would I do with myself, Chris? No, I won't have it,' she said again, with great firmness in her voice. Yet a moment later she was smiling winningly at Guy as he and Angus came back into the box. Perhaps for such smiles he would give up a great deal.

'You were a while,' said Chris. 'What were you talking about?'

'Greece,' said Angus, sitting down beside her.

She would have questioned him further, but the house lights began to dim. There was an expectant silcnce, and Miranda murmured, 'I do hope it's as lovely as *Scheherazade*.'

It began with a melody for the bassoon, slow, haunting and immediately intriguing which touched something deep and restless in her. She felt her insides grip with excitement, and at almost the same moment heard above the orchestra a whistling and hissing from parts of the audience that seemed to grow with the music as if determined to keep up with it.

'Can't people just listen?' Guy muttered. She nodded in agreement and, as if acting on their cue, a man in one of the other boxes jumped up and shouted, in French, 'Listen first – you can whistle later!' This brought silence for a while, and the curtain rose on dancers wearing bold coloured Russian peasant costumes, who moved, not like conventional dancers at all, but like badly managed puppets in jerks and jumps in time to the music, which in its turn changed its rhythms so often that it seemed to Chris that there must be a new time signature every two or three bars. The audience went mad at the sight of it, as if something quite obscene were being enacted on the stage.

'Oh how horrible!' exclaimed Miranda.

'Give it a chance, for goodness sake,' said Guy, angrily.

'Guy . . .' she said, clearly shocked. 'I really don't think you should speak to me like that . . .'

'And you shouldn't speak at all,' he retorted. 'We're trying to listen.'

'What's the point?' she said. 'This is idiotic stuff, an insult. Isn't it?' she appealed to Chris.

Chris shook her head vehemently. She did not want to

get involved in an argument about it. She only wanted to listen and watch. For all that the audience were making a terrible racket, the music itself still triumphed, seemingly inextinguishable. They might shout and jeer, but the music and that odd, jerking, frighteningly primitive dancing would go on and on, relentlessly, just like the indestructible forces of the earth. The drums throbbed on in their extraordinary patterns, despite the cat-calling, and the woodwinds shrieked out at the limits of their registers, making a sound so compelling that not all the booing in the world would silence them. She found herself tapping her hand on her thigh, desperately trying to keep up with the beat, as if she too wished to be stamping on the stage, given up to the energy of the thing. The music seemed to possess her, to express all those deep, unmentionable things in her that she had been trying so hard to forget. But now it lay quite open, she felt, the great gaping red wound of her bodily longing. Every phrase, every shriek of that music seemed to call it out.

Then suddenly Miranda was up on her feet and hissing, as if the infection which had swept across the crowd had now caught her.

'Shut up!' Guy shouted. Chris heard the anger and disappointment in his voice, and at the same moment remembered how he had kissed her, how damp and cold the grass beneath them had been, and yet how he had seemed to lie like fire on her. 'Can't you see this is . . .'

'It's utter rubbish, and I want you to take me home!' she exclaimed. 'It's disgusting. Take me home!'

'No, I want to stay,' said Guy.

She stood in front of him and tried to block his view. He pulled her down into her chair and she gave a little scream.

'Take me home at once!'

'Shut up!'

'I'll go alone then,' she declared and wrested out of his

arms, pushing to the back of the box. She stood there looking petulant, waiting for Guy to relent. 'I will.'

'Go on then,' said Guy, and took her seat at the front of the box.

As he did so, the music seemed to reach a more frenzied stage. Chris looked back at the stage and then at Angus. He had pulled himself right up to the front of the box and was sitting with his hands grasping at the rail, his eyes absolutely fixed on the stage. There was a bead of sweat on his temple, and his foot was tapping out the rhythm just as she was doing. Back on the stage a girl was dancing around and around, almost as though she were mad, as the music grew louder and more indestructible. The crowd was still screaming, but they were powerless against the diabolic force of that music.

'She's going to dance herself to death . . .' she heard him say, as she watched the girl sway and swerve, as if at the limit of her strength, but driven still to dance and dance on. 'It's bloody magnificent!' The crowd grew angrier still, but their anger seemed now to accompany the dance, it had the same frenzy as the music. Despite themselves, the haters were a part of it, a sort of percussion of fear.

Then suddenly, with a giant, clashing, explosive chord, in which the notes fell out like so many pieces of collapsing masonry, it was over. The girl lay prone on the stage. In a moment Chris, Angus and Guy were all on their feet, clapping and cheering as if life itself depended on it.

'For goodness sake, Guy!' shrieked Miranda suddenly from the back of the box. 'How dare you! How dare you!'

They all turned. They had quite forgotten her.

'I really didn't think you could be so selfish,' she went on.

'I didn't think you could be,' said Guy.

Chris found herself looking at Angus, and saw the cool pain in his eyes. The excitement of the music had gone.

They were left with a jeering, abusive crowd and the bitter facts of reality. It was as if the music had thrown a great stone into the glass house in which they all lived, and smashed it utterly. She expected almost to find shards of broken glass at her feet.

'Let's get out of here,' said Chris.

'Yes, yes, please!' said Miranda, in almost a sob.

Chris saw Guy swallow hard, as if he were swallowing his anger.

'All right.'

They left the box and joined the crowd that was storming out of the theatre, belligerent still, despite their expensive clothes.

'An absolute insult!' she heard one woman proclaim. 'It should be banned.'

'What do you expect from Russians, my dear?' said her companion.

'God almighty!' muttered Angus, and pushed through the crowd. They soon lost sight of Guy and Miranda, and Chris almost lost Angus. But she saw him dashing into the street to flag down a fiacre.

'We could walk . . .' she protested. 'A walk would be good . . .'

He held the door resolutely open for her.

'Get in,' he said.

She obeyed and settled herself, waiting for him to join her. Instead, he shut the cab door.

'Angus?' she exclaimed, leaning out of the window. 'What on earth . . . ?'

'I'm going for a drink,' he said. 'You go home and think.'

'Angus . . .'

'Think,' he said.

'I . . .' She was about to let loose a storm of protest but he stood there so stubborn and impassive that she knew it was not worth the effort. 'I'll see you later then.'

'Perhaps...' she thought she heard him say, as the fiacre moved off.

She glanced from the window, but saw he had already vanished into the crowd. She sat back in the seat and felt that there were tears starting in her eyes. Damn it, she did not want to cry, but it seemed impossible not too. Angus had gone. He was making her face facts.

And all the time, as she drove back to the rue du Bac, as she stifled her tears, the pounding rhythms of *The Rite of Spring* beat themselves out in her heart.

30

Guy found Chris alone in her drawing room, sitting on the floor, surrounded by papers which she had spread out around her. It looked very different from the previous night, when there had been a blaze of candles and bowls of scented flowers. All the traces of the party had been carefully tidied up, and in the daylight the uncomfortable, inimitably French furniture looked distinctly shabby. But there was nothing shabby about her. She greeted him with a smile and an outstretched hand, and indicated a chair for him to sit in. He picked his way over the papers and settled himself.

'Tea?' she said. There was a tray of tea things on the hearth. 'It's specially sent from Scotland.'

'Then how can I refuse?' he said.

'My mother – well, this won't surprise you in the least – she doesn't think you can buy tea in Paris so she's sent me a nice large caddy of china tea.'

'No, that doesn't surprise me,' he said, resting his chin on his hand and watching her pour out a cup for him. He knew now exactly why he had come. It was not simply the unforgiving sulk into which Miranda had formed her features that morning at the breakfast table, her mannered show of indifference which had sent him running out of the hotel, like a mad man, almost, fleeing the asylum. That alone might have sent him anywhere – for a long prowl in the Bois de Boulogne or for a quicker comfort in the form of a large cognac in a café. Almost calmly he realized it, as calmly as she was pouring out the tea: that he still loved her. Nothing that he had felt for her had actually died. His feeling had simply lain dormant, like some great root under the earth, storing up the energy and the intensity of it, making it stronger and thicker. He had not ceased to love her at all – he had only thought so.

She passed him the cup of tea – a broad, fragrant cup of lapsang-souchong, and he sipped it, wondering what he should say or do next.

'Well . . .' he began.

'Well what?' she asked.

He had an impulse then to blurt everything out: to tell her of that miserable scene with Miranda, to tell her of his own wretchedness, to tell her most of all exactly why he had come – if of course it were possible to find words for that. Yet he held himself back. She would not want such a bombardment, and neither did he want to hear again what he already knew, that she did not love him. It would only have been a momentary relief to him: a rush of self-gratifying words that would have changed nothing.

'What's all this then?' he said, indicating the music spread on the floor. 'The start of your first symphony?'

She grimaced, and said, 'I'm thinking of having a bonfire, actually.'

'What?'

'Well, that thing last night . . . In comparison, this all seems quite worthless. In fact, just before you came I was wondering quite what I was doing here at all!'

'It's a good thing I called then.'

'To bolster up my arrogance?' she said, rather bitterly. She leant out and picked up a loose sheet. 'This seems so conventional now.' She threw it down and got to her feet. 'That ballet last night, well, it was like a new language, wasn't it? I knew music could be powerful but that was more than powerful – it was like . . . Oh, I don't know . . . like an anarchist's bomb.'

'Yes, that's it exactly,' he said. 'That's why they were all shouting, I suppose. It shattered their complacency. It certainly shattered mine.'

'Did you have a tremendous row about it, then?' she asked.

'Yes, you might say that. She still wasn't speaking to me this morning.' He sighed and added, 'Not something you'd know about, I suppose.'

'Oh, do you think not?' she said with a nervous laugh.

'No,' he said, surprised. 'I'd rather imagined that you and Bretton . . . well . . .'

'Perhaps we all play-act,' she remarked.

'Is there something wrong then?' he found he must ask.

She bit her lip, thought a moment and then said, 'Well, it's all rather complicated, but marriage is complicated, isn't it?' It was as if she had served the ball back into his court. 'Besides, I'm not at all sure if we should be talking about this, given the past.'

'No, I suppose not,' he said. 'But really, if you're not happy, Chris, you should let me help you . . .'

'It's not anything which can be helped!' she exclaimed.

'I hate the thought you should be unhappy,' he said.

'Oh do you?' she retorted, sharply. 'I should have thought you might be pleased, that I deserved it for not marrying you!'

'Do you really think that?' he said, incredulously.

'Oh God, I don't know! Frankly, I don't know what to think about anything any more – everything is so confusing: my work, Angus, and now you, sitting there, looking at me as if . . . as if you still felt the same. I wish you'd go away!'

'Do you?' he said, getting up. 'Do you really?'

He moved closer to her, but she pushed him away.

'Don't, Guy!'

'I only wanted to comfort you.'

'Are you so sure about that?' she asked.

He looked at her, at her angry eyes and at the touch of red in her cheeks, at her pale, freckled, lovely face, at the crimson of her lips, and he felt his insides crumple up with desire.

'No, no, I'm not at all sure,' he said.

'Oh God!' she exclaimed, and turned her back on him. 'I knew it. Oh what a miserable, bloody trick!'

He stretched out and put his hand on the top of her arm. He felt the warmth of her skin through the thin stuff of her blouse and he felt her shake slightly at his touch.

'What is?'

She shook her head, and stood with it bowed, in fact, so that he could see every little hair on the back of her neck. He found himself bending his head towards her and softly kissing the bare flesh. She shuddered but there was no protest, only a faint, choked sob. And she moved her hand to cover his own, as it still lay on her arm. In fact she clutched at it so that the nails dug into his palm.

She knew she ought to cry out, at least make some protest, but it was as if a lock had been set on her mouth. There were no words left. Words were something irrelevant, when only his touch mattered, the fact of the strength of his arms about her, and of his lips on her neck. There was no way in which the thing could be stopped. It was inevitable, every muscle and nerve in her body told her so. Any rational objections were burnt up, like a scrap of paper, in the heart of the fire.

She turned to face him and pressed herself against him, feeling her fast-beating heart against his. Their lips met and they kissed, violently almost, as if they were driven savages. She felt she wanted to cry out already, just at the joy of his close maleness. He pulled at her blouse, and fumbled with buttons with such desperation she felt the muslin would simply tear apart. She did not care. He could rip off every stitch of clothing he cared to. She could think of nothing but being naked with him. She helped him pull away her chemise, and at once he was kissing her breasts, with a hundred frenetic kisses, each of which seemed to burn into her skin.

She led him into the bedroom, and they got quickly out of their clothes. He fell on to her on the bed, pressing his whole, strong, excited body against her, and she saw and felt against her leg the hardness of his desire. Weak with her own desire now, she lifted her legs and let him into her. She could not help crying out with the pain, for he came at her with force, and he looked down at her bewildered, as if he might stop. She gripped at his shoulders and pulled him on to her again, and the pain passed, into something deeper that she had never felt before. The force of it seemed to echo through her, a profound, vigorous thing, dark and powerful, that made her gasp and long for more. And each time he pushed into her, it seemed to grow and grow, until she found herself convulsed by it, as if it had momentarily taken her soul away. She was nothing but that extraordinary feeling.

It passed in a second, and was replaced with a sweet sense of relief, as if her body had been removed of bone and tendon. Guy too seemed to groan with relief and fell flat on to her, panting hard. They lay together, clutching at each other still, bathed with the warm sweat of their exertion. She felt she could lie for ever, and never speak. Words seemed so unnecessary.

But at length he pulled himself away from her and lay beside her, staring at the ceiling.

'You should have said,' he said, after a moment or two.

His words seemed to shatter the world their bodies had created. She felt cold and tired suddenly, and she sat up to pull the sheet over her.

'Said what?' she asked. She sat for a moment, with the hem of the sheet clutched in her hands.

'That you were a virgin.' The word came out uncomfortably.

'Does it matter?' she found herself saying. 'Would that have stopped you?'

'I don't know – I just don't understand it. Bretton, surely, he . . . ?'

'No,' she said, unable to repress the sigh that went with it.

'Why the devil not?' He sounded incredulous.

She rolled on to her side, away from him, and said, softly, 'He's not interested in women.' To say it to Guy was like admitting some fault in herself. She hated to do it.

'What?' he exclaimed. 'Do you mean he's an invert?'

'If that's what you call it, I don't know,' she said.

'And you married him knowing that?' he said.

She sat up and stared at him.

'Of course I didn't!'

'Then how dare he deceive you like this, how dare he? It's sickening that he could do such a thing to you, trap you.'

'Perhaps he loves me,' she protested.

'Loves you? How can he, to do that to you? The . . . God, Chris, you have the oddest notions of love. You wouldn't accept my love for what it was, but you fall straight into the clutches of a filthy pederast, and marry him!'

'He is not filthy!' she shouted. 'You know nothing about this, Guy. It's none of your damned business. I love Angus!'

'You can't, not someone like that. It's unthinkable. Oh, why, why for God's sake wouldn't you marry me?' he exclaimed.

'You know why,' she said.

'You can't say that you don't love me,' he said, sitting up and leaning against her. 'Can you?'

She shrugged her shoulders. She did not know what to say.

'Oh Chris . . .' he said, and rested his head on her shoulder. 'You do, admit it.'

'What makes you such an expert on my feelings, Guy?' said Chris. 'You know nothing of what goes on in my head.'

'I knew you wanted me just then,' he said.

She pressed her hands over her face, as if that might block the tide of feeling coming from him.

'Frankly I don't know what happened just then,' she said. 'We lost our heads, as much as anything.'

'Perhaps not, but we couldn't have stopped it, could we? Something so strong must mean something.'

'Must it? Surely it's like hunger – you simply need to feed.'

'That wasn't just hunger. Chris, you have to face this, we have to face this, that was more than that. When I make love to Miranda it isn't like that. I know you love me. You may not recognize it. I only just realized myself this morning that I still felt the same for you. You must see it now, yourself.'

'I'm not sure I know what love is. How can you be so certain about everything, Guy? With you it's all so simple but from where I am standing . . . I can only see complexity.'

'Things are simple if you let them be. That was simple, that was honest, what we just did, and it was magnificent, wasn't it? You can't deny that.'

'No,' she said. 'I can't but . . .'

'But?'

'But . . . Oh I don't know what! Why do we have to talk like this? There's no point in it. What happened, happened and . . .' She broke off, and looked at him for a moment, lovely in his nakedness. 'Oughtn't we really to try and forget it happened . . . ?' She knew it was a lie as she said it.

'What, and carry on,' he said, 'as if nothing has changed?' He was shaking his head.

'What else can we do?' she said. 'Be realistic, for heaven's sake. What about Miranda? She loves you.'

'I don't care about Miranda. I care about you.'

'There's no point. She's your wife. If we were to carry on, think how much we'd hurt people. Could you live with that, Guy? I don't think you could. I certainly couldn't. This has been quite enough!' She flung back the sheet and got up from the bed. She pulled her wrapper from the chair and put it on, covering herself as quickly as she could. She could still feel his eyes, like a temptation on her bare flesh.

'Can you honestly carry on like this?' he said, gesturing around the room. 'Living with that bastard, colluding with him? That's not like you, Chris.'

'So what shall we do then, Guy? Make a scandal that will shake Rankeillor to the core? Can you imagine what they would say? They'd cut us to pieces with their tongues . . .'

'To hell with Rankeillor!' he said, jumping up from the bed. 'To hell with it. I want you, Chris, and I'll have you. I can't bear to leave you in this bloody trap.' He tried to put his arms around her but she stepped away from him, denying herself as much as him.

'No,' she said. 'Think about it, Guy, be honest. Where would we go? What would we do? You'd be made an exile from exactly what you love.'

'I love you.'

'But you love Rankeillor – I know how much, even if you wouldn't admit it to me. You love it, and what it stands for. You'd be ruining all that. You'd have to give it up to Miranda.'

'I'd have you,' he said.

She shook her head.

'I don't think you would,' she said, with a sigh. 'Guy, this thing between us, it's a phantom, a dream. We can't have it, don't you see? There are other things we have to think of. It wouldn't ever be possible, would it?'

He sat down heavily on the end of the bed, and buried his head in his hands.

'No, no . . .' he said. 'But, oh God, I can't stand the thought of you in this misery . . .'

'Don't worry about me,' she said, going up to him and putting her hand on his bare shoulder. 'I'm stronger than you think.' Almost at once he covered her hand with his. 'You'd better get dressed,' she said, pulling herself gently away from him.

31

Angus awoke in the pale north light of Davie Neill's studio, on the large divan piled with cushions, to find that he was being sketched.

'A sleeping faun,' said Davie, showing him his sketch. 'A pity you didn't take your clothes off – that would have made the thing really authentic.'

'God . . .' said Angus, peering at the bold charcoal image of himself, sprawled across the cushions. 'How come you're so chirpy, Neill?' he asked, thinking of the vast amount of whisky they had drunk the previous night.

'I've just had my luncheon,' he said.

'Is it that late?' said Angus, sitting up quickly, and felt the headache, which he had only perceived vaguely before, assault him like a violent thief, creeping up behind him. He could not help exclaiming at it, and Davie laughed.

'There's some coffee here,' he said.

Angus staggered to his feet and took the cup that Davie offered, but left the saucer. His hands were not ready for such refinements. It was hot and bitter, but the liquid hardly affected his parched throat. The smell, however, pricked up his senses a little. He began to recall snatches of the previous evening – from drunken carousing with Davie, to the cat-calling of the crowd at the ballet; from watching Chris put on her pearl earrings, to walking along a deserted Parisian street, asking himself again how he would begin to tell her what he had decided. He remembered, and at once wanted to be asleep again and oblivious of the nasty facts of his reality. It felt as if a lifetime had passed in the course of it, a futile lifetime, for it had ended – well, he could not quite remember when, but presumably he had simply fallen asleep here, without ever finding the necessary courage to go back to the rue du Bac and face Chris.

'I ought to get back,' he said, swallowing down the last of the coffee.

'Are you still decided then?'

'Bloody, bold, and resolute,' he said, with a feeble attempt at bravado. 'She'll hate me for it but . . .'

'You must do what you think best,' said Davie.

'Do you think I shouldn't then?' said Angus. 'Last night . . .'

'I know,' said Davie, 'but I was thinking . . . Well, she's a fine lass, Angus, and it wouldn't do to hurt her, would it? You wouldn't like yourself for doing that.'

'And what else am I supposed to do?' said Angus, picking up his evening coat from where he had thrown it down last night.

'Come to some sort of arrangement,' said Davie.

'Arrangement!' said Angus contemptuously. 'That word smacks of hypocrisy and that's what I can't stand about the way things are. You saw us last night at dinner – playing that bloody masquerade.'

'All credit to your honesty, Angus, but there's a great deal to be said for covering your tracks,' said Davie. 'Believe me, I know what you're feeling – I've felt it all myself in my time, lad, and I've come to believe that discretion is the only way to deal with this thing.'

'And the ultimate discretion is a wife?' said Angus. 'Yes, yes, perhaps you're right – well, you might be, but with some other woman, an ordinary, silly-headed chit of a woman, but not Chris. She's not the sort of person you can play games with. It feels like meddling with God.'

Davie smiled and said, 'Well, I suppose she's not very ordinary, is she? But there, don't you have a chance, because of that very fact? You've been quite plain with her, and she hasn't gone running back to her mother, has she?'

'But I've forced her into a lie,' said Angus. 'And she deserves better than lies. I'll have to go. If I carry on like this, I don't know what might happen.'

'So where will you go?'

'Greece, North Africa, oh, I don't know yet. Somewhere where the rules don't matter. Somewhere I can be, without feeling my soul is going to explode.'

'God only knows where that might be,' said Davie.

'Well, here it ain't,' said Angus, pulling on his coat.

'Good luck to you then,' Davie called as he left.

He walked back briskly to the rue du Bac, in midday heat which was like the first breath of summer. The street was quiet still, for the French took their time over their lunches, and he hesitated by the gate to the hotel courtyard, hearing the sound of the piano drifting down. It was Chris playing, he knew at once, and recognized it as a variation of the piece he had first heard her play at Royal Circus; that restless succession of rapid notes that had disturbed him so deeply then. It disturbed him now, as he climbed the stairs towards it, drawn by it, as if it were a piece of magic she were performing to keep him deliberately in her web. He felt all his resolutions deserting him.

He slipped quietly in, and she did not stop playing, and as he came into the drawing room he saw how completely in the thrall of her music she was. She was wearing her pale rose-coloured dressing gown, and her hair was hanging down her back, a great pale gold shock of it, that swayed as she played, catching in the light and flashing. The music had reached a violent speed now, and she was crashing out the passages with terrific dexterity, her foot stamping at the pedal. It was impossible to be unaffected by the music, it was like the music of that ballet, driven by the same primitive forces, to express what words could not express – the deep, furtive, animal longings of the body, that went beyond anything the brain could imagine. The music shrieked out desire, like a vixen on heat shrieked out.

Suddenly she brought it to a close with a tremendous pounding chord. The echoes of it seemed to fill the room for some moments, and only when they had quite died away did he dare speak.

'Chris . . .' he began tentatively.

She started and gave out a cry of surprise, that sounded more like a cry of pain to him. He was tempted for a moment to run away at once, before she turned round and saw him, but she turned, and they looked at each other in a long, uneasy stare, as if they were perfect strangers. He felt like a criminal, who had broken into the house to rob or murder her. He had certainly come to do her harm.

'So . . .' she said, at length, sitting down again on the piano stool, 'you've come back.'

'Were you very worried?' he asked.

She gave a brief contemptuous laugh, as if the question did not merit a reply.

'I'm sorry,' he said. 'It was thoughtless of me. It's just I had to think . . . and I can't think here.'

'So you bolted into the night . . .' she said. 'So did you think? Could you think? I couldn't, though you did tell me to, didn't you?'

'I wanted to make you see that it's useless our going on like this.'

'Oh,' she said, flatly, drawing her arms around her in a gesture of self-comfort. As she did it, she disarranged the folds of her dressing gown, and he caught a glimpse of her bare legs. He realized she had nothing on but that dressing gown, and found himself digging into himself for a moment, trying to find the correct response. He should have liked so much to be vaguely shocked and excited by the thought of that, to be suddenly driven by it to take her. Oh for a sudden fit of cheap, straightforward lust! It was a simple enough thing to pray for, after all, there were plenty of men who could not control themselves where women were concerned. Could he not have some of that over-endowment of desire? He knew he could use it and make good of it. If he could do it then, love her as she wanted, he felt he might solve everything.

He decided he would try, one last time, he would attempt the thing. He moved towards her and pressed his hands, which he found were shaking slightly, on her warm cheeks. The gesture seemed to make her jolt with surprise. She looked up at him questioningly, suspiciously even.

'I won't give up without a fight,' he said, and kissed her on the lips. But he closed his eyes as he did, and tried to imagine the face of some perfect boy, a male Chris, lithe and hard, and smelling of sweat and tobacco. Yet he could smell lavender and the smell of a woman, and feel the smoothness of a face that would never be rough with stubble. He pushed his fingers into her hair, and wanted to feel a short crop, not the falling heaviness of hair that went almost to her waist. When he pulled her to him, he wanted to feel a hard, flat body, made like his own, not this thing of alien curves and gentle softness, that seemed to collapse beneath his embrace. Nothing was right there, nothing could ever be right!

He pulled himself away from her, and bellowed, 'No, I can't, it's only damnable play-acting!'

'You ... you...' she stuttered, and then suddenly struck him hard across the face. 'I wish I'd never laid eyes on you!'

'Then you won't care that I'm going away!' he retorted, rubbing his cheek. He had not meant to be so blunt. He had imagined himself explaining carefully with all his reasons, but her slap had knocked the truth out of him. It was an instant response – a way of hitting back.

'What?' she exclaimed.

'I'm going away,' he said. 'To Greece, for a few months, certainly for most of the summer.'

'Oh well, go then,' she said sharply. 'You might as well finish ruining everything for me.'

'It's meant to help.'

'How can it? You're abandoning me.'

'I'm giving you your freedom.'

'Freedom – is that what you call it? I call it neglect.'

'Anything has to be better than this travesty!' he said. 'You must agree. You detest lies as much as I do.'

'Sometimes we don't have any choice,' said Chris. 'Do we?'

'Would you honestly prefer to stay with this ridiculous arrangement, when it's making us both miserable?'

'What choice do we have? We've done this thing, made our contract – we ought to stick by it.'

'Like a pair of filthy hypocrites? God, Chris, you reek of the Manse sometimes. Well, I won't have it. I won't live like this, and I won't let you, even if you think you can.'

'Because I love you!' she burst out, throwing up her hands. 'That's why I want you to stay. Though God knows why, I do love you, Angus. Perhaps you're my disease, my terrible canker. If you leave me . . . I . . .' She broke off.

'You won't shrivel up and die. You're not the type,' he said, harshly. 'You're stronger than I am, Chris, and you know it. There isn't any other woman that I'd do this to . . .'

'No other woman fool enough,' she cut in, 'to meekly accept that her husband wants a separation after only two months of marriage. Who'd stand for that, but a fool?'

'You don't need me, Chris,' he said. 'Not really.'

'Oh don't I?' she said. 'I think that's for me to say.'

'You don't,' he said.

She laughed bitterly at that, and as she did the clock chimed three.

'I have to go,' she said. 'The St Justes are expecting me . . .' She went towards the door.

'Well, I don't imagine I'll be here when you get back.'

'Oh will you not be?' she said. 'Well, be good enough to let me know where you are, won't you? A postcard perhaps – is that too much for a wife to expect from her husband?'

'Chris . . .' he protested. Her harshness cut into him, like blows from a whip.

'Oh go, go, for God's sake!' she exclaimed. 'There isn't any point arguing is there? You've made up your mind. What I think clearly doesn't matter!' She slammed the bedroom door behind her, and Angus hoped it was not her crying he could hear on the other side of it.

Chris had arranged to meet Blanche St Juste and the children under the chestnut trees at the Rond-Point of the Champs-Elysées, and it had taken all the willpower she had in her to get ready to go. She had wanted nothing but a self-indulgent orgy of tears, as if crying might change anything, might bring him to beg at the bedroom door. She had heard him go into the dining room instead, presumably to begin to sort out his papers, and she swallowed the tears, washed her face and decided on defiance. There was nothing she could do to make him change his mind – she had no authority over him, for all the brave words she had thrown out at him. She had done more to destroy what might have been between them than any of his plans. She had slept with Guy – she had been an unfaithful wife, and for that she must forfeit her right to Angus. She could not disabuse herself of the notion that his going was a punishment for her infidelity. She was certain that if she had not been so stupid with Guy, her words would have kept him there. They had sounded hollow even as she spoke them.

So there was nothing else to do, but accept it as a grim fact, and carry on. She chose a smart dress from the press, for the Rond-Point in the afternoon was always terribly chic, and put her hair up into the softest, most fashionable chignon her trembling fingers could manage. She added a frivolous toque, which she had felt ashamed of buying, but of which she was now very glad. It was a sort of armour: like the gaudy silver-gilt breastplates of painted warriors, her printed silk dress and frilled lace collar proclaimed a boastful invincibility. She could not hurt, so long as she was bravely dressed.

Yet as she walked through the Tuileries, past elegant children with equally elegant nursemaids and past young men who lounged on the three-sou chairs and looked her over, she felt quite hollow behind her fashionable armour, as if without it she would crumble into a heap of dust on the gravel path. She felt she had no substance to her bones, as if she had destroyed herself by her own actions, eaten herself up with the worm of her own terrible lust. If only she had not given in to Guy, if only the old Rankeillor code could have settled its cold fingers on her shoulder, instead of Guy's warm lips, then . . . But there had been no restraint, only a few moments of terrible joy.

And now she was strolling through this dazzling place, observing the beautiful figures beneath the trees, glittering in the dappled light that fell through the leaves, a sort of Parisian heaven, but a heaven of surface rather than substance. It was a sight which would have shocked her ardent Calvinist ancestors, she was certain. They would have gasped at the painted faces of the women, and at the indolent staring of the men. For them Paris would seem an ante-chamber to hell, and Chris well set on the primrose path through it to certain damnation. 'Wide is the gate, and broad is the way, that leadeth to destruction.' Well, she had cast away their God, why could she not cast away their terrible morality? Angus's leaving was not a punishment, she told herself, it was simply an inevitability. He was right after all. It had been a charade, this marriage. She would never have let Guy make love to her if it had been otherwise. There was no right or wrong, here, no judgement or punishment, but simple failures and mistakes.

There was little comfort in that, though. A fit of repentance might have been more satisfying. It would have been simple enough to find the God that her parents had so much faith in, and prop herself up with Him. It was easier to believe in her own essential wickedness than in the blundering complexity and painfulness of life. She could flail herself and weep, and return a penitent to her parents. There was a sort of glory in repentance – she had noticed that at school often enough. But what good would that do? She would learn nothing there – of either music or life. She would see only the curtains closing around her again, and she did not think she could bear to go back into that dim world. No, she could not relinquish this life, although the bright light of reality might hurt her eyes. It was a better thing to know the pain of life, and cry and feel oneself torn apart by it. Angus had been right: she was strong, she could survive. 'There isn't any other woman I could do this to,' he had said. It was exactly the sort of tribute she did not want, but it was a tribute, none the less. With Angus, it was always a two-edged sword.

She saw Blanche St Juste now, as she approached the Rond-Point, through a flash of passing carriages. She crossed the road, and waved to her.

'Chérie,' said Blanche, and greeted her with three kisses. The warmth of this greeting, a mark of friendship, was to Chris wonderfully reassuring. When all else had fallen apart, there were still the wonderful St Justes. 'How are you? We've been worried, you know, ever since we found out this morning that we had sent you to a riot! Was it very terrible?'

Had it only been last night? It seemed half a lifetime away, their dinner party and *The Rite of Spring*.

'The music was extraordinary – quite brilliant really – and the crowd were . . . well . . . dreadful. My heart went out to poor Monsieur Stravinsky.'

'I know – and the critics said such awful things as well. We really should have gone last night, so Edouard is going tonight, to show his support. If you want to go again, you must – we've enough places.'

'I'd love to,' said Chris, who realized that otherwise she would be spending the evening alone. 'It needs a second hearing, I think. It's rather a complicated piece.' She sat down beside Blanche, and asked, 'Where are the children?'

'They've gone to the Guignol,' she said, and grimaced slightly. 'Edouard's taken them – I hate the Guignol. I always did as a child, but he loves it. It's Pascal's name-day, you see, so he had to have his treat.'

'Oh – it is, of course. I quite forgot . . .' said Chris. 'I must get something for him.'

'Don't worry, he's quite spoilt enough already.'

'I'll get him something here,' said Chris.

'Don't feel you have to . . .'

'No, no, I must. You've no idea how important bribery is in teaching.'

Blanche laughed, and they walked over to the various little stalls that sold a mixture of sweets, small toys and pretty trash designed to part children from their pocket money. Chris bought a little net bag of marbles and some twisted sticks of barley sugar, while Blanche, unable to resist the temptation to be an indulgent mother, bought some gingerbread and a shining tin drum, which she admitted she was sure to regret buying.

'It will teach him about rhythm,' said Chris.

'It will teach him about noise,' said Blanche. 'Still, it's so pretty, isn't it?' she added, holding it up so that its red and gold enamel sparkled in the sunlight. 'These German toys are so nice, I can never resist them.'

Standing there with Blanche, waiting to spot Edouard and the children emerging in the crowd that was pouring out of the Guignol enclosure, Chris began to feel a great deal calmer. She was surviving quite nicely. Blanche had not guessed that she had been emotionally shipwrecked an hour ago. Perhaps later, when she was alone, she would not feel so, but for now she was managing bravely, and felt quite proud of herself for doing so.

They went to one of the cafés, and drank sirop de menthe, and while the children recounted to Blanche what they had seen at the Guignol, Edouard quizzed Chris about *The Rite of Spring*.

'All based on the pentatonic scale?' he said. 'The whole thing?' She nodded. 'And the forces?'

'About a hundred strong – and the percussion, well . . . I can't begin to describe it.' She caught sight of Pascal's drum and, picking it up, said, 'Well, let me demonstrate. You'd have a rhythm like this . . .' and she tapped out one of the rhythms she could remember, 'for only a bar or so, though, and then, it would all change. Lots in five-four, I think, and seven-eight, but even odder ones than that. You could see the musicians were struggling a bit. They really had to concentrate on it. There wasn't anything in common time – you couldn't anticipate a thing. That's what made it so exciting. There was no form and yet it worked. It worked wonderfully. I wish I had written something like that myself. I envy him terribly for doing it.'

'You want a riot at your first performance then?' said Edouard. 'You may have one yet, Christina. Your music is not easy for ordinary listeners.'

'They'll get used to it. I'm sure now, that's the way things must go. We have to find a new language, all of us.'

'I think you have found your language,' he said. 'I was looking at your opera this morning – those improvements you've made, and really, you're almost there.'

'I'm nowhere near,' she said. 'There's still so much to learn.'

'But you'll learn it yourself. What I mean is, that there won't be much more I can teach you. Beyond a certain point, a composer can only learn by himself. No lessons, even from the finest teachers, can do anything. You are always your best teacher.'

'I don't want to stop our lessons,' she said. 'I wouldn't feel safe . . .'

'This isn't about being safe,' he said with a laugh. 'You know that. It's about risks, always risks. That's what you have to learn – to take risks.'

She sat back in her seat and sipped her drink, contemplating for a moment what he had said. It was as if there were a blank space ahead of her. Beyond a certain point there would be nothing, except of her own making. The pattern of her life, which she had imagined when she married Angus, was gone. Only this blankness remained, when she would have to go on alone and do what she was meant to do – write music, fill that space with her music. 'I'm giving you your freedom,' Angus had said, and the word had frightened her. It frightened her still, that emptiness of her independence, for it all rested on her, and her actions.

'And what if I fail?' she said.

'You'll have the comfort of knowing you tried. Isn't anything else cowardice?'

She nodded, and put her empty glass down on the table with careful resolution.

'You're right,' she said. 'So when should I stop?'

'After the summer, perhaps,' he said. 'We'll see. If you work hard this summer, which I'm sure you will . . .'

'Have you asked Christina about Normandy yet?' said Blanche, cutting in.

'No, no – I quite forgot. You'll come to the country with us, won't you? We've a place on the coast, near Cabourg. It's a marvellous place to work – we usually get up a few concerts in the Casino, and it's very agreeable . . . It would be good for you – and your husband, of course.'

'I should like nothing better,' she said. 'But I have to decline for Angus. He's going to Greece for the summer.'

'To Greece? And you . . . You don't mind?' said Blanche tentatively.

'Oh, il faut être moderne!' she managed to say brightly, and was glad to be in France. Such bravado would not have come easily in English.

32

Chris had been right, but how Guy hated her rightness! To walk away, without so much as a kiss – they could not even permit a kiss of friendship – was an agony to him. It was as if he had torn away one of his own limbs, not his heart, for he could feel that pounding away as he ran downstairs, thudding under his ribs with frustration. Without her, without any prospect of her, he was incomplete, a man grossly disfigured, without a leg or a hand, a useless thing incapable of facing the world. For all the advantages he had – his land, his solid, safely invested wealth, his beautiful wife – he felt impoverished, desiring above all the one damned thing he could not have: Chris. She had made it perfectly clear. It was an impossibility. She would never be within his compass. Always, always she was apart from him, kept from him by an invisible yet impenetrable shield, a crystal wall through which she seemed to shine more beguilingly so that he must, again and again, attempt to break through and reach her, possess her. He was like a man besotted by the jewel house in the Tower of London and there was no more hope of having her than of his having the Crown Jewels themselves. He could only press his face and hands against the glass and stare, and choke down this awful greed. Yet how much harder that would be now, when the keeper had unlocked the cabinet and for the space of a few extraordinary minutes let him hold that jewel in his hand, feel its weight and hold it up to the light so that every facet was illuminated, and the thing seemed infinitely more beautiful and more bitterly desirable. For he had held her now, and kissed her, and known her as he had not done before. To see her locked away again out of the reach of his needy fingers was a thing so painful that he did not think he could stand it.

But stand it he would have to.

He got back to the hotel to find Miranda had a guest: the Baronne de Hulbert, one of his mother's cronies. In fact, coming through the glass doors he thought for a moment it was his mother, so stamped from the same die was the Baronne. It was not simply a matter of clothes and hats but of gestures, of phrases, of the set of the head and shoulders, a particular carriage drilled into them while they had been at school in Boston together.

She turned on hearing him come in and Guy felt a sharp kick of guilt in his guts as if her being there, so like his mother, was in fact representing her. She was, he felt, her ambassador, sent to enquire whether the foul rumours were true: that he had behaved so unspeakably to his darling young wife whom they all so adored and could not bear to think of being hurt. For he felt his defection must be obvious. It was so obvious, so monumental to him, that he was sure that his mother, staying in some country house, had already received a dozen telegrams informing her of the fact and that Miranda, worse still, knew it too. She had heard it, no doubt, shouted by the raucous voices of newspaper boys in the boulevard beneath her window. For a moment he was convinced that retribution was here and that these two women, for all the elegant frippery of their clothes, were in fact a pair of black-robed judges.

He blinked and realized that he was not faced with the grave faces of executioners but with a gracious smile of acknowledgement from the Baronne and from Miranda. He found he would perhaps have preferred to feel the noose around his neck to her greeting. She jumped up from her chair, like an eager child, and ran across to him, the chiffon skirts of her loose gown fluttering behind her, like feathers in the wind. She held out both hands to him.

'Oh Guy, I'm so glad you're back. Did you have a nice walk?' she said, taking his hands in her own cool, small-fingered clasp. Suddenly for an instant she pressed her left hand to his cheek and added in a whisper, 'And I am so very sorry. I was quite horrid to you, wasn't I?'

Her sincerity was unmistakable and her nearness to him was choking. He felt that a soft pillow, softly scented with linen and lavender, had been pushed in his face. She would suffocate him with her devotion, her awful curse of love for him. How could he ever have doubted it? Now those doubts, which when she had been gazing at the dresses at Poiret's had so frightened him, seemed like wishes. Why could she not hate him?

'You do forgive me, don't you?' she added.

'Yes, yes, of course. Will you forgive me?' Had he really managed to say that? It sounded to him like the tinny voice of a gramophone, remote and scarcely real. Yet Miranda heard nothing amiss.

'There's nothing to forgive,' she said, and took his hand and led him over to the Baronne.

'Yes, come and kiss me, Guy,' she said, sounding rather as if he were a six-year-old just brought down from the nursery. He complied and found she smelt of heliotrope, just like his mother. 'And what have you been up to this morning?' she enquired with innocent archness.

'Just a walk,' he said, as steadily as he could.

'Oh this mania for walking!' she exclaimed. 'Your father had that too, you know.'

He managed to smile graciously. Of course he knew – and in his mind, he was suddenly a boy again, going with his father on one of those long walks across the estate. There had seemed to exist a perfect intimacy between them then, his father spinning that peculiar spell of gentle authority over him. It had been impossible ever to keep anything from him, and if he were there still, he knew he would find himself confessing to him. 'You don't need me to tell you that what you've done is wrong.' The phrase formed itself in his mind, an echo, surely, from some occasion in the past when he had teased Isolde or been rude to one of the servants. Yet the voice seemed as clear as life, as if his father were there in person, sitting, in his worn tweed jacket, on the hardest chair that he could find. Guy chose it himself, now, to banish this ghost.

'I called to bring you a card for my ball,' said the Baronne. 'I know you young married people don't like to go about much, but it seemed to me that I couldn't not ask you. Besides, it might not be too long before you can't go out, my dear,' she added with a smile at Miranda. 'It would be a shame to waste your pretty gowns.'

'Yes, wouldn't it?' said Miranda. 'A ball – how lovely. I do so love to dance.'

'I guessed it the moment I set eyes on you,' said the Baronne, getting up, and producing the card from her reticule. 'I shall expect you then.' She handed the stiff piece of pasteboard to Miranda. 'I'm afraid I must go. I've a thousand little things to do this morning.' She kissed them both and left, departing like a rose-coloured, satin-clad ocean liner.

'How wonderful!' said Miranda, tucking the invitation in the mirror frame above the chimney piece.

'I suppose so,' said Guy, thrusting his hands in his pockets and going to the window. The doors ran to the floor and opened on to a small balcony. He stepped on to it and took a few deep mouthfuls of air, hoping Miranda would not follow him. He needed this illusory solitude.

'Guy dear,' she said, however, coming out to him. 'Do you not want to go?'

She leant herself against him and looked up, in the manner of the setters at Rankeillor.

He nearly barked out a point-blank refusal and felt his arm twitching to push her away. Instead he gazed out at the tree-tops that lined the boulevard, and wondered what he ought to say. She was exactly like a dog, the same combination of stupid fidelity and beauty. She could not be made to understand, he suspected, this thing which had happened to him.

'Guy?' she queried.

'Of course we'll go,' he said.

She clapped her hands together with delight.

'I'd better go and dress,' she said. 'It's nearly time for luncheon. Where shall we go today?'

'I don't know,' he said. 'You decide.'

'That lovely place in the Bois, then,' she said, 'on the island. We could go in a Victoria, couldn't we? It's the perfect day for an open carriage – even if it is terribly old-fashioned.' She went forward and leant on the curly, wrought-iron balustrade, with her arms outstretched. 'Oh how lovely it all is here!' She turned and smiled at him, holding out her arms again. 'Why don't you kiss me?' she said. 'To show you really do forgive me.'

'You know I do,' he said.

'But I want you to kiss me,' she said. 'I like nothing better than when you do.' She pressed herself against him, in the same manner which only a few months ago had annihilated him. 'Humm?'

He kissed her on the forehead, which blessedly seemed to satisfy her.

'Perhaps we won't go out at all,' she said. 'We could stay here, couldn't we, and . . . well . . .'

She had wrapped her arms around him and her fingers were stroking the back of his neck.

'Perhaps not,' he said, managing to disengage himself. 'You don't want to waste all those clothes you bought, do you?'

She laughed, and said, 'How wonderfully considerate

you are, Guy! But that doesn't matter really. They're only clothes, and they're so smart they'll keep for a year or so, I'm sure. Besides, there isn't anything I'd like better than to give you a baby. I won't feel properly your wife until we've begun stocking the nursery at Rankeillor.'

'Stocking?' he said, trying not to sound too horrified. At that moment he did not think he could ever make love to Miranda again.

'Yes, I think we should have lots of them,' she said, throwing her arms around him again. 'Lots of beautiful little children!' She laughed, and said, 'Do you know, I never thought I would find myself saying that – but it's funny, being married changes everything, doesn't it? It makes one feel quite different.'

'Yes, yes, it does,' he said, with a certain gravity, and walked back into the drawing room.

'You're very thoughtful today,' said Miranda, following him. 'Is something still wrong?'

He wished she would not ask with such obvious concern, wished that she had not come to sit beside him on the little sofa. It provoked an impulse in him to blurt out everything to her, an action that would be spectacularly foolish. How could he bear to go on lying? He would have to, it was his punishment, to have to be dishonest. He had forsaken the right to ordinary moral standards.

'Oh it's just . . .' he began feebly.

'Tell me, darling,' she said, putting her hand on his knee.

'I'm a bit worried about the estate, that's all.'

'Oh,' she said.

'I didn't want to say anything,' he said. 'I didn't want to spoil your fun. After Florence and . . .' He broke off, appalled at himself, that he could spin this lie and make a show of his consideration for her. It was disgusting.

'You're homesick,' she said. 'Of course.' Her arm was round his shoulders. 'I know. Do you know, Chris said you might be, and I thought she was being silly, but here you are, a miserable exile, and all because of my clothes.'

'I'm being selfish.'

'No, no, I am,' she said. 'We'll go as soon as you like. I'd love to see those gardens in summer.'

'What about the Baronne's dance?'

'Well, there'll be others,' she said lightly.

'We'll stay for that,' he said. 'I'd feel a beast if we didn't.'

She kissed him on his cheek.

'There, a pretty compromise,' she smiled. 'How well we are doing, Guy! A model couple, wouldn't you say?'

33

The air in the Casino concert room was thick with the smell of Gauloises and sweat. It was a fiercely hot morning, and the orchestra was restive, after a long and difficult rehearsal. M. Vincent, the conductor, was finding fault with everything – and that was with music they knew well. Chris, who was sitting in the back row with Edouard, wondered how they would manage when they came to rehearse her suite from *Everyman*. She felt a terrible, crabbing nervousness in her stomach, certain that Vincent would find all the weaknesses and faults in her score, just as he had found them in the musicians. And those musicians too, they would judge every note of it. They more than anyone would be able to see whether her orchestration worked or not.

Vincent let them play on, through the wonderful finale of Edouard's new symphony, and hearing that extraordinary score, so well realized, Chris felt all her terror redoubling. There was nothing in her suite to compare with that. It was a crude, ill-fashioned thing in comparison with these straining harmonies. This music of Edouard's flowed with such elegance that the orchestra could not fail to make a good job of it. Its beauty was as limpid and as inviting as the cool sea that washed the beach beyond the promenade.

The final chord died away and Vincent dismissed the orchestra for a quarter of an hour. Lighting a cigar, he strolled up to Chris and Edouard. In his pale grey suit, with not so much as a button loosened (when everyone else was in shirt-sleeves), the heat of the room and the labour of conducting seemed not to have touched him. Only the flower in his button-hole was slightly wilted.

'Well, that went quite well, don't you think?' he said, settling himself on the row in front and turning to speak to them.

'You're a hard task-master, Vincent,' said Edouard.

'That's why he's no conductor, Madame,' said Vincent to Chris. 'A fine composer. But not a conductor. To direct well, you must be ruthless.'

'Then perhaps I shouldn't be suited to it either,' said Chris.

'But I think you should try,' said Vincent. 'You should take them through it the first time at least. As part of your education – don't you think so, Edouard?'

'It is a useful exercise,' he admitted. 'If you don't mind.'

'Well . . .' The thought absolutely terrified her, but she decided that to admit that and refuse would be extremely feeble-minded. 'I'll have a go.'

'Very sporting,' said Vincent in English, and laughed. He reached out and touched the broad collar of her sailor blouse. 'You look as though you just stepped off your yacht – très anglaise. Frenchwomen never manage such . . . precision.'

'I'm a Scot actually,' said Chris.

'Oh Scottish, English . . . what's the difference?'

'The difference between Normandy and the rest of France,' said Edouard, who had been born in Rouen.

'Phuuhhh,' said Vincent, blowing his cigar smoke upwards. He got up and walked away to speak to someone else.

'I should warn you about him,' said Edouard. 'He's a terrible womanizer.'

'I can imagine,' said Chris, opening the score on her knees. 'Now, help me with this. What do I do?'

'Follow your instincts,' he said, unhelpfully. 'You'll be all right. The orchestra will be glad to see you after two hours of Vincent.'

He was right. When Vincent introduced her to them, and with an embarrassing show of ceremony presented her with his baton, one of the brass section said, in a loud stage whisper, 'Bravo! I'd much rather look at that, than at old Vincent!' There was a gale of laughter and Chris managed to respond, 'I'd rather you looked at my beat than my figure, Monsieur,' and got more laughter.

She wished for a moment she did not have to speak French. She was pretty fluent by now (she had found herself dreaming in it, after all) but she felt she would have been more equal to the task if she could have used English, well salted with a few Scots words, for which it was often hard to find the precise equivalent. This crowd of men were such strangers to her. They had only the language of music in common between them, but somehow she must make them understand her and, more important, understand her music.

The music had been taken from various orchestral interludes in *Everyman* but she had much expanded it, working the sections over and over again until they bore little resemblance to the original source. It was more like an embryo symphony, in four short movements: an overture, with fanfares, and plenty of percussion, with a brief march section; then by contrast, an andante, mainly for the strings, but with an oboe obbligato, rising birdlike above them all; then a demonic scherzo, that had originally been a dance for the students in the dissecting room; and finally a largo, very rich and sad in its colours, with the atmosphere of a highland lament.

She looked down at the score she had opened on the podium – in the neat hand of the copyist it looked unfamiliar, not at all her own scribbled invention. She felt the sweat of nervousness trickling down her neck, and reached for a handkerchief to dab herself dry. The orchestra was still fussing slightly, tightening bows and adjusting the music on their stands. She took a deep breath and raised both hands to silence them, having decided she would beat time with her hand, rather than that silly encumbrance of a baton.

Their immediate silence was gratifying. They were poised like soldiers waiting for the order to shoot, but the result would not be destructive but creative. She hovered there, realizing the monumentality of that moment. She had always dreamt of hearing an orchestra play what she had laboured over, and soon, so very soon, it would happen. It scarcely seemed possible that she, Chris Adam, was at last standing there, her hands raised to bring down the first beat, about to conduct her own music. It was like the moment before a child emerged from the womb. What had been so long internal would now be external, a thing of the world and not alone of her imagination.

She brought down her hands and signalled out the first four beats, and then came the opening chord, as fresh and startling to her as if she had had nothing to do with it. It roared out from them, with more force than she could ever have imagined, the brass blaring out that first fanfare, the drums beating beneath. She felt her skin prickle in the exultation of the moment. It worked, God how it worked! She had done it – she had written down all the right symbols, for these musicians were reading and understanding exactly what was required. It was as if they were reading her mind. Although she leant out to bring the trumpet up to forte at one point, she scarcely needed to. He played out his little theme, which ran counter to the rest of the orchestra, with exactly the bold cheerfulness the phantom trumpeter in her head had displayed.

When the movement was ended, the leader winked up at her and grinned. He was showing his approval, and at that moment Chris felt she had never known or understood happiness before. All the disappointments of her life simply vanished. There was only this wonderful moment, when her peers had judged her and found her not to be lacking, when her dreams had become at last substance.

The brilliant August sunshine had brought the crowds out on to the beach at Cabourg. Angus, after two months of the deserted beaches of Corfu, found the sight rather stuffy, with all the women in their white lace Paris dresses, and the men in English-style blazers. He wondered if, hiding somewhere among them, was Chris, under a striped awning, or the shade of a parasol. He could not quite place her there. It all seemed too idle.

He had not found the courage yet to call at the St Justes' villa, which it was clear lay in the smartest part of the town, beyond all the large hotels and the Casino. He had walked to it, though, through neatly planted pine woods, along a well-made road (for the smart motors which passed him on their way to the beach), past numerous other modern villas, all of which smacked of money, the way that his parents' house in Edinburgh had done. He could imagine his father rather enjoying the place, with its golf courses and tennis courts. But to Angus it seemed bizarre. He had been living in a primitive hotel, in a little fishing port, learning to sail on a strange local boat decorated with an eye, and letting himself grow as brown and tanned as the natives of the place. He had not worn a collar and tie for an age, and now, although the air was cooler here, and it was a turn-down flannel collar of the more informal, seaside sort, he felt stifled. He thought, as he sat on the beach and watched expensively dressed children delicately digging holes in the sand, of the handsome old house above the town he had been so tempted to buy. There he could have happily passed the rest of his days. He had been almost convinced of that, and it had been so absurdly cheap. It was the perfect place for a writer. He liked the wine – he liked the ouzo better – and the utter simplicity of it so much that he had almost done the thing. Almost. He had been held back at the last moment, by the very thing which had brought him to this annoying seaside town: Chris.

He had missed her. It had been as simple as that, but it had been the last thing he had expected. There had been a dozen times each day when he had found himself wondering about her opinion on some matter or other. So often he had pictured her there, sitting beside him in the café on the harbour, listening to the Greek musicians. He had begun to long for her presence to quench his thirst – not a sexual thirst, but a spiritual, intellectual one that seemed in truth far worse. For all the wonder and the beauty of the place, he had found his loneliness eating him up. What was the point of the most glorious spot in the world, when there was no like-minded soul to share it with?

So he had come back, feeling not a little foolish and nervous about facing her. He was not at all sure he would be forgiven for what he had done – all that brave trumpeting about refusing to live a lie, and here he was, after two months, prepared to beg for exactly that. He was certain she would find that very shoddy.

He stretched out on the sand, lying on his back and closing his eyes to the bright sun above him. He wished he could block his ears to the chatter of the beach, thinking he might sleep, for he had not slept the previous night, for all the luxury of his room at the Grand Hotel. He had been thinking all the time what he might say to Chris, how he might begin to explain to her and make her understand. But some demon advocate in his own mind had demolished every line of argument he constructed. He had deserted her, after having promised so much. He could not quite convince himself that he deserved to be forgiven. He opened his eyes and propped himself up on his elbows, realizing it was futile to hope for a little oblivion. Until the matter was settled, there would be no rest for him. He would go directly up to the St Justes'. It was almost lunch-time, and she would surely be there for that.

A little way ahead of him, two men of about his age, their skin still wet from the sea, were sitting side by side, engaged in some earnest discussion as they rubbed themselves down with striped towels. Their closeness seemed undeniable – they seemed almost to publicly declare by it that they were lovers. One of them caught Angus's eye and smiled at him. He wondered what they were talking about, wished even for a moment that he were free and able to plunge himself into an association with them. But he was not free, he knew that now. His very presence there proved it. Chris had enslaved him, not like some bloody tyrant, but in the gentlest, sweetest way imaginable. His soul loved her, he was certain, and of that he would have to convince her. The rest of it did not matter. It might be unconventional, it might be frustrating for them both, but there was too much that was good between them to cast away. He had been profligate with something precious – he would not permit that any longer. He got up and turned his back on the sea and the beach, striding up towards the promenade filled with resolution, his pace double that of every other person there.

'Monsieur Bretton!' The sound of his name called out by a woman broke through to him. He seemed to look ahead of him properly for the first time and saw a tall, slender woman, well shaded by a broad hat and a parasol, waving her gloved hand to him. It took him a moment to realize it was Mme St Juste. She in her turn seemed as surprised to see him. He wondered how Chris had explained his defection.

'You've come for the concert haven't you?' she said, when she reached him. 'Chris never said . . .' There was no note of criticism in her voice. Presumably Chris had given a quite acceptable reason for his absence.

'She doesn't know I'm here. It's a surprise,' he said.

'A delightful one – she'll be so pleased. I'm just off to the Casino to fetch them both – they've been rehearsing all morning. You'll come with me, of course?'

He assented and they began to walk along together.

'How was Greece? You look very bronzé. It must have been terribly hot.'

'Oh I'm a natural lizard. After living in Scotland, the sun becomes something you revere. What is this concert all about then?'

'Well, Vincent has come from Paris to conduct, and they will be premiering Edouard's new symphony, as well as Christina's suite. It's a good place to try things out. Kinder than Paris, you know? And the musicians are good – they're mostly from Paris. There's not much work for them there at this time of year, so they come to Cabourg.' They had reached the pillared entrance to the Casino now. 'We're a little early,' she said, glancing at the clock above the door, 'so we may catch the end of the rehearsal.'

They walked past the various gambling rooms, which were busy, despite the time of day, and a dance hall, where girls could be glimpsed dancing together – the two forming an odd contrast of experience and innocence. The concert room was up a flight of stairs, and as they climbed up, Angus began to hear the music emerging from it. He recognized it at once, which surprised him, for he thought he had a bad memory for melody, and he was certain he had only heard this once or twice, picked out as a solitary thread on the piano. It was that Gaelic-style lament which she had written for the final scene in *Everyman*, but here she had transformed it, into something, well . . .

He found he had stopped in his tracks as the music ran over him, a thing of such haunting beauty and profound sadness that he found himself swallowing down the automatic swell of emotion that seemed to bubble up inside him. Blanche St Juste stood holding the door open to the concert room, and he only just had the wit to follow her in. He could quite easily have stayed there, and let the music invade him for ever.

He saw Chris on the podium at once, her body swaying with the music, as if she were the music itself, and the orchestra had nothing to do with the extraordinary sounds which filled the air. He saw the arms of the string players bending and the puffed cheeks of the woodwind, but it was Chris who had created it all. It seemed to come directly from the tips of her outstretched fingers, straight from her spirit. The music began to die away. No pompous climax here, but the melody alone, played on the flute, rambling slightly, and then finishing on a high, unexpected note, which resolved nothing, but left all in the air, like the half-finished sentence of a dying woman. There was absolute silence for a long minute, and then the violins began to tap their music stands with their bows, and in an instant all the musicians were applauding, not with mere polite gallantry to a pretty newcomer, but with real enthusiasm. Angus could not help joining in. In fact, he found himself running up the centre, determined to congratulate her for himself. The music had removed every last doubt in him. He did not care if she might be angry with him – he only wanted her to see him, and see how the music had moved him. She turned slightly and he saw her face. She had flushed crimson and was smiling stupidly, and, it seemed to him, she was also hastily swallowing back tears. She stretched her hands towards them in a gesture of acknowledgement and he read her lips, saying, 'Merci, merci . . .' Then she turned a little more and saw him.

He threw his arms up and open, in the best gesture of tribute he could manage. For a second, his heart froze, fearing suddenly her coldness, the rejection that he knew he deserved. She did stare – he saw her blink, and then, like a child, jumping from a favourite vantage point, she stepped nimbly from the platform and ran towards him. She flung her arms around him, with such extraordinary force that he might have tumbled back if he had not been standing firmly. He clung to her in his turn. Dear God, he did not deserve such forgiveness!

'Do you hear that! Do you! They like it, they like it!' she exclaimed. He only nodded a reply. He could not quite speak, but instead lifted her off her feet and swung her round. She whooped with delight, and the orchestra boomed with laughter.

'I've done it!' she said. 'Haven't I?'

He set her gently on the ground again.

'The first of many triumphs,' he said. 'Just you wait and see.'

'Do you really think so?'

'Do you need to ask?' he said. 'And I'll be there for them, for every one of them. I promise.'

With a quick hand she wiped away the tear that was trickling down her cheek. In reply she only nodded briefly, but in it seemed to say, 'Yes, yes, I quite believe you.'

34

Have I been rash? thought Chris, looking at the sleeping man beside her, the unexpected stranger in her bed. He was profoundly asleep, like a child, slightly curled up, his breathing deep and regular. He had come back and she had accepted his return without a moment's hesitation.

It was not an eventuality she had much prepared herself for. She had received brief letters from him in Corfu which suggested that he was perfectly happy alone there. She, in her turn, determined not to break, had, with a resolution that surprised her, put him from her mind. In fact that resolution had begun to convince her almost that she scarcely cared what he did. She had even begun to sketch out in her mind how her life might be without him: returning to Paris in the autumn, taking, at Edouard's suggestion, a job as an operatic repetiteur (the best way to learn the real rules of opera, he had said) and making new friends, finding a new lover even. For it had seemed to her, from the distance of Normandy, that her future did not necessarily lie with Angus. As she had put aside Guy, so she could, if she were self-willed enough, put aside him. Indeed, at times, both of them seemed like nothing more than dusty relics of a past that was becoming increasingly distant and irrelevant. As she did not dream in English any more, she did not dream of them. She seemed to dream only of what she might achieve with her music.

Yet on turning and finding him standing there, joining

in the applause, and then opening his arms to her, as if to capture her very soul – well, it had been impossible. All that she felt, all that mess of confusion and desire and sheer hopeless need, had bubbled up inside her and she could do nothing but run to him, throw herself into his embrace and pray that he was sincere. His demon possessed her again, for all the ridiculous frustration it must entail, all the agony of it, she could not be free of him. He was beside her again, deep in sleep, and she was, despite all her rationalizing and fretting, in the pit of her stomach, calm. She lay propped up on her pile of pillows, felt the thick linen of the sheet beneath her palms, and heard the song of the insects outside, as well as his deep, slow breath. She found herself shaking her head at the ridiculous quality of this calm happiness. She felt like one of those pious bodies she had always despised in her father's congregation: so sure in their faith as to be vilely smug. For faith in Angus seemed as risky as belief in God. She had no idea what he might say next, or, worse still, decide next. He had all the unpredictability of a supernatural being and she, beside him, felt horribly mortal, in being able only to worship and depend upon what might be either his whim or his absolute sincerity – which, she could not know. Tomorrow he might be gone again, for all that he said he would stay. She ought not to trust him, and yet, to see him lying there, how could she not?

She could not resist reaching out and touching the thick tendrils of his softly curling hair, quite, quite black in the half-darkness of the night. She thought of her own betrayal and wondered how she would begin to tell him of it. For he deserved that much, at least. Would he understand why she had done it and was it possible for him to understand something which she did not really understand herself? Guy had woken something terrible in her – always he did, every time he touched her. When they had made love, it had been as if they were nothing but animals, that any rule that civilization had devised was there only to be ripped down and destroyed by them. Guy was like the force of the earth itself, something primitive and desperate, which she could not help but respond to . . . God, what a poor, irrational creature she was! She felt so ashamed that she turned away from Angus, revolted by her own slavish dependence on these men, as if neither her soul nor her mind nor her heart could manage without them. Why could she not manage alone?

She got out of bed, and went to the window and unhooked the shutters. She pushed them only gently, but they creaked loudly outwards and she knew that she would wake Angus. She did not turn to see though, but propped her elbows on the sill and stared out into the garden. A rich, warm scent of summer filled her nostrils, a scent of pine and night-scented stocks and of the sea itself, which she thought she could hear in the distance, gently sucking the edges of the long beach. She found that she sighed.

'Ah, what are you worrying about?' His voice, heavy with sleep, floated across the room. 'I suppose I shouldn't need to ask that, really . . . considering.'

'I didn't mean to wake you. These shutters . . .'

'It doesn't matter.'

She turned and saw him climb out of the bed. He was wearing only his pyjama trousers, and seeing his strong bare shoulders she felt a stab of desire. She turned back to the window quickly.

'I'm sorry,' he said, coming up just behind her. She shrugged. 'I am, you know. This won't be an easy thing, I know, for either of us.'

'No,' she said. 'But at least . . . Well, at least you've come clean and . . .' she hesitated. 'I suppose, I should too. I . . . I . . . oh, I don't know where to start. I feel so . . .' She wrapped her arms around herself and began to clutch at the sleeves of her night gown. 'I've been less than . . . Oh

Angus, I did something terrible! I didn't mean to but . . . Oh God . . .'

'You don't have to tell me,' he said.

'I do,' she said. 'It's important that I do. But it's horrid.'

He detached one of her hands from her sleeve and held it.

'Whatever you say, I can't think ill of you,' he said. 'You know that.'

'Perhaps you will when you hear this,' she said. 'It's Guy Lindsay . . . That morning, after our dinner, he came to see me.'

'And?'

'We made love.' How flat it sounded, as if it had been the most mundane thing in the world, and yet she found she was shaking as she said it.

There was a long silence. She heard him swallow and sigh, and then at last he said, 'Well, I suppose that was only to be expected in the circumstances. He's still in love with you then?' His voice had a dreadful control about it.

'Yes,' she managed to say.

'And you, are you in love with him?'

'No, no, I'm not, at least not the way I love you.' The words had tumbled out all wrong, in an incriminating heap.

'What does that mean?' he said, the spark of anger lighting now in his voice. 'That you do love him?'

'No, no,' she protested. 'Look, I didn't choose to marry him, did I?'

'It might have been better if you had done!' he exclaimed. 'So is that what made you come running into my arms this morning? Your guilty conscience?'

'Of course not . . .' she put in, but he interrupted her.

'No wonder you let me go so easily that morning. I thought you would have locked me in the flat, but you simply let me leave. Why, of course, you did – that's exactly what you wanted. Did he come back very promptly?'

'I sent him away, for God's sake!' she retorted. 'Back to Miranda. He wanted us to go away together but I told him no.'

'What superb self-denial,' said Angus.

'I told him to go away because I didn't love him, because I thought that my marriage was more important. Can't you understand that? For all your shortcomings, I was prepared to stick with it – and why else should I do that, unless I loved you, loved you more than was probably good for me? Yes, I could have gone with Guy, gone at the first snap of his fingers, but I didn't! I chose you, Angus, I chose you!'

'But that didn't stop you doing it, did it? It didn't stop you letting him have you?'

'How dare you?' she found herself exploding at him. 'After you've treated me like a piece of meat on the table that wasn't to your taste – how dare you judge Guy for picking that scrap off the floor, and eating it. That's how I felt, you know, like a piece of meat tossed over your lordly shoulder. Not damn good enough for your funny fastidious tastes! Besides, it wasn't like that, he didn't have me. I chose to let him make love to me, I wanted him, I needed him. You may want your strange lovers, well, I wanted too. I wanted that sort of love, I wanted it so much I could not do anything but give into it. And do you know, all the time, I was wishing, wishing deep inside me, that you would do that to me, that you could. Do you understand that?' She flung the last question at him, like a command.

'Why didn't you marry him?' he asked softly. 'If you felt that strongly . . .'

'I didn't – well, I did, but . . . not as I feel for you. Can't you see that, Angus? There was nothing between us, or, at least, nothing that I felt strong enough to throw everything in for. There was nothing solid, nothing of the mind, of the soul . . . But with you, oh, with you . . . it's so different. Despite everything, I can't help but love you. Please believe me.'

He stood, now, just as she had done earlier, his arms wrapped around him. She saw him nod slowly.

'Oh, thank God!'

Suddenly he had reached out and grabbed her hand, and held it in a fierce grip.

'I'm sorry,' he said. 'I shouldn't have doubted you. It was just – jealousy, I suppose. I feel so . . . so uncertain still, you see. When I came back, I wasn't at all certain that you'd have me. I felt I didn't deserve for you to even look at me, but I so much wanted you, wanted you in here,' he said, tapping at his bare chest. 'And when you said that, it was like being in quicksand. Do you see? I was harsh, I admit it, but it was because I was afraid, afraid that I'd lost you to him. He can give you all the things I can't, can't he?'

'I don't want him. It was wrong, not just morally, but, it wasn't right for me. You and I, we're . . . Well, we can't ignore it. For all the mess, there's still something there, something so strong, so wonderful, I scarcely believe it could happen, but it has, hasn't it?'

She clasped her hand around his, and they stood in silence for a moment.

'So, the rest of our lives?' he asked. 'What happens?'

'Who knows?' she said. 'We go on, I suppose, as best we can. But not apart, Angus, please . . . I need you.'

'No, not apart,' he said, holding her gently, in an embrace which had nothing of passion in, but only a sort of exhausted relief. 'I need you too, Chris.'

'So what shall we do, where shall we go?' she said, looking up at him now. 'Do you want to go back to Paris, in the autumn?'

'Not particularly,' he said. 'But of course, if you do . . .'

'No, not particularly.'

'Are you sure?'

'Funnily enough,' she said, 'yes. I do love the place, and the freedom but . . . It isn't us, is it?'

'No, we need to go back to Scotland. I'm sure that's the only place my mind works properly. I fell in love with you there, didn't I?'

'Some might say that was madness.'

'Perhaps – divine madness. What seems foolish, even wicked to the rest of the world, well, you and I, we can see the sense in it, or try to.'

'No, we'll see it,' she said, breaking away from him. 'Let's go home then. I'll make my name there.'

'The hardest earth . . .'

'I've a good sharp furrow, now,' she said, and put out her hand to him. With quiet ceremony, they shook hands on their bargain.

Part Three

35
Edinburgh, January 1915

'You needn't come to the station,' said Angus. 'Really. It's such a foul day. I shan't mind.'

'I want to come,' said Chris. 'It would feel all wrong if I didn't go. You can't just go like that.'

Angus shrugged his khaki-covered shoulders and went on packing up his shaving kit. It was five in the morning, on a bleak winter day, with the rain slashing against the window panes and the wind rattling the sashes. Chris had drawn the curtains open a crack and then pulled them tight shut again. There was no light to let in – just cold draughts, and the bedroom was cold enough as it was.

'You're going to have a long day,' said Angus.

'I can sleep on the train to Rankeillor,' she said.

'Which will you take?'

'The latest I can find,' she said, sitting down on the chair to lace up her boots. 'I don't want to go, but I have to, don't I?'

'Yes . . .' he said. 'Now, have I got everything?'

'Not quite,' said Chris. 'I've got a present for you. It's not terribly exciting but . . .' She went and took the small brown paper parcel from the drawer in the press. 'I thought it might distract you from . . . well, whatever . . .'

'Inspecting latrines, if it's been anything like the last five months,' said Angus, taking the parcel. 'Thanks.'

They both knew that this would not be the case at all. When yesterday afternoon, the pink army telegram had arrived, cancelling the rest of Angus's brief leave, they had known, without saying anything, that it meant he would soon be shipped to France, and the front line. Chris had bought her present with this inevitability in mind. It was a pocket edition of Shakespeare, printed on Bible-leaf paper.

'Better than a Bible to protect you from bullets, I think,' she managed to say cheerfully, as he examined it.

'I'd rather the Bible got shot to pieces,' he said, and kissed her, fraternally, on the cheek. 'Thank you . . . Oh, what's this, then?' he added, pointing to the scrap of music she had written out on the flyleaf.

'I really ought to make you learn how to read music,' said Chris. 'It's the fanfare, from *Everyman*. You should recognize it, you're always whistling it.'

'I am?' he said, and then added, 'Yes, I suppose I am.' He put the book down on the dressing table, and finished his dressing – his dark khaki tunic, with its second lieutenant's pips, and the final elaboration of the Sam Browne belt. He unbuttoned one of the large waist pockets of the tunic and put in the Shakespeare. 'A perfect fit,' he said.

'Shall we go then – unless you want some breakfast?'

'I'm not hungry,' he said.

'No, neither am I.'

He went to the window and drew back the curtain.

'It's vile out there,' he said. 'You stay here.'

'No, I want to come.'

'No, stay here,' he said. 'It'll be better if you don't.'

'Angus . . .' she said, coming up to him and taking his hands. She said nothing more, for he gently disengaged himself from her grasp, as if to tell her that she must disengage herself from him, untangle her emotions.

'I'll go alone,' he said. 'I'd rather go alone.'

'Of course,' she said, moving away again. She found she was swallowing down her emotion. 'If that's what you want.'

'It's much better this way,' he said. 'You know that.'

He made it sound as if he were only acting out of the tenderest of concern for her, but she could not help thinking that there was more to it than that. All week she had been aware of his detachment from her. It was as if he were not quite there at all, not with her in the flat in India Street, but somewhere else she could not reach him, where he did not want her to reach. She had felt all week that they had not actually been together, although they had shared the same bed and eaten at the same table together, and had laughed together at all his silly stories of life with the regiment. The Angus who had just spent a week with her in Edinburgh was not the Angus who had gone off to war in August of the previous year. Rather, this man was a brilliant actor who had come to the house and impersonated him almost to the life. There was, she was certain, something missing.

She stood then in the hall and watched him put on his great-coat and Glengarry cap, this stranger officer husband of hers. Perhaps he was acting for her good and perhaps this coolness was a warning to her. Could he be schooling her for loss? For that was what was happening to everyone. Her poor sister May's fiancé, Archie, and several young men she had known at the Academy were already dead, in a war which seemed greedy for young life. She was suddenly appalled at his fatalism.

'I will come!' she said suddenly. 'I shan't let you talk me out of it.' She grabbed her mackintosh from the press just as the cab driver rang their bell.

'All right,' he said. 'If you insist.'

They went downstairs, Chris cramming on her hat as they did so, Angus overburdened with his extensive kit. The motor taxi was throbbing noisily in the dark street, and Chris noticed one of their neighbours peering out to see who had had the temerity to destroy the quiet of India Street. It was an elderly man who, seeing Angus in uniform, changed his frown to an almost military salutation. Chris imagined he might be the sort of person who had put up a map of Flanders on his wall and had peppered it with little coloured flags. Angus did not notice it – he was too busy stowing his bags in the taxi.

They drove in silence to Waverley, and Chris felt overwhelmed by depression. Perhaps Angus had been right, her going with him was foolish and would not help her in the least. She was possessed with an urge not to let him go at all, to make the cab driver drive endlessly about the city so that he could never catch his train, never go south and get himself killed. She glanced at him, hoping for a smile of reassurance, but he was looking hard ahead of him. She felt like an irrelevance to him, an encumbrance which could not fit in with his life in the army, his life as a soldier.

The station was very busy. There were hordes of men and officers going south, all accompanied by their womenfolk, and there were scenes of hugging, kissing and weeping which seemed quite unlike Edinburgh, almost Mediterranean in their exhibitionism. Angus left her alone for a few minutes while he went to deal with his luggage, and she stood in the midst of it all. The fear and sadness in the air was almost tangible. It was like a low rumbling note of despair, underpinning all the noise, and it shook her at heart. Beside her a girl of about seventeen, her hair not yet up, was crying helplessly on her sweetheart's shoulder. He, not much older, was a broad-shouldered farm boy, handsome in his kilt and innocent in face, and he held her so tightly in his arms that it seemed he intended to crush the life out of her, rather than leave her there alone. From the look of her, she might have wanted that, death rather than separation. Chris turned away from them. She felt she should not be watching.

She watched Angus coming towards her, his coat flapping magnificently, his stick tucked under his arm.

'Ten minutes,' he said.

'Is that all?' she said. 'Oh God . . .' She glanced around her, at that terrible sight.

'You shouldn't have come,' he said. 'I knew this would upset you.'

'Haven't I a right to be upset?' she said. 'I do have feelings, Angus, aren't they better expressed?'

'Then don't,' he said. 'It isn't a good idea.'

'What do you mean?'

'I mean don't feel, or at least try not to.'

She stared at him.

'How can I not feel?' she said. 'I love you, you know that, and you . . .' She did not finish. He was shaking his head. 'You . . . don't . . . ?'

'It's different now,' he said. 'Things are different. Everything,' he gestured around him. 'You don't need me to tell you that, do you?'

'No, you've made it quite clear this week,' she said, 'that there was something, something's amiss but . . . Why tell me now, for God's sake? What happened to that wonderful honesty of yours?'

'I didn't want to hurt you,' he said.

'Haven't you already?' she said. 'All week you've been so odd . . .'

'I tried, I really did, but things just can't be the same any more. Our compromise, it can't work. Not under these circumstances.'

'And why is that?' she retorted.

She got no answer, for someone had shouted out, 'Hello, Angus!' and Angus turned, at once, in the direction of the voice. She saw at once a change in him, as if a lamp had been lit, and was suddenly illuminating him. She saw his eyes flash with sudden excitement as he waved back at the caller. Then she saw who had called out striding towards them.

It was a young man, like Angus, splendidly tricked out

in the uniform of an officer of the Scots Greys, a young man so handsome that heads would turn when he walked past, his beautiful face wearing a look of absolute joy at seeing Angus. He swept off his cap and clasped Angus in a bear hug. Ostensibly a reunion of comrades, Chris knew at once it was not. This glorious boy was the reason for Angus's distance. She felt sick and angry at it, this sudden answer to her last question. There was such an air of perfection between them, these two bonny, well-made young men, so obviously in love with one another. They were, she felt, modern representatives of an ancient, long-suppressed tradition, which no amount of punitive rules could crush out of existence. She had not understood it before, this love between men that he had told her of, but now she saw it plainly, in these warriors, worthy of some Greek epic: men going off to war together, loving each other more than they could ever love the women whom they left behind, crying hopelessly at losing them. But she would not cry. She was too astonished, too jealous, too furious to cry.

'Chris, this is Will Crawford – one of my brother officers. Will, this is my wife, Christina,' said Angus.

'How do you do, Mrs Bretton.' It was an unenthusiastic handshake on both sides. Chris felt tempted to slap him across the face, and then to hit Angus. Why the devil had he not said something before? Why this charade? She might have been able to bear this if he had been honest.

The crowd began to surge towards the trains.

'We'd better go,' said Angus. 'If we're to get a place.'

'Yes, go,' said Chris, feeling her voice was as sharp as vinegar. She made a gesture of dismissal.

'I'll go on ahead,' said Crawford, and they were alone again.

'Go,' said Chris. 'I understand now.'

'You're angry,' he said.

'Of course I am. Why didn't you tell me?'

'I couldn't, I was . . .'

'Well, it doesn't matter now, does it? You had better go.'

'Yes, I had better,' he said, and to her surprise held her tightly for a moment and kissed her on the forehead. 'Be free,' he murmured.

'Angus . . .' she said, panicking at the closeness of him. 'I can't be . . .'

'You can,' he said, letting her go, 'and you will be.'

'What do you mean?'

'I mean be free,' he said, and began to walk off.

'I hate your riddles, man!' she called.

He stopped and turned slightly, and said, 'It's not a riddle. Goodbye, Chris.'

'Goodbye . . .' she found herself responding, as he disappeared into the surge of men towards the trains.

'I've got to go now,' she heard the private say to his sweetheart.

'I know . . .' sobbed the girl and prised herself away from him. 'God bless you, Jimmie.'

'Aye, you too, love,' he said, and vanished, just as Angus had done, into the crowd.

'Oh God . . . no . . .' the girl said.

'Here,' said Chris, fumbling in her pocket for a handkerchief.

The girl took it with gratitude, managed a slight smile, then buried her face in it. The sobs which racked her were so terrible that Chris knew the only thing she could do was to hold the girl in her arms. She shook against her, like a trembling young sapling, which fears it will never hold straight through the storm.

The girl broke away to watch the train steaming out. She turned back to Chris, and said, holding out the handkerchief, 'What do we do now?'

'I really can't say . . .' said Chris, and felt her own pain hit her now, like the pain of a bullet in her stomach. She felt she might double up from it. Angus had told her it was over. That was what he had meant. The bonds that had held them together had been sliced through. 'Be free' had meant, 'Let me be free.'

She found she was walking as quickly as she could out of the station. She had to get out of there, out of the crowd of oppressive, straightforward grief. These women had been betrayed by the war, a generalized, wicked thing which women had always hated, but she . . . No, it was not the war that had taken Angus from her, but the power of love itself, a thing so strong that she, for all her own adoration, could not fight against it and win. A bullet would be no rival to her love for him, but Will Crawford, in all his warrior beauty, was. Angus was more lost to her now than he would be lying dead in some trench as Archie, May's lover, was. She, unlike Chris, still had *his* love.

She ploughed up the Waverley Steps towards Princes Street, taking two steps at a time, no easy matter, for the crowds were still thick. Suddenly she heard a familiar voice calling out to her, 'Oh, Christina, Christina, are we too late?' She looked up and saw, four or five steps above her, Dr and Mrs Bretton were coming down, huddled together under a black umbrella. 'Has he gone?'

She stopped and wondered what she would say to them. She felt very tired suddenly, too tired to speak.

'Yes, he's gone,' she managed to say, and it came out heavily, as if she were admitting to herself by saying it aloud, the full extent of that departure.

'Oh . . .' said Mrs Bretton. 'And I so wanted to give him this,' she added, tapping the brown paper parcel she carried.

'There's always the post,' said Dr Bretton.

'Yes, of course,' said Mrs Bretton. 'Oh, my poor Christina, you look quite upset.'

'Yes, it was a little . . .' She found she was stuttering out the words. There were tears streaking down her cheeks, mixing with the rain. She turned away so that they should not see them.

In a moment Dr Bretton was beside her, and had taken her arm.

'Breakfast,' he said. 'You'll feel better for some breakfast.'

They made their way into the North British Hotel, where in the grill room it was impossible not to notice other stranded families seeking the solace of tea and poached eggs.

Chris allowed her parents-in-law to fuss over her. She was, for the while, a substitute for the son they had not had the opportunity to fuss over. She had not strength to resist them. She felt so deeply miserable, so wounded, that she hardly cared what happened to her. But when a plate of bacon and eggs was put in front of her by the waiter, she found she baulked at it, and pushed the plate slightly away.

'I'm afraid I can't eat that . . .' she said, covering her mouth with her hand.

Dr and Mrs Bretton exchanged a glance. Mrs Bretton leant forward and whispered, 'My dear, you don't think you could be . . . Well, you know . . . ?'

The urge to laugh, albeit bitterly, was strong then. She shook her head instead.

'You never know,' said Mrs Bretton. 'Wouldn't that be splendid?'

'No, it's just I don't feel hungry.'

'Well, drink your tea then, like a good girl,' said Dr Bretton, who found it impossible not to patronize people. She felt like telling them the truth then, in all its sordid detail. But they would probably think she was mad, slandering him so. Angus was a hero in their eyes now. He had quite made up for the past.

'Did I tell you, Christina, the Minister quoted one of

Angus's poems in his sermon this week?' said Mrs Bretton. 'We were so proud.'

'It sounded very fine. He reads well that man,' said Dr Bretton. 'It's a shame you weren't there to hear it.'

When war had been declared, Angus had, in an extraordinary fit of inspiration, written half a dozen poems on the subject, simple poems with a flavour of Burns about them which, when they had been printed in the *Scotsman*, had caught the imagination of the public. Within the space of a few weeks he had become a small, poetic celebrity. The sonnets were not like the usual verse he wrote. He had admitted himself that they were conventional, but he had felt moved to write them, and moving they were, full of love for the landscape and its people. He had even been dubbed a Scottish Housman.

'Which one?' she asked.

'I may not yet from France return,' quoted Mrs Bretton.

I may not yet from France return,
I may not yet come home,
To where the beech hedge glows like bronze
And the thistle bends to the breeze.

The words echoed in her mind, aching in their simplicity. How well he had caught it all, this terrible, necessary business of war, and caught it in a way that stopped the heart in its plain loveliness. It was unbearable to think of, that he could create such god-like things and yet still, like a clay-footed mortal, desert her!

'I think I should go soon,' said Chris. 'I have to pack. I'm going up to Rankeillor today.'

'Oh yes, your sister . . .' said Mrs Bretton, nodding. 'Poor lass.'

'She wasn't the first, and she won't be the last, I don't suppose,' Chris said.

'You're in quite a state, aren't you?' said Dr Bretton. 'Do you know, I don't think it's such a good idea for you to go on living alone. You need people around you, your family, at a time like this . . .'

'I'm sorry?' said Chris, wiping her eyes.

'Lionel thinks you should come and stay with us, when you're back from the country. It does seem a very good idea. We can look after you, and I'm sure it's what Angus would want,' said Mrs Bretton.

'Think of it practically. The rent on that flat in India Street can't be cheap,' said Dr Bretton.

'We've a very nice piano, you know that,' said Mrs Bretton.

'No, no,' she said, managing only just to temper her voice into politeness. 'Thank you but no. I can look after myself quite well.'

'Yes, yes, I didn't mean to imply that you can't,' said Mrs Bretton. 'You run the house very nicely, I'm sure. We think it would be nice, nice for us, really – to have you with us.'

'So what do you say?' said Dr Bretton.

'I'm sorry, but no, I can't,' she said, gathering up her gloves. 'It's kind of you to suggest it, but I really prefer to be alone. My work . . .'

'Well, we shall keep a very close eye on you,' said Dr Bretton. 'We can't have our daughter-in-law going under, can we? We have to think what Angus will say when he gets back. He'll want us to do our best for you, I'm sure.'

Chris rose from her seat and said, 'Angus won't be coming back.' For a moment she had a vision of herself saying that – a Scottish Cassandra, prophesying in a raincoat.

'What?' Mrs Bretton shook visibly. 'Oh Christina, you mustn't talk like that, you mustn't. It isn't helpful.'

'It's realism,' she said. 'I'm going now. Goodbye.'

36

It felt odd for Guy to be wearing his old clothes and sitting in Miranda's sitting room at Rankeillor. He had been back for a day, and he had not yet adjusted. He remembered, as he sat there watching Miranda knitting, with some difficulty, a khaki sock, how it had always taken him a few days to adjust to being there when he had come home from school for the holidays. School had always been harsh and sordid, and Rankeillor so luxurious by contrast. But in one way it was different. When he had been a schoolboy, he had still been ordered around in the holidays, by his parents, and various holiday tutors, but now he had come back to Rankeillor as the master of the place, after two gruelling months as mere second lieutenant, performing less than efficiently on a course at Sandhurst. It was very pleasant indeed not to have a sergeant major constantly dressing him down for his inability to drill. What on earth did drill matter, anyway? He had been sent there by the regiment to learn about bombing, not square bashing. He was not sure he had learnt a great deal about bombing either, but he would be expected when he rejoined his own regiment after his leave to pass what little he had picked up on to them. He had better work a little on his notes, while he was at home. But not yet. He was content to sit there in that old chintz-covered armchair and ruminate, for the time being, glad not to have to do anything in particular.

'Oh bother . . .' said Miranda, and threw down the sock. 'I simply cannot do this!'

'Then don't.'

'One has to do something.'

'You're doing plenty,' said Guy, thinking of her Red Cross clutter that had taken over several rooms, especially, a little to his chagrin, his favourite, the library. He would be there now it if were not for the ominous boxes of bandages and dressings.

'I was wondering if we shouldn't take a few convalescents,' she remarked. 'Officers, of course,'

'Do you really want that?' he said.

'Well, it's rather selfish, this great big house, just for me.'

'I'm not sure it would be very convenient.'

'Lady Ainslie's got over a dozen.'

'Ah, keeping up with the neighbours are we?' he smiled.

'I just want to do something patriotic,' she said.

'You are being patriotic. What about all those concerts in Edinburgh, for Antonia's refugees?'

'Well, that's it, isn't it?' she said, getting up. 'My own sister fills her house up with Belgians, and here I am all alone in a castle.'

'Then ask her for some Belgians. Those children would love the country.'

'I'd rather not. I'd rather have officers. Some of those people, well . . .'

'Snob,' he said. 'I've a good mind to ask her myself.'

'Oh Guy, you wouldn't, would you?' she said.

'I'm teasing,' he said. 'Of course not.'

'Good,' she said. 'I shouldn't want that. But officers, that would be amusing. And one wouldn't have to worry about the furniture.'

'You have an idealized view of officers,' said Guy, thinking of the horseplay he had observed in the mess.

'Why shouldn't I, when I'm married to a perfect example?' she said, coming over to his chair, and putting her arms around his neck. It was clear that she wanted to sit on his lap and be held by him, but he could not, at that moment, manage the insincerity that such an embrace would demand. 'Oh, darling, I'm so glad you're home.' She leant a little closer and kissed him on the lips.

This ought to be overwhelming, he thought. I ought to find her irresistible, this lovely creature throwing herself at me like this. He remembered how every morning he had woken in the narrow metal bed of his room at Sandhurst, as tortured with frustration as if he had been a schoolboy rather than a married man. It was a common enough problem with his colleagues and there was much talk of nice clean tarts in Aldershot, reserved solely for the use of officers. Once or twice it had been so bad with him he had been almost tempted to go and search one out, but he had never quite had the nerve. He had convinced himself that if he contained himself, he might, when he got back, fall in love with Miranda again. His frustration, he had told himself, would have to be borne, as a punishment for his defection. So he had spent a great many quiet evenings, reading the volumes of Trollope and Surtees which she obligingly sent down to him, and with her photograph on the locker beside his bed, at the sight of which the other men always whistled. It had been taken in Paris, by a particularly artistic photographer, with a great deal of her bare shoulders on display, and a grave, sweetly erotic expression on her face. Miranda, in fact, was popular with his brother officers. They liked her parcels of comforts from Fortnum and Mason, particularly the peaches in brandy, which Guy always gave away, because he hated them, but had not quite the courage to tell her that he did dislike them. That was a little like everything between them. Miranda was, in terms of women, just like those over-sweet, over-rich peaches, dressed up in brandy and put in a pretty glass jar – an expensive, desirable thing, which made most men greedy for it. He thought of the eagerness with which his companions had christened their army issue mess tins with those bottled peaches. One of them, an officer in a cavalry regiment, had actually speared one with his sword, and solemnly, and with great swagger, passed the peach from mouth to mouth, so that everyone took a bite. He imagined this scene again, with Miranda being passed from man to man, each taking a vast mouthful of her, while he stood by, not wanting any of her, when he should have been the most greedy.

He had hoped, how desperately, he had hoped it, as he had travelled home for his leave, that he would be greedy for her, that seeing her on the platform at Rankeillor, that the sight of her, after seven months away, would transfix him. He had tried to conjure up the feelings that had caught him when he had first known her, that sense of being utterly drugged by her beauty, so that all he could think was how he must have her. Yet when the moment came, when she ran along the platform into his arms, greeting him as if he were back from the front rather than a course at Sandhurst, he felt the feeble flame he had been attempting to light simply gutter and go out. He was a damp piece of tinder. There was nothing for her obvious passion to burn up.

For the first two nights, he had had the excuse of tiredness, but tonight he would not be able to manage that. She would be lying beside him in bed, quietly expectant. She would stroke his hair, and lay her head on his chest, curling up beside him like a cat demanding affection and attention. What would he do then? What could he do, when he felt nothing, simply nothing?

'Shall we go for a walk?' he said, having managed as graciously as he could to extricate himself from her embrace. He went and stood by the fire.

'You're very restless,' she said, slipping into the chair he had just vacated.

'It's all that drill I'm used to,' he said, and saluted to her with all the smartness he could muster.

She laughed, and said, 'Well, go for a march then.'

'You don't want to come?'

She shook her head. 'No, your walks are too exhausting for me. Besides, I've a few things to do for the dance.'

Tomorrow they were giving a dance and a supper for the people on the estate. This had been Guy's idea, because he had missed the usual Hogmanay party. Miranda, he was certain, thought it unnecessary, but she would do anything to please him. God, how he wished she would not be so pliant! It would make him feel less guilty for not loving her.

'I'm looking forward to it very much,' he said.

'Yes, so am I, actually,' she said. 'You were right – these things are important, especially with the war.'

Why did she not simply fetch a knife and plunge it into him?

Only when he reached the top of Rankeillor Hill did he let up his pace. He was amazed at his own speed and strength – the constant physical exercise of the army had given him unexpected endurance. He was glad to find it so. There were things he was going to face, he knew, that might test him to the very limits. It was odd, this being a soldier, waiting for the action, for the test which would inevitably come. He had seen the newspapers with all their casualty lists; an Oxford friend had died in the first push of autumn last year – and then, of course, there was May Adam's fiancé, a young solicitor from Brechin. That news had come a day or two before he had got home. He ought to go and pay a call at the Manse, he knew. He glanced down at it – the austere grey neatness of it standing always in the shadow of the church. He would go later, if he could find the courage to. For he could not go into that house without thinking of Chris.

He shut his mind to that, and sat down, turning his back on the village to look towards the moors, which he imagined would be bristling with game. The shooting this year had been elsewhere. He wondered if he might take a gun out one morning, to keep his hand in. How ridiculous that was. In a few months, in less, no one quite knew when, he would be shooting not innocent birds, but at the enemy. And who was to say that they, the terrible, faceless, evil enemy, was not, in truth, as innocent and as harmlessly stupid as the pheasants and partridges who clucked amongst the bracken on Rankeillor moor?

They had not been told for what they were being prepared. France was the most likely thing, but Guy had heard mutters of other fronts being opened up. In the meantime, he would have to train the men in bombing techniques, in such delights as making bombs out of empty tins of bully beef, in fact. What would they be doing, and when and where? He wished he knew. There was a dreadful uncertainty in this waiting. It would be better to be in there and at it, with nothing else to think about but the business in hand. He was not eager to be there, for the sake of it, but eager to get it done with, like a visit to the dentist. He grimaced at that – it would be nothing like the dentist's. He thought of the various mortars he had fired during the course, how they had cratered the sand banks, of the rag-stuffed dummies they had blown to smithereens. He wondered if he would have the courage, when the moment came to actually do it. Would he be able to kill a man, with all that military lack of compunction that they had been drumming into him?

He caught sight of the Manse again, and decided he must go down now and call. Perhaps May's grief would put him in a vengeful mood, necessary for a good soldier.

* * *

Phemie answered the door and took him into the drawing room, where he found the startling sight of the Adam women en masse: May, Annie, Mrs Adam, Miss Ronaldson, and even Annie's small daughter. At the centre of them all was Mr Adam, who had begun to resemble, as his beard greyed and straggled, something from the Old Testament. But there was no Chris, thank God.

'Guy, come and sit down, by me,' said Mrs Adam, patting the sofa. 'You're just in time for a cup of tea.'

'How are you managing?' he said to May. He had never noticed before quite how she resembled her sister. She had red eyes from crying but a brave expression.

'Oh . . .' she said. 'You know . . . Thank you for coming.'

'It's nothing, really,' he said sitting down. 'I don't suppose you'll feel much like the dance tomorrow,' he said. 'I'm sorry about the timing.'

'No, no, I shall come,' she said. 'I think Archie would want that, wouldn't he?' She glanced at the others for confirmation of this bold departure.

'You must do whatever you feel is right, dear,' said Mrs Adam unhelpfully.

'I think it's a splendid idea,' said Miss Ronaldson.

'Yes, I think so too,' said Guy.

Then the door opened again. Guy thought it would be Phemie bringing in more tea things, but he glanced up and saw Chris coming quietly into the room.

'Look who's here,' said May to her.

Guy got up from his seat. The sight of her made him panic. He felt his insides churning violently, as if he might be sick. Yes, he was sick, sick with sudden desire for her. Every thought about her, every feeling, which he had carefully stuffed away inside him, came tumbling out to overwhelm his consciousness. She seemed to him in that moment the only thing which could make any sense of anything for him.

They shook hands. He would have liked to have kissed her, but could not, he was sure, have managed to confine himself to her cheek. He remembered with too much clarity making love to her, how she had cried out beneath him with such pleasure. Even as she stood there, beautiful and collected, he could see her face, crumpled up with ecstasy, her hair a golden disorder against the pillow, where now it was neatly put up, with a black silk bandeau running over it. He took in every detail of her, hungry for every last button, embracing her with his eyes. Her dress was black, and plain, with a high white turn-down collar and deep white cuffs. It was the expensive simplicity of a wealthy puritan. He did not think he had ever seen her in black before – and found it magnificent on her. It seemed to make her eyes shine all the more vividly and brought out all the gold in her hair.

She went and sat down between her sisters, her dramatic black clothes blazing out her sophistication. Any trace of girlishness he remembered in her had fallen away in the year and a half since he had last seen her. So much had changed since then – and yet so little. His desire was as acute, if not more so.

Chris had been prepared for his being there. One of the first things she had been told on crossing the Manse threshold was that Guy had come home two days ago. Annie had told her – it was an important piece of local gossip, and it was natural she should be told of it. Annie could not know what effect her innocent pronouncement might have on her. Indeed it had taken a few minutes to sink in, and it had only been as she was washing her hands for luncheon that she realized that sooner or later she must see him. In a place like Rankeillor, there could be no possibility of avoiding him.

Only that morning, as she had tried to concentrate on her packing, as she tried to squash out of her mind what had happened at Waverley, she had found herself thinking again of that day in Paris. It was a thing she had often tortured herself with. It would come unbidden into her mind, to remind her both of her wickedness in doing it and, worse still, of the happiness she had found in it. Even when she and Angus had been at their happiest together – in that winter when they had gone to London, where everything had seemed to go so well for both of them, it would come back to her, that morning, and eat at her soul, like a succubus. She could never exorcize it, no matter how she tried. And now, here was the reality of Guy again, to be faced, and to be resisted. She steeled herself for the sight of him.

But the sight of him still startled her. He rang out like a wrong note amongst her family gathered in the drawing room. He was too strong and vigorous for such a place of faded femininity. She felt she could almost smell the maleness of him – and the clasp of his hand when he took hers was painful. Yet she did not want him to let go. He could have crushed the bones of her hand for all she cared. His touch upset everything inside her, and she found she could say nothing to him. She broke away, and went to sit between her sisters.

Her mother served tea, and the conversation was somehow kept up. She had little to say, and Guy, she could not help noticing, was similarly quiet. She kept staring at him, at the strong, craggy bones which moulded his face, at the coarse, army-short and tow-coloured hair, at the broad hands holding a tea-cup which rattled in his saucer – God, his hands were shaking! Their eyes met as she realized this, and the cup rattled all the more. He swallowed the last of it down, set the cup down at his feet, and said, suddenly, 'I've been following all your successes, you know,' as if she were the only person there.

'Thank you,' she said.

'The symphony sounded simply tremendous. I wish I'd been there to hear it. I should like to see the score. Is it printed yet?'

'No, not yet,' she said. 'But you're welcome to look at the manuscript.'

'Might I have a look at it now? I've only got a week's leave, remember?'

'I'll go and get it, then, shall I?'

She realized he was manoeuvring to be alone with her. When she got up to leave the room, he jumped to his feet, not with the usual automatic politeness of men getting up when a woman did, but with the arching eagerness of a dog waiting for its master to reward it. She could smell his desire, and she found herself running upstairs, as if she were running away from it. In the cool silence of her room, she hesitated – she had a strong instinct to lock the door and never go down again. But something else in her shouted that that was cowardly, that she had to face him, and let whatever must happen, happen.

On the bed lay a copy of Angus's poetry – her father had asked her to bring one, as he, with characteristic carelessness, had given his own away. She picked it up and ran her finger over the dove-grey dust cover, with its elegant black type: Poems by Angus Bretton. She remembered the prickle of pride she had felt when she had first seen that little book. She remembered how she had written to him at once about it, and he had written back. They had been long letters, so full of trust that the idea of betrayal, of sliding affection, would seem impossible to any outsider who might have read them. It would have seemed impossible to them, after that glorious winter in London, and yet that morning she had seen that he no longer loved her.

She threw the book down on the bed, and picked up the battered attaché case in which she kept all her work. Well, what did it matter what happened? What did anything matter any more?

As she went downstairs, someone began to play the piano, to play Schubert, in fact, one of the Moments Musicaux. She knew at once it was Guy – he was the only person there who could play that well, and with that characteristic style. She found she had forgotten the peculiar brilliance of it. How good he was – she had heard many professional pianists now, and yet his playing still impressed her. It was as if the music stemmed directly from his blood – there was nothing insincere about his interpretation, nothing laboured. She stood in the hall and listened, as his fingers slipped through the rapid passages with such ease. She closed her eyes and listened and felt herself shaking with an old desire – to create. How often, when they were younger, had she heard him play and felt that feeling deep in her bones. To hear him now was like finding the source of her own river.

She went to the dining-room door, which was open, and saw that he was playing at the request of her aunt Minna. She was sitting at the head of the table, in that state of peculiar stillness of one listening intently to every note. Guy had reached a slow passage now – a simple melody, with the simplest accompaniment of chords, but full of such feeling that Chris stood there unable to think of anything else but the utter beauty of it.

He released the final chord but no one spoke until it had quite died away. Then, a moment or two later, Aunt Minna said, getting up from her seat, 'You shouldn't be a soldier. It seems all wrong.' Her voice was quiet and rather sad. 'Well, I shall leave you to Chris's symphony . . .' she said, with more of her usual briskness, as she passed Chris in the doorway. 'It would seem hard to follow that.'

Chris nodded and came into the room and put down her attaché case on the table.

'She's right, you know,' she said, as the door closed. 'That was beautifully done.'

'Do you know,' he said. 'The first time I ever kissed you was in this room.'

'I remember.'

'Of course you do,' he said. 'It's all fixed in our minds, every minute of it.'

She nodded, and suddenly he grabbed her into his arms and began to kiss her. She did not protest – it was exactly what every nerve in her body had been crying for him to do. And greedily, she kissed him in return, like a starving child. She felt his hand slip down from her waist and clasp at her buttocks through her skirt, and felt the hardness of his desire, where he was pressed against her. She felt weak and without breath, as if she might pass out from the power of his onslaught, from the power of her own rising desperation.

'We can't ignore, this, can we?' she said, falling against him. Being back in his arms seemed to paralyse her entire being.

'No,' he said, shaking his head. 'Thank God, you've seen it. Oh God, Chris, I think I'll go mad. You . . . I . . .' He broke off and pressed his mouth to hers again. 'I want you,' he said, breathlessly. 'I want you.'

'Yes, yes, I know . . .'

'When?'

'Whenever,' she said.

'Tomorrow – tomorrow night,' he said. 'Yes?'

'Yes,' she answered and returned his kiss, wondering how her body could wait until then.

37

'I've written a little waltz for the band,' said Chris. 'Just a trifle. A Rankeillor waltz.'

'Oh, how enchanting,' said Miranda, kissing her. 'You shouldn't have.'

Guy, who was standing a few paces away, talking to one of the tenants, found he could not help glancing at this embrace. When he had heard the Adams announced he had scrupulously looked away. He did not want to upset himself too much by the sight of Chris making an entrance. His balance felt delicate enough as it was. But hearing her voice over his shoulder, he had to turn and look, and, like Orpheus looking back at Eurydice, he felt as lost at the sight of her. How strange it was to see his wife and his mistress exchanging this social kiss. To any other observer, it must have made a pretty sight – these two handsome women, in their striking evening dresses – the dark-haired woman in white satin, and the fair-haired creature in black. Did she always wear black now, he wondered, looking at the soft chiffon overskirts that floated slightly in the draught of the doorway. His mistress . . . He realized he had not thought of Chris as that before, but if they kept their assignation that night, well, she would be exactly that.

'It was no trouble. You know how I am . . . I like to keep myself busy,' she said. 'I've written out the parts for them. They shouldn't have any trouble with it – I hope.'

'Look, Guy, look,' said Miranda. 'Isn't this delightful –

Rankeillor Castle Waltz – or perhaps we should call it "The Laird's Return"? That would be quite the right style for a country dance tune, wouldn't it?'

'Splendid – quite an honour for us, in fact,' said Guy, noticing how she had rolled the music up and tied it up with a piece of ribbon, as if it were a thing of ceremony.

'It's just a piece of silliness,' she said, smiling. 'I needed something to do. I hate not to work.'

'I like to hear a child of mine saying that,' said Mr Adam, who had come in just after. 'Good evening, Lady Lindsay. You're looking very bonny tonight.'

'Well, I'd better give this to the band,' said Chris, and walked away. Guy's instinct was to follow at once, but he could not leave the receiving line, when the party was in his honour.

'I'm sorry if we're a bit late,' Mrs Adam was saying to him. 'May had doubts at the last minute, you know.'

'Yes, quite,' he said. May was coming in, leaning on Annie's arm. Her eyes were red from crying and went ill with her primrose-coloured dress. But she was managing a bright smile now, when they shook hands.

'Make sure you ask her to dance,' muttered Miranda, when they had gone past, and, turning to the next arrivals, said aloud, 'Oh Mr and Mrs Mackintosh, you've made it – quite a journey in this awful weather, eh? Thank you so much for coming.'

That duty by the doorway seemed interminable and Guy could hardly concentrate on greeting his tenants. When he had had the idea of this party at Sandhurst, it had seemed an attractive prospect, seeing all the old familiar faces from the estate, and hearing their pithy Scots talk. Yet, because of one familiar face, he almost could not stand it. He kept glancing into the body of the room, hoping to catch sight of Chris in her black dress.

'I think that's everyone,' said Miranda. 'Let's go and open the dancing.'

They made a sort of royal progress through the drawing room, to the gallery where the dance would be held, with Miranda leaning on his arm and smiling at everyone, quite the perfect Laird's wife. His mother and Lady Seaton had picked her out for the job, after all. At the entrance, she gathered up Mr and Mrs Adam.

'Won't you help us open the dancing?' she said.

Miranda had been resolutely patriotic when it came to the decorations in the gallery. She had put up an enormous quantity of red, white and blue bunting, as well as every possibly relevant flag. On the back wall, there was even, set against an elaborate draping of flags, a large coloured portrait of the King and Queen, that looked as if it had come free with some popular magazine. The effect was a little strange, to say the least, disfiguring the large paintings and tapestries that were the usual decorations. It was exactly the war, in that respect, imposing on the normal state of things a different set of rules.

He noticed Chris then, standing talking to the band, a dramatic figure against the red, white and blue. He wished he could dance with her.

'What shall we have then?' said Miranda. 'Chris's waltz?'

'Yes, why not?'

'Go and tell them then.'

He walked over to the band, just as Tam Reid was handing Chris a fiddle.

'It's been a long time,' she said, 'I'll send you all out.'

'No, go on, Miss Christina – it's your tune, you should lead us. I seem to remember you had a neat hand at it – you should have, when I taught you.'

Guy had forgotten that she had once played the fiddle.

'Yes, you must,' Guy said, cutting in.

'All right. Trust Tam to bring a spare to taunt me with.'

'Well, when I heard you were home,' said Tam, 'I knew

you'd want to be playing again. So what do you want to start with, Rankeillor?' he added, turning to Guy.

'We'll start with Mrs Bretton's waltz, if you can manage that just now.'

'Och, well, I don't think it's so devilish that we can't,' said Tam. 'Can we, lads?'

'She's going to play then?' asked Miranda, when he returned to her. 'That's a good idea. There's no fun in dancing when there's no one you really care to dance with. She must be worried sick about Angus. Apparently he's going to the front this time.'

'Yes, she must be,' he said.

The band struck up the opening chord, at which it was traditional for the women to make a slight bob of a curtsey to their partners. But Miranda chose instead to make a deep show of reverence, smiling broadly all the time as she did, as if to show her absolute affection for him in a gesture.

'Why did you do that?' he said, as he took her into his arms for the waltz.

'Because I love you, and I'm glad you're home,' she said, stretching out to give him a swift kiss. As she did, the band began the waltz and they began to dance. Chris's waltz was a perfect thing, he realized as he heard it unfold. She had stuck exactly to the conventions, and yet there was more, far more, to it than an old, unconscious folk melody. It was as bitter as it was sweet. He knew then she had not written it merely to distract herself. Rather, it said everything about the impossible situation in which they found themselves. She was speaking in it for them both.

'Guy – this won't work . . .' she said, as later she followed him along the corridor. 'People will notice we've gone.'

'Perhaps,' he said, turning to take her hand and pull her along, as if they were children again, running off for some escapade. 'But they'll never think we might be together, will they?'

'I don't know,' she said.

'Of course they won't,' he said. 'Who would ever think such a thing possible – you, with your handsome husband, the Scottish soldier poet, no less, and me, well, who could conceive of my being unfaithful to Miranda?'

'But you are conceiving of it,' she said.

'I don't consider it infidelity. It would be if I loved her,' he said.

'I don't see the logic of that.'

'Oh come on, Chris,' he said, suddenly, 'what is this?'

'Cold feet, I suppose.'

'I won't have that,' he said, stopping and pulling her into his arms. 'I won't. There's nothing to be afraid of.'

'Isn't there?' she said, breaking away from him. The passageway, only some twenty yards from the party, seemed extraordinarily exposed. 'What if someone finds us, sees us . . .'

'They won't,' he said, turning a bend in the passageway. 'Haven't you heard of keys and locks? And they are all far too busy eating.'

'I don't know how you can take this so lightly, Guy. I'm terrified.'

'Because I'm happy,' he said. 'For the first time in bloody months. I couldn't give a damn about anything. As far as I am concerned, this is all that matters at the moment.'

He began to run up the narrow turnpike stair in front of him, as eager as a boy.

'Where are we going?' she asked.

'To my room – my old room, rather,' he said.

At the top of the stair, he pushed open the first door they came to. They went in and he switched on the light.

'I had them lay a fire in here,' he said, turning the key in the lock. 'I'll just put a match to it.'

'Anyone would think you've a history of this sort of thing,' she remarked, looking around her.

He laughed, as he crouched before the fire, and struck a match.

'Perhaps it runs in the blood,' he said. 'But don't worry, there isn't anything suspicious in asking for a fire in here. I use it as a sort of study. I keep my collection here . . .'

'Ah, yes, your tin soldiers,' she said. 'I remember now . . .'

A hundred little gimlet-eyed figures seemed to stare at her from every surface, their colourful uniforms glistening dully in the soft electric light. She had an urge to turn them all to face the wall. They seemed a little like witnesses.

'It's ridiculous really – I haven't bought any in years. But here they all are, still, all set out with nowhere to go, no real battles to fight. They've been quite useful though. I managed to keep my end up at those mess dinners at Sandhurst because of them. One of the adjutants thought I was quite knowledgeable about military history, for a volunteer.' He laughed. 'You've no idea how scornfully he said "volunteer"!'

Chris sat down on the edge of the bed, and found herself stroking the ancient crimson damask that formed the counterpane. She stared down at her hand, needing to concentrate on something simple. The room, so full of Guy, seemed to overwhelm her. She felt weak with both fear and longing. She could no longer decide what she should do, so sat and stroked the damask instead, feeling the worn softness of the cloth beneath her fingertips.

'Do you want a drink?' She looked up. He was holding an empty glass. 'There's whisky or sherry – only very dry sherry, I'm afraid.'

'Sherry,' she said.

She watched him pour the drinks. He handed her the

sherry and had a dram himself, which he swallowed in one gulp.

'You are nervous,' she said. 'Admit it.'

He sat down beside her, having refilled his glass.

'Yes,' he said. 'But . . . but I shan't let it get in my way.'

'Perhaps we should. Perhaps it means something . . .' she began.

'No,' he said, and pressed his finger on her lips to silence her. 'I won't let you. We have to do this. If we don't, we'll regret it. I know it.'

'How?'

'I don't know. It's just in my bones. Everything at the moment is so uncertain, everything except this one thing between us. I could be dead in a matter of weeks, months . . .'

'No, don't say that,' she protested.

'It's true. You know that as well as I. That's war, isn't it? Well,' he said, having taken another large gulp of whisky, 'I'm not going to my grave without having lived properly, without having found some reason for it all. All the odds are against us, Chris, so we must, absolutely must, take every chance we can. If I've got to go, let me go in . . . in a state of grace.'

She reached out and touched his cheek. The flesh felt warm and strong. Death, even old age, seemed an impossibility. But then she moved her hand and felt the hardness of his cheekbone where it jutted out beneath his eye. She had a sudden vision of a skull then, of the grisly skulls that decorated some of the old graves in Rankeillor Kirkyard, to remind those who lived that they too would die, sooner or later. She felt the tears starting in her eyes, and swallowed hard. What he had said was perfectly true. It would be foolish to ignore it. 'Be free,' Angus had shouted at her. Had he meant the same thing? Had he seen the same sands slipping with appalling rapidity through the narrow neck of the hourglass? Was there anything any of them could do except act according to their deepest, most soul-shaking instincts? She remembered how he had seemed to blaze with love at the sight of Will Crawford, and here was Guy, blazing with love for her. This might be the only time they had left, their only chance.

She leant forward and kissed him on the lips, her palms pressed to his cheeks. He smelt, she noticed, of whisky.

'I couldn't stop looking at you all night,' he said. 'I don't think I've ever seen you look so beautiful.' He bent and kissed the flesh of her shoulders, that was not covered by her dress. His hands were pressed firmly on her bare arms, warmly clutching at them. 'You might have been the only person there.'

'Don't let's talk . . .' she said. 'We don't need to talk.'

He released her and nodded. She got up from the bed and began to unhook her dress, while he sat all the while watching her. She felt no shame in this, for his very looking was like his holding her, there was such gentleness in it. Gradually she discarded each layer, until she stood quite naked in front of him. She saw him shake as she removed the last covering, saw him close his eyes for a moment and swallow hard, as if he could not quite bear the moment. She understood then how very much he did love her, how impossibly he loved her. The way he looked at her naked body was enough to convince her.

She rushed to him and threw herself against him, kissing him desperately, wanting to prove her love for him, as he had just proved his. She clung to him, pressing her bare skin against the dark solidity of his evening clothes, and they fell back on to the bed, and lay together for a few moments, holding each other with such tightness that when he did release her there were red marks on her skin, from the grip of his fingers. He kissed each mark, with reverence, like a pilgrim kissing the wounds of Christ on a holy statue.

He pulled off his clothes, and then grabbed her hands in his, and bent over them, kissing them. She took his chin in her hand and made him look at her.

'You're too wonderful,' he said. 'I almost can't bear it.'

'Bear it,' she said, and ran her hand over his chest, pausing for a moment above his heart. 'I don't want you to die of happiness.'

'Why not? Why can't we die now, knowing what that means? So few people ever understand true happiness.'

'Because I feel too alive to die!' she exclaimed. 'I want life, so much life!'

She threw her arms around him and kissed him fervently on each cheek.

'All right then,' he grinned. 'Life it will be.' And he lifted her up from the ground and threw her the little distance on to the bed, so that she fell on to her back. She could not help laughing, and found that he was laughing too, as he stretched himself out alongside her.

'Take me then,' he said, suddenly, and pulled her over so that she was on top of him.

She straddled him, as he showed her, and guided him into her. The feeling was so intense that she gasped out.

'Guy . . . oh . . .'

'It's extraordinary what you pick up in an officers' mess,' he said, laughing. 'It's very robust. The best way to please a woman, for instance,' he added, rubbing his hands down her back.

'You disgust me,' she smiled, and laid her head on his chest, so that she could hear his heart beating.

He began to push up under her, against her, with slow, powerful thrusts of his body that seemed to set every note of her flesh reverberating, as if it were a great vibrating instrument, made only to respond to such action. In her amazement she straightened her back, and then he began to rock her on him, his hands resting on her hips. She soon caught the rhythm and threw back her head in delight at this entirely physical thing. It was like great music – a wordless, reasonless thing that moved so deeply, that made her cry out in sheer ecstasy. And it grew and grew, a great flood of intense physical pleasure, a sweet sea of it.

Tired suddenly, she crouched over his chest and let him thrust into her. He seemed to go so deep into her, as if he were touching the base of her ribs. He kissed her breasts as he did so, and then as he moved faster and faster, their lips came together again. Then, at the peak of it, she felt a sudden shock inside her, a last deep note of gratification, and he bellowed out with his own pleasure. They lay together for some moments, paralysed by sudden exhaustion.

At last he said, 'How will I ever manage without you?'

She could not answer, but laid her cheek on his chest, and listened to the insistent drumming of his heart. There was no easy answer.

38

Angus, hearing the shout of 'Mail up' and the clatter of the men's boots on the duckboards outside the dugout, looked up, as did every officer in the mess. The arrival of the mail was possibly the best moment of the day, yet they, being officers, would have to wait until the ammunition which arrived with the mail had been safely stored away and the men had been given their post.

'Go and check up on them, will you, Bretton?' said Major Wilson.

Angus was glad of the excuse to get out and do something, rather than endure the collective agony of waiting to see what news and comforts had come from home. Although he was waiting for some oddments that he had asked Chris to send, and his mother was bound to have sent something or other, he was really only waiting for one thing. For four days, he had heard nothing from Will, and was quietly desperate that that evening there should be something, a scribble of a letter, a mere postcard even, just to tell him that he was still alive.

He pulled on his great-coat and swamped his neck in a scarf. It might have been March already, but there was no sign of spring. At least, though, it was not raining. This cold was dry at least, and frosty, not like those weeks in January when he had done his first tour of duty in a front-line trench, when it had never stopped raining for a solitary day. Only two months ago – he found himself sighing at the thought of that. It seemed years ago, when he had first accustomed himself to this bizarre, subterranean life which they shared with the rats.

Outside the dugout the duckboards were glittering with frost, and above him the black, star-spattered canopy of the sky hung there coldly, bleak and uncaring of them, as they blundered on beneath. Further down the lines, to the left of him, there was a good exchange of fire going on, a sound he was so used to now that its rumbling regularity was almost soothing, like the sound of a train passing in the night. There was nothing happening in their sector just then. That would come later.

Weaving along the complicated zigzag trenches, it took him some minutes to reach the gun pits. The ammunition had already been stowed away and the men were sitting round their fires, reading their letters, their dirty faces illuminated by the firelight.

'All organized here, Sergeant Major?' he asked.

'Yes, sir. We got a bit extra too, which should come in handy.'

'Yes, we'll need all we've got.'

At midnight, Angus and Fred Grahame were going to lead a raiding party in an attempt to catch, or at least disable, a mortar gun which had been causing havoc.

'The mail's here, Mr Bretton,' said Angus's servant, Bill Laidlaw. 'Shall I take it down to the mess, sir?'

'No, I'll take it,' said Angus. 'I bet you'd rather stay by this fire.'

'You reckon right, sir,' said Bill, handing him the bag. 'All night, if possible.'

> 'I don't want to be a soldier,
> I don't want to go to war,
> I'd rather stay at home,
> Around the streets to roam,
> And live on the earnings of a lady-typist,'

one of the privates began to sing, hearing Bill's comment.

> 'I don't want a bayonet in my belly,
> I don't want my bollocks shot away.
> I'd rather stay in Scotland,
> In bonny, bonny Scotland,
> And fornicate my bloody life away!'

'Hear, hear!' said Angus, as he slung the mail bag over his shoulder and began his return to the officers' dugout.

'Ah, postie Bretton!' exclaimed Fred Grahame, as he came in. 'Good and heavy, is it?'

'Yes,' said Angus, putting it on the table. His first instinct was to scrabble in and see if there was anything from Will, but he decided that he would not. Instead, he let Grahame do the scrabbling, sorting out the various letters into the five piles for the occupants of the dugout.

'Is that the lot?' Angus asked, when the bag was apparently empty. He had hopes of a postcard being lost in its dark depths.

'Yes, you greedy beggar,' said Grahame, laughing. 'Haven't you got enough there?' he added, tapping with his forefinger Angus's two large parcels and the little wad of letters on top of them. 'I hope there's some of your wife's shortbread in there, by the way.'

'She said she'd send some,' said Angus, flicking through his letters again, in case he had not recognized Will's hand the first time. It was a ridiculous false hope though. Will's handwriting was as distinctive to him as the features of his face. Angus could no more have failed to pick it out, even by the inadequate candlelight in the dugout, than he could have failed to recognize Will himself. 'Are you sure there's not a postcard or something knocking around in the bottom?'

'No, doesn't seem to be. Are you expecting one?'

'Just something from a friend – a chap I trained with. When I got sent to you lot, he went up to the First Battalion. We've kept in touch pretty regularly but . . . well, for the last few days there's been nothing.'

'Ah . . .' said Grahame, grimacing. He had caught his meaning at once. 'Well, he's probably simply run off his feet. There are some lunatic senior officers in the First, you know – they're probably keeping your pal on the hop. More likely them than our dear neighbours yonder.'

'Yes,' said Angus, 'probably.' It was a blatant lie, a palliative of the worst sort, but such lies were how they got along. The truth, which lay so visibly all around them, was not something anyone much cared to discuss. It was far more comforting to think of Will being worked off his feet by a battalion tyrant than to think . . . to think the unthinkable. 'Well,' he said, digging in his pocket for his penknife. 'Let's see what we've got in here then.'

Grahame and Angus went to sit on one of the bunks, and sliced through the string on their parcels, and ripped back the paper with enthusiasm.

'I hope she's got those sardines for me,' said Grahame. 'I've such a bloody craving for them.'

'Anyone would think you were the pregnant one,' said Angus. Grahame's wife was expecting.

'It's brain food,' said Grahame.

'What the hell do wc need brains for here?' said Angus.

'Good point . . . Ah-ha – Bingo!' exclaimed Graham. 'Four tins, no less. Good show, Nell.' He held one up reverently. 'Ah noble sardine . . .'

'Do I bow or kneel?' asked Angus.

'Kneel, kneel, definitely,' said Grahame, kissing the tin. The Major, who was deep in a fresh copy of the *Field*, glanced across at them, and smiled indulgently. Angus and Grahame had a reputation for larking. 'Right, let's see what you've got. I'm willing to trade one tin of sardines for one round of petticoat tails.'

Angus always felt a vague sense of shame when he opened Chris's parcels. He knew that he had no right at all to keep on making demands on her, but there was no one else he could ask to send out the things which made life there bearable. He might have asked his mother, but she would never have managed to send the right things. She would have sent stupid books and the wrong tobacco and hand-knitted socks that could not be worn. Chris understood his needs, and obliged him in a way that was on the verge of heroic. He had told her to be free and yet almost every day he wrote asking for some little thing. In fact their exchange of letters resembled nothing more than those between a shopkeeper and his customer. He could never manage to write honestly to her, he found. His letters seemed bald lists of requests, punctuated with brief accounts of what had been going on, written in the manner of a schoolboy reporting the way the house rugger match had gone, and then finished with profuse thanks for the parcels. He could not begin to express to her how it actually was. He felt he had no right to do so. It would have been too easy to pour out the very cold depths of his anxiety, the slow revulsion of his soul at what he was involved in, but he could not, when that was all he could give her, that agony that was quietly rotting him inside.

That evening's parcel was, as usual, perfect: the tins of his favourite pipe tobacco from a particular Edinburgh tobacconist; the rounds of home-made shortbread, with peel and split almonds in it; a slab of black-bun, left over from New Year, and maturing nicely; a bottle of unblended malt whisky from the Blane distillery and, wrapped about the bottle, in its straw cradle, was the chamois leather waistcoat he had requested. Round the neck of the bottle she had added a label saying 'Drink me' in the fashion of

Alice's Adventures in Wonderland. At the sight of this, Grahame roared with delight.

'What a sport she is, your Chris!' he said. 'It's a shame she and Nell can't meet up somewhere. I'm sure they'd get on famously.'

Angus smiled in vague agreement as he folded the note she had put inside. It was, as ever, brief. She had no great facility with words on paper.

Dear A, Here are the things you asked for. Jeanie is making more Black-Bun, so when it is ready, I will send it. Am working very hard – have started some settings of Donne, for tenor, piano and string quartet. Our refugee concert raised over 200 guineas – and there were v. good notices in the paper, which I enclose. May is starting as a probationer at the Royal Infirmary, so will probably come and live here – a good thing, as it will stop your parents asking me to give it up and move to Blackford Road. There was a letter yesterday from Blanche – they have got out of Paris – she says it's dreadful, with Zeppelin raids, etc. They are in Montpellier, now, and she says she will send you something. She was full of questions about you and wanted a photograph of you in uniform to show les enfants. Must finish and get this in the post. I'm going to lunch at Royal Circus – Jack has a week's leave. Chris

He glanced through the newspaper cutting:

A highly successful concert, organized by Mrs Jack Rosenberg in aid of the Edinburgh Belgian Refugee fund, featured two new works by Miss Christina Adam (who in private life is Mrs A. L. Bretton, wife of the celebrated Scottish soldier poet). The first, a choral setting for female voices and string quartet of

John Milton's famous poem 'Blest Pair of Sirens', was particularly effective and was very well received. During the present crisis it is interesting to record that it is not only on the military but on the musical front that this nation is advancing against its old rival. We have no need to have recourse to the Teutonic pomposity of Wagner and his like when such bright stars as Miss Adam are rising in our native firmament.

He opened his other parcel. There was a pair of useless-looking gloves, some religious nonsense and a long rambling letter from his mother.

We went to hear Christina's music at Mrs Rosenberg's concert. It seemed very odd and modern to me, but the others seem to think it very fine. I wonder if she isn't doing too much – she struck me as rather pale and exhausted-looking. Your father agreed. I cannot help thinking this might mean *very* good news for you – we must pray that it might be. I'm sure it is exactly what Christina wants and needs . . .

He did not read on. His mother's well-meant delusions were torture.

His other letters were from his sister and from Chris's father. Now that the brief excitement of opening parcels and letters was finished, he was left again with the old anxiety about Will. What on earth had happened to him? If he were dead . . . No, he was not going to think that. He settled back in the bunk to look at the two remaining unread letters. Which would be the best distraction?

He did not have a chance to decide. A runner came in from Staff HQ and handed a packet of orders to Major Wilson.

'I wondered when we'd see those,' said Grahame.

'Perhaps they're telling us to clear out,' said Angus, in a fit of blind hope. It wasn't exactly likely, even though they had been in the line for over a fortnight without relief.

'Gentlemen,' said the Major. 'Your attention for a moment, if I may.'

'Sir?' said Angus.

'We're still on for tonight,' said the Major, 'but O one hundred hours instead. Got that?'

'Yes, sir. I'll go and tell the men,' he said. It would not be easy. Another hour of waiting would be the last thing they wanted. He hesitated a moment and stuffed the bottle of whisky in his great-coat pocket. It would be a welcome treat for them, a tiny incentive.

'It's a good thing for you that sardines don't have the same effect, isn't it?' he remarked to Grahame.

'One has to make a few sacrifices for one's country,' said Grahame. 'And I'll buy you a schnapps, I promise, when we get to Berlin.'

At five to one, Angus ordered his platoon into their positions, having issued them all with a dram. He had had one himself, but it did not seem to do much good, as he waited on the firing step, glancing constantly at his watch. It was ominously quiet on the other side, as if they were waiting too, waiting for the first silhouetted tin helmet to emerge above the parapet. And that tin hat would be him, armed ineffectively with wire cutters and a rifle.

'I don't like the look of this at all, sir,' said Sergeant Frazer.

'No,' said Angus. 'It could be very nasty indeed. But what else can we do? Orders are orders, aren't they?'

He listened to the voice saying that and loathed it. It was not his voice, certainly. Would Angus Bretton really have said, 'Orders are orders,' in that resigned, dutiful tone? Orders were orders, but these were bad orders, contemptible orders, orders which ought to be disobeyed. Why didn't he do that? Why didn't he suddenly throw up his hands and tell the platoon to stand down? If he did that, lives could be saved and limbs remain unmangled. Why not? Because it was useless. He would probably be court-martialled and shot for that, and his men, under some other officer, would be sent again and again on such ridiculous, criminal excursions into No Man's Land, until there was not one of them left. There was no escape, what ever way you looked at it. Death was an inevitability, it seemed. Of course they would all die, but not as old men, in their beds. It was as if some power had decided that all these men, himself included, were not to survive, but were to be exterminated, like rats, as if they were not men at all, but a sort of pestilence covering the earth that had to be got rid of. It was like something out of the Old Testament, a pointless destruction like the Flood. But this time it would not be harmless old drunken Noah who would be saved, but those arrogant, red-tabbed staff officers who issued such damned stupid orders as this raiding party.

He glanced at his watch again. It was one o'clock. He began to climb his ladder and then, half hanging off it, gestured to the men and called out, 'Let's wake up those bloody bastards then!'

He climbed up the last few rungs, and crawled on to the parapet of No Man's Land. He wasn't going to be so stupid as to stand up yet. The mortar gun lay directly to the north of him, about a quarter of a mile away. Only a quarter of a mile, and yet that vast mess of barbed wire and vandalized trees made it seem impenetrable. How the devil were they going to get across?

Some time later – he could not say when – he found himself, along with Sergeant Frazer, under heavy fire, attempting to cut through the mass of barbed wire, which had been wreathed round the gun placement. Amazingly, though, the fire seemed to fly over them, and they carried on, lying on their stomachs and crawling forward on their elbows, towards their objective. Angus wondered if he had been hit, for he was utterly exhausted, as if the blood were already flowing out of him, trickling out behind him in fact, but he felt no pain, although the wire had scratched his face and hands. He flicked the last of the wire aside with a deft movement of his bayonet. Surely they were not going to let him get this close to it. He glanced to his side.

'Here . . .' he said. 'I'm through.'

He crawled the last foot or two up the parapet, and looked, very tentatively, into the trench. One glance revealed that there was one man left, looking out the other way, his gun trained on their covering fire. Their volley of grenades had done a good job. There were a few bodies on the floor, but no one else. It seemed extraordinary. Was that the last man left alive, or was he the last to remain there, the others having abandoned the trench? Or had they gone to fetch re-enforcements?

Going as softly as he could, he heaved himself over the parapet. The moment he landed the soldier turned, looking vaguely surprised. There was nothing Angus could do other than plunge his bayonet into his stomach. If he had hesitated, the soldier would have done the same to him. He stabbed him again, remembering, oddly, an occasion when he had begun to dissect a corpse which had sighed when he had made the first cut in the viscera. This man sighed too, and crumpled on to the floor as Angus pulled out the bayonet.

For a moment he was lost, watching the death of this unknown man who he had just killed. It was the first time he had killed a man so directly. It had been appallingly easy. Nausea surged up in his gullet.

'Good work, sir,' Frazer said behind him.

Frazer's voice brought him back to the task in hand.

'Let's get a charge under this gun, then.'

He fumbled with the explosives, while Frazer covered the entrance to the trench.

'Are you done, sir? I can sense 'em coming back.'

'Then let's get out of here.'

They scrambled over the parapet and back through No Man's Land, much faster now than they had come, running almost with a sort of desperate confidence, that having got so far they would get back in one piece. But Frazer's instinct had been correct – the Germans had reclaimed the trench, and a sudden rain of machine-gunning pursued them. Angus prayed desperately that the charge he had set would not be disabled.

Angus hurled himself into their trench as a shell exploded at his heels. Fortunately it was one of the shallower bits, and he only fell about seven feet, and landed on his back on a duckboard.

'Trying to break your neck, are you, Bretton?' asked Major Wilson, helping him up.

'Has she gone?' he asked, breathlessly. He need not have asked, for that moment a violent explosion drowned everything, and seemed to shake the very earth. Everyone cowered for a moment, and then Major Wilson looked up through his periscope.

'Good work,' he said.

'Where are the others?'

'We're just getting them in. A lot went down. You and Frazer were damn lucky.'

'God . . . How many?'

'Can't say just yet. Go and get a drink, you two. I'm needed elsewhere.'

Angus and Frazer slumped down on a pile of ammunition boxes and gathered their breath.

'How did we manage that?' said Angus, incredulous,

exhilarated still, at having achieved it and remained alive. 'We should be bloody dead.'

'I dinna ken, sir,' said Frazer. And then they saw how, as over the parapet, taking advantage of the relative calm the explosion had brought, came the remains of the raiding party. Some managed to crawl over, helped by a mate, their wounds still fresh, but some were well dead. The last to come, for he had got the furthest, was Fred Grahame, who was only just recognizable.

'Christ . . .' Angus heard Frazer say.

'Was that bloody worth it?' said Angus. It felt a crime to be alive.

'I couldna fucking say,' said Frazer, getting up wearily.

Fred Grahame was lying at their feet, his corpse waiting unceremoniously while the still living were attended too. Angus reached down and touched his cheek, unable yet to credit what had happened.

'Mr Bretton?'

He looked up. A staff ADC was standing over him, a captain like Fred Grahame, but clean and unblemished.

'Yes?'

'General Claude wants a word. You too, Sergeant.'

They followed the ADC to their dugout where they found the General, smoking a cigar and looking, despite everything, extremely comfortable. He probably regarded this excursion as an evening's entertainment. Angus felt an instant prickle of dislike.

'Major Wilson tells me you chaps have just done rather well,' he said.

'Hardly, sir,' Angus said. 'Most of my platoon have been knocked out in one way or another.'

'Nevertheless, Mr Bretton, the objective has been achieved, has it not? The gun is disabled.'

'Yes, sir, for all the difference it makes. They'll put another there soon enough, I imagine.'

'Well, that needn't worry you, need it?' said General

Claude, imperturbably. 'You'll be relieved tomorrow. And I think you could probably do with some rest, couldn't you? You seem a little, er, nervy to me, Bretton.'

Angus wanted to retort, 'No, not nervy, General, angry!' but Frazer gave a warning glance.

'That'll be all,' said the General.

Frazer saluted smartly, like the regular he was, but Angus's was half-hearted.

'You like sailing close to the wind, do you, sir?' said Frazer when they were outside again.

'We've got enemies on both sides,' said Angus. 'But frankly, I'd rather deal with that lot,' he added, gesturing in the direction of the German lines. 'At least it's logical that we should be fighting them!'

39

The following day, Angus found himself in unaccustomed luxury, about ten miles behind the lines in a château. Once he had settled what remained of his men in reasonable billets, he walked, with Bill Laidlaw, who had escaped with only a few shrapnel wounds, up an avenue of poplar trees, to a house that would have looked almost normal had it not been for the clutter of army vehicles parked outside it.

'This looks all right, sir,' said Bill, who was not insensible to the very occasional advantages of being an officer's servant.

'The place is crawling with Staff,' observed Angus, as a car passed them, with a pair of brass hats in the back. 'So long as General Claude isn't around.'

They got to the front door where a slightly officious sergeant major enquired what their business might be. He looked them over, as if quite disgusted by their somewhat disreputable state.

'The billeting officer sent me up here. Bretton, Second Battalion Scots Guards.'

'Got you, sir,' he said, consulting his list. 'If you go up those stairs to the west wing, you'll find Corporal Summers. He'll find you a bed.'

'Good. And some food?'

'Lunch at one o'clock, sir, in the dining room,' said the sergeant. They went on towards the stairs, and the sergeant called out as an afterthought, 'Oh, best khaki, if you please, sir, in the dining room. The General doesn't like things slipping.'

'The General?' said Angus, turning back.

'General Claude, sir,' said the sergeant major. 'Staff HQ here, sir.'

'Oh . . . I see,' said Angus, and climbed the stairs wearily.

The family who owned the château had left everything there, rather trustingly, Angus thought, but there was something wonderful about being put in a room with real walls and real pictures hanging on them. It was a plain enough room – a room for a family tutor, he imagined, or a poor relation, but there was a large cherrywood bed, and a view over the gardens. Angus threw the window open and rested his elbows on the sill. The luxury of being able simply to lean out of a window was immense, even if it was a brisk March day.

'I'll go and see about a bath for you sir,' said Bill.

The bath when it came, was only tepid, but, having not been able to wash properly for a fortnight, it was heaven. Then he shaved off his half-grown beard, cut his fingernails and struggled into his best khaki uniform. He looked at himself in the glass – a reasonably presentable young officer again, whose most pressing need was to see a barber and get his hair cut. Last night, and all the long nights before it, seemed faded here. He was amazed how easily he could put the memories aside, and think eagerly instead of what he might get for lunch. If the place was full of Staff officers, the food was bound to be good.

He went downstairs and into a large sitting room, which had once clearly been the grand salon of the château but was now functioning, to all intents and purposes, like a gentleman's club. There were easy chairs, and recent newspapers, and a waiter, almost immediately, came up to see what he wanted to drink. It seemed faintly absurd that this standard of civilization could be kept up only ten miles away from the front. Angus sat down, ordered a brandy and soda, and strained his ears for the sound of the guns, the guns which had become so much part of his reality of late. But he heard nothing of them, only the tinkling, of all things, of a piano, upon which someone was playing a ghastly sentimental tune of the sort Chris had taught him to despise. He picked up a copy of the *Illustrated London News* and flicked through it. He was almost surprised to find it carried stories of the war. In this glass bubble of a place, he might have imagined that even the newspapers carried no trace of the war. Had it not been for the illustrations in that magazine, he might have believed that the war had stopped altogether. Yet perhaps it had, at least the war he had experienced, for the pictures in the *Illustrated London News* bore no resemblance to any aspect of life at the front he had seen. One in particular showed the piper of some regiment, pacing up and down in a stretch of No Man's Land that was as level and as free of rubbish as a suburban street, and playing to spur on, over the top, the men, who waited with singularly eager faces in the trench below. In reality he would not have managed to stay upright for more than a minute, before being got by a sniper. 'A tremendous show of spirit' the picture was labelled. He shut the magazine and wondered if he was dreaming, after all.

The door opened at the far end, and he thought he saw Will come in. He decided at once that it was an hallucination, like the rest of this ridiculous place, and took a deep drink of his brandy. It was only some other good-looking, golden-haired officer, he told himself, and then looked again, as the man walked down the room, towards him. It was Will – and Will looking as fresh and as fair as he had the first time he had seen him, sitting on the other bed in the hut they were to share at training camp. It was not the mangled, defaced Will, the trench-dirtied and bloodied

Will, that his imagination had recently insisted on conjuring up in front of him, but Will, angelic and whole still, looking as if the war had never touched him. He looked indeed as if he had just stepped down from paradise.

Angus leapt up and signalled vigorously to him. Will stopped, and Angus saw him take stock for a moment, and then he grinned, and came striding over.

'God, I thought you'd had it, for sure!' he said. 'This is simply . . .'

'I know,' said Angus. 'I thought just the same.'

They embraced, after a fashion, in one of those brief, masculine squeezes that were just about permissible in public. Angus felt he could scarcely bear to release him, for to hold him in his arms was to touch the core of life itself, to find a meaning suddenly, when everything had been so terribly meaningless. In that moment, in that brief instant of closeness, he felt he understood at last what it was to love. It was true, he had told himself that he loved Will, that the constant, quiet aching of his spirit was because he loved Will so utterly, but it had been like faith in a god he had never seen. This was the moment of revelation. The clouds had parted, and he saw the perfect truth of it, felt it in every fibre of his being. Will was alive, when he had been so certain he was dead. It was like a resurrection – but without the empty tomb, the abandoned grave cloths and the wounds to prod doubting fingers into. What need did he have of such clumsy signs to signify their immortality? For that was how he felt they were suddenly: untouchable, inviolable – saved, indeed, from anything that the damnable war could do to them. Their love had triumphed over the evil of it. They were alive, and together again, which was enough of a miracle to suggest it was no miracle at all, but something rightful and sacred, at which all assumed laws must bend and bow.

* * *

'Do you know,' said Will, the next morning. 'There's a tennis court here.'

'What?'

'A lawn tennis court – in not bad condition. How do you fancy a game?'

Angus laughed. The suggestion seemed so absurd and yet attractive.

'Lawn tennis?' he said. 'Don't you know there's a war on?' and he picked up the pillow and attempted to hit Will with it. But Will dodged him expertly. 'I don't think lawn tennis is entirely patriotic,' he added and lunged again with the pillow.

'You're just afraid I'll beat you, aren't you?' said Will, leaping away again, wonderfully nimble in his nakedness.

'I happen to be a crack player, actually,' said Angus.

'Oh yes?' said Will, and went to push the window open. 'God, look at it – it's perfect out there . . . You wouldn't think folk were blowing each other up would you?'

Angus joined him at the window. Together they stood, their bare flesh touching, and gazed at the mist that was rolling across the château parkland, magnificently illuminated by the first sunlight of the day.

'I can almost smell spring,' said Will, breathing deeply. 'I can feel it, can't you?'

He was right – there was something in the air, a deep, distant smell of cracking earth and waking roots that stirred his blood and made him feel strong – thc force of spring, which would change everything and bring explosive life to every sleeping bud and branch. The pale, ice-green promise of that parkland seemed to whisper at its very power. It was stronger even than the war, that rebirth. It never failed, even when tiny man spat and stamped on its first shoots. It was uncheckable, and Angus and Will, because they were young in body and spirit, could not help but rejoice at it. After all they had seen and done, there was still the indestructible energy of spring to make them run and laugh and be human again.

And so they dressed and ran out into it, armed with warped tennis racquets, and balls so ancient that Will was prepared to bet that they were those sent by Henry V to the Dauphin. The court looked a little as if it had been abandoned for years, although it could have been in use only a summer ago, by smart Frenchwomen in pretty tennis dresses, who were a far cry from the two unshaven officers in crumpled khaki shirt-sleeves who had taken possession of it now.

'We shall have to imagine the net,' said Angus.

'You'll imagine it lower on your side and higher on mine, I suppose,' said Will, groping for a coin. 'Heads I serve.'

Will won the toss and they began their mock battle. They found they were well matched as players, which was gratifying – it seemed to Angus just another sign of their rightness together. Indeed, what was this whole glorious business but that, a wonderful sign! For he ought to be exhausted, he ought to be demoralized, he knew, after a tour of fourteen days in a front-line trench, after crawling through No Man's Land two nights ago and seeing most of his platoon wiped out. Yet here, with Will, in this enchanted domain, he felt complete and strong, his body and his emotions perfectly satisfied. For once in his life, he was whole and perfectly happy. How calm that made him. He felt as if he had come home and found at last his family.

'Well done,' exclaimed Will, as Angus, with a skill that surprised him, served an ace and won the set. In his astonishment he threw his racquet into the air and whooped for joy at it. It was so lovely that morning, so sweet and flawless, that he was sure he would never forget it as long as he lived. He looked across at Will, who was standing still at the other end of the court, his face ruddy with exertion. Oh that they could go on like this, in this paradisical state, until the end of time itself!

'I'll finish you yet,' said Will. 'Just you wait and see.'

'Perhaps I should stop while I'm winning. The novelty, you know, I rather like it.'

'I'm afraid I can't allow that,' said Will, stretching up, as if to serve again. The beauty of his body struck Angus, as if he had never seen it before. He was such an elegant creature, too good for a simple whim of nature to have created. He seemed like the work of a great craftsman rather than the accident of his parents' love-making. Or perhaps it had been a great strong love between them, to make something so entirely magnificent as Will, a love as strong as that which now fastened them together. God, how he did love this man!

'Well?' said Will. 'Another set?'

'Not until I've kissed you,' said Angus, walking down the court to where he stood.

'Am I your prize then, your victory crown?'

'If you are, I scarcely deserve you. You're too good a thing for me.'

'No,' said Will, kissing him on the lips. 'No, no, there's no difference between us. It's a perfect balance, an absolute equilibrium.'

Angus returned his kiss, pressing his lips to Will's, feeling the stubble against the hand with which he had cupped his chin. He smelt of cigarettes and sweat and of desire. His love was tangible to Angus then, and in his kisses, he returned it.

Suddenly the yapping of dogs surrounded them and they broke away from each other.

'What the devil!' exclaimed Angus, finding two ugly hounds snapping at their heels.

'The hounds of hell . . .' said Will, under his breath. His face washed pale suddenly. 'Christ . . .'

Angus turned to see what Will was staring at. Across the lawn, coming at them in a rapid stride that his plump body looked ill able to sustain, was General Claude. Behind him came his ADC, a very smart young officer, running with much better form.

'You saw that, didn't you, Haslemere?' shouted the General. 'You saw that, didn't you?'

'He's like a schoolmaster, isn't he?' said Angus, pushing away one of the dogs which kept leaping up at him.

'This could be serious,' said Will.

'I don't give a damn. The man's a fool. What can he do to us?' said Angus, shoving his hands in his pockets.

'Gus . . .'

'Don't worry,' said Angus. 'Good morning, General. Isn't it a lovely day?'

'I might have known!' exploded the General. 'I wasn't impressed with you the last time we met, sir, for all your daredevil activities. What do you mean by this disgusting exhibition?'

'Disgusting? I'm sorry, sir, I don't know what you mean.'

'I saw you kissing him, Bretton, lathering all over him, as if he was a girl. You saw him, didn't you, Haslemere?'

'Yes sir,' said the officer. 'I'm afraid I did.'

'So what do you mean by it, Bretton?' the General barked on.

'What do I mean by it, sir?' said Angus.

'Let me remind you, you hold a commission in his Majesty's army, Mr Bretton, you are both an officer and a gentleman, and you are supposed to behave as an officer and a gentleman.'

'I rather thought I was a human,' said Angus. 'I don't care for your labels, sir.'

'My labels!' roared the General. 'Labels! It's clear to

me that you have absolutely no respect for His Majesty's army. How else could you so blatantly contravene King's Regulations?'

'Is it against King's Regulations to be in love, General?' retorted Angus. 'Is that what this bloody war has reduced us all to – automata, under King's Regulations? Well, King's Regulations or no King's Regulations, I am a human, who will behave decently and kindly, despite all your efforts to make a murderer of me. I will not forget what I am!'

'You call yourself decent! Why ... why...' Words failed the General, and instead he lashed out at Angus with the stick he was carrying. Angus dodged the physical blow, but the General's words stung his ears. 'You are nothing but filth! Filthy excrement!'

'Right, I'm not letting you get away with that!' shouted Angus, and punched him in the face, a good, hard, prize-fighting punch that sent Claude staggering backwards gratifyingly, and which Angus hoped would at least dislodge a tooth or two.

He realized, as Claude toppled gracelessly into the ADC's arms, that he had better absent himself before he succumbed to the temptation of slugging the General again. He began to run back to the château, with Will at his heels. He did not stop running until he had got back to his room.

'Angus ... What the hell are we going to do?' said Will, closing the door behind him. 'That's an arrestable offence...'

'They both were, let's not mince words.'

'Yes but ... God...' said Will, sitting down on the bed. 'A general – you just punched a general.'

'Someone had to.'

'Angus ... please ... You've got to get out of this somehow. You could go and apologize or...'

'I won't apologize to that man,' said Angus. 'Don't you

see I can't? You of all people must see I can't! You heard what he said.'

'He's an ignorant old fool,' said Will, 'and people like that have to be humoured, unfortunately.'

'No!' exclaimed Angus. 'I won't, I won't do that any more. You mean too much to me to live a lie any more, to let them get away with their damnable notions of what's right and wrong. I've been a coward all my life, Will, I've never stood up to be counted and it's about time I did.'

'I don't want you to,' said Will, jumping up and putting his arms around him. 'God only knows what that might mean. You mustn't go on with this. I can't stand the thought of it . . .' He pressed his hands to Angus's cheeks. 'Please.'

Angus felt weak when he was so close and so lovely. How could he refuse him anything, and yet the principle of the thing hung like a great shining sword over them.

'You could say you're neurasthenic,' said Will. 'You'd only have to bribe a doctor or two. I've heard it done quite often. They couldn't make anything stick if you were proved to be mad.'

'No,' said Angus, breaking away from him with difficulty. 'Oh God, I know this isn't easy, but it's the only thing I can do. Our cause – it needs a sacrifice.'

'Our cause? It's not a cause . . . Don't be ridiculous, Gus.'

'It is,' said Angus. 'This isn't just you and me, but everyone like us. We have as much right to be as we are as any men or women alive. It's our right, and we have to prove that, and we can't, not by cowardice, attractive though that is. Believe me, I'd like nothing better than to be able to do that, to grovel to that disgusting man and save ourselves from whatever, but I can't. I've crossed a line now, a line I should have crossed years ago.' He reached out and caressed Will's fine gold hair, savouring the feel of it. 'It's because I love you – because I understand what love is now, because of you – that I can do it.'

'I wish to God you wouldn't,' said Will. His voice was dense with raw emotion. 'But I do see . . . Christ, though, why us? Why should it have to be us?'

'We're a generation of sacrificial lambs, that's why,' said Angus.

There was a furious thumping at the door. He kissed Will, briefly but fiercely, and then unlocked the door. Two military policemen stood on the threshold. He held up his hands to them in a gesture of surrender.

'Second Lieutenant A. L. Bretton?' He nodded, and the sergeant went on. 'You are charged and under arrest under sections five and eleven of the Army Emergency Act. Do you understand, sir?'

'Perfectly,' said Angus.

The sergeant came into the room and turned to Will.

'Second Lieutenant W. B. Crawford, you are charged and under arrest under section five of the Army Emergency Act. Do you understand, sir?'

Will nodded. Clearly he did not trust his voice. Angus noticed how his cheek muscle quivered yet his back was as straight as a poker. He felt his own belly griping with sudden fear. He may have been righteous, but he was still afraid. He had remembered the lecture on military law that they had been given as part of their basic training. The sentences, baldly written out on a blackboard, had appalled him then. Striking a superior officer on active service: death, for both officers and men.

'If you'd like to come with me please, gentlemen, we'll have as little fuss as possible,' said the sergeant.

Lambs, they were, a generation of sacrificial lambs.

40

Miranda, on stage, was in her element. She had all the ease of a seasoned performer appearing on a far more illustrious stage than the rudimentary platform that had been put up at one end of the hospital recreation room. Her behaviour suggested there were great velvet curtains decorating it instead of a few yards of bunting and that there was a full orchestra in the pit rather than simply Chris to accompany her on a less than adequate piano. In every gesture, in every phrase of every song, she created this illusion and convinced her audience with it. From her seat at the piano Chris could see how enchanted the men were by her. Where before they had been drab-faced, bored convalescents who had been bullied into the recreation room by the nurses, they now wore expressions of rapt concentration, their eyes fixed on the delicate, ninon-clad figure in front of them, who seemed, so uncannily, to address each one of them as an individual. She was caressing these boys with voice and gesture, commanding them, with such sweetness of demeanour, to love her, to adore her.

> 'My heart is sair, I dare na tell,
> My heart is sair for Somebody
> I could wake a winter-night
> For the sake o' Somebody.'

The songs she had mostly chosen were popular songs of

the moment – sugary ballads and jaunty ragtime – but to finish, at Chris's suggestion, she had agreed to sing some of the old Scots songs, with words by Burns. The effect on the audience was extraordinary. They fell utterly silent as she sang. The simple but beautiful melody exactly suited Miranda's voice, and her sincerity was such that Chris wished that she had never suggested that particular song:

> 'Ye powers that smile on virtuous love,
> O sweetly smile on Somebody!
> Frae ilka danger keep him free,
> And send me safe my Somebody.'

When the song was finished, there was one of those profound pauses before the men burst out into applause: a tiny, powerful moment that was not simply astonishment but a sort of paralysis, as if their collective soul had been frozen by the force of the music. It was the gasp that attends a meeting with the divine – for Miranda had been divine. She had achieved in that song what all artists set out to do. She had, for a moment, lifted those men, those boys – and Chris could not help noticing how young they all were – from the commonplace and disagreeable world of wounds and hospitals, into another realm entirely.

As the applause boomed around her, and Miranda dropped seductive curtseys on stage, Chris suddenly felt so flooded with exhaustion that she would have liked to have rested her head on the piano keyboard. This was no surprise to her. It happened constantly these days, and was accompanied by a wave of nausea. Now that came on particularly strongly, triggered by the smell of carbolic which hung in the air. She braced herself against the back of her chair, gulping hard, thankful that she had a chair back to support her and was not sitting on a piano stool. She should never have agreed to do this. Working with

Miranda was a trial enough for her conscience – but to be feeling ill as well . . .

Feeling ill . . . Heavens, how oblique she could be with herself! All the evidence of her body suggested, no, stated that this was not simply a bout of some unknown sickness, but no illness at all. Yet she could not admit that appalling fact to herself. The thought that she might well be carrying Guy's child did not bear contemplation and yet continually her body prodded and slapped at her mind to tell her that she must contemplate that dreadful possibility as more than a possibility.

Well, she would not, just yet, she told herself sternly, taking another deep gulp of air, and turning over her copy. It was time for the next song – thankfully the last – 'Scots wha have wi' Wallace bled'. It was not a song often sung by a woman, but Miranda had her heart set on it as being a suitably rousing and patriotic end to the concert. Glancing at the words now, Chris wondered, having seen all those young men with their bandages, whether it was quite appropriate. These men had already bled for their country – was it really fair to expect them to do any more? Yet she supposed they would be sent back on active service if they recovered sufficiently. That was the nature of war, the war which in her heart she could never think of as anything but a dreadful piece of folly which they all rashly embarked upon.

> 'Lay the proud Usurpers low!
> Tyrants fall in every foe
> Liberty's in every blow!
> Let us Do – or Die!'

Miranda sang out, like a Valkyrie, with thrilling intensity. The audience began to cheer when she had finished. 'Liberty's in every blow . . .' The phrase echoed in Chris's mind. Was it for liberty that the soldier she could see from the corner of her eye had been scarred so horribly across the face? Was it for liberty that he would be sent back the moment he was fit again?

Miranda came dashing down the steps from the platform, and over to her. The applause continued.

'Come on, come on, you must come up too,' she said, grabbing Chris's hand.

Chris tried to resist, but she could not. Miranda almost pulled her up on to the stage to take a bow. The platform was not high, but she felt too dizzy to stand and the noise of the clapping seemed aggressive and almost physical in the intensity with which it assaulted her. Her legs felt weak and treacherous, and she felt sick again, violently sick this time. She made a brief bow, and bolted off again. Miranda followed.

'Don't be so modest.'

'It's you they want . . .' said Chris. 'Go on. I'm . . .' She could not go on. She had to cover her mouth with her hand and began to walk as quickly as she could towards the door. But her vision was swimming, and her legs felt powerless As she reached the door, she found she was stumbling badly. A nurse sitting just by the door jumped up and said, 'Let me help you.'

Chris nodded frantically, and allowed herself to be taken into professional charge. In fact, as the nurse put a steadying arm about her waist, and took her arm, she felt her remaining strength desert her, and she would have fallen if the nurse had not supported her.

'I think I'm going to be sick . . .'

Quickly the nurse helped her through the swing doors and along the glittering expanse of tiled corridor.

'You've chosen a good place to be taken ill, Mrs Bretton,' said the nurse, as she took Chris into a small room off the passageway. Chris caught sight of a slop bucket on a dresser and lunged at it, tasting bile already in her mouth. She retched painfully for some minutes, bringing up nothing but green bile, the sight of which repulsed her all the more. She felt tears starting in her eyes, not just from the pain, but from her own fury at her weakness.

'I think you'd better lie down and rest for a few minutes,' said the nurse, helping Chris on to the bed. 'I'll get one of the doctors to take a proper look at you. There's a pail just here if you feel you need to vomit again.'

She bustled off efficiently, taking away the dirtied slop pan. Chris sank her head back on the pillows and stared up at the white ceiling of that little cell of a room, lit by a window high in the ceiling. She found she was shivering, and pulled the blanket over her.

The doctor came, a kindly, balding man, with cold hands, who, when he had finished his examination, said, 'I imagine you've guessed you're pregnant, Mrs Bretton.'

She nodded and managed a smile. For the nurse was beaming at her, as if that would be the best news she could imagine.

'That'll give your husband something to fight for, then, won't it?' said the doctor. 'What regiment is he in?'

'Scots Guards . . .' said Chris mechanically.

'Splendid,' said the doctor. 'My boy's in Cameronians,' he added. 'Well, I think you ought to rest here for a little while – and eat something if you can. Nurse, will you see to that? Yes, definitely something for your next letter . . .' he mused. 'You'll enjoy writing that, I'm sure.'

'I hate writing letters actually,' Chris said. She felt an urgent need to show a little defiance in the face of these circumstances. She was not going to fall willingly into simpering motherhood now that she could no longer deny the fact of it. It was a damned nuisance, this child, and a damned piece of stupidity of hers to have allowed it to happen. She thought of all the parcels she carefully packed up and sent to Angus, the little packages that were lame attempts to assuage her constant guilt. What should she say now? 'By the way, I've another little parcel to send to you – it's a baby.' She imagined him unwrapping a naked, squalling child from folds of brown paper and string. Round the child's neck would be an amusing label like that she had so recently attached to a bottle of whisky: 'I am a little bastard that will be passed off by your unfaithful wife as your own child.' How on earth would Angus react? For all his telling her to be free, she could not imagine how he would take this very concrete evidence of her taking his advice.

The door opened and Miranda peered round.

'Can I come in now?'

'Yes, of course, Lady Lindsay,' said the doctor.

Miranda breezed in, saying, 'Don't tell me, Chris, don't tell me! You're expecting aren't you?'

Chris nodded lamely. Miranda, a prophet in pink ninon, sat down on the end of the bed, and took her hand.

'How utterly marvellous!' she said. 'I'm so jealous, really.'

41

'To the first charge, of grossly indecent conduct, how will you plead?' said Major Wilson.

'Not guilty,' said Angus.

'And to the second charge, of striking a superior officer whilst on active service?'

'Guilty, sir.'

'You understand that this second charge carries a maximum penalty of death?'

'Yes.'

'Well, given that it does, wouldn't it be safer to admit the first charge, Bretton?' said Wilson. 'If you were to plead guilty to both, there might be some room for some leniency there. I've seen it happen on many occasions.'

'With proper judges,' cut in Angus. 'Yes, perhaps, but a field court-martial, with staff officers on the bench? They want blood.'

'Well, I don't see that you should open a vein for them, Bretton,' said Wilson.

'I don't see the point of doing otherwise. Besides, there's a principle at stake here, isn't there?'

'For God's sake,' said Wilson, throwing up his hands. 'This is no time for principles! How the devil do you expect me to construct you any sort of adequate defence when you talk like that?' He reached for the pack of cigarettes on the table and lit himself one. 'You have to take this thing seriously.'

'Do you think I don't?'

'I've no idea,' said Wilson. 'It seems like a game to you sometimes, but believe me, Bretton, this is life and death. Don't you care about that?'

'How can you ask me that?' said Angus, leaning across the table. 'You've seen what I've seen. You know the reality of this war. Death is not something we can ignore any more. We live with it now. The skulls roll out at our feet and every one of them tells us that it's our turn next. Don't deny it.'

'I don't. The odds are poor for us, but this . . . This is suicide. Do you want to die that much?'

'Perhaps.'

'Why?'

'Because . . .' He leant back in his chair for a minute and thought. 'Because it isn't necessary for me to live any more.' He found himself smiling slightly. Wilson, across the table, looked horrified. 'I can't expect you to understand that, I suppose.'

'No, for God's sake. What about your wife?'

'My wife will be better off without me,' said Angus.

'I wonder if you shouldn't ask her that.'

'I'm of no use to her now.'

Wilson was shaking his head.

'This bloody fatalism!' he said. 'What am I do with you? How can I defend you when you talk like this?'

'Then don't.'

'I couldn't do that. It's a matter of principle.'

'Ah, you see,' said Angus. 'I'm not the only one.'

'I can't understand your principles,' said Wilson.

'I don't expect you to. You couldn't. You're not made like me. I'm fighting for my right to be as I am – and that's a cause that's worth dying for.'

'You do want to die, don't you?'

'I want to die decently and for a good reason,' said Angus.

'Is this a good reason?'

'In my mind, yes,' he said, getting up from his chair. 'You see, I've had plenty of time to think about it in here. Amazing how clearly you can think in a cell like this. No wonder monks live in whitewashed rooms – this might even be a monk's cell, mightn't it?' he said, gesturing around him, at the bare white room. 'No crucifix though. Anyway, the thing is, five days here have made me see it all so clearly. I see that I will die, sooner, very probably, than later. I might have died last week, when I went on that stupid raiding party, but I didn't. But it's only a matter of time. And if I do die, I'll be blown up into smithereens by a mortar bomb and what for? What for? To tell the Kaiser he should behave himself? Is that worth dying for?' He finished, pressing his palms on the table-top and leaning over to Wilson. Wilson's face was twitching but he did not answer. 'Is it? Is it really?' Angus demanded of him. He looked blankly in reply. 'But I can die for this. I can die for the right to love whom I please.'

'You can't die for something as ridiculous as that . . .'

'Is love ridiculous?' retorted Angus. 'You have a wife, Wilson. Don't you love her?'

'But that's natural . . . This is . . .'

'It is natural. It's as natural to me as it is for water to flow down a burn over the rocks. I am what I am, as you are what you are. If we are forced to deny that, then we are living in a tyranny, and I will not stand for that! I will, if necessary, lay down my life for that. That's a decent end, as far as I'm concerned. I don't want to be a mangled corpse in a dugout for no damn good reason. Just imagine how you would feel if you were told it was wicked to love your wife as you do. Just imagine that.'

There was a long silence, and Wilson stubbed out his cigarette with some vehemence.

'What am I to do?' he said. 'I feel it's my duty to defend you. We've served together. If I don't do my best to get you out of this mess, I wouldn't be able to live with myself. You're a good officer, and a good man, despite everything. You don't have to do this. Can't you simply be reasonable?' The sincerity in his voice was undeniable, and it shook Angus, pained him. Death meant leaving such good people behind for nothingness.

'No,' he managed to say at length. 'The time's past for that, I'm afraid. But thank you for trying, for being so damn human.' And he reached across and pressed his hand over Wilson's for a moment.

'I'll never understand you,' said Wilson.

'Perhaps not. But you've accepted me, haven't you?'

'I suppose I must. But, God damn it, there must be something I can do for you.'

'Get Will off. Do everything you can for him.'

'Is that all you want?'

'I know he'll be in good hands with you. You're the best defence a man might have.'

'Oh Bretton, for heaven's sake . . .'

'No, just do it. It's just as I said – it isn't necessary for me to live any more, but Will, he's a candle that has only just been lit.'

'You're young yourself, Bretton . . .'

Angus shook his head.

'I'm just a flare,' he said. 'I was made to light up a dark sky for a few minutes, to shine intensely and then . . . nothing. I was never meant to get old.'

'You're the bravest, most stupid man I ever met,' said Wilson.

'You may be right,' said Angus, 'but I can't change it. I've had my life. I've tasted the sweetness and the bitterness, at full strength. Who could ask for more than that? That, and a death that might mean something.'

The court-martial lasted a little over quarter of an hour, and in a hasty travesty of justice Angus was found guilty on both counts and sentenced to death. When he returned to his cell, it was as if he had never left it. The calm white of the walls embraced him, and through the high window fell an intense shaft of warm spring sunshine. Angus went and sat on the floor, so that it washed over him. He closed his eyes, and remembered, not with regret, but with great happiness, the room which he had slept in as a very small boy in an old house in the New Town, before his parents had moved to the pompous prosperity of the house in Blackford Road. An attic room, it had been, not unlike the one he had slept in at Royal Circus, he supposed, but as a boy it had seemed vast, and always washed in the same intense golden light that he soaked himself in now, as if it were hot water. He had been sure he had seen ghosts there, not ghosts of the night, but sunlight ghosts, passing palely before him, like the strangely dressed and faded people in old family photographs. Perhaps he would join them when he was gone, those silent-footed maids who had seemed to smile at him, and beckon him into a world of fantasy, a world severely condemned by his parents downstairs. There, with those sepia shadows, he had seemed to know the possibility of anything, to know the richness of life before he was of an age to understand it, and to know there was more than the present, but also the past and the future lying always in layers above and below each moment. In the world of his imagination he had lived so many lives, that to relinquish this one seemed such a small thing. And yet, he found there were tears on his face, that dried only slowly, despite the sunlight.

42

'You'll have to tell them,' said May.

'No,' said Chris. 'They'll only fuss.'

'They've a right to know. It's their grandchild.'

'And I've a right not to say anything until I choose to. Besides, what does it matter to you?' She knew she was being over-sharp with May but the prospect of the Brettons arriving shortly for tea was making her nervous. They had invited themselves, of course.

'I really think you should tell them, that's all. I don't think it's right,' said May. In her VAD uniform she looked starchy and authoritative. Mentally Chris placed her firmly in the Bretton camp and then wondered if being pregnant gave one delusions.

'Yes, I know, but if you knew them as I do,' she said, 'you would know why.'

'All right.'

'So you promise you won't say anything?'

'No, of course I won't. But why are you so secretive, Chris? Anyone would think you didn't want the baby.'

'I'm not sure I do. It's a nuisance.'

'Oh, how can you say that!' exclaimed May. 'What would Angus say?'

'What Angus might say or think is hardly the point,' said Chris. 'He doesn't have to carry it, does he?'

'He is its father,' said May. How Chris longed to contradict her. But she wondered if she would even be able to make May believe any of it. She would not be able to begin to understand that Angus might love another man better than he loved his own wife, and as for the facts of her own sister's adultery . . .

The bell jangled, and as Jean went to open it, May tweaked at the napkins and cups arranged on the tea table, with the anxiety of a young bride entertaining her mother-in-law for the first time.

'Hello, Jean,' they heard Mrs Bretton saying to the maid. 'Your mistress is expecting me.'

Chris stirred herself to get up from the armchair. She was still exhausted.

'Hello, my dear,' said Mrs Bretton, fluttering in. She kissed Chris. 'Apologies from my husband. He has a patient he can't leave.' She turned to May. 'Hello, Miss Adam – how pretty you look in your uniform. How are you finding it?'

'Very interesting, thank you.'

'I should love to do the same myself, but I'm a little old for it,' she said, sitting down on the sofa. 'Now I must ask you, Chris, have you heard anything? I've had nothing for a week, and I'm, well, worried . . .'

'I've had nothing either,' said Chris, and saw the alarm cross Mrs Bretton's pale face. 'But I'm sure he's just terribly busy.'

'I suppose so,' said Mrs Bretton. 'But one can't help but worry, can one?'

'I don't think we should give into that too much,' said Chris.

'No no, you're right. It isn't very patriotic, is it? So, tell me, how did your concert with Lady Lindsay go?'

'She was a huge success – the men loved her.'

'But poor Chris fainted,' said May.

What a devil that girl could be! Chris shot an angry glance across at her.

'You fainted – oh, Christina . . .' said Mrs Bretton significantly.

'It was nothing like that,' Chris said, and heard to her relief the bell jangling again. 'Oh, I wonder who that might be. Have you asked anyone, May? Perhaps it's Antonia.'

She hoped rather desperately it was. At least then she would feel she would have an ally.

Jean came into the room. She looked diffident as she stood by the door.

'Yes, Jean, who is it?' asked Chris.

'It's a telegram, Mrs Bretton.'

She held it out – it was pale buff in colour. Mrs Bretton put her hand over her mouth and made a faint exclamation of horror. Chris decided that this was ridiculous and melodramatic. She would read it calmly outside. It was probably something perfectly trivial.

She got up and took the telegram from Jean.

'Excuse me for a moment,' she said, and followed Jean out of the room. Just as Jean was about to go back into the kitchen she said, 'Make a good strong pot of tea, will you, please.'

'Yes missus,' she said, and then added, 'do you think . . . ?'

'I don't want to think,' said Chris. 'I shall read it first.' She went into her bedroom and shut the door. She sat down on the bed and looked at the still closed telegram.

With trembling fingers, at last she opened it. It took only a moment to read. Died of wounds. What else did there need to be said? She folded it, and swallowed hard. Died of wounds – that was all. Well, she would have to tell his mother now. That was all she could think of.

There was a tapping at the door. It was May.

'Chris, Chris, is everything all right?'

She got up and opened the door.

'No,' she said, softly. 'Don't go back to the drawing room yet. Get Dr Bretton's surgery on the telephone. He has to get over here now, do you understand? I have to tell Mrs Bretton . . .'

'Tell her what? What's happened?' said May. 'It's Angus, isn't it? Oh God, he's not dead is he?'

'Yes,' said Chris. 'Yes, he is.' She was using every ounce of her strength then.

'Oh Chris, oh, I'm so . . .' May's voice cracked at once into a sob. How easily her tears came. Well, let her cry in my stead, she found herself thinking. I can't cry yet. I'm too . . . She did not know what she felt, only a sudden coldness, harsher than the bite of any winter she had known. Angus was dead. Angus was dead.

She repeated it to herself softly as she walked along the hall back to the drawing room. She opened the door and went quietly in. The afternoon sun had filled the place. The pots of daffodils and narcissus she had placed under the windows were glowing with intensity in that spring sunlight, light that was as rich as a slice of aspic. But she felt no warmth from it. Rather its beauty angered her. It opulence was inappropriate.

'Christina?'

She looked down at the little woman on the sofa, tracing, for the first time, Angus's features in her still handsome face. 'Is it . . . Is it . . . ?' She broke off and buried her face in her hands. 'Oh please God, don't let it be . . .' Chris could see her shaking, the muslin ruffles at her wrists trembling.

'I'm afraid I've some very bad news . . .' She was astonished at her grave, calm, professional voice. It was the voice of a nurse or an administrator, one trained to give such news, not a widow. 'Angus has been killed.'

Mrs Bretton looked up at her, her face already stained with tears.

'Oh no, no . . .'

'I'm afraid it's true,' she said, and stretched out the hand in which she held the telegram.

Mrs Bretton snatched it and read it over several times, and each time her sobs grew louder and more intense. It was if as someone were standing there applying a whip to her back.

'May's telephoning for your husband,' Chris said.

'Oh Christina, oh . . .' Mrs Bretton staggered to her feet. 'Oh what shall we do? Whatever shall we do?' She threw herself against Chris, demanding an embrace. Chris held her, but she felt useless and tired. 'I don't think I can bear this . . . I really don't . . . and you . . . How will you . . . ? With the baby and everything?'

'The baby?' Chris broke away slightly. 'How do you know about that?'

'Your sister told me, just now. You see, we were worried. News like this, well, something might . . .'

'She shouldn't have done that!' Chris found she shouted it.

'What does it matter?' said Mrs Bretton. 'I'm glad to know. There's a comfort in it – you must remember that. We should thank God we have something left of Angus – his child.'

'Oh God!' exclaimed Chris, and turned away from her. 'What has God to do with anything? There is no God!'

'My dear . . .' Mrs Bretton began, and then tears overcame her again, and she sank into a chair and wept bitterly. Wept for what, Chris wondered, for an illusory Angus who bore no relation to the man she had known? Would she cry if she knew the truth about him? And what would she, Chris, his mock-wife, weep for, when the tears came? Another illusion? He was a golden shadow passing through their lives. She wondered if even Will Crawford had known him, known the real essence of Angus Bretton, whatever that might have been. And now that shadow was gone and could no longer charm or infuriate them by turns – that creature one could not help loving, because of his beauty and his brilliance. They would never have the chance to puzzle him out now. He had been destroyed.

She reached out and grabbed the top rail of a chair, noting how, as her hand fastened round the carved wood, her knuckles went white with the fierceness of the grip. She felt violently angry then, angry enough to pick up that chair and hurl it across the room towards one of the windows. In fact, she felt she could have broken the window with a single cry of rage. She had a sudden vision of the window collapsing inward, with a hundred shards of glittering, deadly glass flying across the room, making chaos of everything. But how could there be more chaos, in this room? It was as turbulent as the heart of a tempest, for all the quiet sunshine and abandoned tea-cups.

The next morning, Chris hauled herself up on to her pillows, after a very restless night, as Jean brought in a cup of tea for her.

'How did you sleep then, Mrs Bretton?' she asked.

'Oh . . . well, not too bad, I suppose . . .' She felt a first, fierce wave of nausea bubbling up inside her as Jean put a tray over her knees.

'Tea and dry toast, missus, that's what you need,' said Jean. 'Your letters are all there too,' she added, as she went to draw the curtains. 'I'll come and make up your fire in a minute.'

'Don't bother with that,' said Chris.

'But I must. Mr Bretton told me I was always to make sure you had a fire in your bedroom. I couldn't ignore that now, could I?'

'No, no, I suppose not . . .' she said, wearily. It was so typical of Angus to have seen to such a detail for her comfort.

'The doctor would want that too, I'm sure. You have to look after yourself properly, Mrs Bretton, for the baby.'

'Don't worry, Jean, I shall . . .'

Jean smiled approvingly and left Chris to her dry toast and letters. The toast, to her surprise, brought some relief to her nausea, but she did not think the letters could bring her much comfort. They would probably be the first of the condolences. She had seen the letters that May had got from Archie's commanding officer, and various of his friends. She was rather afraid to pick them up. The first seemed very plump. Opening it, she saw at once why – it contained another envelope, with a letter wrapped about it. The letter slipped away, and she saw the inner envelope was addressed to her, in Angus's familiar hand.

Oh God . . . She swallowed hard for a moment, and deliberately took up the covering letter:

> Dear Mrs Bretton,
> Your husband asked me to send you the enclosed letter. I hope it may prove some comfort to you in your time of grief. I was with your husband during his last hours, and I have to report that he faced death with extreme bravery.
>
> Yours sincerely,
> Rev. Gerald Mackenzie (Chaplain, 2nd Battalion, Scots Guards)

That was much as she might have expected. She opened Angus's letter now, and found another envelope, with a longer letter wrapped about that.

> Chris,
> By the time that you read this, you will know I am dead. You will not know the circumstances of it, as I believe it the policy of the army in such cases to fob off relatives with their own version of the truth. You will be told, I think, that I died of wounds. Well, I shall, but they will be inflicted by a firing squad, not

enemy guns. I know that is bluntly put, but I promised you, Chris, that I would never lie to you again. So this is the truth about my death.

I am writing this in prison – in a converted stable, in fact, about ten miles behind the lines. Yesterday I was court-martialled and found guilty of indecent and licentious behaviour and of striking a superior officer whilst on active service. To that latter charge I pleaded guilty, and it is for that I am to be shot. As to indecent and licentious behaviour – that was a simple kiss, given to my poor Will.

Of course, I might have wormed out of all this. I might have got myself declared insane and packed off to an asylum, but I could not. For the first time in my life, I think I have acted honourably. I am dying for what I believe in – my rights, and any man or woman's right to love as they must. I suppose it is a sort of martyrdom, but there will be no cult around me, because no one will know, except you and Will, and the few other witnesses to this little . . . whatever you like to call it. But I will know, and that's what really matters. I had thought I would die anyway here, I could feel it in my bones, and at least this death means something, when so many I have seen mean nothing.

The chaplain has just been here. I think I confused him. He can't understand a man dying for something that he considers wickeder than hell itself. There was a look of repulsion in his eyes which convinced me all the more that I was right to do it. Yet I got him to agree to take this letter and post it, without it going through the censors. His conscience will be paining him for days, I imagine. He did not think you should know at all, but he doesn't know you. But I didn't tell him about the letter to Will, which I enclose. I made sure he got off. He's been sent home as neurasthenic.

If you could see him and give him something of mine . . . I know that's an unreasonable thing to ask you, but I ask it of you as my dearest friend. He will suffer so much over this. He will think I do not love him, but really, I do, or I could not face death.

Oh Chris, how hard this is, to say goodbye to you. What we had was not common – it was something entirely exceptional. It was the greatest friendship I have ever known in my life. That you wanted more, I know. and I had no right to trap you in a place where you could not have all that your rich heart deserves. You'll be free again now – there is some good of this business. For what we had together, I thank you. It is not every man who can die, knowing he lived with genius. Don't let anyone stop you from your music, Chris. While the world is so corrupt the force of art is all we have left to fight with. Yours is a good sword, a bright, clean sword – use it. But really, do I need to say that to you?

Goodbye, and good luck, always,
Angus

She discovered she was crying, the tears welling up in her, surprising her with the intensity with which they shook her body. The voice of this letter had spoken so clearly to her. It was as if Angus had spoken it himself, standing, as he had often done, at the foot of the bed, in his dressing gown. Yet it was the voice of a dead man who had spoken, and she felt cold and afraid that the world could play such tricks upon her. Angus was dead and yet his words, as powerful as life, had sprung up in front of her. She looked back at the letter, but could hardly read it for her eyes were blurred by her tears. She could scarcely understand a word of it – so strange it was, with its talk of executions and martyrdoms. Martyrdom. It made her remember a coloured reproduction of the *Martyrdom of*

St Sebastian that had hung in the nursery of the St Justes' house in Normandy. She had noticed it because the languid saint, tied to the tree, his bare and perfectly muscled flesh punctured at intervals by arrows, had reminded her a little of Angus. It had been such an absurd image she had laughed at it – that a martyrdom could be made so elegant, so serene. It had seemed like a piece of play-acting. Now, it seemed as real as anything. She could imagine Angus tied to that tree, beautiful, inaccessible, dying with the grace of good conscience, from the arrow-heads of his enemies. And she was left to look up at him, like someone kneeling at an altar, left to mourn for that which she had never been allowed to love fully. She understood only one thing then: the great, cold, empty place that lay in her heart where Angus had been.

43

It was still, that morning, and hot already despite the early hour, as the two hundred ships steamed slowly out of Mudros harbour. Guy, standing on the deck of SS *River Clyde*, could not quite believe they were at last embarked on the invasion. While they had been preparing for it, he had not quite believed in it either. There had been an unreality about it all, as if drilling his men in full pack and making them climb rope ladders up the sides of ships were merely an elaborate army game to keep them occupied. He had doubted it even as he had dutifully marked up on the map he had been issued each new piece of intelligence about the Turkish defences, and had passed round to his platoon those useful leaflets on how to identify the Turk. They could recognize, it stated: 'A country Turk of the village class to a certain extent by his dress. He wears as a rule a red fez, with a small coloured turban, a pair of very baggy bloomers of bluish cotton stuff which are girt above the knee.' He had laughed when he had read it – it was a fancy-dress enemy they were to face, it seemed. The leaflet had gone on to tell them how, when they reached Constantinople, 'soldiers should beware of the Europeans inhabiting the low-class districts near the docks, cinematograph-show keepers, grog-shop keepers and the hangers-on of disorderly houses'. Constantinople! Was that really where they were aiming for? He had heard it said enough times in briefings, but he had no sense of it in himself. Constantinople was so distant and fabled a place it seemed to exist only in the imagination of men, and on maps. To him, it was the place of Grand Viziers and Mozart's *Abduction from the Seraglio*, and, more mythical still, of the last days of the Roman Empire. It was extraordinary Byzantium towards which they were sailing, and with their guns and bayonets they were to lay siege to it.

He doubted it still, even on the last morning, that first morning, as they sailed for the peninsula on which they would attempt their landing. It had all been so thoroughly organized. They were heading for V beach, and there would be a bridge of boats formed to carry them from the *Clyde* to the shore. There had even been holes cut in the side of the ship to increase the number of men who could disembark at once, and they would all go charging up the beach, wave after wave of them, and overthrow the surprised Turks in a matter of hours. They would continue to push north, joining up with the French and all those Australians and New Zealanders, who had come halfway across the world for this show, and they would all fight on until they reached Constantinople itself. That was the plan, at least.

Yet on such a day this, with the sunlight intense on the oily calm of the sea, with those silent ships processing out of Mudros harbour, beneath the craggy gaze of the island hills, Guy could not believe it. There was too much quiet excitement here – even the regulars had the look of children going to the Sunday School treat. When they passed another ship, everyone cheered, and then the cheers died and they fell into that strange, expectant silence. What did they all expect?

'I don't believe in it,' Guy told himself. 'Because if I did, I'd be too damn afraid.' Yes, that was it – he wore his own amused disbelief, in the same way the others wore their euphoria. These emotions were only masks, like the comedy masks of ancient Greek actors, with the lips permanently fixed in a manic smile that could be read by the most distant spectator in the theatre. Nothing that was real was allowed to show. That would destroy the illusion, and by God, they needed illusions – the best and showiest they could find. Yes, it was a great splendid adventure this, like something out of Homer! They were going to capture Constantinople from the infidel! He tried to convince himself, but a bitter little taste of doubt remained. He could not quite master himself.

He leant back against the warm cast iron of the bulkhead behind him, and closed his eyes. He felt the engine throb and wished he might sleep. He had not slept much recently, despite all the intense physical activity of his days – and when he had slept it had been fitfully, restlessly, punctuated by disturbing erotic dreams, the vivid memories of which tormented him during the day. It was not as if he needed any more torture of that kind. His conscious mind managed to supply enough. Just to think of Chris was to turn a knife in his guts, a double-bladed knife of guilt and desire. When Miranda's letter had told him that she was pregnant he had felt such a mixture of disgust at himself and sheer joy at it that he thought it would poison him slowly. He would so liked to have strutted into the mess and announced his good news. He was moved more deeply than he ever could have imagined at the thought of their child growing slowly in her womb and he had longed for a letter from her, telling him herself how it was all going on. But of course it did not come. Chris did not write letters, even at the best of times, and these were not the best of times. He had supposed, as calmly as he could, that she was mourning Angus, the man under whose name his child would masquerade. He could not bear the thought of that: couldn't bear the thought of his child being Bretton instead of Lindsay and could not stand the thought of her mourning Angus. He hated the jealousy that ate him up but he was powerless to prevent it. In the darkest parts of him, he found he was glad

Bretton was dead and she was free of that appalling mock-marriage. He had her back to himself now.

He realized, standing there, that he had never actually forgiven her for refusing him. If he had, his love would have died utterly, instead of springing up again, as it had done, like some indestructible rampant climbing weed that lies for a season or two dormant and then grows on the most unlikely, infertile soil. He was still furious at her for it, for if she had taken him then, he could stand there legitimately dreaming of his wife and the child that would come. He wanted to wear her colours going into battle, not those of foolish, adoring Miranda, whose photograph he carried for form's sake. He did not need to carry Chris's image though, for she had possessed him, and lay inside him, a presence more powerful to him than any little scrap of printed pasteboard might conjure up. It angered him that she should possess him so thoroughly and yet remain out of his grasp. Damn her for her wretched ambitions, damn her for liking Angus bloody Bretton, damn her to hell for all of it, for being so near to him and yet always so . . .

His anger died as swiftly as it had come. He had no right to be so angry with her. It was not as if she had behaved like a common flirt. It was rather that she was extraordinary, and driven by things which he could not begin to understand. Yet it was with painful simplicity he longed for her, like a peasant yearning for the complicated grace of the Madonna.

The order came for everyone to go below, and Guy, with the burden of his full pack, made his way down the steps to the hold, which had once held tons of coal, but was now crammed with two thousand men, most of whom were eating, as the general order had specified, a last hot meal before leaving the transport. It was typical of the army that this should be Irish stew at six o'clock in the morning, and it did not promise to be appetizing, but

Guy, having had his canteen filled, found he ate with the same appetite as the rest of them. There was a feeling it might be a while before they tasted anything as palatable again. They had all been issued with three days' worth of iron rations.

His platoon, forty men in all, seemed cheerful and aggressive, quite ready to get at it and give Johnny Turk a good going over. They toasted the prospect of this in mugs of strong brown army tea, nauseating with sugar, and as Guy sipped his own, he remembered from nowhere, it seemed, drinking pale bonfire-smelling china tea with Chris in her flat in the rue du Bac before he had first made love to her. How clearly he remembered that cup of tea – it was as if it were the very same stuff that filled his enamel mug then. Was he destined to remember every moment with her with such clarity, or was it some strange review of life that his mind was launching itself upon? It was a commonplace, of course, that the whole history of a man's life passed in front of him at the imminent prospect of death, but the sharpness of the memory startled him all the same. Perhaps he was marked for death that morning. He glanced around him and wondered how many of his companions were as well.

The meal finished, and they got into their places for landing, all in neat marching lines, facing the same way. The ship began to make elaborate manoeuvres. As they rolled and swung about, the noise of the bombardment became louder and louder.

'That's just our covering fire,' Guy heard someone say.

'Bloody glad to hear that,' responded his friend.

But for the most part the tense silence of waiting was kept up. Suddenly the ship made a great groaning shudder and ran ashore. The lurch this created would have been violent enough to throw men to the floor if there had not been such a press of them. There was no room to fall, though the instinct to duck, even within the iron sides of the collier, was keen enough, for the gunfire was virulent now. Through the open sally ports through which they were to make their exit, the smoke of the guns drifted in, an acrid, terrifying smell.

And still they had to wait, unable to see, but only hearing the banging and crashing, accompanied by the ever thudding, inexhaustible guns as the boat bridge was formed. It took half an hour longer than had been planned – they were further out than they were supposed to be, the whisper came down to them, the beach shelved more steeply than they had thought.

At last, at five minutes past seven, the order was given for the first wave to go ashore. They cheered them, as they went, and Guy felt a deep, shuddering inward relief that his regiment was not scheduled to go until later in the day. But the relief soon turned to dry-throated fear, as the men clanked away down the gangplanks to the dreadful accompaniment of the bombardment, which seemed to grow louder and louder.

They waited two hours, in fact, two hours in which the hold of the ship became furious with heat and the smell of sweat through khaki serge was as strong as the smell of fear. Some injured men managed to get back aboard, when there was a brief gap in disembarkation, and lay, like bleeding animals, helplessly waiting for attention, while the rest of them stood in line, waiting for their turn 'out there'.

Cape Helles was the name of the landing place. Cape Hell seemed to Guy, even then, a better name. Those wounded men were a terrible portent, he was sure enough of it now, of what would come.

At last they were called. The sergeant manning the port pushed the man in front of Guy along the gangplank with a firm hand on his back. It was an unnecessary gesture. They were all moving along as if they could do nothing else, for they could see only a few feet in front of them for the smoke. Forward was the only way they could go, and fast, because it seemed the faster they went, the better the chance of avoiding the hail of bullets.

So he hurtled down the gangplank, which was not difficult, with the weight of his pack, and suddenly the man in front of him was splashing and flailing in the water. God, they were yards from the beach still – the gangplank ended in about five foot of water! Guy squatted down and slipped into the water and attempted to grab the man in front of him, who looked as though he might drown at any moment. He got him to his feet though, and pushed him forward, just as the sergeant major had done.

He turned back to his platoon, who were negotiating the end of the gangplank with similar care. He and Sergeant Meaker, another tall man, thankfully, stood and handed them off, while bullets fell about them like rain – but at the tail of them he noticed one of them get shot and go tumbling over the chain guide rails.

'That was Ramsay,' said Meaker.

One down, Guy could not help thinking, as they made their way to the shore, and forty to go. For as they waded up through the water, the number of bodies floating around them became more and more apparent as the water shallowed out. The water itself was red. Guy wondered for a moment whether to simply drown himself rather than go on. What was the fucking point? Especially as he saw Sergeant Meaker stumble on the foreshore, reaching land only to be met by a bullet. He fell flat on to his face and Guy joined him. The rest of the men, or at least those who remained, joined him too. There was a sort of safety in lying utterly prone on the bloody sand.

'What are we going to do now, sir?' said Wishart beside him.

Guy groped for his field-glasses and stared through them, as best he could without lifting his head. Through them he saw a magnified and misted vision of men running across the beach, only to fall back, as if crashing into invisible walls of glass. It seemed quite hopeless to go anywhere. He shuffled a little on his belly and looked to his right and saw a slight ridge behind which there was clearly good shelter, for there were men hunched beneath it who looked to be alive. Or at least he hoped that was the case, and it was not simply a heap of corpses. But if that was the only shelter they could find, it would have to do.

'West,' he said, to Wishart. 'Up to the right there. Do you see that ridge?'

'Just about, sir,' said Wishart.

'We'll crawl,' said Guy. 'Go slowly, play dead. No bloody heroics.'

'Right sir,' said Wishart and passed the message on.

It was not sand or shingle they crawled over, it seemed to Guy, but a greasy smooth slope of marble, which to move over with any sort of speed needed enormous strength. He could feel exhaustion flooding him. It equalled the despair he felt as gradually the platoon was picked off, like so many innocent pheasants. He would never go game shooting again, he vowed then. He would let all the birds on Rankeillor Moor die as they should.

Beside him Wishart cried out and faltered. Guy grabbed him and began to pull him with him towards the ridge. It was only another three yards or so to safety, and Guy was determined Wishart would make it. But his weight, for such a lean man seemed unimaginable, and the distance interminable.

'Here, you look as if you could do with a hand,' a rich Irish voice sounded in his ear. Guy, who had almost pressed his face to the sand, looked up, and let the Irish sergeant take Wishart.

'He's dead, sir, I'm sorry.'

'Oh God...' It was almost impossible to speak, his

mouth was so dry, as if he had swallowed sand. He fumbled for his water bottle.

'Is this safe?' he said, sounding, he realized, like a pathetic child.

'As safe as can be here,' said the Irishman. 'You can rest a bit now. We can't get any further than here without getting killed, and since you've got this far . . . We'll get dug in soon.'

Guy took a long draught of his water and stared out towards the shore. They were still unloading men.

'This your first time then, sir?' asked the sergeant. Guy nodded. 'Might as well be mine,' the sergeant went on. 'This makes those bloody Boer snipers look like children.'

Guy sat gulping air and water in equal quantities. He was too amazed that he was still alive to say anything at all.

44

Mrs Bretton lifted up the christening dress out of its tissue and held it up for Chris to admire.

'It's at least sixty years old,' she said. 'Certainly all my husband's aunts were christened in it. Isn't it lovely?'

It was made of soft, cream-coloured silk, elaborated with a great deal of butter-coloured lace, and Chris knew it was expected to provoke her to reverent appreciation. She was supposed to feel terribly proud that her child would be given the honour of wearing such a sacred family object, as well as a sense of thrilling maternal anticipation at the advent of the child itself. She was supposed, like Mrs Bretton and her own mother, to be attending to that apparently exciting business of knitting and sewing baby clothes, assembling what they called a layette, and which she could not help considering a nuisance. True, the child would need clothes, but why did there have to be such a fuss about it, such an endless consideration of ribbons and bows?

'Yes,' she said, and managed a half-smile. Mrs Bretton was tweaking at the lace ruffles and Chris, suspecting that the open drawer of the chest from which she had taken the gown probably held a few other sentimental treasures for her to admire, sat down gently on the end of the bed with her arm hooked round the wooden bedpost for support. She had not imagined it was possible to feel so constantly tired, but she did. She felt like a numb lump of flesh, from which the brain and the animating spirit had been removed.

Why else would she be there, enduring Mrs Bretton's well-meant torture? If she had had the will to resist she would have resisted. But what else better had she to do? She could not write. She had written nothing since she had heard that Angus was dead. There seemed to be no music left in her. Instead, her whole being was consumed with the dreadful punishment of this child. She was utterly subjugated by it.

'Angus looked so bonny in this,' said Mrs Bretton, and held it against her breast for a moment as if it still contained the child Angus. 'I can remember that as if it were yesterday . . .'

The quiet regret in her voice jangled the nerves of Chris's own pain, and she found herself gripping the bedpost a little more firmly. It would have been so easy to break just then. She could not disguise however the sharp exhalation of breath that her body forced upon her.

Mrs Bretton turned and said, 'Oh Chris, I'm sorry, I didn't think, did I? This must be terrible for you.' She dropped the dress on a chair as if it were a useless old rag, and came to Chris's side. 'I only thought that thinking of the future a little might be a comfort . . . Oh, but how silly of me!' She was half sobbing as she said it, and reached for her handkerchief.

'No, no, it wasn't silly,' said Chris, putting her hand round her shoulder.

'Yes, it was,' said Mrs Bretton, and gave into her tears fully. 'Oh Christina, why on earth do we bring children into the world if . . . if . . . they're just going to be snatched away. It seems so wrong . . .'

'It is wrong,' said Chris, staring across at the rose-patterned walls of Mrs Bretton's bedroom, with its decoration of family portraits and photographs. Angus, at every stage of his life was there – from the naked baby on the fur rug, to the young officer, swanking in his new uniform.

Chris had had a copy of the same photograph, but she had stuffed it away in a drawer, unable to look at it any more. Now his eyes, those mesmeric eyes, even in the crude imprisonment of a studio photograph, looked across at her while his mother cried bitterly beside her.

'I simply can't see the point of it,' said Mrs Bretton. 'This war . . . It's so . . . so difficult. I ought to be able to resign myself to losing him, because he died for his country. I should be proud, shouldn't I, but I can't be. I just feel utterly . . .' She broke down again, and Chris held her. 'I can't say this to Lionel you know,' she said, gathering hold of herself again. 'He doesn't understand, he doesn't feel as I do. Only a mother can feel the wickedness of it. I'm certain of that, you know, that it's wicked, this whole war is wicked. You understand me, don't you, Chris?'

'Yes, of course,' said Chris.

'That's because you're a mother too, now,' said Mrs Bretton, suddenly reaching out and touching Chris's cheek.

'Men have freemasonry, and women have motherhood,' remarked Chris.

'Perhaps,' said Mrs Bretton, smiling slightly. 'You mustn't expect to feel the same any more, my dear.'

'I don't,' said Chris, and levered herself up from the bed, and walked over to the wall of photographs. Angus's picture was beckoning her. She wondered if she ought to tell Mrs Bretton the truth, whether that was the moment, whether knowing the truth would help her. She looked at the Angus in the photograph, who seemed so serene, so straightforward, and decided she could not destroy that image. Mrs Bretton might be destroyed with it.

Yet she longed to tell someone. She felt heavy with dreadful secrets that seemed to be quietly poisoning her. She longed for the fresh wind of honesty but it seemed impossible. She could not tell Mrs Bretton that Angus had died at the hands of a firing squad – a fact she could hardly bear to think of it herself. Even thinking of it for a moment made her feel physically sick. Angus had once shown her an engraving by Goya of an execution, of a man about to face a barrage of rifles, his hands raised up in horror, a terrible expression on his face. At the time she had only looked at it for a second, for it had terrified her, but now it haunted her, transformed into nightmares, where night after night she watched Angus being shot. She could not tell Mrs Bretton that. The poor woman was suffering enough.

She turned away from the pictures, feeling suddenly the stifling heat of the room, as if there was no air left in there to breathe. She longed to be out of there, somewhere cool and open. She wanted to be up on Rankeillor Hill, and, as she looked out over the coloured fields and ancient trees, be dreaming of all the music she might write, to be again in the uncomplicated state of innocence she had felt before Guy had come back from Vienna. She wanted then so much to be untried again, untouched by life, like a child, in fact, standing on the shore of life, looking at the sea as a beautiful, tempting prospect again, long before the tide had crept about her ankles. How lovely it had seemed then – and yet, in truth, how cold, how dangerous, how complicated it was! She felt so out of her depth, with the current so strong, that she felt certain she would drown. Certainly, she would never get back to that shore.

She went quickly to the window and pushed up the sash, letting in a sharp breeze that whipped up the muslin curtains that lay on the glass. The wind on her face was like a balm. She felt instantly strengthened by it.

'Are you all right?' asked Mrs Bretton.

'I am now,' said Chris, breathing in deeply. 'Just a bit faint suddenly.'

'It is rather close in here,' she said. She glanced at the watch. 'Goodness – is that the time? I shall have to get ready, shan't I? The appointment's at three and' – she went to her looking glass on her dressing table – 'I'm sure I look a perfect fright.'

Chris was glad of an excuse to leave the bedroom. She went downstairs and met Dr Bretton at the foot of the stairs.

'We shall be late,' he said.

'She's just coming,' said Chris, taking up her own hat and gloves from the hall table where she had left them before lunch.

'I'm glad you've decided to be sensible about this house business,' he said. 'Of course, you know we'd rather you came here, but . . .'

Chris smiled wanly. She was glad she had at least had the strength to resist that, and suggest the compromise that she take a house instead of the flat in India Street. Dr Bretton had been violently opposed to his grandchild growing up in a mere flat. She had thought the choice of a house would have been left to her, but Dr Bretton had insisted they help her look over the various possibilities, as if she were an imbecile, incapable of choosing one for herself.

Mrs Bretton joined them after a few minutes, and Dr Bretton drove them over to the New Town. The motor was a recent acquisition and Dr Bretton could hardly be described as an experienced motorist. Every jerk and swerve would make Mrs Bretton gasp, to which he would respond, in a tone that suggested he was reining in his temper, 'Now, dear, there is nothing to be worried about. You are perfectly safe. I have complete control.' Chris, sitting in the back, could not help thinking that, had Angus been there, he would have been highly amused by this. In fact they would probably have been choking down their laughter. How could she reconcile that Angus with the man who had martyred himself? Swiftly, she damped down that train of thought.

They turned into Ann Street, which, because it was June, was heavy with lilac and fresh greenery.

'Number Seven – it'll be the one with the removalist's van I imagine,' said Mrs Bretton, peering out of the window. 'There, isn't that pretty?'

Chris blinked, staring at the house, its door and gate open. There was a voluptuous pale pink clematis trained over its elegant portico. She recognized it – it was Dr Stewart's. A house in Ann Street – she had not thought which house, when Mrs Bretton had told her about it. In fact, she had not even remembered that he had lived there until now. She had put that business so entirely from her mind, and now . . .

As they got out of the motor, two workmen in brown overalls emerged from the house carrying a sideboard, and behind them, fluttering anxious attendance like a butterfly, was, unmistakably, Mrs Stewart.

'Please do be terribly careful . . .' she was saying. Then she caught sight of Chris and the Brettons, and her face became one of transparent panic.

'Oh I'm so sorry,' she said, trotting up to them, 'I know we're supposed to be out and you're supposed to have an empty house to look at but I'm afraid . . .'

'That's quite all right . . .' began Dr Bretton, but Mrs Stewart exclaimed suddenly, 'It's Miss Adam, isn't it? Well, clearly not Miss Adam any more.' She finished with a vague gesture to acknowledge the now prominent bump under Chris's loose dress.

'No, Bretton,' said Chris, taking her proffered hand. Chris presented the Brettons to her and then they went into the house. Chris went reluctantly, with a vague, twitching fear growing inside her, which she squashed with the rationalization that Dr Stewart would most likely not be there.

'We are in such a dreadful mess still,' said Mrs Stewart. 'Shall I show you upstairs first, perhaps? Most of the furniture is out of there.'

She began to climb the stairs, and Dr and Mrs Bretton followed her, but Chris could not, for she was trapped in the hall by a removal man lugging out an armchair from one of the rooms downstairs. As she waited for him to pass, pressed against a door, she realized she was leaning on the door to Dr Stewart's study, the very room from which she had rescued *Everyman*. Before she could do anything about it, the door, which was not properly shut, yielded against her back with a great creak and she almost fell into the room.

'Yes, what is it now?' growled a bored, irritated, unmistakable voice. She turned to face him and found she was actually shaking with fear and that her throat was dry. She stood rooted to the spot while she watched him turn to her, and saw his face register surprise and then a sort of chilly amusement as he realized it was her.

'Well, well,' he said. 'This is a surprise, is it not?'

Her impulse was to run away still, but she conquered it. She would not let him win this time.

'Yes, quite,' she managed to say brightly. 'What a charming room. I'm thinking of taking over your lease, you know.'

'Oh that's why you're here, is it?' he said. He looked at her again, with sharp eyes, observing every detail of her with careful contempt. 'I'm glad to see that you are at last reduced to the proper lot of a woman,' he remarked.

'That smacks of jealousy,' she said.

'Why on earth should I be jealous of you?'

'Because I am a better musician than you,' she said. 'Your music is banal and unoriginal.' Saying that gave her an extraordinary surge of strength. She ceased to be afraid of him and the past. She walked, as calmly as she could, into the room and looked about it. It was a beautiful room, plain but elegant, with its two tall windows overlooking the front garden, and she could quite picture herself in it. For the first time in months she could imagine herself working again. 'What's the acoustic like in here?' she asked.

'Do you think I care what you think of my work?'

'No, I don't imagine you do. You never cared much for my opinion before, did you?'

'Because you were a silly chit who did not know what was good for her,' he said.

'Oh, was I supposed to give in gracefully, give in gratefully?' she retorted. 'What an honour I passed up – to be raped by the great Dr Stewart!'

'Will you keep your voice down,' he said, moving imperceptibly but menacingly closer. 'My wife . . .'

'Yes, your poor wife!' she exclaimed. 'Perhaps she should know exactly what kind of a devil you are.'

'As if she would believe a slut like you!' he said, sharply.

For a moment she went cold with fear. She had always distrusted superstitious belief, but it seemed too deep in her to resist sometimes. She had often bracketed Stewart with a devil – now he seemed the Devil himself, endowed with supernatural knowledge. She had behaved sluttishly, the child in her womb was proof of that, and she was rocked by the accusation. It took her a second or two to grip on to reality and convince herself that he was only throwing about words to taunt her, words which he could not possibly know that he had aimed so well. And as she did that, she overturned in her mind the guilt that had tormented her. She had only felt guilty because the world demanded that she should. Why on earth should she feel guilty for something that had been so profound, so good, so utterly full of meaning? Why should she feel guilty when she had done something to make something new? For the first time, she realized that the child inside her was not a faceless nuisance or a monster made of their wickedness, but a fresh soul, an individual man or woman, who might achieve anything.

'Oh don't waste your breath!' she said to Stewart, feeling the last vestiges of her anger and fear die away. She no longer cared what became of this inadequate man. The past seemed so unimportant when suddenly the future stretched out with dazzling possibilities. She felt alive, for the first time in months, and she felt the life of the child in her. She was certain she could feel its tiny heart beating.

'Then, you won't say anything?' he said, with a touch of desperation at which she could not help laughing. He seemed no more frightening then than a painted dummy in a knock-down booth at the fair. 'You won't?'

'What do you think?' she said.

But there was no opportunity to answer, for Mrs Stewart herself came in with the Brettons.

'Ah, here you are . . .' she said.

'Just renewing an old acquaintance,' said Chris, beneficently. 'Dr Stewart was my tutor for a while at the Academy,' she explained to the Brettons.

'It's a lovely coincidence, isn't it?' said Mrs Stewart. 'I should love to think of another musician living here – you write too, don't you? I remember – you came to get a score. Henry has written such beautiful things here. There must be a muse in the house, mustn't there?'

'Only you, my dear,' said Dr Stewart, with oily gallantry.

Mrs Stewart gave an appreciative smile, and said, 'I'm sure you'd like to see the rest of the house.'

'Yes, please,' said Chris.

As she followed Mrs Stewart about the other rooms, she decided that she would take the house. It would be the start of a new life for her and the child whom she could so easily imagine playing and growing there. As they walked around, she felt new music stirring in her and she felt a longing to be in soon, and at work again. It struck her as a good place for building, for making. Yes, a new life, her child and herself, and her music. She could not hope for much more than that. Guy was a complication about which she could not yet bring herself to think.

45
Cape Helles, September 1915

'Sometimes,' said Cruikshank, 'I don't see the point of eating. Whatever you put in, comes straight out again.'

Guy, flicking away a green fly that was hovering over his mess tin, smiled bitterly and said, 'Best place for this muck, in a latrine . . .' With reluctance he stirred the brown, near-liquid mess of bully beef. He had no inclination to eat it. What Cruickshank had said was right. In an hour or so he would be joining the latrine queue. Like everyone else on Cape Helles, he had the trots. He was lucky, though, it was a mild enough case. He was not like the three men in his unit that he had despatched on that morning back to Mudros, one of them so debilitated they had had to carry him. Another day in the dugouts and he would probably have died. For now it seemed that the Turk was not their principal enemy but enteritis.

Cruickshank and Guy were sitting in the relative cool of their dugout eating this reluctant lunch. With a tray made out of an old ammunition box over his knees to carry his mess tin, and the prudently covered mug of water, Guy leant back against the dugout wall and imagined for a moment what he would like to be eating. Fruit, he decided, the best that the kitchen garden at Rankeillor could offer: those large white and fragrant peaches that grew under glass on the south wall, and which came to the table on a bed of beautiful leaves. With them there would be some sweet, cold German wine, the bottle beaded with icy water, and possibly a dish of blackcurrant ice cream . . .

He stopped. It was stupid to think like that, even for a moment, for returning to reality was painful: bully beef, hard biscuit and water.

'If we get that part of the tunnel finished tonight,' said Cruickshank, 'we could give the men those tins of pineapple.'

'I thought we were keeping them for Christmas,' said Guy.

'Are you daring me to stay alive that long?'

'You've managed this long,' said Guy and took a mouthful of food. 'Another four months of this will simply fly past.'

'The devil it will,' said Cruickshank. 'Look, why not? The men deserve something.'

'A chunk of pineapple each?' said Guy. 'It seems a bit thin to me.'

'Are you expecting new supplies?'

Guy shrugged. The post was erratic. Parcels had a habit of going astray.

'Then we'll give them out tonight. To celebrate.'

'All right, Major,' said Guy. They often called each other by their newly acquired ranks – the loss of officers had been such that they had risen meteorically. Another few days of fighting such as they had had at the beginning of August and Guy felt sure he would get to be a lieutenant-colonel. Either that or he would be killed.

Death had become a dry fact to him. It was impossible for it not to be. There were several major topics of conversation amongst them: dysentery, food, lice and death, and of these four, death seemed the most common. Not a day went by when he did not see or hear of someone dying, and sometimes it was worse than that. The chances of his own survival seemed slimmer and slimmer the longer he remained there. Death seemed only a matter of time.

He felt his bowels griping again, and put aside his tray.

'Time for a stroll in the gardens,' he said.

'I'll see you there anon, I imagine,' said Cruickshank, toasting him with his water mug.

The latrines lay down a short side trench back from the line. It was primitive in the extreme – a matter of two buckets covered with box lids, with such sharp edges, one had to be careful not to slice a finger open lifting them off. Usually there were shells falling about, but the Turks had been suspiciously quiet for the last few days. He was glad, too, to have the place to himself except for the ever-present swarms of obese, green flies. Gingerly he lifted the lid on one of the buckets, and was relieved to see it had been recently emptied by whatever poor sod was that day's latrine orderly.

As he sat and let his body purge itself with its usual violence, he felt his usual despair at the weakness of his body and the humiliation of the situation. To be reduced to this – sitting on a bucket, with flies buzzing about his head, passing blood and slime, knowing that the thing could only get worse, although it was painful enough as it was – painful enough, in fact, to bring slight tears to his eyes. Christ, was this really what his life was supposed to be, this living hell, this stagnant midden of a prison, filled with rotting men, who were both dead and alive? He longed then for Rankeillor, for its clean soft beds, and hot baths, for those large, civilized meals in the dining room, for that life which he had enjoyed so carelessly, without much thinking about it. In the grim stink of that latrine, it seemed as if he had never known these things, that he had lived all his life in this savage, bloody place. And he would live the rest of it there, no doubt, for there was not much chance of getting out of the place alive. Not much chance at all.

He left the latrine and made his way through the claustrophobic, narrow, high-sided trenches towards the front line and the mouth of the tunnel he called Cruickshank's folly. It had been Cruickshank's idea to excavate under No Man's Land, towards the Turkish front line. There was something about it that tempted fate. They would, Guy thought, have been better expending their effort on making some really solid underground dugouts, to prepare for the coming winter and the likelihood of a brutal enemy bombardment. But Cruickshank was acting engineering officer, and had had approval from on high – in fact Sir Ian Hamilton himself had approved it. It would be spectacular if they succeeded.

For the first ten yards or so, it was possible to stand, but after that it was necessary to get down on hands and knees and crawl, as the tunnel sloped steeply downward. At this point, Guy, like the others, shed his shirt, for the heat would soon be unbearable. It was a relief to be rid of it and the lice it contained. He crawled down, past the chain that was laboriously clearing the spoil, pushing along the sacks of excavated earth from man to man until the last one dragged it back to the mouth of the tunnel, where it was heaved up to reinforce the parapet. The men lay prone to do it, their bodies dusty and their faces blackened and eerie in the dim light of the slush lamps which lit the tunnel.

'Heard anything from the other side lately?' he asked, when he reached the diggers at the earth face.

'Nothing much, sir,' said Private Mackinnon.

'They're too bloody quiet today, aren't they?' said Guy.

'Little heathen bastards,' said Mackinnon with feeling as he thrust his pick into the earth. 'We'll give them a nice surprise, won't we?'

Perhaps Cruickshank's folly was not such a folly. It gave them all something to do, after all, and the thought of eliciting some small revenge on their persecutors was quite comforting. And it was good, mind-numbing, body-numbing work. Guy joined the men who were filling the spoil bags – hardly an easy task to do on hands and knees but he forced himself. It was not the time for taking officer's privileges. Besides, he needed the distraction of the work for himself. It was a case of work or go mad . . .

It was not long before he was dripping with sweat and his guts were aching again, ominously. Private Gordon caught sight of him wincing with sudden pain.

'You should report sick, sir,' he said.

'I'm not that bad, yet . . .' he said. He felt his bowels leap again. It was like having a vicious animal in there, gnawing at his entrails, except now it was not gnawing, but biting. Another trip to the latrine was necessary. He put down his shovel and began the crawl back. No one commented on this. Such disappearances were a commonplace.

The pain as he crawled was terrible, and he wondered if he was going to get to the latrine in time. He scrabbled forward as fast as he could, but the slope up seemed steeper than ever and he felt as feeble as an old man. The dust filled his nostrils and he thought he might choke. He paused for a breath and heard Mackinnon at the far end of the tunnel call hush. He could feel the men behind him freeze at it, for it meant he had heard something ominous. There was a sudden, horrible, intense silence and then . . .

He found himself swinging, in mid-air. He stared up and saw the vivid blue of the autumn sky. He was being hoisted upwards, swaying from side to side. For a moment a childish notion of floating up to Heaven swam into his cloudy mind – for surely this was death – and then he felt the pain, a harrowing agony that made him cry out. It was as if his legs were burning up like dry tinder tossed on to a roaring fire. He could feel the pain eating at the very bones of them. Was that Hell snatching at him? He closed his eyes and prayed for oblivion again, but instead there was a violent lurch and he found he was lying in a sort of shallow box, that had cracked into something. He half opened his eyes, frightened to look, and found he was dangling over the side of a ship. For a moment he thought he was in a coffin, but then remembered that no one got a coffin at Cape Helles. At last he realized, as with one last jerk he was pulled up to deck height and brought aboard, that he was lying on a stretcher and was being loaded on to a hospital ship. A woman of all things, white-coiffed like a nanny, was bending over him. He grabbed at her hand, anxious for reassurement. He tried to speak, but nothing came out.

'Don't try and talk,' she said, and put a soothing cool hand on his forehead. 'We'll get you something for the pain soon.'

He was carried under the shelter of an awning, and after a moment or two the same nurse appeared with a syringe.

'You'll just feel a slight prick, Major Lindsay,' she said, and plunged the needle into the flesh of his upper arm. 'There you are – nothing to it, eh? That was morphine.'

'Morphine . . .' he managed to say.

She smiled and went away. He looked around him, but only for a minute or two. With relief, he fell asleep.

It seemed like an instant before he woke, but he realized at once, as he looked about him through sleep-hooded lids, that it could not be. He saw he was lying in a bed, with sides raised to stop him falling out, and he could feel smooth linen under his body. He realized he was clean and deloused, but apart from that he could feel little. His body was oddly numb, as if it were only his mind that had woken up. With great difficulty, for it felt like pulling up a heavy weight, he propped himself up on an elbow to see where he was. He was in the hold of a ship, fixed up like a hospital ward, with shiny white paint and rows of other cots like his own. In the air there was the sweet, safe smell of disinfectant, and at the far end he could see the white-clad figures of a pair of nurses. It seemed extraordinarily calm and cool. He could not see a single fly. How far, he wondered, were they from the Dardanelles? For the ship was moving – he could hear the throb of the engines and feel the slight motion of it from side to side. Had he honestly got away from there, got away with his life?

He attempted to sit up and could not. The lower part of his body felt lifeless and it worried him. He rested on the other elbow and tried to flick off the cotton sheet which covered him. It took a few tugs to free it and he saw firstly that his right leg was entirely cased in plaster. Then he was aware of a terrible throbbing at his left knee and pulled away the last fold of the sheet. He blinked, for he could see nothing below his knee except a great gauze dressing. His lower leg appeared to have quite gone, and yet, how ridiculous that was, because suddenly he could feel it all right, feel the livid pain of it, right down to his little toe, and yet, there was nothing of it . . .

I must be hallucinating, he thought, and sank back on to his pillow. He would look again in a minute and see it there, just as it had always been, right down to the last hair and birth mark on his calf.

He waited as long as he could bear to, and then struggled back up on to his elbow. Cautiously he looked down. There was nothing there below the knee. He was shaking with panic now, and looked up to see a nurse coming towards him.

'Nurse . . .' he called out. 'Nurse!'

She trotted to his side and started to rearrange the sheet, but he tussled with her, pulling it away again, and pointing down.

'I can't . . . I can't see my leg. I can feel it . . .'

In a moment she had her arms around him and was lowering him back on to the pillows.

'You have to rest,' she said. 'You've lost a lot of blood.'

'My leg . . .'

'I'm afraid it had to go. There was nothing else we could do. The other will be fine.'

'My leg!' he said, reaching up and gripping her shoulders. 'My leg!'

'Now calm down, you'll wake the others,' she said, deftly disengaging herself from him. Quickly she tucked the sheet around him, firmly, as if she meant to restrain him. 'Do you need more morphine?'

He lay there shivering. In the things he had seen and faced, he had never felt such fear as then.

46
The Manse, Rankeillor, January 1916

Chris, sitting in her old bedroom, at the ink-stained deal table, was finishing the last few pages of the fair copy of the *Songs by Donne* to send to her publisher in London. It was a job she hated. It bored her to have to spend so long over clear handwriting and blot-free pages when she would rather be fixing her mind on the next piece of work. However, it was an absolute necessity, especially now she was writing so fast. The pages of a score were illegible to anyone else until she had deciphered them by writing them out laboriously in her best hand, as if in a copybook.

She had reached the final note of the last setting and with a slight flourish marked a good black double bar line to end it before reaching for the blotting paper. For a moment she savoured the shrieking dissonance she had finished it with – it was the sort of thing that always mystified her critics, who liked music to end comfortably. But these songs were not comfortable. Into them she had poured out all the darkness inside her and the results were bleak, painful, but powerful – she was certain of that.

She finished blotting and then, as a last thought, picked up her pen and added her name and the date, and below that she wrote, 'Dedicated to the memory of Angus Bretton'. It was a final valediction. He would have been pleased with those songs.

There was a quiet stirring in the crib behind her and she

got up and went over to it to see her son waking quietly up. She smiled, amazed that he should be so obliging as to sleep while his mother worked. He was not always so considerate, but that afternoon, perhaps he guessed the importance of getting the thing finished. Certainly, he had such an intelligent face that Chris felt certain he knew. Their instinct seemed reciprocal. He stretched out his little arm and she put out her finger for him to clasp it with his perfect miniature fingers. They were, even now, good strong fingers, and she wondered what instrument they would take to.

She picked him up and held him against her, loving as ever the feeling of his warm head against her swollen breasts. She would feed him later, but for now she would just hold him. It was nice to have a quiet moment with him, for her mother and Phemie were forever fussing over him when they were downstairs, as if he were the only baby they had ever seen. She sat down with him in the armchair (a recent addition to the room – it had never been there when she was a girl) and addressed him.

'Well, Robin, I've finished that, so I shall write some music for you now. What would you like? Commission me.' He looked quizzical, and again, so wise, as if he knew everything. 'Another symphony? Do you think your mother is ready for that?'

He gurgled as if in assent and Chris laughed at her own absurdity. She lifted him up and toddled him on her lap, dancing him along to some unheard music. She whistled to him, which he loved, but only for a minute or two because his face soon crumpled up in a wail, which signalled he wanted to be changed.

'Right then,' said Chris, getting up. She carried him through to the temporary nursery where Peggy, his nurse, was sitting by the fire mending.

'Nothing lasts, does it?' she said, as she handed him

over. The sight of Peggy seemed to stop him crying at once.

'I'll get him changed, Miss Christina,' she said. She was Phemie's niece, and had lived in Rankeillor all her life, until she had come to Chris just before Robin's birth. Her mother had been a nursemaid at the Castle and had looked after Guy, presumably in the same calm and kindly way that Peggy now looked after his son. Guy, Chris knew, would approve, if he had been in a position to approve.

She winced when she thought of him, as she always did – a definite, heart-slicing pain. She tried always not to think of him, to close a door on that part of her. It always proved impossible. Guy was always there, hovering over her shoulder, it seemed, every time she picked up Robin – Guy, the father of that miraculous child who had changed so much, who had given her back the reason for life. In Robin's face she saw him, in his fiercely kicking legs and arms, which promised to grow long and muscled like Guy's. He was so absolutely Guy's, that child, and she longed for the moment when she could hold him out to him and say: 'Look, look what we've done together, look what we have created!' The impossibility of that made the desire for it all the stronger. She wanted to shout the truth of it out, especially when her parents or the Brettons scrutinized Robin's little face for signs of his paternity. 'Those are definitely Aunt Isabel's ears . . .' Mrs Bretton had said.

Sometimes she tried to forget it, but her actions seemed to thwart every effort in that direction. Why else would she have come to Rankeillor for Robin's first Hogmanay, if it had not been for thinking Guy would want that? He was a Rankeillor child, after all, conceived there, in the house his ancestors had inhabited for centuries. If she had married Guy, Robin would be the heir to all that, a celebrity in the neighbourhood, instead of merely one of the Minister's grandchildren. It terrified her that Robin would hate her when she told him the truth, when he was old enough to understand. He would be old enough to understand, but very likely not to forgive. She had brought him into a life of ambiguity, to be the son of a man who could never have been his father. How she dreaded those questions which would surely come: 'Tell me about my father.' She would not be able to lie to her own son, would she?

She watched him, lying on the table, blissfully unaware, being ministered to by Peggy.

'I'm going down to the post office,' she said. 'Is there anything you need?'

'Oh no, miss,' said Peggy, deftly putting on Robin's fresh nappy, with an ease which Chris had not managed to acquire.

'I'll be back in time for his five o'clock feed,' she said. 'And bath time,' she added, especially to Robin, who particularly enjoyed that.

She spent a few minutes parcelling up her score and then threw on an old coat and hurried down towards the post office in the growing dusk of three o'clock.

The post office at Rankeillor was also the grocer's and also the source of all local gossip. One could not hope to make a brief visit there. That afternoon the place was buzzing with a sense of excitement that was as tangible as the smell of paraffin and coffee that always filled the air of the shop. Even as Chris approached the counter, Babbie Thompson, the sub-postmistress, was leaning forward, eager to give her the news.

'The Laird'll be home tonight!' she said, after very few preliminaries. 'Isn't that something?' Chris was not allowed to answer the question, as Babbie carried on breathlessly. 'Yes, there was a telegram this morning, from her Leddyship, to get the mansion house opened up again. She must be fair relieved to have him out o' that hospital, eh?'

'I should think so . . .' Chris managed to say. She put a discreet hand on the counter to steady herself. For she felt it herself, a surge of wonderful relief. She had tried to distance herself from the details of Guy's injury, telling herself it was a slight thing and that she should not worry. She had not allowed herself to worry about it. It would have overwhelmed her. Yet hearing now that he was well enough to come home – how long, in truth, had she secretly hoped for that? 'That is good news.'

But it was dreadful news too. As much as she wanted to see him, she knew she could not. She would have to get back to Edinburgh as quickly as she could, for if they met, well, she could not say what might happen. It was best to avoid him. Avoid him at all costs. Her heart rebelled at that. Of course it was the right thing, the sensible thing. She ought to go straight back to the Manse and start packing. But defiance was bubbling up inside her. She needed to see him. Every nerve in her ached with the need to see him. They needed to talk so badly. How could she run away? She would have to stop running away now, because she knew it, for the first time, perhaps, with such devastating clarity, that she loved him. There amongst the chatter and clutter of Babbie Thompson's shop, she knew she loved him. How simple it seemed now she had admitted it to herself. It was a simple, beautiful, undeniable truth, no matter what the world might say. She had faith in it.

'That's one and eleven,' said Babbie Thompson.

Mechanically, Chris handed over a half-crown.

'And how's the wee one today?' she asked.

Robin was going to see his father.

'Oh fine, fine,' said Chris, smiling.

She walked out of the shop and into the dusk. She did not go straight back to the Manse but wandered over to the Castle gates, the gates by which he had kissed her so passionately. In the distance the lights of the Castle were glowing like a beacon, squares of warm gold standing out against the sombre stone of the walls. She stood there for some minutes looking at the house through the complicated screen of those great wrought-iron gates, as the sky above her drifted imperceptibly from violet grey to black, while the breeze rattled the leafless branches of the trees along the carriage drive. How simple it was, for all the complications, how utterly simple! She understood then how Angus had felt, and how, when possessed by such strength of love, anything was possible. The words of his last letter echoed in her mind: 'I am dying for what I believe in – my right and any man or woman's right to love as they must.' No, she could not run away, she could not any longer ignore her love. She must love as she must. That was what Angus had done, and so would she, whatever that might mean! She leant against the gate, feeling the sharp blade of an iron lily flower in the palm of her gripping hand. She pressed her cheek to the cool belly of the leaping deer that decorated the gate. 'As pants the hart for cooling streams, so pants my heart for thee . . .' Well, she would see him soon, very soon . . .

She began to walk back to the Manse, a little afraid still, but at least knowing she had found her courage. It was time, after all, to give their son his bath.

At last the journey was nearly over, and they were on the branch line that went from Perth to Forfar by way of Rankeillor. It had been a dreadfully long affair, with his mother and Miranda fussing over him, as if he were a child. They had wanted him to stay in London for a few days, but he had been adamant. Miranda had taken a house in Bryanston Square, a great stucco monstrosity, very smartly and horribly furnished, which she appeared to love, but one night there had been enough to convince him how alien it was. He had to get back to Rankeillor as soon as he could. It was the one thing he was certain of. There had been quite a scene about it. Miranda and his mother seemed to think he had lost his intelligence instead of his leg. They patronized him, like the nurses had, and their attentions cloyed. He thought he would suffocate if he did not get back to the space of Rankeillor. He wanted to be back in his old room, with the ancient red damask hangings, the smell of dogs and the ranks of little soldiers. There, he was sure, or at least he prayed he was sure, he would find some equilibrium again. As the train drew into the station, he hoped desperately there would not be any sort of reception arranged for him. He wanted so much to be alone and not to have to speak a word to anyone. He stood anxiously at the door, propped up on his crutches, and the moment it had stopped, he began to fumble to get the door open.

'Let me, Guy,' said Miranda, trying to get him to stand aside.

'I can open a bloody door, for God's sake!' he snapped. He was pre-empted, however, for Henry Blaikie, the station master, had come to open it. He stood there, smiling respectfully up to Guy, offering his hand.

'I can manage, thank you, Blaikie,' Guy said, and heard the coldness in his voice. He had not meant it. Blaikie was a good man, but he had to show them he would manage alone.

'Of course, sir,' said Blaikie and stepped back to let Guy manoeuvre himself out of the carriage.

'Be careful, Guy . . .' Miranda said.

He nearly shouted at her, but bit his tongue and concentrated on getting out. The moment he was sure of his balance, he pounded on his crutches across the platform towards the exit. He had no intention of lingering at the station. Outside, the carriage was waiting. Mackie was off driving an ambulance in France so they had reverted to horses. The sight of the old carriage, bought during his father's childhood, reassured him. Nothing had changed here, not even Davie Watson, the head groom, who had been in charge of stables ever since Guy could remember. He even thought he recognized the horses.

But he had changed, changed horribly. He saw that in Davie Watson's face – his old, comfortable face registered shock at the sight of Guy. Guy, the skeleton, the cripple, standing up only because the crutches were holding him. He felt his face muscles twitching. He could not help it. It happened all the time now, as if demons were pulling his nerves.

'Davie . . .' He managed a slight signal of acknowledgement.

'They never told me about the leg, sir,' said Davie at length. Guy found he was smiling. It was typical of Davie to be so blunt and he was glad of it. Most people stared at his leg and then avoided the subject. 'You'll have to learn to ride side-saddle.'

'What an excellent idea,' said Guy, feeling at last a little calmness in him. He was right to have come back. His instinct never failed. He glanced up suddenly at the starry sky, and grinned. 'Christ, it's good to be back!' Rankeillor would cure him.

Yet as soon as it had come, his optimism evaporated. In the carriage, Miranda insisted on tucking the carriage rug round him, as if he were some bed-wetting old man. He pushed her away slightly and saw his mother, who was sitting beside him, frown.

'Miranda is only trying to help you,' she said.

'I don't need help. I need to manage alone.'

'I know, Guy,' said Miranda, 'but it's so cold in here. You must let me worry.'

'Don't,' said Guy. 'Please! I'm alive, I'm here. There isn't anything to worry about any more.'

That was utter rubbish, but it silenced them. They could not know, could not begin to know, what was going on inside him. Only those who had been there could know, and God, there were so few of them left. Yes, he had survived it, but he often thought it might have been better to go with his comrades, to know only dark oblivion, to be a forgetful corpse. He saw them in his mind, those maggoty lumps of flesh, only half buried in the sand, he could smell the stench of them still, as clearly as if a phial of that noxious perfume had been dropped on the carriage floor. He found he was shuddering at it. He could never get away from it. Even here, in the old brougham that his grandfather had bought, the ghosts were with him. One sat next to Miranda now, a half-rotted skull on a lumpen khaki body, grinning at him, his bony arm outstretched, the digit beckoning him to join him.

He looked away. He would not give into that. He had got this far. He was still alive, and he would not give in. He was nearly home. Inside the castle, these demons would not follow him. It would be against all heaven that they should.

But they did follow him – or at least that particular one, the corpse who had been sitting next to Miranda. Guy knew it was not real, but it followed him with all the fidelity of one of the castle dogs. He wondered if it wasn't Cruickshank. It would be Cruikshank's sort of humour to haunt him when he was supposed to be greeting the servants. It even stood next to Mrs Malcolm, the housekeeper, and put out its hand for Guy to shake. Or was it beckoning to him again and asking him to come back, to face the death he should have suffered?

Guy wanted to shout out 'Go away!' but then all the staff and his mother and his wife would think that he was mad. Well, he was mad, he knew, for he was looking at a half-rotted corpse standing alongside Mrs Malcolm, and wondering whether it wasn't Cruickshank. He could not see such things with clarity and be sane. He was mad, he knew that, but what could he do about it? Was it something he simply had to bear, like the lifeless, aching stump that was left of his leg? Was it part of the price he had to pay for being alive? That price seemed so high.

Cruickshank's corpse was suddenly gone, and Guy felt weak with relief. He looked frantically about the hall, at all the familiar things there, smelling now the wood-smoke of the fire, and the sweet figgy polish that was so characteristic of the place. No more corpse stench.

After he had seen the servants they went into the billiard room, which he found odd, for it was not a room that Miranda or his mother ever used.

'I thought it might be easier for you,' Miranda began, as she sat at the tea table, 'if we had the business room turned into a bedroom – and the little ante-room for a dressing room . . .'

'What?' Guy said. 'Why?'

'To save you the bother of the stairs,' she said.

He stared, utterly astonished by the suggestion. To be confined to the ground floor of his own house . . .

'It would only be for a while,' said his mother. 'Until we had a lift put in.'

'A lift?'

'Yes, we already have one for the luggage, don't we?' she said. 'It might be rather messy but . . .'

'No,' said Guy. 'No, I won't hear of this.'

'Be practical, darling.'

'You call that practical?' he said.

'Well, the stairs will simply wear you out,' she said.

'They will not,' he retorted. 'Good God, what do you think I am, some sort of ridiculous cripple?'

'Well, my dear, if it's not too insensitive to point out, you are an amputee,' said his mother. 'And one has to face the thing realistically.'

'What the hell do you know about being realistic?' he said, and reached out for the crutches that were lying by his chair. He had to prove her wrong, but it seemed a tremendous struggle to get out of the deep armchair. He had not realized how tired he was.

'Guy, will you mind your tone,' she said, exactly as if he were a boy.

'What will you do if I don't, Mama, take away my crutches?' he responded. 'I'm going upstairs now . . .' he went on, and noticed how Miranda had half risen in her chair. 'Alone.'

'If you're sure . . .' she said.

'Yes, quite sure.'

As he made his way over to the door, he saw his mother reach out and put her hand over Miranda's.

The stairs were difficult. He had not thought of it before, but they were turnpikes, broad enough by usual standards, but requiring immense care on his part to make sure the crutches were safely placed on each step before he heaved himself up to the next one. How heavy he found he was, as if his bones were made of lead. He felt that his shoulders ached and that his armpits were sore where the leather-covered top of the crutch rubbed against them.

And then, when he had managed two flights, and got to the long passageway that led to his old room, a nice level passageway, except for a few steps up, he suddenly saw his haunting corpse again. It was dancing in front of him now, dancing round him in fact, tormenting him with a jig on two ghastly, skeletal legs.

'For Christ's sake, go away!' he cried out, feeling dizzy as the figure whipped round and around him, filling the air with that stench again. 'Go away!'

He lost his balance and found himself lying flat on his stomach, falling with a great bellowing groan of rage. He stared down helplessly, his nose in the thick Turkey runner that lined the passageway. He could feel tears in his eyes but would not look up at the shadow that he felt had fallen over him. He could not bear to see that thing again.

'Sir, are you all right?'

It was a girl's voice, tentative and innocent, a real Rankeillor voice.

He looked up. It was one of the maids, a girl of about fifteen, neat in her black afternoon dress and frilled apron.

'Just a little slip – I'm not used to these yet...' he managed to say.

'Shall I help you up?'

With anyone else he might have refused, but he did not think he could manage to get up on his own.

'Thank you...'

When he was standing again, she asked, 'Can I do anything else for you, sir?'

'Yes, actually, you can,' he said. 'It's Florrie, isn't it?'

'Aye, sir.'

'Could you have a fire laid in my room?' She looked puzzled, so he explained. 'My old room – the red room.'

'Oh aye, sir, of course. I didna know that was your old room. Shall I have the bed made up in there, as well?'

'Would you?' he said. It was like entering into a conspiracy. He wondered where Miranda and his mother had planned for him to sleep. Probably on the floor below in one of the soulless but opulently decorated guest bedrooms, until his prison in the basement was ready. Well, if he was to have a prison, it would be of his own choosing.

She walked with him to the room, and opened the door for him.

'Och, it's awful cold in here,' she said. 'And the dust sheets are still on...'

'That's all right,' he said, coming in after her as she hastily moved round, pulling off the dust sheets.

'It'll need a dust too,' she said. 'All these wee men...'

'My tin soldiers,' he said, picking one up. It was a Napoleonic grenadier, bright with enamel paint.

'I'll just go and get some things for the fire, sir.'

'Yes, thank you . . .' She went towards the door. 'By the way, Florrie, please don't tell anyone you saw me fall, will you?'

'Of course not, sir,' she said. 'I won't be a minute.'

He sank into one of the newly unshrouded armchairs, the tin soldier still in his hand.

'Don't you dare come in here, Cruickshank,' he muttered. 'I've nowhere else left to go . . .'

'I'll never leave you now,' he heard it whisper, and felt a distinct bony finger run along the back of his neck, tickling him like a fat Gallipoli fly.

47

He was in the tunnel again, sweating, shitting himself and feeling the paralysing weight of earth, pressing down on him like a living, malicious thing, and he could hear the muffled, choking cries of the others, cries that were fading fast. He opened his eyes, which were stinging with the swirling dust, and looked down at the slope upon which he was lying, belly down. There was a stream of liquid, thick, dark liquid, running up it. How could something run up a slope, he wondered, and touched it with his finger. It was blood, thick, fresh blood, running as if it had just spurted from a newly open wound, and the level of it was rising. Where there had been an inch before, there were now five inches, and there would soon be ten. He could feel it lapping against him. In a moment he would drown in it. He began to struggle against it violently, pulling himself, or at least trying to pull himself, along, up the slope. But he could not move – there was a pair of hands on his shoulders now, restraining him, kindly hands. He looked up and saw it was his father, looking exactly as he remembered him – dark-haired and bearded. He looked a little like the King, and he was shaking his head, a little regretfully, perhaps, but the order was clear. Then he spoke: 'Dulce et decorum est pro patria mori . . .'

Guy woke with a start, his limbs jerking as if electricity had been applied to him. He stared up at the blackened oak frame of the bed, at the carving on the canopy of leaves and fruit, and realized he was at Rankeillor. He was dripping with sweat and his throat was dry. He had to drink. He flung himself out of bed, and then, as he went crashing to the floor, remembered, with fury, about his missing leg. It had felt as if it were there. He shivered on the floor, clammy still with sweat, but in the grip of the cold. He could hear the rain beating against the window. It was January at Rankeillor, and he was alive – just.

He crawled across and gathered his crutches and pulled himself on to them. He cursed himself for falling asleep. He had not meant to – in fact, he reckoned he had kept awake until four or five, and then it had been impossible to stay awake any longer. He screwed up his face and tried to exorcize the image that lingered in his mind, but it was no good. He stood in the middle of the room, feeling it was only the crutches that held him up. He was exhausted, but he could not permit himself to sleep.

Suddenly he was aware of music playing a few rooms away. He recognized the tone of the piano – it was the Broadwood upright in the old schoolroom, the piano he had spent hours practising on. And the music was Schubert, his beloved Schubert, one of the impromptus. For a moment he wondered if he was still dreaming. Could that be his younger, innocent self playing?

He made his way towards it, drawn by it, like a Caliban spellbound by Prospero's music. For this was magical stuff, sane and beautiful, and therefore not of this world, for the world was dirty and corrupted. It was the stuff of heaven itself. It calmed him as nothing had in weeks and yet as he reached the door he hesitated. Perhaps it was another trick. Perhaps it was death calling again, this time so sweetly disguised that he could not resist it. If it had taken the form of his father, why not Schubert as well, why not take the voices of the things he loved to tempt him into oblivion? Why not?

He opened the door slowly and saw it was Miranda. She was wearing a pale, soft-looking dress, the full sleeves of which shook as she played. Was she real? Had she ever been real to him, this beautiful creature, who played so perfectly, her technique so brilliant it made him think of a piano roll? She was nothing but a doll to him, an automaton, who performed as his wife. She meant nothing real to him.

She broke off, realizing someone had come in, and spun round on the piano stool to see who.

'Oh . . .' she said, and jumped up. Immediately she was at his side. 'Did I wake you? I didn't mean to. I thought you should be allowed to sleep . . . after such a long journey.'

'What time is it?' he said.

'After ten. You looked so peaceful.'

'You should have woken me,' he said.

'You need rest. You mustn't drive yourself so hard. You're a convalescent,' she said, taking his arm.

'You don't understand, I don't want to sleep,' he said, wresting himself away from her. He stumped across the room, and sat down in the window seat. He was sweating again and he wanted the draught from the window to cool him. 'What were you doing in here?'

'Well, the piano tuner came a few days ago – I called him specially. I was sure you'd want all the pianos in tune again. I was simply checking he'd done this one. It's nice – surprisingly so. You learnt on it didn't you?'

'Yes. You needn't have bothered about the pianos,' he said, annoyed by this wifely attention to detail.

'Why not? You'll want to play, won't you?'

He shook his head, and stared out of the window. How often had he sat on that window seat staring out when he should have been trying to get something by heart for his governess? He wished he could be that child again, a child of six or seven, with nothing much more to be afraid of than losing his supper or having an extra psalm to learn. How comfortable those fears seemed now.

'Surely,' said Miranda, coming over to him. 'Oh you mustn't sit here, dear, you'll catch a chill. Let me fetch your dressing gown . . .'

'No, I won't be playing again.' It had hardly occurred to him before, but he knew it for certain now. He could not play any more. 'I can't.'

'Oh, what nonsense!' she said. 'You might as well say you won't breathe.'

'I might not do that either.'

'What do you mean?'

'I mean . . . I mean . . .' He wondered if he could explain to her. She was so untouched by the reality of it, like her namesake, she lived on a magic island. She would only think him mad and pity him all the more. How he loathed that sweet pity in her eyes. He saw it now. It was not love – at least, not as he understood it. 'I just can't,' he said, and got up again. She insisted on helping him.

'Let's get you somewhere warm. Do you want some breakfast?' He nodded meekly, the will to resist gone suddenly. 'Good, well, what would you like? Coddled eggs? I know how you love those. And later, only if you're feeling up to it, we could ask Chris to bring her little boy up for you to see.'

'Chris . . .' He could not help sounding startled. 'Is she here?'

'Yes, with little Robin,' said Miranda. 'Antonia says he's a beautiful child. I haven't seen him yet.'

'Robin,' he said.

'Robert, properly,' went on Miranda. 'So would you like to see her? It can wait of course, I think she's here to the end of the week. I didn't know myself until Mrs Watson told me. Shall I ask them up?'

'No, I'll go down myself.'

'In this weather?'

'Yes,' he said.

'All right, I can drive the Lanchester.'

'I'll go alone,' he said, detaching himself from her.

'But I haven't seen the baby.'

'Then see him tomorrow,' he said, sharply. They had reached his door now, and he pushed it open. 'I want to go alone.'

'If you insist,' she said. 'I don't know why though. She's my friend too.'

'Please, Miranda,' he said. 'Just leave it, please.'

'Very well,' she said, clearly offended. 'Whatever you like. I'll have Malcolm bring you up some breakfast, shall I?'

'Yes, if you would,' he said and shut the door in her face, and leant on the back of it for a moment, as if he were afraid she would pursue him. He staggered over to the bed and fell on to it, abandoning his crutches with a clatter. He found he was shaking at the thought of seeing Chris – not just from excitement but from fear, a deep, childish, sickening fear of rejection. For how could she love him now when he was nothing but a skin sack filled with demons? She would loathe him, surely, just as he loathed himself.

The news came quickly enough to the Manse. Effie, who had been down to the shop early, announced it when she brought in a pot of tea to Chris and Mrs Adam in the middle of the morning.

'Oh dear, how dreadful,' said Mrs Adam. 'I'd no idea it was so bad, had you, Chris?'

She shook her head, not daring to speak. All she had heard was that he had suffered severe leg injuries. Antonia had told her that and she had explained that Miranda's letter had said nothing more specific. It had not crossed her mind, or rather she had not allowed it to cross her mind, that that might mean amputation. But hearing it now, she wondered how she could have been so stupid as not to imagine such an eventuality. It was the very stuff of war, after all, that men should lose their legs. Other men, though, she found her instinct shouted out, not Guy, please, not Guy . . . She found she was staring across at her mother through swimming eyes. Mrs Adam did not see her. She had bent over Robin's crib, to look again at that small, perfect, unspoilt body as a reassurance.

'I'm going for a walk . . .' Chris said and was unable to disguise the sob in her voice.

Mrs Adam looked up at her and stretched out her hand.

'Oh my poor lamb,' she said. 'You've always been so close.'

'It's just a bit of a shock,' Chris said. 'I need some fresh air.'

'Well, Robin and I will be fine,' said Mrs Adam, returning her gaze to the sleeping child. 'Won't we?'

Chris strode up Rankeillor Hill, conscious with every step how easy it was for her to walk up it, how steady and evenly she could place each step, despite the frozen snow that lay in treacherous little patches as she got higher up. It was a bitter morning, despite the sun, but the cold did not bite into her as savagely as her anger. She found she was furious at the injustice of the war . . . No, it was more than injustice, it was evil. It was as if the Devil were commanding all the armies in the guise of those elderly, pompous-looking generals whose photographs appeared in the illustrated newspapers. There was no reason for it. It was not a just cause – it was a wicked, wasteful cause, that could kill so many good men and break so many others. For it had killed Angus and it had broken Guy, condemned him to a life on crutches, so that he would never be able to get to the top of Rankeillor Hill again, and look over the valley and the village, to the distant hills beyond. And there was no sign of it stopping – there had been well over a year of it now, but there was nothing but stalemate, and more agony. For she knew, as she stood, with tears of anguish and rage pouring down her face, that she was not alone. A hundred thousand souls were like her, crippled by grief for what had happened to those they loved – and for what great gain? What power had she, or any of them, to stop it?

'You may not be able to do anything, but you must register your dissent.' The notion swam into her head, phrased as Angus might have phrased it. 'There's no point in being silently angry. It looks like consent, and you don't consent, do you?'

'No,' she said, aloud. 'I don't. I will not.'

She rubbed her face with her handkerchief and took a deep breath. She had a voice after all – her music – and with it she could speak more plainly and more profoundly than ever she could with words. With music she could go straight to the bitter black heart of the war and show it for what it was. At least then she would feel she was doing something.

It was too cold to linger on the hill so she began to retrace her steps. As she turned from the lane into the road she saw the Castle Lanchester sitting outside the Manse. She swallowed hard at the sight of it, glad of the opportunity of a few minutes to prepare herself for the sight of Guy. But although she tried to imagine how he might look now, it was old images that flooded her mind as she walked up the path to the front door of the Manse. She could see a boy in a bathing costume running across a beach, his fair hair catching in the sun like a cap of gold, and then, later, there was a young man striding up Rankeillor Hill, always able to walk faster than she, and later still, a man, naked and beautiful, making love to her, pledging himself with every muscle of his body. She could not imagine him maimed in any way and yet in a minute she would have to face that terrible reality . . .

In the hall she heard Miranda's voice, bright and clear as a bird in the spring, saying, 'Oh what a darling you are!' and then Robin's crying.

She rushed into the sitting room without thinking of anything but her son's crying. She saw Miranda standing with him in her arms, attempting to calm him.

'Oh dear, I don't think he likes me,' she was saying and, seeing Chris, 'Well, here's Mama, Robin . . .'

'Here, shall I take him?' asked Chris.

'I think you'd better,' said Miranda. 'He's magnificent. Antonia was not exaggerating.'

'Thank you,' said Chris, taking him from her. At once he stopped crying.

'That's always the way,' said Mrs Adam, from the fireside.

'May I?'

It was Guy, sitting in the quietest corner of the room, and Chris, with all the fuss over Robin, had hardly noticed his being there. Or perhaps, she reasoned, she had not wanted to see him there, for now she did, she felt she could see nothing of him but the crutches and the pinned-up trouser leg, nothing of him but the ruined thinness of his face and the exhausted droop in his shoulders. It had hardly seemed to be him at all, but some grotesque stranger who had asked to hold her child. She looked hard and yet could hardly recognize the old Guy.

'Of course,' she said, and laid Robin in his lap. As she did so, his hand, hidden by Robin's shawl, grasped hers and she felt her heart jump with sudden exultation. That touch was like a kiss and the disguise of the stranger fell away. She looked into his eyes and saw the same agony and joy which she felt. She watched as he touched the head of his son with a hand that trembled, and saw the strong resemblance between them, as obvious almost as a painted sign announcing it. And how, how much she would have liked to announce it, to say, simply, 'Your son, Guy . . . our son, Guy.'

'Oh, he does like you, doesn't he, Guy?' said Miranda butting in between them. She crouched down beside him and looked down at Robin, stretching out a protective arm over Guy's shoulder. Chris saw Guy flinch at it, and she felt repulsed, as if Miranda knew everything and was deliberately pushing them apart. She retreated and sat down.

'It'll be your turn next, perhaps,' said Mrs Adam, blandly to Miranda.

'Oh I do hope so,' said Miranda, squeezing Guy's shoulder.

Robin began to cry again.

'Perhaps you'd better have him again, Chris,' said Guy.

'I think he needs to sleep,' said Chris rising. 'I'll take him upstairs to Peggy.'

By the time she reached the top of the stairs, Robin was wailing fiercely enough to bring Peggy out of the nursery. She took him from Chris, and seeing the tears which Chris had been unable to prevent, said, 'Oh Mrs Bretton, is aught wrong?'

'It's just . . . oh . . .' Chris could not finish, but instead shook her head and dismissed Peggy with a furious gesture, before bolting into the sanctity of her own room.

She sat down on the bed and wept, choking with unmanageable, inexpressible emotion. It was like breathing in poison gas – she felt she could not breathe, as if all the air were barbed with particles of such misery that it would destroy her. For it was all so hopeless. Yes, she loved Guy, loved him with every part of her being, loved him as she had not thought it possible to love, and what a glorious thing it had been when she had realized it! It had been so glorious and blinding, that light of self-knowledge, that she had never felt the cold shadow of impossibility that lay over them now.

48

'Chris has gone back to Edinburgh,' said Miranda. 'It's a shame. I was hoping she'd come and dine with us. You'd have liked that, wouldn't you?'

Guy put down the book he had not been reading and looked at her. She had just come in from an excursion to the village, but she was dressed as if Mayfair had been her destination, in a dramatic fur-trimmed coat and an extremely jaunty hat. He felt sour with irritation at the sight of her and even more so at her patronizing tone when she had said, 'You'd have liked that, wouldn't you?' It had not been put as a question, but just as a general platitude, rather as one might address a dog on the subject of a walk. Guy felt he was as inarticulate as a dog, if not worse, for he did not have the recourse of a good howl. He could easily have howled – let rip a great bellow of rage, to express the sudden pain that her news had produced in him. She had slipped away from him again and yet he had not the means to express his misery at it. He could only sit, his tongue paralysed, while Miranda took off her hat.

'Guy?' said Miranda. 'What is it, dear? You're so very quiet . . .'

She crouched beside him, the hat still in her hands. He reached out and touched one of its curling feathers with his finger, watching it tremble. He wanted to push her away – he was still angry with her for not letting him go to the Manse alone – but he felt utterly powerless to do anything, to change anything. She was too strong in all her sweetness for him to overcome. If he had pushed, it would have been pushing at a lump of cast iron. She would not have moved a fraction of an inch, not for all the pushing in the world. She was both his guard and his prison. She would not let him out of her sight for a moment. He remembered how she had come and put her arm around him when Chris had put the boy in his lap, how she had thrust herself in between the three of them, as if she knew exactly what was going on. Perhaps she did.

'Guy? Why won't you talk to me?'

'Because . . .' he managed to say, but his throat was dry. Her face was full of expectancy and he found himself shaking his head. She sighed slightly and got up and walked away.

'I wonder,' she said, 'if you didn't come out of hospital a little early, sometimes. Perhaps we should see some specialists . . .'

'No! No more fucking doctors!' he exclaimed, finding his voice suddenly.

She blenched visibly at that, her nose wrinkled slightly in disgust.

'Really, Guy, I know you feel strongly but . . .'

He began to heave himself out of the chair.

'But?' he countered.

'But . . . that sort of thing, it won't help.'

'Did I offend you? I'm so sorry,' he said with heavy sarcasm. 'It's only a word.'

'I don't like such words,' she said primly.

'Jesus, Miranda, have you any idea?' he said. 'Any idea at all?'

'I'm trying very hard to understand.'

He shook his head.

'There's no way that you can. No way.'

'But why won't you let me try? Why won't you talk to me about it?'

'You haven't the stomach for it,' he said, and stumped

to the other end of the library. 'I should hate to offend your delicate sensibilities, Miranda!' he flung back at her.

'I'm your wife, Guy,' she said, pursuing him. 'And I want to help you.'

'No, you are not. This isn't a marriage, this is a sham!'

God, he had said it, at last. It felt a little like throwing a bomb over to the enemy, the same mixture of terror and exhilaration. You never knew what the enemy might throw back.

'I beg your pardon?' she said, drawing herself up stiffly.

'A sham,' he said, again, and thumped one crutch on the wooden floor for emphasis. 'A bloody, fucking sham!'

Yes, it was definitely a bomb, one of those home-made Gallipoli bombs, with explosives stuffed into an empty bully-beef tin, a bomb which one could never be sure would land on target or even explode.

He watched her react, time slowing, just as it always did before a large explosion. He saw her swallow, and then bite her lip.

'You don't really think that, do you?' she said, at length, in a voice that trembled with suppressed tears. She reached out for a chair back to steady herself. He turned, crippled with the bullets of his own self-hatred. How could he have said such a thing? It might have been less brutal to hit her, or even to stab a bayonet through her pretty stomach. Her pain rang out, a horrible high, misshapen note.

'Whatever makes you say such a thing?' she wailed. 'Guy . . . oh Guy . . .' She was crying now and he turned back to see her collapsed in a chair, her face buried in her hands. 'What are you saying? Whatever do you mean? Is it something I've done?'

'No,' he said, realizing he could not stop this thing now he had started it. The battle was underway, but like all battles there would be no glory in it. 'Nothing you've done.' She looked up at him, her eyes reddened already with tears. He braced himself, gripping at his crutches. 'The truth of it is, I don't love you.'

'What?' Her voice was thin and bewildered.

'I don't love you.' She shook her head vehemently. 'I don't.'

'No,' she said, getting up and going over to him. 'No, don't say that . . . please . . . I can't bear it. You're lying. Tell me it's not true.'

'I'm trying to be honest with you. I can't lie any more,' he said. 'I have to be honest. I don't love you.'

'No!' she screamed it out now. 'No, that can't be true!'

'It is. I'm sorry but it . . .'

'You're sorry?' she shrieked. 'Sorry – is that all you can say?'

'Look, I know this isn't easy, but I think it's better that way.'

'Oh is it?' she said, and began to pound her fists against his chest. He did nothing to stop her. He half wished she might pummel him to death. He deserved as much.

'What is going on in here?'

Lady Lindsay's voice rang out in the library. Miranda stopped at once and ran sobbing to her side.

'What has happened?' she went on. 'Miranda, dear, what is it?' She put her arms around her as she wept inconsolably. 'Guy, what have you said to her?' She looked at him accusingly, her eye bright with vengeful anger.

'He says he doesn't love me!' Miranda burst out.

'Oh Guy . . .' said Lady Lindsay, shaking her head. 'What on earth has gotten into you?'

'I thought you brought us up to tell the truth,' he retorted, furious suddenly at being spoken to like a schoolboy.

'Guy doesn't know what he's saying,' said Lady Lindsay to Miranda. 'He can't. He isn't well.'

'He meant it,' said Miranda, breaking away and facing him again. 'Didn't you? You meant every word of it.'

'Now I think we should all calm down, and . . .'

'No,' said Guy. 'She's right. I meant it, and what's more, I don't intend to carry on living like this. I'm leaving.' The thought had only just occurred to him, but he seized on it, like an abandoned rifle in a trench.

'You are what?' said Lady Lindsay.

'I am leaving.'

'No, Guy, you can't, you can't possibly,' said Miranda, rushing at him and fixing him in her arms. 'I won't let you do that. I won't.'

'You'll be better off without me,' he said, managing to remove himself from her grip. 'Find yourself someone else.'

'Guy, for heaven's sake!' exclaimed Lady Lindsay. 'How can you say such things?'

'Because they have to be said,' he said, harshly, as he walked towards the door.

'But where will you go?' said Miranda pathetically behind him.

For a moment he paused and closed his eyes. He saw Chris stretching out to put the boy into his lap, her eyes full of happiness at the sight of him. Despite everything, she wanted him, loved him. He had known it with the touch of her hand. That was where he would go, even though the world might spit at him for doing it. He had no other choice. He ignored the sound of Miranda's tears and swung forward on his crutches, away down the passageway.

The rain came down ceaselessly, driving against the windows of Chris's work room, the long, thin, grey lines of it shadowed against the pale walls opposite. The room was cold and the light fading, as the afternoon drew on, but Chris did nothing about it. She was sitting with her legs stretched out on the sofa, a rug wrapped about herself, too tired to stir and put a match to the neatly laid fire or light the lamps. The grey indeterminacy of it suited her mood. She could not work, and neither was she inclined to go upstairs to the warm yellow sanctuary of Robin's nursery. He was better off with Peggy just then. She was certain she would upset him, for she was sure he could sense all her moods, as if they were still physically connected. She did not wish him to feel the misery she felt, that black oppressive cloud that had hung over her since seeing Guy three days ago. It felt like a bereavement, that awful knowledge of her loss. For she could not have him, now that she wanted him so much. He might as well have been dead.

So she sat in a sort of stupor, having cried so much she could no longer cry. She could only sit, with that terrible heaviness of heart, pressing down inside her, until she thought she could not bear to go on any longer, yet always knowing that she must go on, that life itself rolled on relentlessly, that there was Robin and her music to think of and to comfort her. Yet she knew nothing could adequately fill Guy's place.

She rested her head back on the high arm of the sofa and closed her eyes, willing herself to think of something else, but could not. He was haunting her, and without being able to prevent it she imagined him bending over her to kiss her, with warm, adoring lips. God, how weak her body was always to think like that, but with Guy it seemed that she could not separate her physical need from her emotional desire. She needed him, it was as simple as that, all of her needed him. He was as linked to her as closely as the child they had made, linked by an invisible bridge made of both flesh and spirit.

She heard a motor grumbling up the street and then coming to rest outside the house. Stirred by dread that it might be the Brettons, she got up and went to the window.

It was a taxi, so it would not be them, she realized with relief. She saw the door being flung open before the driver had got round to open it, and an arm brandishing a crutch was thrust out on to the pavement. She blinked. It could not be. She was dreaming, surely . . .

But he staggered out and straightened up, fending off the attentions of the driver – Guy, standing there, looking across the small front garden to the windows, looking, it seemed, straight at her, as if he could see her lurking by the window. How could it be Guy? She heard his voice giving orders to the taxi driver, who was removing suitcases from the back of the motor, and yet she still did not believe it. The rain was playing tricks on her eyes, or her mind was playing tricks. She heard the gate squeak open as it always did, and saw him coming up the path towards the front door, the rain dripping from the brim of his felt hat. She heard the bell jangling, and Jean's quick steps crossing the hall to answer, but still she did not move. She could not bear the thought of a disappointment. She would wait.

'Is Mrs Bretton at home?'

Yet suddenly she was pushing open the work-room door and dashing into the hall, to see him standing on the step, fumbling awkwardly for money with which to pay the taxi driver. At the sight of her she saw him slump on to the crutches with sudden relief. She put out her hand to him, and he grabbed it. It was wet and cold, but it was real. It was Guy. He had come. She had longed for him, and he had come.

She took him into the work room and he flopped down on to the sofa, as if he had no strength left in him.

'I didn't think I was going to get here,' he said. 'My mother was running round the house like a harpy, threatening to lock me in my room. But I was so abusive she had to let me go.' He rubbed his face. 'Lord, Chris . . . I feel a complete . . . but I had to come. I couldn't stay there.'

'Do they know where you've gone?' she asked, as she knelt to light the fire.

'Oh they think I'm cooling my heels somewhere. They don't know about you . . . yet. I've given them enough shocks for one day.'

Chris sank back on her heels and watched the newspaper and kindling burning up swiftly. She felt his hand on her shoulder.

'Do you mind that I've come?'

'No,' she said, without turning. 'I wanted you to. It's just I wish things didn't have to be so difficult.'

His hand pressed harder on to her shoulder.

'I shouldn't have come.'

'Of course you should have,' she said, turning round. 'I wanted you to. I wanted nothing else.' She reached out and stroked his cheek. 'This is where you should be, even though . . .'

'Though we'll be despised for it?'

She nodded. 'I can't help being afraid of that,' she admitted.

'There's no reason why you shouldn't be. I know exactly how you feel. When I told Miranda that I didn't love her, I felt . . .' He broke off and leant back. 'I felt obscene, as if I'd done something utterly dreadful instead of trying to be honest. You see, I want to sort things out, sort things out in me, and this was the first step . . . but, oh God, it's not going to be easy is it?'

'No,' she said, getting up and sitting beside him on the sofa. 'But it would be wrong of us not to try. We must learn not to mind what the world says, find a little courage.'

'I could do with plenty of that,' he said heavily. 'You ought to know – I see things sometimes now, and there are nightmares . . .' He broke off. 'I'm not what I was. You should know that.'

'What do you see?' she asked, as calmly as she could.

'Things I don't want to see. Things from ... you know...' She saw his face twitch. 'I know that they aren't real. I'm sane enough to grasp that, still, I think, but it doesn't stop them coming. And at night ... oh God, Chris, do you really want me to stay? You don't know the half of it. I'm not...'

She took both his hands, and said, 'I don't care. I want to help you. If I didn't, I wouldn't love you, and I do.' She saw the tiny flicker of relief in his eyes. 'I love you,' she said. 'That's all that matters,' and she passed her hand across his forehead.

He pulled her against him, and kissed her.

'If anyone can make me sane again, it's you,' he said.

49

He lay in darkness, in terrible heat like an oven. He could not open his eyes, and raised his hand, with difficulty, to rub them. When he did, he found them caked with dry earth, which he had to flake away before he could open them. He opened his eyes to the guttering light of a slush lamp, and saw what he had already known, that he was in the tunnel again. Or was it a grave now, because now he could see, dimly, neat heaps of skeletons, like those in an ossuary in a continental town. There was a curious order to it all, with caverns carved out to take the bones, and he realized that he was in some vast subterranean labyrinth, lit with a thousand vaguely flickering lamps, which had been made to take all of them, all the dead, all his comrades, and his enemies too. They were all here – a hundred thousand of them, more, stacked up in chambers that stretched out in every direction. And he was there, not yet rotted to nothing but a skeleton, but in time he would be, and would not be able to move or see. He would be nothing but bone and then eventually dust. If he did not get out, he would be properly dead.

He began to crawl frantically, wondering how he might get out of there, but every way he crawled was blocked, not by a wall of earth but by a group of people, all in funeral clothes, carrying long tapers. Miranda was there, and his mother and father, and Roddy, and Cruickshank, of course, in a silk hat, with black gloves over his bone fingers. Miranda was wearing a long thick veil, but through it he could see her tears, stuck to her cheeks, glinting like diamonds. When he begged them to let him past they shook their heads, altogether, in solemn unison, and he had to scuttle back and find another way. If there was another way, for he was growing so tired, and when he glanced down at his hands, pressed like animal paws in the earth, he saw that the flesh was falling away from them, to show the bone underneath . . .

Guy's scream rent through the silence of Chris's exhausted sleep. She found him threshing around beside her, gasping for breath, flailing his arms, so that she was hit as she tried to get him into her arms to shake him into consciousness. It took some doing and then he stared suddenly at her, his mouth hanging open, his body hot beneath her hands, beads of sweat on his temple. He gasped and then fell on to her, crying bitterly. He squashed his head on to her breasts and sobbed, his whole body shaking with misery and terror. Ineffectually, she tried to calm him, stroking his head and back, but she realized she was doing so as much for her own comfort as for his. She could not know what he had seen, but she felt his fear in the pit of her stomach and she had to find all the strength she had to murmur reassurements to him.

At length he managed to speak.

'I . . . I am alive, aren't I?'

'Yes,' she said. 'Very much so. I can feel your heart beating.'

He sighed and pulled himself away a little.

'Could you light the lamp?'

'Of course,' she said, and groped for the box of matches on the bedside table. She struck one and lit the candle. She turned back to find him staring at his hand.

'There were bits of flesh falling off them,' he said. 'I could see the bones.' She stretched out and touched his shoulder, rubbing it gently. 'You let me fall asleep,' he said.

'I'm sorry . . .' she said. 'I couldn't help falling asleep myself . . . I did try.'

'It doesn't matter,' he said, with a great sniff, rubbing his hand across his face. 'It was rather a lot to ask you . . . and I can't help myself sleeping either . . . but, oh God, when I do, it's . . .' He broke off, covering his mouth with his hands. He groaned heavily and shook his head. 'I want to sleep – just normal sleep . . . do you know?'

'I can't know exactly,' she said. 'But I did have dreadful nightmares at one time. After Angus died . . .'

'What were yours?'

'It's rather hard to explain,' she said, pulling the covers back over her. 'I don't know if it would much help you . . .'

'Tell me. If I'm not the only one, then . . .'

'All right. It's to do with how Angus died.'

He nodded. 'Like my tunnel.'

'Tunnel?'

'I'm always back there, in the tunnel, where the explosion was. What happened to Angus then?'

'Do you really want to know?'

'I think you should tell me,' he said.

'I should,' she agreed. 'I haven't told anyone this, you know. He died . . .' She paused and corrected herself. 'He was executed by a firing squad.'

'Oh God . . .' said Guy, sinking back on to the pillows. 'Oh Chris, my poor . . . Why? What did he do?'

'He hit a general. That's all – well, not quite all, but that's the gist of it.'

'Oh Chris,' he said, and pulled her gently down beside him. 'I had no idea.'

'Nobody knows. I only know because he wrote to me, to explain. The authorities told us it was just wounds.'

'Why did he hit him?'

'Because . . .' She turned over to face him. 'I know what you thought of Angus, Guy, I can't. . .'

'I don't judge so lightly now,' he said. 'Besides, I think it's jealousy as much as anything. I still envy him, you know, giving you his name – giving our son his name . . .'

'There's nothing to be jealous of. I didn't love him, not the way I love you. We were . . . What were we? The best of friends, I suppose. He loved someone else too. That's really why he died. For love. Funny, you don't think of people dying for love, but Angus did, for his right to love whomever he pleased.'

'You mean another man?'

'Yes. Does that disgust you?'

'Not now,' he said, with a sigh. 'When the world has gone mad, it's the only thing left, isn't it, and it doesn't matter how it is, so long as it's right, and true . . . Like us, I suppose? Why else would I be lying here, committing adultery so calmly, if I didn't think that this was all that was left that makes sense? Those old rules are all blown up. What's that wonderful thing of Matthew Arnold's?

'Ah, love, let us be true
To one another! for the world, which seems
To lie before us like a land of dreams,
So various, so beautiful, so new,
Hath really neither joy, nor love, nor light,
Nor certitude, nor peace, nor help for pain;
And we are here, as on a darkling plain
Swept with confused alarms of struggle and flight,
Where ignorant armies clash by night.

'That's it, isn't it?'

He sighed and pulled her close to him, so that she lay, her back pressed against his chest.

'You should set that, you know,' he said.

'I was looking for some words,' she said. 'Those might be the ones.'

'I wish you would . . .' He sighed. 'I haven't talked liked this for months, for years, it seems. Nobody talks like this in the army, and then, well, what did anyone talk about at Cape Helles? You couldn't talk about the truth, because it wasn't safe to. It would drive you out of your mind. We had gallows humour instead. And then, in the hospital, well, you don't talk. You're patronized by nurses who are more concerned about the state of your bedpan than your soul. But here I can think, I can breathe . . . It seems extraordinary.'

She rolled over so that she looked up into his eyes. It was extraordinary, this quiet comfort between them, this absolute normality of lying together in bed, at night. It was as if they had done it for a hundred years before, and would for a hundred after. The common life between them fell into place like some pre-ordained ritual. There might be storms coming for them outside the walls of the bedroom, but for now she felt safe, and she could see that Guy felt safe too. She could feel it in fact, for his heartbeat, as he came close against her to kiss her, was even again.

The next morning after breakfast, Chris politely but charmingly excused herself.

'I always work in the mornings,' she explained, getting up from the table. 'It's my routine. I have to try and stick to it. Do you mind? It's just I feel I could do something very constructive this morning, and I've done so little work lately . . .'

'Oh, have I inspired you?' he said, reaching out to catch her as she passed him.

'Very possibly,' she said, and gave him a kiss. 'So I had better seize the day, hadn't I?'

'Yes, of course you must,' he said, but inwardly he felt a terrible reluctance to let her warm body slip from his arms. He wanted to see her face constantly. It was so reassuring.

'There's a fire lit in the drawing room – and I'll only be across the hall, if you need me,' she said, seemingly reading his mind. He resolved then he would not disturb her. For all her kindness, he suspected she would not want any interruptions.

'Well, I've got the *Scotsman*, haven't I?' he said, with a certain amount of bravado. It seemed a great many hours until lunch.

The drawing room was sparsely furnished, like the rest of the house, and was more like a library in character. Books were the only thing in any profusion, and he realized, looking over the shelves, that they were mostly Bretton's. He could not imagine Chris buying such outlandish stuff. In fact, when he had settled in a chair by the fire and began to get the measure of the room, he realized it was not a drawing room at all, but essentially a study, with a large oak desk under one window. Bretton's desk, he imagined, a desk waiting for its owner to return and continue working at it. He knew that Chris had taken the house after Angus's death, but he could not help feeling she had arranged a space for him, all the same, with his books, his desk, his favourite chair. Was he, Guy, now sitting in Angus Bretton's particular chair? It had the feeling of a shrine to the martyr – for that was how she had spoken of him, wasn't it? Even as she told him she loved him, there was reverence enough left for Angus Bretton to disturb him. He wondered if the drawers of that desk were full of his papers, kept like holy relics. When she had been in his arms last night, safely within his grasp, he could accept what she had said, but now, alone again, in this odd room that smelt of Bretton, he felt all his old jealousy revive. And there, suddenly, was Cruickshank again, smiling his odious smile, and behind him, as clear as the day, Bretton, himself, dressed in evening clothes as he had been the last time he saw him in Paris, on the night of *The Rite of Spring*. Except that today he stood there with a neat bullet hole through his head, and a sort of aura about him, the cheap painted nimbus of a plaster Jesus, in fact. He lifted his hand as if to give a benediction and then, thankfully, the two figures vanished. Guy sank back in his chair, breathless with panic. All his security seemed to be slipping away. She loved Angus still, he was certain, not like a man, though, but like a saint, a martyr, and she had made this little shrine to him. How could he ever compete with that? He had been her first choice, and he would always be there, in the back of her mind, in the corner of her heart. He could never have her completely. There would always be Angus, the martyr, hovering, giving off a far worse stench than Cruickshank. He felt his insides grip with fear.

The doorbell was jangling and he heard the maid go to answer it.

'Oh good morning, Mrs Bretton,' she said. 'I'm afraid the mistress isn't to be disturbed just now. She's working.'

'That's all right, Jean,' said Mrs Bretton. 'I've just brought a few wee things for my grandson. Perhaps you could get Peggy to bring him down to me.'

'Yes of course, ma'am.'

'I'll wait in here . . .' And in a moment the woman had bustled into the drawing room. 'Oh . . .' she said, seeing Guy. 'I didn't know Christina had visitors.'

She was a small, delicately boned woman, dark-haired like her son, and it was clear, seeing her, where his good looks had come from. In fact the resemblance was enough to make Guy doubt her reality at all. Perhaps she was another vision. He sat motionless in his chair, unable to respond. She, in her turn, was clearly waiting for him to do her the courtesy of getting up, but he saw her notice first the crutches and then his leg. Quickly she formed a bright, cheery smile, which he had seen often enough from patronizing hospital visitors, and came over, extending her hand to him.

'I'm Christina's mother-in-law, Mr . . . er?'

'Lindsay . . .'

'Oh, are you Sir Guy Lindsay?' she said. He managed to nod. 'So very pleased to meet you.' She shook his hand with furious enthusiasm. 'I've just come to see little Robin. I'm afraid I'm a dreadfully doting grandmother. I've just found the most lovely rattle at Maule's – ah, that sounds like him, doesn't it?' she finished, as Robin's crying broke out in the hall outside.

Peggy Logan came into the room holding the child, and Mrs Bretton fell upon him, like a swooping, flapping eagle plucking a defenceless lamb from a hillside. She clucked and chattered over him, rocking him in her arms, crooning to him until he was quiet again.

'Ah, that's better,' she said, and glanced over at Guy. 'I suppose I spoil this one terribly, but I can't help it. He's no father, after all . . .'

Something snapped inside Guy. Bretton might be a dead saint, but that child was his, and he had half the making of it. Certainly Robin was nothing to do with that vulgar little woman.

'Yes, he has,' he said. 'That is my son and I'll thank you not to spoil him. Take him back, Peg.'

'Sir . . . ?' She looked simply dumbfounded. Yesterday, when Chris had taken him up to the nursery to see Robin, Peggy had looked mildly surprised to see him, but had seemed to quite accept Chris's explanation that he was staying in the house. She had probably not had a whiff of a suspicion that he might be sharing her mistress's bed. The Logans were a famously God-fearing family in Rankeillor, after all, and it had been Peggy's mother who had used to terrify Guy as a child with her descriptions of hellfire.

'Your bairn?' she said, incredulously, contemptuously even, as if he were quite deranged.

'Yes. Now will you take him?'

Mrs Bretton held Robin a little more tightly against her. Clearly she had no intention of surrendering him to Peggy.

'I don't know why you're slandering yourself and Christina so,' she said, her voice shaking somewhat. 'Really . . . You're a married man.'

'It's no slander, it's the plain truth,' he said, and pulled himself up on to one crutch. He noticed she retreated a little, shaking her head. 'Yes it is, I'm afraid. No, I'm not afraid. I don't regret it for one moment. That's one of the best damn things I've ever done. What I do regret is that everyone should assume he's bloody Angus Bretton's son. That's my child.' He edged towards her but she retreated, still shaking her head. 'Don't you understand, woman? My son! Not your grandson!'

He found he had bellowed it out and Robin immediately began to scream. He could not help laughing.

'You see, he has my lungs!'

Mrs Bretton gave him a vicious, disapproving glance and returned her attention to the child, desperately trying to calm him. But Robin seemed determined to scream and scream, ripping the air with his infantile fury. In a moment it brought Chris running into the room.

'Oh, what's all this?' she said. Mrs Bretton at once surrendered the child to her. In a moment Robin was quiet again.

'My dear,' said Mrs Bretton, 'this man – he's been saying such horrid things . . . that . . . Robin's his child . . .'

'Oh Guy . . .' said Chris. He saw her grimace and it maddened him.

'It isn't true, surely?' said Mrs Bretton.

He watched as Chris stood there, with Robin in her arms, rocking him gently, calming him, stroking his thin, pale hair. It was a beautiful, powerful sight and he could hardly bear it.

'If you dare deny it . . .' he said. 'I won't have him passed off as Bretton's. He's mine as much as yours!'

Gently she handed him to Peggy.

'Take him back upstairs, please.' Then, when Peggy and Robin had gone, she turned to Guy and said, 'I wasn't going to.'

She said it quietly, but there was a sharpness in her voice that felt like cold steel slipping into him. In the heart of his anger, Guy felt afraid. He had not meant to make her angry with him – he could not stand the thought she should be angry with him. Yet neither could he bear it that a dead man should claim both his son and her affection still.

'Christina, surely . . .' said Mrs Bretton. 'This can't be right.'

'It's absolutely true. Robin is not Angus's son. I'm sorry, you must be very disappointed, I know . . . but . . .'

'I don't understand . . .' bleated Mrs Bretton.

'I don't think you could,' said Chris, simply.

'You've lied to us.'

'You've only assumed,' said Chris.

'You lied to Angus,' said Mrs Bretton, her voice becoming shrill with anger. 'You deceived my son. How could you do such a thing?'

'You never knew Angus,' she said. 'Not as I did. He would have understood. Our marriage was exceptional. We didn't have ordinary rules.'

Exceptional: that word, which she had said so calmly, almost joyfully, in fact, crashed against Guy's heart like a battering ram. Exceptional! How dare she say that?

'I simply don't know what to say . . .'

'Then shut up and go home!' burst out Guy.

'Well . . . well . . .' Mrs Bretton gave up attempting to speak and made for the door. 'Oh Christina, I really can't believe . . .' She gave a profound sniff, shook her head again and went.

When they heard the front door close, Guy exclaimed, 'Good riddance. What an appalling woman!'

'Guy, you idiot!' Chris said, vehemently. 'How could you be so stupid?'

'I couldn't stand seeing such a dreadful creature pawing over my son. I won't have it.'

'You shouldn't have been so blunt.'

'What else am I to do? We can't keep lying, for God's sake. I should have thought you of all people . . .'

'We might have told her a little more kindly.'

'Oh damn kindness!' he shouted. 'You didn't want to tell her, really, did you? It's because you rather like the idea, I suppose, of him being Angus's after all.'

'What on earth do you mean?'

'"Our marriage was exceptional."' He flung back her words. 'Exceptional! God, you really do love him, don't you, for all you say?'

'Yes, you know I loved him, but not . . . Oh Guy, I thought you understood this now. I explained last night. We loved each other as friends.'

'You loved him more than that.'

'What if I did? He's dead now – you're the one I love now.'

'Oh yes,' said Guy, gesturing about him. 'What about all this? This is virtually a shrine. You want him to walk back in any moment and start writing that dreadful poetry, don't you? You don't really want me. You want him, don't you?'

'I want you! You know that. Why are you being so perverse?'

'Because I have to know that it's all of you that's loving me. I have to have all of that. I can't cope unless I know that there's nothing left for him. I need all your love just to keep going. Do you understand that?'

'You know you have that. I've told you,' she said. 'Will you stop being so . . .'

'Prove it,' he said, coming close to her, and putting his hands on her shoulders. 'Prove it to me.'

'What do you want me to do?'

'Say yes, at last. Tell me you'll marry me.'

'Guy, you can't marry me.'

'That doesn't matter. I'll get a divorce. When I do, will you marry me?' He knew it sounded like a threat and that he shook her slightly as he asked it. But he had to know. If she rejected him again . . . 'Will you?'

'Yes,' she said, and when he sighed with relief, she added, 'you didn't really need to ask me that, you know.'

50

The offices of Carluke and Carluke W.S. were in North Charlotte Street, with only the most discreet brass plate to announce the fact. Guy, negotiating the steps up to the front door, could not help remembering how the last time he had been there, it had been after a trip to a military tailor's where he had ordered his mess suit. He had gone on to Carluke and Carluke to deal with his will. It had been rather a jolly occasion. The place had been full of the high-minded patriotic excitement which had infected them all, like a mysterious disease, in the first month of the war, and the business of checking over his will had been a laughable precaution. In fact it had seemed that the act of being so sober-minded as to think his will might come into force was really invoking a sort of protective magic. 'If I deal with this now, I can't possibly come to any harm, can I?' he remembered thinking. A man with his affairs in order was surely immortal. Death had seemed such a remote, clean thing then, that if it came it would be neat as well as glorious. Never for one moment had it occurred to him that he might find himself again on the steps of Carluke and Carluke struggling with a pair of crutches to push open the heavy front door. He wondered at his utter naïvety, at all their naïvety. Could humans forget so easily how dreadful wars were? Perhaps they had to forget or another would never have been permitted.

He gave the door a final shove with his shoulder and almost fell into the long entrance passage, immensely irritated by this small complication. Why was nothing easy nowadays? He watched the elderly clerk come running up to greet him. Why should a white-haired man be allowed to run and he stand there, a helpless cripple, exhausted by the simple business of opening a door?

The clerk recognized him.

'Sir Guy, Mr Carluke is ready for you upstairs . . .' he began, and then he took stock of Guy's crutches. 'Perhaps you'd care to wait in the library, sir,' he added hastily, opening a door. 'Mr Carluke won't be a moment.'

It was a stuffy, gloomy room despite the big windows. Endless law books in dreary, uniform bindings lined the walls, and the chairs were upholstered in some repellent black stuff that looked indestructible. The atmosphere of respectable Scottish law seemed to hang in the air: heavy, wordy, and most probably unyielding. Guy pulled out a chair from the table and dumped himself down on it. He had walked up from Ann Street, or rather hauled himself up the hill, and he wished he had not. Even such a short walk had tired him out.

'Well, Sir Guy, this is an honour indeed.' Mr Carluke came in, his hand extended, his manner nicely obsequious to an old and wealthy client. 'Or should I say, Major Lindsay? I never know whether a military title takes precedence . . .'

'The army has no use for me any more,' said Guy. 'And I have no use for it.'

'Of course,' said Carluke, a little nonplussed at this. 'What can I do for you this morning, then, Sir Guy?' he asked, sitting down opposite him at the table.

'I want to talk about divorce,' Guy said.

'Divorce?' One of Carluke's bushy eyebrows went up. 'I see . . . Er, I am to infer that you are seeking a divorce?'

'You are,' said Guy.

'Well, this is somewhat outwith the normal practice of this firm . . .'

'I don't care about that,' said Guy. 'I want to know how one goes about it.'

'Are you certain this is what you want?'

'Would I be here if I wasn't?' said Guy. 'Besides, what business of yours is that? I employ you as my solicitor, to carry out my wishes.'

'Yes, of course, but in a matter like this . . . Well, divorce is not a thing to be embarked upon lightly, Sir Guy. The law, not to mention society, does not look kindly upon the dissolution of Christian marriage. I would be neglecting my duty if I did not suggest to you in the first instance that you seek a reconciliation with your wife. You may be angry with her. Perhaps she has committed some indiscretion which has upset you. Would it not be better for you to forgive her rather than take this very drastic step? It would be more Christian.'

'I don't regard myself as a Christian,' said Guy. 'So you can spare me the sermons. Just tell me how I would go about freeing myself, if you please.'

'Very well,' said Mr Carluke rather coldly. 'If you are irrevocably set on this.'

'I am.'

'Well, there are two grounds under Scottish law for bringing an action of divorce, which are desertion and adultery. Do you believe your wife to be guilty of either?'

'No,' said Guy. 'She's done nothing like that. I don't think so, anyway.'

'Then I'm afraid you have no grounds to bring an action. Marriage cannot simply be dissolved because you dislike it. There must be evidence of fault.'

'There is fault,' said Guy, with growing impatience. 'On my side, on both counts, I suppose.'

'Ahh . . .' said Carluke. 'We are getting to the heart of it, I think.' He smiled very slightly and said, 'I regret to inform you that there is no recourse in law for adulterers to regularize their position. You may not bring action for divorce, even though you have created the grounds for it. Only your wife may do that.'

'Then I'll ask her . . .'

'No, you may not. That would be collusion, a very serious offence. Collusion invalidates an action for divorce. Lady Lindsay must decide entirely of her own accord whether she wishes to bring such an action against you.'

'What?' said Guy.

'I'm afraid that is the truth of the matter. It may not suit you, Sir Guy, but personally I believe it is a good system. Divorce on the terms you seem to require would be an encouragement to immorality. Divorce as the law now stands is a desperate remedy for those who have been sinned against – innocent spouses such as your own, I feel I have to say. If what you say is true, she would be quite justified in bringing an action against you, but I suspect she would rather not.'

'So there is absolutely nothing I can do?' said Guy, slumping back in his chair, feeling a tide of despairing anger rush over him.

'Nothing,' said Carluke. 'Except perhaps to go back to her and ask her to forgive you. That would be a far better thing.'

'Oh would it?' said Guy with heavy sarcasm. 'What the hell would you know about it?' He had meant to sound defiant, but his voice was half choked. He could easily have wept as the implications took hold of him. He had never imagined it would be so difficult to disentangle himself from Miranda. She would never bring an action. He was painfully certain of that.

Carluke had got up from his chair and was standing over him like a kindly but authoritarian schoolmaster about to give out a punishment.

'I'm sure you'll come to the right decision,' he said. 'These are difficult times, I know, but we should never forget what's right and wrong.'

Guy stared up at him, at that plump, Presbyterian face, rising above an impeccable stiff white collar.

'You forget,' he said, pulling himself up on to his crutches, 'you are speaking to a man who has been given a gun and told to kill as many people as possible, by his own government. What can I know about your quaint old notions of right and wrong? If you knew what I'd done and what I'd seen, you wouldn't dare to speak to me like that. I've killed better men than you, I imagine, far too many of them. Doesn't adultery seem a very little thing after that? I'm a murderer – what do I care about morality?'

Had he shocked him? He could not tell, and he decided not to wait to find out.

Outside a rainstorm was whipping about Charlotte Square, making that elegant space seem as bleak as a Siberian plain. The rain lashed his face and hid his tears as he pushed through it, past the grey stone terraces. He could not go back to Chris yet, bleeding still with this dreadful news. There was a pub near there somewhere, he remembered. Yes, he had gone there with Roddy once, when he had been about eighteen after a visit to Carluke and Carluke. Of course. He stopped, vividly remembering it – a sparkling sunny day, with the sunlight flashing through the trees in the square gardens. 'God, God, God how I need a drink!' Roddy had exclaimed, and they had run across the square and into Queensferry Street to Mathers Bar. Mathers Bar . . . He pushed on towards it.

A few minutes later he was standing at the bar with a pint and a glass of whisky. He caught sight of himself in the mirrors on the wall – a ragged ex-soldier, propped up on his crutches, drinking whisky far too quickly. He wondered that he didn't see his ghosts there, but saw only himself. A man in uniform did appear – a sergeant, whom he did not recognize, and whom he realized was simply another customer.

'What happened to you, pal?' he asked Guy.

'Oh, Dardanelles...' said Guy and took another swig of whisky.

'Fucking show, that,' he said.

'Aye.'

'Buy you another one?' he asked as the barmaid hovered.

'No, let me,' said Guy, digging into his pocket.

'Well, I don't mind if you do, sir,' he added.

'What would you like?'

'Whatever you're having.'

'Two malts, please,' said Guy, slapping a coin on the counter. 'You're on leave from France then?'

'Aye. I should be at home with the wife and bairns but... Well, sir, you know how it is, don't you?' Guy nodded. 'It's a different world, that it is,' said the sergeant. He raised his glass to Guy. 'Cheers, sir, thanks.'

The whisky burnt cheerfully in the pit of Guy's empty stomach.

'A pleasure,' he said with sincerity. He gestured towards an empty table. 'You can tell me all the latest...'

'Oh dear,' said Chris, looking at Antonia. 'This is not going to be easy.'

Antonia was sitting in her favourite armchair by the fire in the little sitting room at Royal Circus, her feet carefully up on a footstool and her hands neatly folded on her swollen stomach.

'I'm not as delicate as I look,' said Antonia. 'You should know, you've been pregnant.'

'I think you might be rather cross with me.'

'I think you're judging me, unfoundedly,' smiled Antonia. 'What on earth have you to tell me that's so very awful, that I shall hate you for it? Besides, I'm incapable of hate these days. I feel nothing but serenity. You're perfectly safe.'

'I'm not so sure,' said Chris, taking the chair opposite. 'It's to do with Miranda.'

'What's my daft little sister done now?' said Antonia, gently rubbing her stomach.

'She's done nothing. It's Guy . . . and . . .' Chris stared down into her lap. Antonia, at eight months pregnant, struck her as rather terrifying, like some infinitely wise earth goddess, with her half-spectacles perched on her elegant nose. 'It's all such an utter mess we're in . . .'

'Oh dear . . .' said Antonia. 'What is going on? You sound . . .' She leant forward and stretched out her hand to Chris. 'What has happened?'

Chris looked at her friend. Her voice was kind, her eyes gentle and reassuring.

'It's Guy and I . . .' she managed to say. 'We're in love. Desperately in love . . . hopelessly . . .'

Antonia nodded and sat gently back.

'I might have guessed, I suppose.'

'How?' said Chris.

'Because I've often thought that Miranda and Guy weren't so well suited. Well, rather, and this does sound perverse, doesn't it, but that they were so well suited that it couldn't be right. It felt like a novelette to me. Isn't that an awful thing to say, but I always did wonder. Of course, you'll think I'm being wise after the event but . . . you see, I suppose I think that love isn't easy, shouldn't be easy. It needs proving by a struggle, like Jack and I and my breakdown. Now Miranda never struggled – she just fell into his arms and swanned off, like something out of a musical comedy.'

'Oh thank God you understand!' said Chris, and found she was crying. 'Oh how stupid to cry but . . .' She pulled out her handkerchief.

'Cry all you need to,' said Antonia. 'Why else would you be here, if it weren't to cry and to find I understand? I am your friend.'

'But she's your sister and he's left her,' said Chris. 'He's staying with me. Can you understand that?'

'Guy wouldn't have done that lightly. He's not a frivolous man, is he? It may have hurt Miranda – I'm sure it has, but she'll heal. She's very strong. It used to amaze me sometimes how she could shrug off things when I could feel myself collapsing.'

'Guy wants a divorce.'

'He may have trouble with that,' said Antonia. 'I should think she will want to hold on to her position. You know how she likes it, being Lady Lindsay.'

'And she'll hold all the more tightly, because we've wronged her.'

'You're being very stern with yourself.'

'I feel abominable. You see, it's been going on for some time . . . and . . .' She found she was crying again, hopelessly, into her handkerchief. She heard Antonia move to her side and put her arm about her shoulders.

'Tell me it all,' she said.

'All right,' said Chris. And so, sitting there, with Antonia on the sofa, she confessed every detail of it.

'It's shameful, isn't it?' she said, when she had finished.

'Do you really think so?' said Antonia.

'No . . . I don't know what I feel, except that it's an indestructible thing and that I couldn't ignore it. He's like something in my blood.'

'As Angus never was?'

'Yes,' said Chris. 'Not that Guy is convinced of that. He's so jealous of Angus. That's why he wants a divorce from Miranda, so he'll have the certainty of having me as his wife, and Robin as his son. I suppose I don't mind what happens so long as we can be together, but he's so fragile he needs every prop we can find. It's not just his leg . . . he seems half mad as well.'

'Shell shock,' said Antonia with a slight sigh.

'Is that what they call it?'

'Jack deals with nothing else. The war has destroyed as many minds as it has bodies, it seems.'

'Perhaps I should get Guy to talk to Jack.'

'It might help – he's due for some leave next month. Do you think poor Guy can hang on that long?'

'I don't know. His moods are very unpredictable.' Antonia nodded. 'I told you it was a mess, didn't I?'

The door opened and the maid came in.

'Lady Lindsay is downstairs, Mrs Rosenberg. Shall I send her up, ma'am?'

It felt like nemesis, and Chris found herself screwing up her face, with a sharp intake of breath. She tried to be calm, but panic was galloping over her.

'You don't have to see her,' said Antonia softly.

'I ought to though, oughtn't I? I should try and explain.'

'All right,' said Antonia, and told the maid to let her come up. 'You're very brave,' she said, when the maid had gone.

'I don't feel brave,' said Chris, 'but this has to be done.'

Miranda came in a few moments later, bravely dressed, Chris could not help noticing, in a crimson coat with a fur collar and hat.

'Ah you're here too!' she said, seeing Chris. 'I was going to call on you next.' Her voice was brittle and bright. It was easy to see that a performance was being put on. 'I was going to ask if either of you had seen my irritating husband. The silly boy has run away and I can't find him anywhere.'

'Miranda, sit down,' said Antonia.

'Well, have you?'

'Yes,' said Chris. 'I have.'

'You have?' said Miranda. 'How did he seem? To be frank, I think he's gone perfectly mad. He's said the most horrid things to me.'

'Sit down,' said Antonia, again. 'Chris wants to tell you something.'

'Oh yes?' said Miranda, finally allowing herself to sit down. 'This all sounds very ominous, as if he's been run over by a bus or something ridiculous. Frankly, I shouldn't care if he had, the way he's behaved . . .'

'Then why on earth are you looking for him?' burst out Chris.

'Because . . .' She broke off, stared at Chris for a moment, and went on. 'Because it simply isn't on. He isn't allowed to desert me. It isn't playing the game at all.'

'A game, you think it's a game?' said Chris.

'It's only an expression. What has got into you, Chris? What is all this?'

Chris took a deep breath. 'Guy has left you because he doesn't love you.'

'I know, he told me. But how do you know?' she added, a flicker of suspicion crossing her face. 'Have you had a full confession from him? I know you're old friends, but . . .'

'It's more than that,' said Chris, swallowing hard.

'More? What does that mean?'

'There's no other way to put this but bluntly,' Chris said. 'It means that we're lovers.'

'I beg your pardon?'

'Lovers,' said Chris again, firmly.

'You and Guy?' Chris nodded. 'No! No!' said Miranda jumping up. 'I shan't have that. That's . . .'

'It's true. I'm sorry but it's true.'

'You stand there, calmly admitting you're having an affair with my husband, and you say you're sorry? Good God . . .' She threw up her hands, appealing in a glance to Antonia. 'Do you hear this, Toni?'

'I know it hurts,' said Chris. 'And I know how angry you must feel, but there was no other way. There can't be any other way. Guy needs me. His call goes too deep for me to ignore. Please try and understand. I didn't want to hurt you. I would love it to be any other way than this, but it can't be, can it? Guy needs me and I love him too much to let him suffer any more than he's suffering already.'

'No, no,' said Miranda, covering her ears with her hands. 'I shan't have this.'

'You'll have to try and accept it,' said Antonia.

'What are you taking her side for?' said Miranda. 'How can you? I'm your sister, remember . . .'

'Do you really love Guy that much?' said Antonia.

'What do you mean?'

'How much do you really love him?' Antonia went on. 'You said just now you wouldn't care if he didn't come back. You don't really care about Guy, do you? It's what Guy brings you, isn't it? I know you, Miranda.'

'How hateful you are!' she exclaimed. 'How can you say such things?'

'Because they're true. Think about yourself clearly for once, Miranda,' said Antonia. 'Does it really matter to you if he's gone, or is it only your wounded pride? Do you wake up at night longing for him, longing to talk to him? Are you sick with fear for him, for his mind? Are you?'

'You're trying to trick me with your clever questions,' said Miranda, coldly.

'No, I am not!' said Antonia. 'I'm just trying to be plain with you for everyone's sake. What do you honestly think about Guy now?'

She thought for a moment.

'I hate him. I hate all of you, especially you . . .' she finished with a sob and extending a trembling finger towards Chris. 'I never thought you'd be a viper.'

'She's not,' said Antonia, sternly.

'Oh this is simply ridiculous!' she exclaimed. 'It's as if I've done something wrong, which I haven't. I've only tried to be a good wife. It's Chris you should be speaking to like this. What have I done?'

'Nothing. This isn't about right or wrong, or blame or anything like that. It's much more complicated,' said

Antonia. She sat down beside her, and her tone became confidential. 'It could have happened as easily to you as to Chris or to anyone. If Jack had been married to someone else I shouldn't have been able to help myself. I should still have loved him. This sort of love you can't stop. Let him go.'

'Let him go?' said Miranda in a horrified whisper. 'Do you honestly think I should?'

'You're not a cruel person,' said Antonia taking her hand. 'You wouldn't imprison him, would you, against his will? Besides, you'd be imprisoning yourself as well.'

Suddenly Miranda burst into tears and pressed her face against Antonia's shoulder. Chris sank down into a chair and stared across at them, astonished by Antonia's vigorous defence. She felt like a criminal in the dock, who had just escaped punishment because of a brilliant advocate, and she wondered how she could ever repay such a remarkable act of friendship.

51

It was one o'clock in the morning, but there was no possibility of their going to bed. Guy was still too angry. He was pacing the drawing room – as much as a man on crutches could pace – pulling himself up and down it, turning, with almost parade-ground precision, after four paces and then launching down the room for another four paces before turning again. Occasionally he would stop, take a deep drink of claret, and then set off again, expostulating. Chris could say nothing to make him stop. It was almost as if he intended to carry on until he dropped down from absolute exhaustion.

Chris did not know where the energy came from. She had no strength left for herself, and she would have slept if for a moment the regular rhythm of the crutches and then Guy's boot pounding the wooden floorboards had ceased. The noise was the only thing keeping her awake now, that and the occasional crescendo when his angry muttering turned into a shout. She sat in the armchair, unable to escape this display of appalling mania. For what could she do? She could not go to bed and leave him there in that state. He might do anything to himself. She could not risk it, though her body ached with tiredness and her head throbbed with an incipient migraine.

She closed her eyes, praying silently to whatever gods that remained to her, that he would stop soon, or at least show some sign of wanting to rest. And then suddenly he bellowed and she flashed open her eyes to watch him clattering to the floor, his crutches flying across the room so that one crashed against the fender and the other against the side of the desk. He landed flat on his belly with a great slap, so hard she almost felt the pain of it herself.

In a moment she was crouched beside him on the floor. He rolled slowly on to his side and looked up at her pitifully, his anger turned to misery. She could see the tears starting in his eyes.

'It's . . . it's . . . not fair!' he gasped, and clamped his arms vice-like around her waist, and, burying his head in her lap, began to cry, shaking so much with his sobs that she was shaken too.

She sat stroking his hair, wondering what she could do or say to comfort him. Nothing, it seemed, or he would have been comforted and calmed hours ago. She had said all she could say. Now she was too tired for words, too tired almost to stroke his hair. There was nothing more she could do than be there. He would have to accept his exile for himself.

Exile. A brutal word, but Guy felt it like that. What else could have reduced him to such a senseless rage? They should have been happy that it was all over at last and that he had his freedom. It should have been a moment of triumph, even, after the dreadful humiliation of the divorce court that afternoon, to know that they had survived that hurdle and at least could begin to chart out some sort of future for themselves and Robin. But instead there was this fresh agony to deal with.

The events of the afternoon still made her shudder. There had been an old custom in the Kirk for sinners to have to sit in front of the congregation on successive Sundays and do public penance for their misdemeanours. When her father had described it to her she had thought it terrifying and barbaric. She had never expected to have to experience something similar, but in the Court of Session she knew that the spirit of the stool of repentance was alive and well. Even though Guy had not denied anything in the charge of adultery in the action Miranda had brought, the court insisted it be proved, and Chris, who had been named as 'paramour', had to give evidence to supply this proof. She had been questioned by an officious advocate who had seemed to relish the task of humiliating her, and although the court had not been crowded, she could still sense the frisson of disapproval in the air as she meekly affirmed that, yes, she had been the mistress of the defender for some period of time, and that, yes, he was the father of her child. She had noticed the newspaper reporters scribbling down her words, and a terrible black thought had loomed into her mind: 'I shall be more famous for this than for my music.' It had been an odd feeling to surrender, by telling the truth, all claim to respectability. By being honest they had made themselves reviled.

She had returned to her seat, her soul feeling bruised by the eyes of everyone in the court, to hear the judge excoriate Guy's character in his summing up. She had been afraid that he might not be able to stand such a moralistic torrent, but his expression was hard and impassive, as if he cared not a whit. Chris supposed that after gunfire this was nothing. But then his lordship had gone on: 'Therefore I order that the defender pay to the appellant, two-thirds of his income, per annum as aliment, and that the mansion house at Rankeillor be retained for her sole use, with all the expenses of upkeep, etcetera, to fall also upon the defender,' at which Guy had visibly blenched. In fact, Chris had thought he was about to protest very audibly, and clearly the judge thought so too, for he went on, firmly, looking very pointedly at Guy. 'This, in my opinion, satisfies the need for reparation which is an established principle under Scots law.' And that, it seemed, was that.

'You have to accept it,' Chris murmured now, bending over to kiss his forehead.

He pulled himself away from her, and sat up, rubbing his hand across his face and staring bleakly at her.

'How?' he said. 'Tell me that.'

She gathered what inward strength she had and said, 'By thinking of it rationally. It might even be a good thing.'

'A good thing?' he said. 'How can it be that? I might as well have lost the other leg.'

'You don't need the house.'

'I do.'

'Why?'

'Because . . . because . . . Oh, for a hundred reasons. It's part of me, it's something in my blood.'

'Is it more important to you than me, or Robin?' she asked.

'No, but . . .'

'No,' she said. 'No buts about it. It's the price that has to be paid.'

'Then it's too damn high!' he snapped.

'Then it is more important, isn't it?' she said, moving away slightly. At that moment she felt so fragile, so full of doubt, that she did not want to hear his answer.

'No,' he said, laying his hand on her arm. 'It's only that I'd hoped, dreamt, so much, of us all being there. I want you and Robin and Rankeillor. I want it all.' He said it plaintively.

'You can't always have what you want,' she said. 'Compromises have to be made.'

'Can't she compromise?' he said. 'Can't she see that she has no right to the place? It's mine. She's no claim on it.'

'She has the claim of law now.'

'The law is an ass. No moral claim, I mean. I'd buy her a house – set her up in all the style she wants. She can have her country house – so long as it's not Rankeillor. But she knows what it means to me. That's why she asked for that, specifically. It's malice.'

'Perhaps she's entitled to a little malice. We should be grateful she decided to come to court at all.'

'Yes, yes, yes, I know, but ... God, Chris, I've had enough, absolutely enough! We're not common criminals. We simply made a mistake, but the law insists on far more than its pound of flesh. This makes Shylock look decent, doesn't it? I resent it, I really resent it! How on earth do they think they can drive a man off his land, the land where his ancestors have been for hundreds of years? It's appalling...'

'Shush...' she said, stretching out and pressing her finger to his lips. 'No more fulminating. It's a waste of your energy.'

'I know,' he said, with a grimace. 'I just...'

She nodded, and said, 'I know it isn't easy, but perhaps this might be a chance for us. We can go somewhere and start again entirely. I can't say I was too happy with the state of my country this afternoon, or at least with the way it chooses to see things. Perhaps somewhere else...'

'That sounds like running away.'

'Try and be positive, for goodness sake,' she said, a little exasperated. 'Do you realize what it will be like if we stay? Things are going to be difficult. Why should we have to suffer that as well, after all this? If we went away...'

'Where to?' he said, contemptuously. 'To the Colonies, I suppose, that's the usual dumping ground for black sheep.'

'Perhaps... They've given women the vote in New Zealand, you know. That can't be such a bad place.'

'And everyone would heave a sigh of relief to see that we've gone,' he said. 'They'd probably even pay our passage. No, I won't have that.'

'France then?' said Chris.

'God, no,' he said. 'What the hell would I do there? Besides, aren't you rather overlooking something here? I still have to run the estate.'

'What about the factor?'

'I don't trust him. How am I to make sure the place isn't bled dry by madam if I'm abroad? My father always said that delegation was fatal. And the principle of the thing – why should I be driven out of my own country just because of a few disapproving wifies? It's a ridiculous idea.'

'It doesn't seem so ridiculous to me. What about Robin? I don't want a question mark hanging over him. We might be able to ignore snide remarks but a child . . .'

'I think it would be worse to deprive him of his birthright,' said Guy. 'Scotland is where he belongs. He's my heir, after all.'

'He's a child, Guy, and people can be very cruel. I don't want people calling him a bastard.'

'If they do they'll answer to me for it,' said Guy. He reached out and pulled over his crutch. 'No, I will not be driven out.'

'All right, we'll stay here.'

'No,' said Guy, heaving himself up, with all the painful effort of a man determined to be independent. 'Not here.'

'Where then?' said Chris.

'Rankeillor,' he said.

'Guy . . .'

He smiled suddenly.

'I don't know why I didn't think of this before,' he said.

'What?' said Chris, already dreading what he was going to say.

'The shooting lodge. The judge didn't say anything about that, did he? It might need a little work on it, but it's a good solid house.' Chris closed her eyes and shook her head. 'A splendid house, in fact,' he went on. 'I was always supposed to have the use of it, you know, and

Miranda has never set foot in the place. Why on earth didn't I think of it before?'

'Because it's a stupid idea!' burst out Chris, jumping to her feet. 'Can't you see that? It's obviously stupid!'

'It's better than running away.'

'I want to run away!' she said bitterly. 'I'm exhausted by all this! I've had enough.' She turned quickly away so that he should not see the tears that had run down her cheeks.

'Oh Chris, I know.' She felt his arms fold round her. He was holding her strongly, supportively. Involuntarily, she relaxed. 'That's better. You see,' he said, turning her gently back to face him, 'I need this. I know it will be hard for you, but I need it. Just thinking about it makes me feel strong. And if I'm strong again, then no one can touch us. I won't let them.'

'Are you sure you want this?'

'I'd bleed dry without it. I'd be no good to anyone, especially not to you and Robin. Can you understand that?'

She nodded, but she was not sure she was being entirely truthful. He bent and kissed her.

'We're going home,' he murmured, squeezing her.

'I hope so,' thought Chris.

52
Rankeillor, March 1916

When she had taken Robin from his cot and quietened him, Chris went to the window and dragged open one of the curtains. They were old and heavy, made of ginger-brown stamped velvet that had clearly once hung in the Castle, but had been relegated to the shooting lodge when they had fallen out of fashion. The whole house was furnished like that, with strange, musty relics of previous moments of good taste. It felt like a graveyard to Chris, in which her own furniture, like herself, sat uncomfortably.

Guy loved it of course. Yesterday he had dashed about the place, getting in the way of the furniture movers, directing where every piece and packing case should go. Chris had found herself hiding from it all in the kitchen, exhausted, with Robin grizzling and bad-tempered in her arms. For she no longer had Peggy to rely on. Peggy had given in her notice, a decision which seemed all too understandable to Chris, especially when she was forced to witness the dressing down Guy had given the poor girl about disloyalty. It was easy, so easy sometimes, to want to give Guy notice. The last month in Edinburgh had seemed to test her own loyalty to the absolute limit, but it seemed, looking out that morning, that the test was only beginning. She was his wife now, Lady Lindsay, as he liked to remind her, and she felt consumed by him, just as she had always feared she might be. His love was so powerful she could not ignore it, and she knew she loved him, but there was a dark whisper of despair in it all, as she felt her liberty, indeed her very identity, being chipped away. And what was this house, with the moor rolling out in front of her, with the pale billows of morning mist still hovering over it, but a sort of prison?

But you walked into that cage willingly, she told herself fiercely. You knew it would be difficult and so you had better simply accept that it is difficult.

She realized that Robin needed changing and wondered where Guy had got to. She had woken to find Robin screaming, but no sign of Guy. It was a sign of how tired she had been to sleep through his getting up and dressing – it had woken Robin and not herself. She put Robin down briefly on the bed, put on her dressing gown, and gathered up his various necessities into a basket to take downstairs to the kitchen. There was no bathroom in the house, as there was no electricity. There was a pump in the kitchen, and a large boiler on the range. That was all – and no Peggy. She scooped up Robin, who was howling by this time, and wondered if she ought not go and beg Peggy to come back. It was a five-mile round walk to the Logans' farm, but she would willingly make it. She did not think she would be able to look after Robin competently alone. She could perhaps persuade her to come for a few days, at least until a new nurse arrived from the agency she had contacted from Edinburgh.

Looking at the kitchen though, which was vast and cold, with the fire burnt out (of course Guy would never have thought to light a fresh fire), she wondered how easy it would be to get anyone to come and work in such primitive conditions. Jean had quit, not because she disapproved, but because she could not face life in the country. 'I've never stepped out of Edinburgh in my life,' she had explained. 'I wouldn't know what to do wi' myself.' And for a moment, looking at that kitchen, Chris could not think what to do with herself, but Robin continued to howl and remind her of her priorities. So she changed and dressed and fed him, and thankfully he seemed inclined to sleep again. She dressed herself, and brought Robin downstairs again in his wicker crib, deciding that she would wean him soon.

After some struggle she relit the fire in the kitchen and looked at the meagre supply of food in the larder. She realized she would have to go down into the village and put an order in at Babbie Thompson's – a thought which terrified her. She did not have a willing messenger to take down a list for her. She would have to face them all, the rank of gossips in the post office. They had avoided the village yesterday and the absence of locals coming to help them settle in had been extremely noticeable. At least, Chris had felt it acutely. Guy had seemed neither to notice, nor to care.

She put the kettle on the range and decided she would put off going to the village for as long as she could. Perhaps she could even get Guy to take a list for her. They were sure to treat him more kindly. Men were always regarded as poor dupes in such cases whereas she was the really wicked one, in Rankeillor terms, a home-breaker, an adulteress herself, who had had the temerity to parade a bastard child as if he were legitimate. No, she could not face Babbie Thompson's shop.

She washed up the teapot and cups from yesterday in the stone sink under icy water and then heard someone knocking at the front door. She went to open it tentatively, drying her hands on her apron, dreading who it might be.

It was her father. She could not help a slight gasp of surprise, especially as he held out in his hand a bunch of perfect, freshly picked primroses. Behind him stood the familiar shabby Manse pony trap, with the placid old mare Heather, neatly tethered up.

'The first I've seen this year,' he said, handing them to her.

'Oh . . . oh . . .' She could not speak, but looked down at the pale soft yellow flowers, still spotted here and there with dew. 'Oh . . . I'm sorry!' she exclaimed suddenly. 'I'm so sorry . . .' She sounded like a child, she realized, on the verge of tears at confessing some offence.

'Now, now, you're not to cry, I won't have that,' he said, putting his hands on her shoulders. He sounded as if he could not stand the thought of it.

'No, all right,' she said, managing a smile. 'Come in then. I've just put the kettle on.'

'I'm just ready for a cup of tea.'

They went into the kitchen and he pulled up a chair to the fireside, scraping its legs on the stone flags, while she searched in the china press for a vase for the primroses. All she could find was a cream jug with the Lindsay crest printed on it.

'How's wee Robin?' he asked, glancing at the cot.

'Missing Peggy, I suspect,' she said. 'There, how do those look?' she added, arranging the flowers.

'Very bonny,' he said. 'I could go and speak with her for you.'

'No, she won't want to come back. Guy was rather . . . savage with her for giving notice.'

'Oh, was he?' he said, suspiciously.

'It's just he gets angry about things. He can't see things straight always. It's part of his illness.'

'He's not savage with you, I hope,' he said.

'No,' she said, and realized she was not entirely convinced by her answer. There was a sort of savagery in forcing her to live there, after all, when she would rather be anywhere else.

'Are you sure?' he said, picking up her unease.

'Oh, I don't know how to explain,' she said, sitting down opposite him. 'It is all so very complicated. Guy will get better, I'm sure of it, I have to be sure of it, but for now I have to be here and bear with him, don't I? He needs me. Without me, God knows what state he'd be in. I have to do this, because I couldn't do otherwise, even if it does seem abhorrent to everyone else. I have to because I love him, that's the simple fact of it. I suppose it feels abhorrent to you, that I should have broken up a marriage, and . . .'

She broke off and went to lift the kettle from the fire, glad not to have to look him in the eyes as he reproached her, for she was certain he would. He would do it kindly and with understanding, and make it far worse for her.

'Do you think it does?' he asked, after a pause.

'Well,' she said, a little confused by the question. 'I haven't behaved as you would have liked, have I? As you would have expected of me?'

'Oh Chris,' he said, with a slight laugh. 'I have never known what to expect of you.'

She stood, the open tea caddy in one hand, the spoon in the other, too startled to go on.

'Sometimes,' he went on, 'you seemed like a changeling to me. I could never read you, never quite understand you, like I could Annie or May. It was always as if you were a stranger to me – a wonderful stranger in our house, who would never quite behave like the others. And then you started to write music, to pull down music, almost, from somewhere I couldn't hear it, strange music, music that went in so deep that . . . aahh . . .' He broke off and waved his hand slightly. 'I can't describe what your music does or says, can I?'

'I thought you didn't care for it,' said Chris, crouching down by him. 'I thought . . .'

'Oh I care for it, care for it very much. But at first it frightened me. It upset me, it seemed to undermine everything I thought certain. It seemed to go right into the dark places in me, the places I wouldn't admit to having. You've so much more courage than I, to go in there.'

'I don't have courage,' said Chris. 'I just have ... instinct.'

'And instinct doesn't sit well with our notions of morality, does it?' he said. 'It makes me wonder whether those notions are so hard and fast as we'd like to believe. You're not a wicked person, Christina, and neither is Guy. In my heart I can't really believe that, and I can't stand up in my pulpit and condemn you for doing wrong, when I can't help thinking you've done right, that you've done a brave thing.'

'You do?' said Chris, her throat dry. 'But that flies in the face of everything... Your faith ... everything...'

'Yes, it must seem like that,' he said. 'But I'm an old man now, and one of the blessings of old age is a little wisdom. I've been thinking a lot these last few years, with the war and all this, and I've begun to see clearly at last that the God I set out to serve doesn't live where I thought He did. He's not in the kirk, not in my sermons, not even much in the Bible. He can't be pinned down by words, I know that, and He certainly doesn't operate a heavenly law court to judge our sins.' Chris sank back on her heels. 'No, he's in us all, he's the good in us, the force in us that makes us love and create and be happy. Do you see?'

'Yes, but... You know I can't believe in God?'

'Yes, certainly, not the notion of God we brought you up with. I don't believe in that. No, perhaps God is just the name you put on it. Think of all those other folk, with other gods. Perhaps what music is to you is Allah to another.'

'You are extraordinary, you know,' she said, reaching up and touching his cheek.

He shrugged at the gesture and looked away saying, 'Where's that cup of tea got to then?'

'Of course,' she said, getting up. As she made it she asked, 'What does Mother think of all this?'

'She doesn't know,' he said. 'You're the first living soul I've told. There, you see what a coward I am!

'You're not a coward at all,' she said. 'There aren't many ministers of the kirk who'd say what you've just said to me. But I can imagine it would be hard to tell her. Her view of the world is so simple.'

'I tried to make her come up with me today,' he said. 'But she won't hear of it. We'll work on her though. I should imagine she'll not be able to resist seeing little Robin for long.'

'I don't expect her to,' said Chris. 'I don't expect any of them, really. After all, I've broken all their rules. I was just dreading going down to Babbie Thompson's with a grocery list though . . .'

'I'll take it down for you,' said Mr Adam and added, with a malicious twinkle in his eye that surprised her more than anything than he had yet said to her, 'that should give the old wife something to talk about, shouldn't it?'

'Let me in, Malcolm, for God's sake, I'm only going into the estate office. I'm not going to take up residence.'

'Yes, sir, I know, but her ladyship gave very strict instructions . . .'

'Her ladyship is not here, though, is she? And you, let me remind you, have been employed by my family far longer than by her.'

'Yes, sir, I know that, sir, but I wasn't speaking of your wife, I mean your former wife. No, her ladyship your mother gave the order.'

'She's here?' Guy was surprised.

'Aye, sir, did you not know?'

'No, clearly I didn't,' said Guy with mounting exasperation. That his own mother should ban him from the house like this, even when Miranda was not there. 'Kindly tell her I should like to see her a moment.'

‘She said you weren’t to be let in.’

‘I know, I know! But try, will you, for goodness sake!’

Malcolm’s natural obedience to the Laird surfaced at last.

‘Of course, sir, I’ll go and try.’

‘So I should hope!’ Guy could not help muttering as he followed him into the hall. ‘I’ll be in the office,’ he called as he pushed open the door.

The estate office was the room nearest the front door, placed there presumably so that visiting tenants did not tramp mud into the Castle carpets. Guy felt going in there that he was just like a tenant now, only there on sufferance. How dare Malcolm try and turn him away! But it was inevitable that he should. He was only doing what he had been told and probably he disapproved as much as any of them.

He sat down in his old chair at the desk, wondering if his mother would deign to see him. Probably she would be unable to resist the temptation to give him an almighty lecture and he braced himself for it, while thinking how he was going to get the estate papers from the estate office up to the Lodge. He hoped Davie Watson would be more co-operative. Surely he would have to be allowed the run of his own stables? That was really nothing to do with the house. He could imagine, though, it was the sort of detail that that devil of a judge would relish settling against him, no doubt with some Latin tag, known only to Scottish lawyers. Well, he would go to the stables when he was finished here and try and get something sorted out.

He looked up at the map of the estate on the wall opposite him, with all the farms and features carefully delineated, with the Castle at the heart of it all and the Lodge in the far eastern peripheries, a good hour and a half’s walk from the village. It had seemed an interminable walk and physically he was exhausted, but mentally, he was raging, raging more now that he sat there, looking at that map and all it represented. Yes, he was back at Rankeillor, but the citadel which represented it, which was in truth all the place to him, was still denied him. He would see it every day and it would anger him all the more, especially since Miranda did not seem inclined to live there at all, but in London. He supposed he should be pleased that she was not there, but the fact of its being wilfully left empty infuriated him all the more.

The door opened and his mother came in. She looked him over rather contemptuously for a moment as he struggled to stand up and he at once wished he had not bothered to make the effort.

'Well?' she said.

'If I'd known you were here I'd have called last night,' he lied brightly.

'Certainly you would,' she said. 'I didn't think you would be able to keep away for long. If you are stupid enough to come back to the Lodge . . .'

'Do you think it's stupid?'

'Of course it is!' she exclaimed.

'Don't you think Father would want me to be personally managing the estate?'

'How dare you drag what your father would want into this?' she said. 'He'd be disgusted, utterly disgusted, at the way you've behaved.'

'You mean that you are.'

'Yes, of course I am. How couldn't I be? It's utterly contemptible, all of it. You did not even have the courtesy to tell me what you intended, to ask my advice.'

'I should have asked your advice?' he retorted. 'Oh, and what advice would you have given me, eh? Bad advice, very bad advice.'

'I should have told you to stay with Miranda.'

'Exactly, bad advice.'

'I should have advised you to stay with her, and if you were unhappy to have found some comfort elsewhere, rather than losing all sense of discretion and marrying your mistress.'

'Oh, is that all that offends you?' he said. 'That I've been indiscreet?'

'You've been more than indiscreet, you've been scandalous. You've muddied our name, you've muddied your father's name, and the damage is irrevocable. You've dirtied this family.'

'You make it sound as if I'd married a whore.'

'She has behaved as good as one by all accounts.'

'You've never liked Chris, have you? You've never been able to stand her, have you? Why, for God's sake? What's she ever done to you, that you think you can be so bloody rude about her?'

'Because – because she's simply not good enough,' she said. 'She never has been and she never will be. Look what a mess she's made of your life. She's ruined your marriage and trapped you. She's made a fool of you – and there'll be worse to come, just you wait and see.'

'No,' he said, slamming his palm down on to the table. 'I won't have you talking like this. Chris is my wife now, Mother, and you owe her some respect for that. If there were any justice she'd be mistress of this house, just as you were. She's my choice and you'll have to accept that, if you can. And if you can't, it doesn't matter, because it's not going to change because of anything you say.'

'No, how can it?' she said coldly. 'Nothing I say has ever mattered much to you, Guy.' She rose from her chair. 'You had better clear out these papers. Miranda, I'm certain, won't want to be bothered with details of business. You can do that little for her, at least. I have to go and pack myself.'

'Where are you going?'

'Away,' she said. 'And I do not suppose I will be back. Isolde and Frank have a very nice little house at Southam just waiting for me. It is not what I planned, and I imagine your father would be rearing up out of his grave at the thought of my not living out my last years here, but... Strange times, eh?' she added, with precise sourness as she went to the door.

Guy gripped at the arms of his chair, trying to remain calm. He was not angry any more but afraid. That last remark, about his father rearing out of his grave, was too literal a reality for him. He had seen him, after all, enough times in his nightmares, so why not now, standing in the room where he had spent so much of his life? Yet instead of the sensible tweed suit it would be white grave clothes that he would wear, and his hand would be outstretched, to point a sharp, accusatory finger at Guy. He began to feel choked with fear at the thought of it and did not wait to see it but, with all the strength he could muster, got out into the forecourt of the house again. He looked up at the great stony façade, gasping for air. In that last moment, he had felt the air was thick with ghosts. He could not live there with them even had he been allowed to. His exile was absolute.

53
June 1916

Chris opened the letter abstractedly. She was watching Guy, who was just visible through the screen of flapping white sheets made by the washing line. He was fiercely hoeing the vegetable garden. It was not easy for him to do this, but he was insistent. He was obsessed with the vegetable garden, determined, in fact, it should rival any in the village, if not that of the Castle itself. Gently she had tried to tell him that the bleak space behind the Lodge would need a vast amount of work to make it even mildly productive, but he had rather sharply informed her that he needed something to do, and why not this? He had even quoted Voltaire at her: 'Il faut cultiver notre jardin,' and had proceeded to fill the house with gardening manuals and seed catalogues. 'By the time of the Rankeillor Games, I shall be able to enter most of the vegetable classes, and next year perhaps the fruit.' She had wanted to retort that he would never manage to grow fruit up there but she could not bring herself to puncture these dreams. He was bound to be disappointed, yet he could not be convinced of it. The garden had taken over almost all their existence. Mhari, the girl whom Chris had managed to recruit to help clean and look after Robin, had been transferred to garden duties by Guy. Even Chris was expected to buckle down to weeding, which she resented extremely, but she never saw Guy so happy these days as when a seedling had first poked its small green head through the soil.

On a morning such as this his enthusiasm was perhaps understandable. It was the first real warm weather they had had, and Mhari was playing with Robin on a rug spread on the lawn. Chris had been there herself, before she had got up to go and fetch the post, and had tried to persuade Guy to leave the potato beds for a moment and come and join them. Hoeing the potato beds was far more important than dawdling around, he had said, and had added quite callously that it would be a good thing when Robin was old enough to help them by scaring birds. She winced when she thought of that and decided that it was more than enthusiasm, this garden business, it was a mania. Whatever lucidity Guy had left seemed to be slipping away fast, under an onslaught of trivial horticultural tasks. She half expected to find him there in the middle of the night, fiddling around with flowerpots and green string. The days were so long now that he did not usually come in till ten o'clock, and when he did he expected to make love, with a fierce energy that astonished Chris, who was generally exhausted. She liked his love making, but its intensity frightened her sometimes. It was almost as if he were not making love to her at all, but propitiating the earth goddess with his semen. There was a distance in his eyes which saddened her. She had thought they would grow closer but he seemed more and more a stranger, as each day passed. She had not yet been able to tell him she suspected she was pregnant again. She had no idea how he might react – with delight perhaps at the prospect of another bird-scarer for his garden?

It was his strangeness that was wearing her down most of all. She felt she might be able to stand the petty humiliations that life in Rankeillor inflicted on her constantly, if she felt that Guy was in some way recovering. But she could see no signs of it. Only this strange, obsessed man, frantically hoeing his potato beds as if life itself depended on them. She could not help noticing every clumsy, unskilled movement he made with the hoe. It was an agony to watch him so unnecessarily punishing his body. She could see the pain of it in his grim face, but he would not permit anyone to intervene. This was his thing and he would go on with it. Nothing else mattered to him, except making love, and drinking large amounts in the Rankeillor Inn, which he did periodically. He would arrive home very drunk, usually helped by someone else, and on those nights would always have nightmares. At least there were fewer of those, she thought to herself, and looked down at her letter again.

The heading announced it was from the Royal Glasgow Choral Society, which surprised her at once, and she glanced down to the foot of it to see that it was signed 'Henry Bradley, principal conductor'. She did not know that he had been appointed to the post.

'Dear Lady Lindsay,' it said:

> I am honoured to have the pleasure to inform you that you have been chosen by the commissioning committee of the Royal Glasgow Choral Society to provide a full-scale work for SATB and orchestra to be performed at our forthcoming autumn concert. The fee for this work will be two hundred and fifty guineas. Please let me know at first opportunity whether you would be interested in accepting the commission. The choice of libretto would, incidentally, be entirely in your hands.
>
> Yours respectfully,
> Henry Bradley

She could not help exclaiming with delight. It seemed too miraculous to be credited, so she read the letter again just to be certain. Yes, it was perfectly true – it was a commission, for a full-scale work for chorus and orchestra! That was the stuff upon which reputations were made.

'Yes, yes, of course I'll take it!' she said aloud, laughing. 'Dear old Dr Bradley!' He seemed the last person in the world from whose hand such a piece of manna would fall but it meant that her music had really impressed him, that she had broken through to her sternest critic, broken through enough for him to recommend his choir commission something from her. She wondered which piece it had been – the symphony, or perhaps 'Blest Pair of Sirens'? She could not remember having seen him in the audience but in the excitement she may not have noticed.

Exalted, she ran across the lawn and through the washing into the vegetable garden.

'Guy, Guy, you'll never guess what's happened,' she began, but stopped, because he did not look up from his hoeing. 'Guy, do you hear me?'

He did not look up, but went on pushing the hoe into the earth, manipulating it with exquisite awkwardness, moving his arms only below his elbows.

'Guy?' She asked again, going closer to him. 'Do you hear me?'

'Yes, of course I do,' he said, still without looking up. In fact he shuffled himself a little further away from her on his crutches. 'What is it?'

'You could look at me,' she said.

'I can hoe and listen at the same time,' he said, carrying on. 'Now get on with it. I've a lot to do this morning. There's the lettuces to be pricked out remember.'

'Damn lettuces,' she said. 'I've been given a commission.'

She expected him to look up then, to smile and congratulate her. But he went on stolidly hoeing.

'Guy, do you understand, a commission?' she said again, feeling cold inside. How could he not react to something as wonderful and as important to her as this?

'Yes, of course I understand,' he said, at last looking at her. But it was a hard, irritated glance which lasted only a moment. 'Very nice.'

'Very nice!' she exploded, and grabbed him by the shoulders. 'Guy, are you quite mad?' He pushed her away, with so much force that she stumbled and almost fell into the carrot bed.

'No, I am not,' he said. 'I am far more sane now than I have been in months. I should have thought that was obvious.'

'I don't think it's obvious at all,' said Chris. 'This isn't curing you, Guy, this damned garden, it's obsessing you, making you madder than ever.'

'I am not mad!' He shouted it this time. 'How dare you say that?'

'Because you are. I should know, I live with it, every day, every night, watching it get worse and worse. You're like a stranger now. If only you could see yourself.'

'I can see myself perfectly, thank you,' he said, resuming hoeing.

'I do wish you'd stop that,' she said.

'And I wish you'd go away,' he said. 'Or at least do something useful. Have you watered the tomato plants yet?'

'Oh for heaven's sake,' said Christ and walked straight back into the house.

The dim light of the kitchen made her blink after the sunlight. It was dry with heat from the range and the pot of soup she had set to boil needed attention. She did it automatically, as she did all the household tasks, which even with Mhari's help seemed to take for all eternity. There were tears in her eyes but she could not give in to them. If she had given in every time she had had a run in with Guy recently she would not have had time for anything else except crying. But she wavered on the brink of it, as she stirred the broth, wiping her hands across her eyes. The joy she had felt on reading that letter was utterly evaporated, for how could she possibly in these circumstances write a full-scale choral piece in time for the autumn? There seemed to be no time for music, no space for anything but this dull domestic drudgery and dealing with Guy. And if she were not dealing with Guy, she would be worrying about him, even when she scoured pots or bathed Robin or mended holes in his socks! She had been reduced to a sort of nothingness and that letter was nothing but a cruel joke, blowing up in her face. For how could she work, how could she do anything here except survive from day to day, going from one chore to another? How could the miserable drudge in the Lodge have enough mind or spirit to write a full-scale choral piece? How on earth could she presume such a thing, when all she was fit for was bearing children and watering tomato plants?

How she would have liked to tie Guy to a chair and make him watch as she systematically smashed every flower pot and uprooted every vegetable. But what good would that do? She had a horrible feeling that he would only start the whole thing again. The garden was his sustaining idea. Perhaps he no longer needed her at all.

Yet he did need her. She knew that, and she knew she could not leave him. One day the tower he was building in his imagination would come crashing down and he would have to face the facts of his life again. She would have to be there when that happened, wouldn't she? She was the only one who could pick up the pieces, after all.

She walked back to the kitchen table where she had left the letter. She felt herself twitch with anger at the sight of it. Why did she have to sacrifice herself for Guy? Why could he not be sacrificed to her need for once? She knew he could not help himself, but it was still impossible to bear, to feel the leech of his need always on her, sucking away at everything until she was nothing but a husk, draining her until she must write back regretfully declining the commission.

How could she decline, how could she even begin to do such a thing? It might not be betraying Guy but it was betraying herself. It would be like taking a knife to her wrist, a sort of spiritual suicide. Which ever way she turned she could not avoid pain, either for herself or for Guy. She folded up the letter and put it away in a drawer as if that might put the problem out of her mind.

Of course it did not. The day dragged, the heat building up, but Guy would not stop hoeing. Chris observed with despair that he worked over the same row again and again. The sweat was pouring off him, but he would not stop, except to drink the occasional glass of water Mhari took out to him.

Chris sat with the girl and Robin in the shade of the beech hedge. Mhari was reading a novelette, and Chris, unable to resist the temptation, had fetched her manuscript notebooks from the top of the virtually untouched piano. She had remembered Guy's suggestion that she set 'Dover Beach' and had dug out a copy of the poem from Angus's books. How much more sane he had seemed then. Then he had been aware of his illness, now he stoutly denied it, though it was obvious to everyone. Most of Rankeillor, she suspected, considered that the Laird was being punished by madness for his sins.

No, I'm not going to think about that, she told herself, and stared down at the page of poetry:

> The sea is calm to-night.
> The tide is full, the moon lies fair
> Upon the straits; – on the French coast the light
> Gleams and is gone; the cliffs of England stand,

Glimmering and vast, out in the tranquil bay.
Come to the window, sweet is the night air!

Only, from the long line of spray
Where the sea meets the moon blanch'd land,
Listen! you hear the grating roar
Of pebbles which the waves draw back, and fling,
At their return, up the high strand,
Begin, and cease, and then again begin,
With tremulous cadence slow, and bring
The eternal note of sadness in.

There was music in every line of it. Her mind seemed to wash through with the very sea of it, the cold wetness slapping at her imagination and awakening it. She could hear it set for tenor, in very free fashion, like an ancient folk song, full of plangent harmony. A choir could not sing those words, they would muffle them. The choir must have another text, and it occurred to her that it should be the words of the Requiem Mass, in Latin, for what was this poem, but a requiem for certainty? She felt a thrill of excitement at it, and relief to find she could still have such ideas, that her mind should already be humming with threads of melody and layers of harmony. She remembered how, suddenly, she had felt up on Rankeillor Hill, in January, before she had seen Guy again, how she had been certain she must express her anger at the war and find some music to convey that. Well, would this not do that? Would this not be her tremendous act of dissent, because in it she could reach all those others who suffered impossibly as she and Guy and Angus had suffered?

'Have you watered those tomato plants?'

She looked up and saw that he had at last decided to stop. He stood looming over them, his shirt stuck to him with sweat, his chin thick with stubble.

'I'll go and do it, shall I?' said Mhari.

'Better doing that than reading silly novelettes,' he said.

'Don't be unkind,' said Chris, when she had gone. 'She works very hard.'

Slowly he lowered himself down beside her.

'It's a waste of time reading that sort of rubbish,' he said. 'She could help me a lot more if she stopped.' Chris decided she would let this pass. She was glad enough he had stopped. 'What are you doing?'

'Oh just making a few notes for that commission.'

'You're not taking it?' he said. He sounded surprised.

'I haven't decided,' she admitted.

'Well, I won't allow it,' he said.

'I beg your pardon?'

'There's no point you doing it. You don't need to do it, do you? That sort of thing isn't important.'

'Oh God!' she could not help exclaiming. 'I didn't think I would ever hear you say that, Guy Lindsay. Of course music is important. You know that. You love music.'

'It's peripheral,' he said. 'it doesn't feed anyone, does it?'

'You're afraid of it, aren't you?' she said. 'Because it makes you feel things, is that it?'

'I've felt enough to last me the rest of my life,' he said. 'I just want some peace and quiet in my garden. Can't you understand that?'

'Of course. But that doesn't have anything to do with my accepting this commission does it?'

'Yes it does. I won't allow it, that's all.'

'I don't know what gives you the idea you can make such decisions for me,' she said, feeling her temper slipping from her.

'I'm your husband, aren't I?' he said, getting back up on to his crutches.

She gazed up at him, at this monstrous version of him,

and wished she could knock him off the crutches and stun him back to normality. But she wondered if it were possible to do such a thing. Perhaps he was a lost cause. If he was lost to music, then . . .

'Would you seriously forbid me from doing it?' she managed to say.

'I do forbid it,' he said. 'I need you here, in the garden.'

She blinked, bit her lip and let him go. She sat for a moment, rigid with absolute anger, her fingertips digging into the grass, even through the blanket. If she had had a weapon then, she felt she might have used it against him, not just from fury, but out of a sort of mercy. Surely Guy was better dead than living out this futile, alienating travesty? He could not be happy, she was certain of that. He filled her with both pity and hatred, for this thing, that had taken him over and destroyed the man she had once known, now seemed to have stretched out its destructive hand to those around him. If she stayed there, and let him have his way, she felt certain she would go mad too. Was she not halfway there already, to think of killing him? She had to preserve herself, if only for Robin's sake – and for the sake of the child she might be carrying.

She picked up Robin's crib and took him into the house, making a series of rapid decisions. When Mhari came back into the house again, she asked, 'Do you think your mother would mind coming up and doing the cooking and cleaning? She'd be well paid. I have to go away for a while and I shall need some help with Robin, if you would like to come with me.'

Mhari's mother, Mrs Crumm, was an imperturbable widow. If anyone was qualified to keep a mad-house it was she.

'Where to?' asked Mhari.

'Glasgow. I've some work to do there.'

'I dinna see why not,' said Mhari with a shrug. 'What about . . .?' she gestured vaguely towards the garden.

'I don't suppose he will notice we have gone,' said Chris, 'if your mother remembers to water the tomatoes.'

54
July 1916

It was raining still. It had been raining for four or five days, with a relentless heaviness that seemed intent on flooding the garden, washing away all the top soil and young plants. Everything was drowning. Guy knelt down in the mud that had been his carefully tilled earth and wept, as the rain beat down on him. He snatched at a carrot top and yanked it up to reveal a tiny, rotten stem that would never have turned into anything of any consequence. It was all ruined, the whole damn garden was ruined!

He dug his hands into the earth, the earth which he had found so absorbing, and stared at the filthy treachery of it. He scooped it up in his hands, and pressed it under his nose so that he might learn the stench of it, to avoid in future. He knew the smell at once though, even through the damp, rain-soaked scent, he recognized it – it was the tunnel smell. Even now, in this damp sod, he could smell the dry, dusty earth of Cape Helles and he could see the exact colour of it, and feel the texture of it beneath his fingers as he crawled up towards the exit to get to the latrine. Yes, that was it, and then there had been silence, that ominous silence, and such fear in the air that you could have cut it with a knife. Then . . .

Then for the first time, he actually remembered what had happened. He heard the explosion again. It had been so strange, that sound, a whisper and then . . . a great bowel-crunching, heart-splitting, throat-constricting boom that had shaken the earth. And all at once the tunnel had begun to collapse. He had turned slightly to look back and he saw it fall in, earth cascading from the ceiling and burying his companions. He had seen them all suffocated and could not move because he had been trapped himself from the waist down. He had heard their dying, choking cries, their hopeless attempts to breathe still. They sounded in his ears now, along with the drumming of the rain. He had lain there while so many – twenty, thirty of them – had died, and he had been the only one to survive. He remembered being dragged out now, seeing the grim faces of his rescuers. He was gasping for air, just as he had done then.

He did not know how long he sat there, on the damp earth, but he found with time he was breathing normally again and his heart seemed calm in its beating. He felt extraordinary, as if to know was to accept. He had seen it and felt it all again, and it had frightened him just as much, with his guts knotting themselves up inside him, but he felt he had cast out a demon. He knew now why those dreams came to him, what they meant.

He slapped his hand on to his chest, in the bare space where his shirt was undone, and smeared the mud against him, like a fox hunter blooding a novitiate on the forehead with the quarry's paw. He turned his face up to the rain and let it wash over him, as every muscle in him seemed to lose its grip on his frame. He stretched out his arms and palms to catch the drops and opened his mouth to it. He was free, free at last from it.

Almost free, he realized, as he turned to face the Lodge. There were other ghosts still.

'And I'll face them now,' he thought as he grabbed on to his now muddy crutches.

The walk down to the Castle was more exhausting than ever, but he pushed on, although the wind seemed almost against him, as if it were determined to blow him away from confrontation. He found he had to pull the bell chain at the front door with two hands.

Malcolm seemed to take an eternity to open the door, and when he did Guy found he was drooping on his crutches.

'You'll let me in today, won't you?' he gasped.

'Of course, sir,' said Malcolm.

'I want a bath, please, Malcolm,' said Guy. 'In my father's bathroom.'

'Very good, sir,' said Malcolm.

How easy it had been. Malcolm, excellent servant that he was, knew when not to ask questions but obey orders.

He laboured up the stairs after Malcolm, acutely aware, now he was out of the rain, of the discomfort of his soaking clothes.

'I'll just fetch some towels from the linen room, sir,' he said, opening the door to the dressing room. 'I'm afraid everything is under dust sheets.'

'Probably just as well,' said Guy, observing the mud that still remained on his boots. 'There should be some clothes of mine here.'

'Certainly, sir. I'll find you something suitable. I shan't be long.'

Alone in his father's dressing room, Guy dared his ghosts to come, but they were oddly reluctant. Even his father would not come, though this was so much his room. Guy found he had only memories, and not visions to contend with. He stood looking about him, resting on his crutches, his good leg weak with incredulous amazement at it. Was he really as free as this? Wasn't something else going to happen?

Malcolm came back with towels and some clothes – a smart white linen suit he had had made in his last year at Oxford and which would hang loose on him now.

'I'm not sure how much hot water there'll be, sir,' said

Malcolm going into the bathroom. 'With the house not being open, officially . . .'

It was an austere room. His father had had no concessions to vanity. There was not even a mirror there.

'A trickle will do,' said Guy, sitting down on the white-painted stool.

In the end it was only a few inches, but it was enough, and Guy got out with tingling flesh having scrubbed himself with his father's most ascetic back brush. He dried himself and went back to the dressing room, supported on newly cleaned crutches. Malcolm was pinning up the spare cloth of his left trouser leg.

'I was wondering sir,' he said, as he helped him to dress, with exquisite tact, not as a nurse but as a valet, a luxury which Guy could not help enjoying again, 'if it isn't offensive to ask, have you not considered having a wooden leg? I've read great things of them.'

Previously Guy would have been offended. The idea had disgusted him at first, although it was highly practical. But he realized now he had liked to make a show of his disability to himself. He had wanted it to be a constant punishment for living, like the nightmares and the visions. All of it was self-inflicted punishment.

'That's a very good idea,' he said. 'I shall look into it.' He did not need to punish himself any more. He had had enough. Silently he told his father this, in case he was lurking there, outraged that he should make such free use of his room. For he was certain now, it was his father who was at the root of all this, the father who had taught him it was better to feel guilty than happy, who had enslaved him to a notion of duty and family that was nothing more than suffocating.

For what was this place, in reality, but simply a collection of beautiful things, carefully arranged? Perhaps his ancestors had been there for a very long time – but did that honestly matter? It was only a house, after all.

'Can I wait here until the rain's stopped?' he asked Malcolm.

'Of course, sir,' he said. 'It is your house, sir – properly, that is.'

Guy shook his head.

Malcolm left him, looking a little puzzled perhaps, and he began to make a slow pilgrimage about the place. For the first time in his life, he looked objectively at it, as a stranger paying a call while the family were away. He could not identify himself with the family that had made this place. He realized, to his surprise, that he no longer belonged here. He was something else entirely now. He searched for what that might be and could not find it. He felt like a shadow stealing along the passageways and into the shrouded rooms.

He turned at last into the gallery and walked along its drugget-covered floor to the piano, which was hidden under a special drab canvas cover. He put his hand on it and saw, not in front of him, but in his head, where ghosts of the past should be, a young man and girl sitting there playing piano duets. It was odd, because he was one of the players but he was observing himself, sitting there, shoulder to shoulder with Chris: Chris with her hair down, a great floppy bow restraining it, and wearing a girl's sailor shirt. He could hear the music, echoing through the room, and their laughter as they played, not with brilliant technique, but with absolute spirit, with all the helpless heedlessness of youth. Then the piece finished, and he remembered the smell of her hair and how even then he had felt it would be more than interesting to kiss her. No doubt he would have done, had not Isolde's German governess been sitting in the corner, with her tatting.

He pulled away the cover and sat down at the piano, pushing up the lid. In his eagerness, he let his crutches fall to the floor behind him. It was not badly out of tune – one or two notes revealed that much. He began with a chord or two from nowhere in particular. He stopped though, suddenly surprised at himself. He had not thought he had it left in him, but his fingers felt adept, and the tone of the instrument was sweet, its action responsive. He had forgotten how lovely this piano was. He had forgotten, indeed, just how many hours he had spent there, practising, dreaming of being a musician. He had never thought of Rankeillor as his destiny then – it had been Roddy's, not his. He had never dreamt of owning it, so why should he mourn not being able to have it any more? There were far more important things to mourn – Chris, for example.

Her absence then struck him, as it had not done before, as a terrible physical pain. It was as if every nerve in his body had come alive and was screeching with agony. She had gone, slipped away in an afternoon, and he had done nothing to stop her. In fact, most likely he had driven her away. He remembered now what he had said to her: that he had no need of music, that it was peripheral and unimportant. Had that really been him speaking, or the mad man speaking, the one who had taken him over and made him stand for hours hoeing and digging in that wretched vegetable patch? It had felt like a stranger, but he knew it had been himself, a dark, bitter, unyielding part of himself, that he detested and regretted. Bitterly regretted.

He played a few more chords, and found his hands shook slightly as he did so. He wanted to break into some virtuoso piece but was not sure that he could. Snatches of scores were in his mind but the old, instinctive playing was gone, or at least so deeply buried that he would have to work and dig to get it out again. It was more than being out of practice. It was as if the dirt in the tunnel had crushed the music in him, as well as his leg, or at least tried to crush it, for he knew it was still there, waiting for a voice again.

She had said he was afraid of it because it made him

feel. She was right, as she was always right. Well, he would feel now, he would unearth himself again and hear the beauty that he feared, the beauty he had not believed he deserved any more. But he did deserve it, because it had formed him. If there was anything that had made him, it was those long hours at this very piano when he had seen, so clearly, that the finest thing he could ever be was an interpreter of great music. That was why he loved Chris so dearly, because of what she made as much as what she was. They were two sides of the same coin – she creator, he interpreter.

He swung round on the stool and began to pull open the drawers of the music cabinet that stood by the piano. Somewhere in here was her first set of salon pieces. He had bought them, just as he had promised her, although he had felt guilty about it. He had not even told Miranda about them. There they were in the bottom drawer. He pulled it out – an elegant buff-coloured volume, with sparse, very chic French lettering: 'Cinq Pièces de Salon par Christina Adam. Paris, 1913'. He opened it and put it on the stand.

He began to play them through. It was not easy for him to play well at once. His fingers were stiff and the number of mistakes he made annoyed him. He had always prided himself on his easy sight-reading, but this tested him. Yet for all the roughness he could grasp at the spirit of it, at the restless melancholy in it – a world where there were no easy harmonies or obvious modulations, where the phrase never resolved itself with a simple answer. It was as sharp as it was sweet and there was no happiness without irony.

Of course she had had to go. How had he dared to tell her she could not write, that she had no need to, when these simple things made more sense of what he had felt over the last few months than anything? He might as well have put his fingers about her throat and throttled her. He felt as wicked as if he had, for making her come back there and live in that dreadful house, while he tortured her with his madness. He wished he could have stopped himself and lost his anger then, as he had lost it now.

He pulled his arms around him to comfort himself. The room was cold suddenly, as it always had been, even in the height of summer. There was only one torture left for him – and in some ways it was the greatest yet, for it depended not on his own will but on hers: whether, in short, he could persuade her to come back to him, or, rather, persuade her to let him go with her, wherever she might choose to go.

55
Glasgow, July 1916

It was extraordinary how easy it had been. A month and she had the first draft of it lying in front of her. A month of absolute concentration though, in quiet lodgings near Kelvingrove Park, with a kindly landlady supplying meals and pots of tea at regular intervals. There had been no distractions. Robin was in a nice nursery room at the top of the house with the now doting Mhari to indulge his every babyish whim, and she could not hear his cries from the large cool sitting room on the first floor. In fact these external matters had hardly intruded upon her at all. Not even the symptoms of her pregnancy had distracted her. They were there but they were not reality. Reality was the work, was 'Dover Beach', the music of which seemed to come springing from her with such speed that it seemed hardly to be anything to do with her at all. Sometimes it had felt like nothing more than musical dictation – writing down those passages which rang so clearly in her head. But when she considered she had really written nothing of substance since Guy, it seemed that this music was a dammed stream in her, that had only been waiting for an opportunity to be released.

Guy ... she winced as she thought of him. Like everything else, she had pushed him out of her mind, but now that she had stopped working it could not be avoided. She looked at her score and hoped desperately that it was worth what she had done. For she knew, having felt the ease of its birth away from him, away from that awful house, that she could not have done it if she had stayed, that the music would have rotted inside her like a grievance, while she weeded the garden and meekly took the orders that he seemed, in his madness, compelled to give. The music was good, she was certain of that, but she wondered if the price were not too high. She had done something unspeakable in leaving. To abandon a sick man, for all her muddled justifications, was a great crime. It was as simple as that.

She got up from the table, pushing away the score, as if it were suddenly hateful to her, that marvellous child of her imagination. How had he managed the nights without her? What agonies had he gone through alone, because of her selfishness? She had had a letter from her father, her unlikely ally in all this, telling her not to fret, that Guy was not seen too many nights in the Rankeillor Inn, that he seemed still concerned only with the garden. But her father, for all his perceptiveness, could not know how he really was. Perhaps nobody could, except Guy himself.

She glanced back at the score, filled with the foreboding that it would be her last, her swan song. She would have to go back after all. It was only a temporary escape for a specific purpose, and after this was finished she would have to do what she had promised in marrying him. One last great song and then silence, as she tended to him and his children, for the rest of her life. Was that how it was supposed to be? She had to go back to him, she knew, not just from duty, not because of promises, but because she did love him – of that simple fact she was certain – but the thought that she might never be able to write again was too much for her. Was the price of her love to have to turn her back entirely on music? Could the two things ever exist together? She remembered how she had seen so clearly, when he had first asked her to marry him, that they could not. Yet that seemed a world a hundred years ago instead of less than five, a world which had not guessed at Angus or the war, or any of the complicated shades of feeling that had wrapped themselves about her to restrict her movements.

She opened the score again, and turned to the closing section, which she had sat up until three in the morning to write. It was really a coda to the whole piece, with no choir, but a solo soprano singing a pure line of sound, a lament without words to the rumbling, tense accompaniment of the timpani, then the full orchestra coming in with a great redemptive melody that had seemed to boil up in her, like some deep well of optimism which she scarcely understood. It had flowered and run away from her, as she had never expected it might. She had been astonished at her own skill in making the thing, and exhilarated. She had touched beauty there, made beauty, no less – how could she stop now, when she had found this great power in her? She could not.

She gathered up the score and decided she would take it to show Dr Bradley, anxious for a practical distraction. It was better he should see it early on so that in the case of his taking a violent dislike to it she could steel herself to the thought of its not being performed. She was aware its modernity might upset him. It was far more extreme in its dissonance than anything she had yet written, and perhaps not at all the thing to suit the Royal Glasgow Choral Society. It would certainly make a change from the *Messiah* and *Elijah* for them.

Dr Bradley lived not far away, near the university, where he was now a senior lecturer, in a large but drab house that seemed to have taken its decorative style from the Academy. She had called on him briefly when she had arrived, an odd enough experience, with all his old disapproval of her carefully put aside. She had felt able to forgive him for anything he had said in the past when he told her how impressed he had been by 'Blest Pair of Sirens'.

Now his solid old housekeeper opened the door to her and told her that he was taking a choir rehearsal, a fact that was clear to her at once from the sound of *a cappella* voices that drifted into the street to greet her.

'I don't mind waiting,' she said. The housekeeper nodded and took her upstairs, the sound of the choir's music swelling round them as they walked up, perfectly amplified by the high, empty stairwell.

The housekeeper showed her into the back drawing room, which had its large folding doors half open to the other room, so she had a good view of the singers, and of Dr Bradley conducting them.

The sound was wonderful, from a small force of men and boys, a church choir of course, rehearsing the anthem for tomorrow's service. She wished the Church of Scotland had permitted itself such glorious indulgences as choirs such as that, and then found herself wondering if Rankeillor could muster such a choir. Her father would love music like this every Sunday. It fitted well with his strange new theology, though whether the village would ever take to this popish practice she had no idea. How odd to find herself thinking of Rankeillor here, as those perfect voices rose and fell and wove about in ever more lovely and complex patterns. She closed her eyes to let the music fill her, but in her mind she saw the village with astonishing clarity: the Castle, and the Manse, the church, grey-stone without, white-washed within, and then moorland and the hills. It had all formed her, that particular landscape. And at the centre of it, as if at the dead centre of her heart itself, she could see Guy, looking at her with all the intense passion that she could not prevent herself from responding to. God, how she wanted him, how she ached suddenly for him.

The music stopped, and she found there were tears streaking down her face. She fumbled for her handkerchief, feeling tired and hot, suddenly, as if her own strength of emotion might crush her.

'That wasn't bad,' she heard Dr Bradley saying. 'It wasn't bad at all.' She could not help smiling at the characteristic deprecation in his voice. 'But . . . well, trebles, you do need to keep sharper in that final passage. I could feel you slipping, or at least wanting to slip into flatness. But it will do, for now. I'll just go and fetch next week's anthem . . .'

She realized, hearing the choir begin to chatter, that he had left them and was coming into the back of the room. She had to struggle to compose herself.

'Oh, I'd no idea I'd find you here!' he said. 'What a very pleasant surprise.'

'I couldn't resist sneaking in to listen,' she explained. 'And I think they were more than not bad.'

'Well, you have to keep them on their toes,' he added in a confidential whisper. 'Do come through. We shan't be much longer.'

'Thank you.'

'In fact,' he said, 'I know what we shall do.'

So she went with him into the main drawing room, hoping that her tear stains were not visible.

'Now, gentlemen, I have the honour to present to you Miss Adam, or rather Lady Lindsay, who composed "Blest Pair of Sirens" which of course you know well. I rather thought we might give her a rendition of it now, since you still have copies of it. That should stop you boys falling asleep, shouldn't it?' he added particularly to the trebles and altos for whom the piece was written. 'And give the old men a rest . . . But Mr Maclennan, perhaps you'd take the piano part?'

He turned back to Chris, smiling still.

'Perhaps you'd like to direct?' It was graciously said,

and a great tribute, she realized. This choir was clearly his pride and joy, and to be asked to conduct was an honour.

'I've never heard it done with boys' voices – we had women in Edinburgh . . .' she managed to say.

'But it should be for boys' shouldn't it?' he said. 'No vibrato?'

She nodded, amazed that at last they should understand each other. He had accepted her utterly. He ushered her to the music stand.

'I wonder if you don't have a spare copy,' she said. 'I can't remember my own markings I'm afraid . . .' This amused the choir and got them on her side. But she felt unaccountably nervous, standing there, as if she had not enough power in her to do it. All those days and nights of concentration were catching up with her, she supposed, and rested one hand on the music stand to steady herself. With the other she signalled to the accompanist.

The introduction was quite long – it had been written for string quartet and the piano arrangement irritated her. She would rewrite it when she had the chance, for more choirs would sing it with a decent piano accompaniment than with a formidable string quartet. She was aware, though, as she listened and beat time, that she was in fact struggling to keep time. She was puzzled at herself. She never lost time, but her mind was swimming suddenly and she could not focus properly on the boys in front of her. She dropped her hand and clutched the stand with it, certain that her legs would give way, and as she did she felt a terrible stab of pain in her stomach, like a contraction, but in fact far more painful.

'I'm sorry,' she managed to say, and then could not help exclaiming as another, far sharper wave of pain assaulted her, at which she could do nothing but double up. A moment later she crumpled on to the floor, in an ungainly heap. She could not open her eyes for the pain, and she felt so hot that she might burn up into a cinder. Everyone in the room seemed to be crowding round her and she was fighting for air, for consciousness even.

'My dear, what is it,' she heard Dr Bradley saying to her.

'Mis . . . carriage.' She forced the word out. She knew it, for it felt now that her womb had been ripped open and she was certain she was bleeding. She felt indeed she would bleed to death, as every ounce of will and strength seemed to desert her, and the world faded about her.

56

Inside the nursing home, his courage suddenly failed him. The disgusting smell of disinfectant and the sight of the bland-faced nurse at the reception desk, in her white, starched headdress, the very ordered cleanliness of it, curdled his blood. He expected to be seized upon and examined and frowned over, as he had been for all those months. He found his throat was dry as he went to answer the nurse's enquiring glance.

'My wife . . .' he said. 'Lady Lindsay. I was told she was brought here.'

'Of course, sir,' she smiled. 'This way please.'

She took him along a passageway, of which all the walls were painted with shining white enamel paint that glistened in the strong sun that came in through the windows. It had all the terrible serenity of hospitals, a serenity that disguised the obscenity of death and dying.

'If you'd like to wait here, please, Dr Skirving will be along shortly.'

He nodded and went through the door that she held open for him.

The waiting room had the same white sunniness, with gaily covered chintz chairs and pot plants scattered about. A man jumped up, a stocky little fellow, with neatly dressed grey beard and moustache. In his arms he was holding Chris's attaché case.

'Dr Bradley?' he ventured. 'My wife's landlady told me . . .' He broke off, feeling the oppressive warmth of the room pressing down on him. He had to sit down. '. . . that you'd brought her here. Thank you . . .'

'Sir Guy?' said the man. 'I didn't know you were in Glasgow . . .'

'I wasn't,' he said, 'at least not till today. I came . . . Well, it seems it's a good thing I came.' Bradley nodded earnestly. 'What's wrong – her landlady only said she'd been taken ill. Have they said anything yet?'

'She said it was a miscarriage,' said Dr Bradley, putting down the attaché case.

'What? Oh God – I didn't even know she was pregnant . . .' He pressed his face into his hands, trying to ride the pain of this revelation. Why had she not told him? Why? Because, the answer slipped into his mind, you would not have been listening.

'I suppose I had better go,' he heard Bradley say. 'Now you are here. Perhaps if you have a moment to tell me how things go. I am on the telephone – they have my number here.'

Guy looked up at him, struck by the emotion in his voice.

'Of course,' said Guy. 'But you're welcome to stay. Frankly, I'd be glad if you did.'

He shook his head. 'I couldn't intrude.'

'It wouldn't be an intrusion,' said Guy. 'You obviously care, don't you?'

'Indeed,' said the man, looking away slightly, as if embarrassed by having to admit to feeling. 'Your wife was one of my students, one of the best I have ever had the pleasure of teaching. She is an extraordinary talent . . .'

At that moment the door opened and a woman came in, wearing the long white coat that signified she was the doctor. She was a tall, imposing woman, mature, her face both handsome and authoritative, with small gold half-glasses perched on her nose. Guy at once felt terrified by her, as if she were, with her diagnosis, going to tell him how his cruelty had caused it all. He ran his finger round his collar and leant back into the chair, anxious for its support. He could read bad news in every line of that woman's face and he did not know how he could bear it. To have come so far and now to have to face this. The indiscriminate bullets on V beach seemed more kindly.

'Yes?' he managed to ask.

She drew up a hard chair and sat down opposite him. From the corner of his eye he saw Bradley sit too, perch anxiously, in fact.

'Well,' she said. Her voice was soft, that of a Highlander. 'Your wife has had a miscarriage, complicated by severe haemorrhaging and an infection of the womb. We've had to perform an emergency hysterectomy – that is, take out the womb . . .'

'And?' Guy had to ask.

'It went well. She's lost a lot of blood, but she's strong, and the signs are that she will pull through. But unfortunately, there'll be no more children, Sir Guy.'

'But she will be all right?'

'I think so. She's feverish still, but . . . Basically, it's a good constitution she has.' She reached out and patted his arm.

'Can I see her?'

'She's not conscious.'

'Just let me see her, please.'

'A few minutes can't hurt.'

He attempted to get up.

'Do you want a hand?' asked Dr Skirving.

'Yes, yes, please,' he said, and found as she helped him up on to his crutches that he could no longer stop himself crying. He felt like a child being helped out of its cot, but he did not resist her help. He was shaking too much to make a decent job of it.

He glanced over at Bradley, who was sitting with his mouth pressed against his folded hands, as if he were praying. Perhaps he was, and Guy hoped, from some ancient superstitious part of himself, that such gestures had some effect.

They went slowly back along the corridor, Guy feeling as if he were walking on the crutches for the first time. Then he had been rigid with the fear of falling on the floor. Now he felt he might fall into a far deeper abyss if he were to lose Chris. Dr Skirving had not given him certainties, after all. The odds still felt deeply stacked against them.

Chris was lying in a small side room, with the blinds down to keep out the light. At first he hovered at the threshold, too frightened to go in, for she looked so pale and still. But then she moaned slightly and moved her head, so that her hair, which was spread out over the pillow, glistened slightly in the dull light. He thought of all the times he had seen men die – of all the men in the tunnel, each of whose dying voices he had heard slowly silenced by the choking earth. He thought of all those bodies lying on V beach, some of them twitching just a little, as if to expel the last drop of soul. Was he facing that again here? Any moment, would Chris suddenly be gone, stolen away somewhere, like all those other victims of dreadful chance? If that were so, then it would be his turn surely, for there would be no reason to go on any more. He looked about him, feeling the ghosts again tickling at his shoulders, but he saw nothing. There was nothing but Chris and himself in this little white room, with all the past and the future hanging in the balance of the moment.

'Don't,' he whispered to her. 'Please don't . . .'

'Come and have some tea,' said Dr Skirving behind him. 'I'm afraid you are in for a long wait.'

In the waiting room, he found Dr Bradley had gone, but he had left Chris's attaché case lying on one of the chairs. Guy sat down in the chair next to it and reached out for it. It was a disreputable old thing, that looked as though it must have served her father when he was theology student at St Andrews. It had his initials, certainly, E.J.A. He scrabbled to open the buckles and drew out the solid pile of manuscript paper he found inside.

There was a covering sheet, hastily written in pencil, by her: 'Dover Beach, Christina Adam, July 1916.'

He knew she could read a score and hear it playing in her head. He had known that for years – why else had he brought her back Mozart operas from Vienna in orchestral versions? He had envied her that, he recalled, even as he had bought them, from that excellent music shop in the little street down by St Stephen's Cathedral. He wondered if it was still there, whether it had her music in stock. It would be something to go and find out, find out together. Perhaps one day they would, after the war, if Vienna was left after the war, if any of them were.

Of course they would be. He forced himself to believe it and turned to the first page of 'Dover Beach', intent on deciphering the symbols into sounds in his head. And if he could not now, then there would be a time when he would hear it properly, with her sitting beside him again, just as he had once imagined it. She had to pull through for the sake of this, for he could see, even with his lack of skill, that this was something extraordinary. He picked out the line of a violin solo and followed it. That alone was beautiful – and then a solo tenor took it up, and sang the opening lines of the poem, the poem he had suggested she set:

> The sea is calm to-night.
> The tide is full, the moon lies fair
> Upon the straits; – on the French coast, the light
> Gleams and is gone; the cliffs of England stand,
> Glimmering and vast, out in the tranquil bay.

He blinked in his astonishment at hearing it so clearly in

his mind. How well it was done, how exquisitely! She had taken the poem he so loved and turned it into something more wonderful than he could ever have imagined.

He clenched his fists, willing life into her, with all the strength in his body. She could not die, she could not be allowed to die. If he had to go to hell and back to save her, he would gladly have done it. Not for himself, though, nor even for Robin, who needed her perhaps more than he did, but for this, for such miracles as this. For she, with this, could make sense of the senseless and give comfort where there could be none.

57

She found she was reluctant to wake up. Drowsiness hung round her comfortably, wrapping her like layers of warm bedding from which there was no urgency to escape. She had a dim sense that she was somewhere unfamiliar and that she did not particularly want to find out where. Rather she would sleep again.

But an encouraging female voice was speaking to her.

'Are we waking up now, dear?'

She pulled open her eyes for a moment and saw the woman standing above her, her face framed with a nimbus of glowing white linen. A nurse, she supposed, and then, remembering, thought, 'Of course a nurse . . .'

'That's good,' smiled the nurse, and said, 'you've had a good long sleep.'

'Have I?' Chris managed to say. Her voice, she found, was slurred, and it hurt to speak. In fact she became aware that all of her hurt, and that she felt as though she had been squeezed through a mangle.

'Ohh . . .' she sighed. 'What happened?'

'I'm afraid you lost the baby.'

Chris closed her eyes again. She had known anyway without asking, but to hear it said, however gently, released a spasm of emotional pain far sharper than anything her body was suffering.

The nurse's cool hand pressed to her forehead.

'I shall have to take your temperature,' she said, and in a moment she had put a thermometer into Chris's mouth which seemed so large and uncomfortable that she had to resist the temptation to spit it out.

'Good,' said the nurse, at last taking it out. She glanced at it. 'Very good, your temperature's right down. Now you can have a drink.'

The nurse propped her up efficiently on some pillows, and Chris realized how weak she actually was. Her body was as limp as a washed-out rag. The nurse had to hold the water glass to her lips for her. There was no possibility of her fingers gripping it, and although the water was refreshing, the effort of drinking seemed enormous.

'I'll get you some beef tea,' said the nurse. 'And I think you can have your visitor now.'

Chris scarcely cared what she said. She had sunk back into the pillows, her head irresistibly rolling to one side. She wanted to sleep again desperately. She did not like this consciousness at all.

'You can see her now for a few minutes,' said the nurse coming into the waiting room. 'Only a few minutes though. She's only just woken up.'

'Oh thank God,' said Guy.

He had been there since seven that morning. They had sent him away last night, though he would happily have slept in the waiting room, although he had known he would not sleep. So he had gone back to her lodgings, and tried to kill time there, amongst all the disturbing distractions of her things, attempting to sleep in her bed, with her nightgown still neatly folded under the pillow. He had in fact fallen asleep, and had a brief but vivid nightmare, the first he had had for days, in which he had been trying to drag her unconscious body out of the tunnel. He had woken in panicking sweat and decided to go straight to the nursing home, his heart pounding with terrors about prophetic dreams. He had to walk there, because at six on a Sunday morning there were no cabs to be had. The streets had been eerily silent, in sunshine that was already clear and intense. He had felt a little like the only soul alive.

He got up on to his crutches and followed the nurse.

They had piled up the pillows behind her so that she looked less corpse-like, but she was as motionless. She was also looking away from him.

'Chris . . .' He said it tentatively, as if he were testing his voice in an unfamiliar acoustic rather than greeting her.

She stirred slightly and rolled her head towards him. He saw the confusion in her face as her eyes focused on him.

'Guy . . .?' It was the faintest whisper.

'Yes, it's me,' he said, coming forward, and sitting down on the chair the nurse had put by the bed. He wanted to grab her pale hand as it lay on the cover and kiss some life into it, but it looked too fragile.

'How come?' she said.

'I came to find you,' he said. 'I couldn't stand it without you.'

'You've come to take me home?' she asked.

'No,' he said. 'Not unless you want to go back.' She closed her eyes and he saw her body relax slightly. 'It was a stupid mistake. I don't need Rankeillor. I need you.'

'I know . . .' she said, and with obvious effort stretched out her hand towards him. He bent over it and kissed the palm of her hand, and as he did so he felt her other hand gently touch his hair. After a moment her hand slipped away again. 'I'm so feeble,' she said.

He reached out and touched her cheek.

'Only physically,' he said. 'You'll pull through. I'm certain of it.'

She gave him a faint smile at that and said, 'And you . . . you're . . .'

'Halfway mended, I think. I remembered it all. It was

like casting out a demon, and things made sense again – things like loving you and Robin more than anything.'

'I shouldn't have gone,' she said. 'I'm sorry. And I should have said about the baby . . .'

'It doesn't matter now.'

'It does.'

'It doesn't. You matter, Chris. You and your music.'

'That's enough for now, I think,' said the nurse coming in. She was carrying a vase of deep purple-red roses. 'These are from Dr Bradley,' she said, putting them down on the table by the bed. 'He delivered them on his way to church.'

'Well, I had better go then,' said Guy. 'I don't want to but . . .'

'You can come back this afternoon,' said the nurse. 'At three.'

'Then I'll be here,' he said, and leant over and kissed her gently on the lips to say goodbye.

When he kissed her, for all that it had been tenderly, she felt his strength again, the old strength of life in him which it had been so difficult to ignore. Now it felt as if he were breathing the same life back into her, as if they were both made out of the same element.

She watched him leave, but only with passing regret, because she was conscious now that any separation between them could only ever be a temporary one. The threads which had bound them now seemed plated with gold, and indestructible.

The honey scent of Dr Bradley's roses drifted over her. She would never have been able to predict such a thing as his sending her flowers. They looked like prized blooms from a well-tended garden. An extraordinary tribute . . .

She closed her eyes and drank deep of the smell. It made her relax completely, until only her mind seemed awake, and goodness, how awake. Sounds were forming:

harmonies as rich and as sensual as the smell of those flowers. It began to make her panic though, for she had to get them written down, however roughly.

Without much thinking about it, she called out for him, as loudly as she could.

The nurse came running in at first, and then she heard, unmistakably, coming down the passageway, the urgent clatter of his crutches. He burst in a second later.

'Chris, Chris, are you all right?' he said.

'Have you got a notebook?' she said. 'Some paper?' She found her voice was a mere hoarse whisper.

'Somewhere . . .' he said, beginning to dig in his pockets. 'Why?'

'Just write this down,' she said. 'Please . . .' He had brought out a small pocket book and a stub of pencil. 'Two staves – key E major . . .' He stared at her. He looked quite bewildered. 'You know that one, don't you?'

'Yes, yes, of course,' he said. 'I was just terrified, I thought you were going to dictate your will.'

'No,' she said. 'This is much more important. E major, now, have you got that?'

'Yes,' he said, scribbling, 'just about. These lines won't be too straight.'

'Doesn't matter . . . six eight time, first chord is a minim – bottom note D, then A sharp, then C, then D, then F with a double sharp, A sharp again, C sharp, then D. Have you got that? Show it to me.'

'Yes, I think so,' he said. 'Here.'

She looked at it quickly.

'Good . . . next chord then, another minim. C, G and B, then C, E sharp, G, B and C . . .' She found she was gasping for breath a little, from the effort, but the chord sequence was still ringing in her ears. 'Have you got it?'

'I think so. Shall I just write down the letters? I can put it on to manuscript later for you.'

'Yes, yes, that's fine, so long as they're written. Next

chord, minim, B, F, E, B, D ... A natural here, B, again ...'

He looked up at her suddenly, smiling.

'Who'd believe you?' he said, shaking his head.

'I want to get well,' she said. 'This seems to me the best way to do it.' She closed her eyes for a moment and listened for the next chord. 'Aah ... crotchets now ... I think ...'